BAR MAID

BAR
MAID

a novel

DANIEL
ROBERTS

Arcade Publishing • New York

First Edition

This is a work of fiction. Names, places, characters, and incidents are either the products of the author's imagination or are used fictitiously.

Arcade Publishing books may be purchased in bulk at special discounts for sales promotion, corporate gifts, fund-raising, or educational purposes. Special editions can also be created to specifications. For details, contact the Special Sales Department, Arcade Publishing, 307 West 36th Street, 11th Floor, New York, NY 10018 or arcade@skyhorsepublishing.com.

Arcade Publishing® is a registered trademark of Skyhorse Publishing, Inc.®, a Delaware corporation.

Visit our website at www.arcadepub.com.

10 9 8 7 6 5 4 3 2 1

Library of Congress Cataloging-in-Publication Data is available on file.
Library of Congress Control Number: 2021938314

Cover design by Erin Seaward-Hiatt
Cover illustrations © 4x6/Getty Images and Edge69/Getty Images (silhouettes); © Beastfromeast/Getty Images (painting); © Boris Zhitkov/Getty Images (texture)

ISBN: 978-1-950994-27-4
Ebook ISBN: 978-1-950994-28-1

Printed in the United States of America

BAR MAID

Chapter One

"YOUR FIRST DAY OF college should be a life bookmark," Charlie Green said to his fellow counselor, the Very-Brown-Eyed Counselor, on their final night of camp.

"Tonight could be a life bookmark. You know, for us," said the Very-Brown-Eyed Counselor, blinking into the bonfire they'd made.

"Tonight doesn't feel like a bookmark. The last night of senior-year summer job? Maybe a dog-eared page that your finger finds every decade."

"I don't want a dog-ear, Charlie. Sigh."

Charlie was grateful for the crackling fire. It filled silences after the Very-Brown-Eyed Counselor said things like *sigh* and batted her lashes, showing Charlie her impressively huge brown eyes. Her real name was Lucia, and she was the only girl he'd ever felt truly comfortable around; it pained him that he couldn't give himself to her romantically. Worse, he felt shallow, obvious. A *guy*.

"You want a marshmallow, Fuchsia?"

On the first day of camp, her nametag had read LUCIA. IT RHYMES WITH FUCHSIA.

"Of course I do. If you weren't here, I'd probably eat the whole bag.

But I don't want your last memory of me to be the chubby girl with her face full of marshmallows."

"Who's to say this will be a last memory? Maybe we'll know each other forever, become these famous pen pals."

Camp Shining Star was a camp for overweight middle-school kids. Charlie, tall and skinny, had interviewed for a counselor job that winter. They usually only hired larger counselors, but he'd won over the head counselor with his stories about last summer's job, Space Camp, where he'd consoled an unstable Apollo mission astronaut, who'd arrived drunk for a speaking engagement.

Charlie knew his tipplers. His mother was at her most endearing during the third glass. The stories about Paris. About being nineteen in Paris. In her moist, smoky eyes Charlie could almost see the famous carousel, in view of the Eiffel Tower, where she'd met Charlie's father. Charlie knew how to speak to winos.

"It must be hard for you," Charlie had said to the astronaut. "So few people have seen what you've seen."

"You don't know darkness," said the spaceman, "until you've walked the rock alone. Part of me wanted to stay up there."

He smelled like Scope and gin. It was all he took from those six hot Floridian weeks. Scope and gin, the smell of outer space.

"I promise never to associate you with marshmallows," said Charlie to the Very-Brown-Eyed Counselor.

"How romantic, Charlie."

"I'm sorry. Maybe we'd have a future if it weren't for—"

"Monica Miller."

"She's my girlfriend, Fuchsia."

"Remember the night you admitted you have more fun with me? That the 'Very-Brown-Eyed Counselor' was your cup of tea?"

You are that very cup, thought Charlie, *but you don't know what it's like inside Monica Miller's eighteen-year-old bedroom. Girl smells. Girl clothes. Girl darkness, which is lighter than true darkness. A forgiving light. And the bed is soft, but not cloyingly so. And her long and thin eighteen-year-old fingers fumbling with my belt.*

"Our campfires have been so beautiful. So easy," said Charlie. "Your brown eyes, generous and pure. Monica Miller's eyes can look mottled in the New York daylight."

Lucia ran the computer lab at camp, teaching kids BASIC programming and setting them up with games. She was going to college out west, to study computing. They'd argued about the machines. Charlie found them limiting, lonely, a blinking cursor stuck on a screen, though he did admire the colorful Apple sticker on the Very-Brown-Eyed Counselor's camping bag. It was the sort of sticker that a hot girl would slap on her book bag in a vacant act of rebellion.

Charlie watched her hold her hands up to the campfire built for two. Its heat had reddened her cheeks, and its light gave her roundness some angles. *Hell*, thought Charlie, *everyone's skinny on a late summer night*.

"Our brown eyes are cool, Charlie."

"I know, I know, I've just never kissed a blue-eyed girl and have a theory that it tastes different."

"If I had blue eyes, I'd let you kiss me. Just for you to see what it's like."

"My most cherished prophecy is that on my first day of college I will fall in love with a light-eyed girl, exit college, and enter *life*."

"I can't wait for college."

"My mother thinks that being eighteen is magical, and that anything can happen. Of course, she wants me to finish school, but I really do see myself having a life-changing escapade on the first day. The biggest life bookmark of them all."

She licked a finger and rubbed away marshmallow from Charlie's chin.

"Maybe on my first day I'll find an apartment somewhere magical," said Charlie. "Like above an old bar that predates the Civil War. Imagine living above a place like that."

"I like your one-way ticket to Paris fantasy better."

"Yes," he said, inspecting her face for his parents' homeland, remembering that he'd found something appealingly French about her nose.

"Tell me about your cute little French dad," she said, closing her eyes and moving closer for a kiss, "and your wine-loving mother."

"What are you doing?"

"Please. Just one."

He let her kiss him, participating by shuffling his lips, until he got into it. Monica Miller was a bossy kisser, but this girl was aimless, slow. They were by the lake, near where they stored the kayaks. The boathouse keeper was asleep on a lawn chair in plain sight, the camp's newsletter *The Skinny* splayed on his lap.

"Wow," she said, her eyes still shut after it ended, both of her hands in his.

"We're holding hands," said Charlie.

"So what do we do now?" she asked.

"I don't know. I'm confused. Look at the boatman, how calm he is. He's not confused."

"He's asleep. Maybe we could sleep out here tonight?"

For the first time this summer Charlie could imagine a romance with her. If only he hadn't devoted so much time, so many letters, so many thoughts to Monica Miller. And then there was the long-awaited night before college. They'd both written about it.

Champagne at the Adam's Rib bar, then back to her parentless apartment. She'd already shopped for lingerie.

"I have a girlfriend," said Charlie.

"Why do boys kiss me and then say that? Target practice on the girl who could lose twenty pounds?"

"I'm sorry," he said, and meant it. She had such a good, soft heart. A marshmallow heart.

"You should know, Fuchsia," said Charlie, "that I'm going to tell Monica Miller about this."

"Don't you *Fuchsia* me."

Charlie wanted to be true to his word and tell Monica Miller about the kiss—but only after they'd slept together. He would tell her in the morning. It was more of a morning revelation than a night one, but then she might counter with her own story, and it wouldn't be a singular kiss with a tender girl, it would be about the Columbia University philosophy major who built his own furniture and rode a Vespa.

"You don't get it," said the Very-Brown-Eyed Counselor. She upended the bag of marshmallows into the fire. "This is how a real diet starts, with a broken heart."

*

Charlie waited on a parking lot log for the yellow cab that his mother had dispatched, while the other campers and counselors reunited with their parents. The final morning of Camp Shining Star was Weigh Out Day. Per tradition, most of the counselors dressed in costume. Against a carnival backdrop, parents held their breath as their kids stepped on the scale. Not one of the campers had asked for Charlie to be their scale chaperone, something he'd blamed on his thinness. He was surprised to feel a tap on his shoulder.

"Hey, Mr. Charlie?" Georgie was ten. Crewcut and freckles. His arms and legs raw from mosquitos.

"Big day, Georgie. You excited?" asked Charlie.

"Can you go with me?"

"To weigh out?"

"Yeah."

"I'm expecting a taxi. But screw it, they'll wait for us. Taxi drivers pretend to be impatient, but they like nothing more than a running meter. Wouldn't it be fun to be a cabbie in Europe?"

"Oh, I'm not sure. My grandmother drives a school bus."

Charlie held Georgie's hand as they walked back to camp and into the clamor.

"They're playing the music so loud," said Georgie.

"They want everyone to be in a good mood, and you *should* be, Georgie, no matter what."

"If I gained? My life is over."

"Don't be silly," said Charlie. "One day you'll be loved by a beautiful girl, and this camp will seem distant and absurd. That's what a beautiful girl can do for you: solve your youth."

"I just want to be thin."

There were families, some elated—dads finally able to carry their daughters on their shoulders—and some silent, even sniffling, shoulder to shoulder, helping the wounded back to the station wagon, wondering how the hell a kid could gain ten pounds at a $10,000 ten-week fat camp. The counselors dressed as gangsters, ALF, cowgirls, Prince. They were taught to applaud everything, gains and losses. At Camp Shining Star, no one was a loser, and everyone was a loser.

"I had a few Skittles last night," Georgie told Charlie.

"Good. You followed your heart while all these other kids fasted, or worse."

"I wish I knew how to make myself puke."

Georgie's parents were already inside the weigh-in cabin, at scale three. The scales were large enough to weigh a golf cart or a cow, with red digital numbers overhead to broadcast the news. Charlie knew that scale three was unforgiving, but scale five—off-limits, so it could be recalibrated—was a gold mine of shed pounds. He told Georgie to wait with his parents while he plugged in scale five. No one was watching him. All eyes were on the numbers, every counselor clapping or consoling.

By the time the machine had started, Georgie was stripped to his underwear, in a prayer circle with his parents.

"It's going to be okay," Charlie said to the family. "Georgie, just take a deep breath, close your eyes, and step right up. Now, when I count to three, you should open—"

"Sweet Jesus in heaven," yelled Georgie's dad.

"You did it, honey," said the mom, the entire family jumping up and down on the scale.

"Fifteen pounds. *Fifteen pounds*, you skinny son of a bitch."

*

"Hi," said the Very-Brown-Eyed Counselor. She'd been watching him drink from his silver vodka flask, toasting the late summer day. She was wearing her Madonna costume: half a wedding dress over black leggings, lace arm warmers, bows in her hair.

"You look great," said Charlie.

"I wanted to say goodbye."

"Did your kids lose weight?"

"Most of them."

"I only had one. Georgie."

"How'd he do?"

"I put him on scale five."

"Charlie, you're not doing him any favors."

"He probably did lose weight. I just want him to be happy. Screw college. I'll go around the world, rigging scales so people can be happy. I'm serious."

"Come here," she said.

Charlie got up from his log and she hugged him, her clunky crucifix digging into his chest. He felt her tremble, felt a tear make the jump to his cheek. *What wetness under the morning sun*, he thought, until a car horn broke the spell. A New York yellow cab had pulled into the parking lot. After a long country summer, the dirty car looked out of place. They stared at it together as if it were a flying saucer, vibrating inches off the ground.

"Here," Charlie said, handing her the silver flask. "Take a sip from it in college, maybe at graduation, and remember this summer."

"Who's RG?" she asked, looking at it.

"Rose Green. My mother."

The taxi driver rolled down the window and tapped his watch. "It's a long ride back to the city, kid."

"Well, this is it," said Charlie.

They hugged again. An adult hug. A vise. This time it was Charlie's tear that made the jump. Two eighteen-year-olds holding on for their lives, steeling themselves against what was waiting for them. Adulthood, rapacious adulthood.

"Are you okay?" she asked.

Charlie nodded. Through wet eyes he focused on the endless pine trees and the overgrown Cherokee path that receded into its kingdom.

"Just have a good date with Monica. I mean it. I'll be fine. And you'll be fine." She patted his belly. "Skinny," she said, then walked away, intoning Madonna's "Like a Virgin." A song about survival for sure. *She's going to make it*, thought Charlie. *We both will?*

"What kind of camp was that?" the cabbie asked Charlie. "When I was asking for directions, the guy at the gas station said it was a camp for fat kids."

"It was a camp for beautiful kids."

Chapter Two

"Charlie, where are you going without your juice?" asked Angelina, holding out a glass of freshly squeezed orange juice. For fifteen years she'd been juicing breakfast oranges for the Greens.

"I'm out of practice," said Charlie. "At camp they gave us a can of fruit punch for breakfast."

"*Estupido*," said Angelina.

Angelina was from Puerto Rico. No kids of her own; a quick, snickering mouth; tight gray curls atop her head; fair skin. She contended that the original Puerto Ricans were all light skinned and all middle class: "Fishermen, servants, chauffeurs, shop owners. Work six days a week, sleep one day a week. The best people on earth. *La Dignidad*."

"I have so much to do before tonight," said Charlie. "Look at this list. Three full yellow legal pad pages. A record."

"What happens tonight?" asked Angelina.

"I meant that I have so much to do before college tomorrow."

"*Ay Dios*. Watch him get into trouble with some girl tonight."

"No girl, just—

"*Dios*."

Angelina didn't like girls. She came to the Greens in 1970, just after Charlie was born. She was a house nanny at the San Juan Loews, where the family spent a Christmas holiday, and made the plane trip home with them, chastising the stewardess for the candy wrapper she'd found beneath the boy's seat, and debriefing Mrs. Green about the exact type of juicer she'd require for the household.

Charlie shared Angelina's love for the 1970s and her healthy mistrust for the 1980s. The former meant the Concorde, which the Greens flew once, the flight nearly empty except for them. Angelina cherished the experience. Charlie was shocked that she didn't cross herself before takeoff.

"*Dios* is on the Concorde," she'd said.

He'd timed her retelling of the adventure to her numb cousins in Brooklyn, the story coming in at two hours and fifteen minutes, the flight two hours and fifty-nine minutes.

Charlie believed that the 1970s were best represented by the Green family, at warp speed, wrapped in British Airways' complimentary cashmere throws, while Angelina received a manicure from the in-flight beautician. That and when they saw Yul Brynner in *The King and I*, the preshow dinner at Adam's Rib. It had been Charlie's first time there. He remembered watching, his chin on the table, a pat of butter melting on a slice of pumpernickel bread.

Angelina was wary of the latter decade, though. *Los eighties*. The AIDS, the Iran hostages, and the black dye in Mr. Reagan's hair. "A man should go gray," she'd tell Charlie. "You remember this when you are old."

"I won't mind having gray hair. You'll see," he'd say.

"You write me a postcard about it."

"You'll teach my wife how to make banana bread, like you taught my mom, right?"

"Go brush your teeth."

*

When Charlie thought about the Monica Miller date, he turned red with promise. Things would go well, with a skip in his step as he approached the restaurant's famous burgundy canopy. Then he'd bring himself to the moment when she walked into the barroom, and the cheer vanished, in its place a wholly unpredictable night.

Keep to the list, thought Charlie. *Your list will take you to the promised land of her bedroom, where you'll be warm together under a crocheted blanket from her childhood.* At the top of his list was a visit to the electronics store to buy Sony's Boodo Khan Walkman, the world's loudest and finest personal cassette player, complete with the largest consumer-class headphones. Deep into the afternoon, dressed and showered, he'd pop in the pre-date mixtape and sit on a bench on Fifth Avenue, outside Central Park, his eyes locked on the canopy of Adam's Rib, a mere block in the distance. In the absence of his older brother John, the Boodo Khan would be his trail guide: a metal square with Japanese lettering, two splashes of color, a green Play button and a red Stop button, and a leaden volume wheel. Less a machine than a *place*.

"May I see it?" Charlie asked the electronics salesman.

He'd asked the same question on the other side of this summer, about the same Japanese packaging that remained on the highest shelf of GOING OUT OF BUSINESS, the decade-old signage that covered the original name of the local electronics store.

"It's $970," said the salesman, a surly Israeli who wore no fewer than three Stars of David.

"I know," said Charlie. "I made the money myself."

"How else do you make money? Are you a magician? Feel this," said the salesman and placed the metal brick in Charlie's palm. "This Walkman is like a tank. You couldn't hear a war with these on."

"Were you in a war?"

"Of course I was. I tell you what, I'll throw in the batteries."

He'd have $190 left for tonight's date, the fruits of his fat-camp labors gone by tomorrow morning. John had said it was good to go to college penniless. Less is more. Pack lightly. Toss a single duffel bag onto your unmade bed. They'll think you're dangerous.

"$950," said Charlie. "With the batteries."

"Geez Louise. I've seen you in here with your nanny. I should charge you a thousand."

"$950. You haven't sold it all summer."

"Okay, okay. You win. Next time we bargain, you let me win. That's how the world works. You always get what you want?"

"No. Never."

"It's good to lose a lot. Makes you strong."

Charlie watched the man fumble with the batteries and their compartment. It took him minutes. It would have taken Charlie seconds. The shopkeeper was equally inept in June. The backward Duracells had annoyed Charlie then, but the summer had made him sympathetic to all who stumble on their path.

"You must have to know how so many things work," said Charlie.

"I fixed tanks in the army. In Israel. You should join. Bring your Sony Walkman."

"Maybe I will. What are the uniforms like? I like countries who still equip their soldiers with swords. Somehow it's less violent."

"You don't need a sword, my friend. You need a gun, and uniforms are crap. They are to be torn off in peacetime."

I'll miss this shopkeeper, he thought, *and all of the shopkeepers who saw me at five years old, eleven, and eighteen. Thank you, shopkeepers. I'm sorry Angelina scolded you, and I'm sorry I stole lemon drops. I don't think my college has a Madison Avenue. John said as much.*

John also said Charlie needed a civilian uniform for college. After blasting "With or Without You" on his new acquisition and chasing Angelina around the kitchen with the leathery headphones, begging her to experience the booming sound, he settled into his room and called his older brother.

"You need to commit right now," said John. "Choose your uniform carefully. Memorize it. Never waver. That way, people don't have to think, they just know it's you. And girls like consistency. To them it means you'll last a long time in bed."

John's uniform at Princeton had been camouflage army shorts, a purple polo shirt, and sandals. Now a second-year banker on Wall Street, he rotated his suits but made certain the ties were always a shade of yellow. John had a crush on his supervisor, Shannon Chang, and believed that on the five hundredth or thousandth day of his yellow-tie streak she would ask him to a post-work cocktail.

"I'm going with my navy-blue blazer," said Charlie.

"With just a smile and a navy-blue blazer, almost every door will open," Charlie's grandmother had told him, in the final months of her life, when terminal lung cancer allowed for an all-you-can-smoke existence that she described as a preview of heaven.

"Then at least rip off a couple of those shiny buttons," said John. "You don't want to come across as rich. That's a huge detriment in college."

"But it's not in life?"

"Of course not. College isn't life. It's more like war," said John.

In addition to the blazer (the two buttons removed), he'd selected a black Calvin Klein V-neck tee, pulled at the neck to suggest torso muscles that didn't yet exist. For pants, he went with the stiff Brooks Brothers jeans that his mother called dungarees. Shoes were easy: penny loafers with buffalo head nickels crammed into the slots. He wore the same socks and underwear as his father, sourced from a pre-school shopping day at Saks Fifth Avenue, during which Rose Green bought a year's worth of staples for her "boys." Charlie put up a fight, but he actually liked the quality of the knee-high socks and the drawers. He tried never to imagine his father in them, on crinkly examination table paper, some doctor making small talk by commenting on the golden toes.

"I should wear the uniform to my date tonight, right?" he asked John.

"Of course you should. Break it in. Why are you taking her to Adam's Rib? Least sexy place in New York."

"It's incredibly sexy."

"If you're seventy. You told Mom you're staying with me?"

"Yes."

"She's not stupid."

"Why wouldn't I want to spend the last night with my brother?"

"You *should* want to, but you're spending it at Adam's Rib with a B-minus brunette."

"Monica Miller, in the light of Adam's Rib, is an A-minus."

"By the way, losing your virginity isn't really fun. It's something you have to do before getting to the good stuff. Like how you have to run the faucet at home before the cold water comes out."

John was shorter than Charlie, stocky like their French father, George Green—*Jee-Jee* for short. John had Jee-Jee's smile as well—great dimples that girls loved. A fretted nose. A modest beer belly. He was comfortable. Easy. So many people called him their friend.

"I think I'll be good at it," said Charlie.

"Everyone thinks that. And wear a bag. I saw your girlfriend at a club downtown. Warhol was there. That means AIDS. That means wear a bag."

"She didn't sleep with Warhol, did she?"

"No, idiot. No one sleeps with Warhol. He's only had sex once, and that was with Jackie O."

"Then how did he get AIDS?"

"Immaculately."

*

Charlie passed Jee-Jee's blue and yellow entryway dish, a little bit of Provence chipped by car keys and loose change. He could usually make out the fawns and other garden creatures who lived on the bottom, but today it held a disposable camera, a University of Pennsylvania parking sticker, his father's driving gloves with LE MANS stitched in red thread below the knuckle holes, and a *Les Misérables* cassette. Tonight is all, thought Charlie. Twelve, maybe fourteen hours till he'd hear his father ask, *Allons-y?*

"How are you feeling, Charlie Bear?" asked Rose Green, char-donnay no. 1 in her hand.

"I found a tape measure on my bed. John said you were planning to change my room?"

"Well, sweetheart, your father has always dreamed of a billiards room, but don't worry. You'll always have a bed here. Forever and ever."

"In which room?"

"We'll probably end up keeping everything just like it is today."

I'm not going to sleep on a pool table, thought Charlie. *It will mess up my back, which will mess up my sex life, if I have a sex life. Which I will, I pray to God.*

Paint cans on the stairs. The goodbye-Charlie dish teeming with the end. *They want me gone*, thought Charlie. *Fine, then. Maybe Monica Miller and I will stay at the Plaza Hotel tonight and never leave. Like Eloise but with bottles and sex.*

"I'm staying at John's tonight," said Charlie. "For old time's sake."

"I have dried apricots for you, in case you decide not to sleep over."

"No, I think I will sleep over."

"It's your last night, so you can spend it however you want, just be careful."

"Why would I have to be careful at John's?"

"Just know that the apricots are waiting for you." She kissed his forehead. Charlie could tell she wanted more. A forever hug. *Please don't know about tonight*, he thought.

"Have fun with your brother," said Rose Green, touching his warm cheek with the back of her cold hand. "I love you."

"Me too." He sounded defensive. *Does she know?* He decided she didn't. It was the only way to proceed.

"College," said Rose Green. "Exciting." She went into the kitchen to pour chardonnay no. 2, then out to the backyard to join Jee-Jee under the Japanese tea lights. Charlie watched them: his father with *Le Monde* and a cigarillo, his mother looking on lovingly, reverentially, wondering exactly when her husband's better senses would prevail and he would pour himself a pastis.

"The shower you take before you lose your virginity is more important than the shower you take before your wedding," John had said. "A new bar of Irish Spring. New razor. No cologne. Extra deodorant, but it has to be cheap. You should smell like a workingman. And don't overdo it with the mousse."

The shower had been a great one. Thirty minutes of hot water. Then a thirty-nine-cent deodorant he'd picked up at Woolworth's. His uniform suited him: the missing buttons did the trick, and the Boodo Khan fit perfectly in his blazer pocket, the huge headphones around his neck.

"So, this is it," said Charlie to his parents.

"This is just the beginning," said Jee-Jee.

"You look very handsome," said Rose.

"Thought I'd dress up, in case John takes us somewhere fancy."

"You kids are so fancy," said Jee-Jee. He'd grown up poor, in a happily crowded French countryside house where he wore hand-me-downs, no questions asked, and mended the holes in them, no questions asked. Each child came with a sewing kit. As Jee-Jee liked to say, "Growing up, we had no questions to ask. Everyone knew what to do."

"There are worse things than fancy," said Rose.

"It's only the blazer that makes it fancy," said Charlie. "And two of the buttons are missing. Girls appreciate that deficiency."

"Well, you have fun tonight, Charlie Bear."

He'd watched her fill a tumbler with half a bottle of wine. Now that glass was empty. He wanted better advice than *have fun*. Maybe something closer to home, like, don't drink too damn much, too damn quickly, Charlie Bear.

*

The Adam's Rib bar smelled like roast beef and asbestos, the frigid air born of huge whirring air conditioners, forced from shafts by old airplane propellers, Charlie imagined. And the amazing lighting, like sepia, straight out of a 1940s war movie. Like an Abbott and Costello movie. *Abbott and Costello Join the French Foreign Legion.* But before they're in uniform, they're at some swanky Egyptian joint, hanging out with the Andrews Sisters, served by portly waiters wearing fezzes. Potted palms and red leather banquettes. The pyramids might as well be in the distance. But before dealing with the Sphinx and its riddle, have a Yorkshire Pudding and an end cut of prime rib. The Adam's Rib bartender will set you up. He might even answer the riddle with a wink and a smile: "They pour some of the roast beef juice into the Yorkshire puddings while they're cooking. That's the secret."

John had told Charlie he should get there one-and-a-half drinks early. "Be caught writing something when she enters."

"What should I write?" asked Charlie. "I could write another short story about the Adam's Rib bartender."

"It doesn't matter. Just put it away quickly after she sees you. Some part of her will think it's a note for another girl. And bring the fake ID I made for you."

"People look at me like I'm cursed. You gave me JFK's assassination day."

"It's plausibly implausible."

"Monica Miller never gets carded."

"Of course not. She's always annoyed, which bartenders mistake for adulthood. Just bring the ID. That creepy steakhouse bartender can turn on you any second."

"He's not creepy. He's wondrous."

Charlie had never been to Adam's Rib on a plain old Tuesday night. He'd been there on Fridays and Saturdays, Sundays, and once on a Thanksgiving Thursday. The pre-theater clamor was gone. A brunette walked in, and Charlie almost choked on an ice cube, but it turned out to be an older woman in black stockings.

"My parents told me they might want a bottle of Krug tonight," Charlie told the Adam's Rib bartender. The Greens had a house account that went unchecked. It was Jee-Jee's job to look through all the credit accounts for overcharges and fraud, but according to him life was too short for double-checking anything under a hundred dollars, a fact Charlie knew well. A bottle of 1984 Krug was $94, and Jee-Jee's eyes would glide right over it.

"And if for some reason that my parents don't show," Charlie said to the Adam's Rib bartender, "I'm sure they'd be fine with my girlfriend and I having—"

The Adam's Rib bartender stopped him. Held out a hand into which Charlie deposited his fake ID.

"Well, let's see," he said, straining to read. "I suppose that the numbers don't lie," the Adam's Rib bartender said, but then he shook his head. "You know, it's not the worst thing in the world to just be your age."

Then he stared too deeply into Charlie's brown eyes and the boy became five, in a playground, stuck on a slide. Pee in his pants.

"Sorry," said Charlie.

"One bottle of Krug Champagne will be on its way," said the Adam's Rib bartender.

Thank you, thought Charlie. *Please don't hate me. Kids needs lies. You were once a kid, right, Adam's Rib bartender? No, not you.* Then he felt something warm near his cheek and spun around.

"It's you," said Charlie to Monica Miller.

He'd practiced saying, "A sight for sore eyes." She was dressed up, looked grown up in a little black dress. John said that every guy wanted to date a girl who could do justice to the little black dress. Everything good emanated from it. Good nights, good sex, a good life.

"You're tan," said Monica.

"Camp."

He kissed her shiny lower lip. Her upper lip was a small crescent, just like her parents' upper lips, but the lower one was pulpy and red. *Thank God for the lower lip*, he thought.

"I sort of missed you," she said and tugged his ear.

They'd begun dating in the spring, after they'd met during a school play, a bizarre Old West retooling of *Romeo and Juliet*. It was an integration of his all-boys' school and her all-girls'. He'd gotten a part as a heard-but-never-seen narrator. Monica was the stage manager. Their first kiss was on opening night, in the infinite and infinitely soothing darkness of backstage, while the stage whispers of star-crossed cowboys and Indians bounced off of the gymnasium's rafters.

"I missed you, too," said Charlie. "I got Krug for us."

"I can't believe you're going to college tomorrow. Are you sure you want to stay over tonight? You're going to be so tired in the morning."

How could she possibly think tonight was anything but a mandatory event? Her blitheness bruised his solar plexus, a place he perceived to be the temple of his soul. It was where alcohol went to cause or solve problems.

"I definitely want to stay over," said Charlie, "and I definitely want to be tired. Who knows, maybe I won't make it to college. Maybe you and I will take a trip instead. Some nights can last a lifetime."

"That's a sweet idea, but, as you know, I start NYU next week."

NYU isn't really a college, thought Charlie. *It's more like an intellectual experiment in Greenwich Village with too many pigeons.*

"Don't you wish NYU had a sprawling green campus?" asked Charlie. "I don't want you to be stuck in concrete."

"Aw, I'll be okay."

"John said grad students camp out in Washington Square Park, just waiting for a new crop of freshman girls."

"Oh, speaking of grad students, my friend from my summer internship, this guy, Barry, I told you about? He's having a party uptown at the bar he works at near Columbia. I thought we could stop by. He's really cool."

"I'm sure he is really cool, but I thought tonight it could just be us."

Charlie had asked the Very-Brown-Eyed Counselor for advice about this Barry person. Monica Miller had ridden around town on the back of his Vespa, and Charlie wanted to know where her hands stayed during the ride.

"Just don't think about it, Charlie," she'd said.

"Barry really wants to meet you," said Monica.

"But he doesn't know me."

"He knows you through me, silly."

"You spoke about me?"

"Of course. You're like my boyfriend."

The Adam's Rib bartender whistled "April in Paris" and refilled their flutes. "Nice night in the big city," he said. "Or so they tell me."

"God, this place is so weird," whispered Monica.

"We love this place, don't we?"

"It's a little stuffy. I was almost going to say that we should buy a six-pack and sit on a stoop. Remember when we did that, and you told me a story about everyone who passed by, including the dogs?"

"I could tell you Adam's Rib stories."

She asked the Adam's Rib bartender for an ashtray.

"Smoke 'em if you got 'em," said the bartender.

"You're smoking?"

"Sometimes. Barry and his girlfriend—well, ex-girlfriend, now—we all used to smoke, like, a cigarette or two after dinner. It's not like it was a *thing*."

"I guess there's some sort of elegance to it."

"I don't know. I really like it when I'm drinking. I'll probably quit in five or ten years. Or when I have kids."

"Five years?"

Two Haircuts walked out of the dining room, to the bar. Haircuts was what Charlie called them. They were always kids in suits, with suspenders, horn-rimmed glasses, or yellow ties; kids who dressed or looked like John. All of them had gotten a haircut within the last twenty-six days. John himself had verified this: on Wall Street, anything less than fourteen haircuts a year was unacceptable.

The blond Haircut was an athlete in college but had let himself go, just like John and his beer gut. Although John had assured Charlie that girls actually liked beer guts: "It makes them feel safe and a little superior. They'll pat it after sex."

Blond Haircut was wearing Polo cologne, a lot of it. His friend was short, fat, balding. His wrist was adorned with a rope bracelet, an ID bracelet, and a preppy-looking striped Swatch.

Blond Haircut. Swatch Haircut.

The Haircuts were staring at Monica Miller because that was what Haircuts did. The blond one lit her cigarette with a pack of Adam's Rib matches.

"Mind if I bum one of your smokes?" he asked her.

"Of course not," she said.

Blond looked over at Swatch and raised his eyebrows.

"So, what are you guys up to?" Blond Haircut asked them.

"We're on a date," said Charlie.

"Lucky man," Blond Haircut said, and Monica Miller smiled.

"What are *you two* up to?" she asked.

"Dinner with the boss while his wife is out of town," said Blond Haircut.

"We should probably get back to the table," said Swatch Haircut.

"Okay," said Blond, smiling at Charlie's date. "If you insist, although I like it better out here for some reason." He put out his cigarette and touched her hand. "Thanks," he said.

"Sure," she said. "Bye."

"Fucking Haircuts," said Charlie.

"They were harmless preppies."

"*Haircuts.*"

"Charlie, your little language can get a little annoying."

"I just hope I never turn into one. If you ever see me wearing all sorts of crap on my wrist—"

"I like a watch on a man, or a bracelet, but definitely not both. You'd look good with a leather strap, like the kind Bono wears in 'With or Without You.'"

"Our song."

"I think it's everyone's song this summer," said Monica Miller, peering back into the dining room.

"Doesn't this place smell incredible?" asked Charlie. "Nixon could be back there. Sinatra!"

"You're cute when you get excited. It reminds me that you can be normal."

The champagne was working, thought Charlie. Monica Miller asked for a refill. Some nights she'd only have one drink, and those nights usually ended with a cursory kiss: "You don't have to walk me home, Charlie, really."

He'd end up at Mariella's Pizza in the Ten O'clocks on a Saturday night, kids coating their stomachs with a slice before the clubs. To end one's night amid others' beginnings was for Charlie the definition of precocity. He could handle the sadness of eating pizza next to old men and their first few sections of the Sunday *New York Times*. He'd eat one slice at Mariella's, get one to go, buy his own paper, then read the travel section in bed. Sometimes the phone would ring, and it would be Monica Miller apologizing for their flat ending. They'd make a date for the following weekend, and Charlie's heart would swell.

"One day," he'd say, "I want to share with you the Saturday night loneliness of Mariella's. One day we'll read the paper in there together."

She'd try to understand, saying, "I know we will. One day." Like Charlie, Monica Miller was Jewish; both her parents were shrinks. An only child, she was the captain of her life. *No* came easily to her, but so did the occasional sympathetic smile, and sometimes her hand through his hair. *If only she had lighter eyes*, thought Charlie. He didn't want to be damned to a lifetime of mud. The dark mud in his eyes would combine with the hazel mud in Monica's, one day producing more mud on the blue planet Earth.

"They're really more green," Monica would say. "Like your pretty name."

"I guess I could see that." But he could only see it when her contact lenses made her eyes red and teary; then, purely by contrast, there would be some green grass poking through the mud. Then he thought of another boy adoring her irises and panicked.

"I actually love your dark eyes," said Charlie.

"They're hazel, Charlie."

"I'm sorry. That's what I meant. Hey, let's raise a glass to the Adam's Rib bartender."

"I feel bad for him. I think he's too old to be doing this job."

"He loves his job."

"That's crazy. Most normal people hate their jobs. My parents treat one or two blue-collar people each year for free. It's called pro bono, but it's not pronounced like Bono from U2."

"I think the Adam's Rib bartender is one of the happiest people I know," said Charlie.

"You don't even know his name. You only call him 'the Adam's Rib bartender.'"

"That's one of the amazing things about him. He doesn't need a name. Like how God doesn't need a name."

"Bartenders aren't gods."

"They are to me. At least this one is. There's really something magical about him."

The Haircuts had returned, this time with a bottle and wineglasses.

"Gentlemen," said Monica Miller, spinning around slowly on her barstool, recrossing her legs. Charlie had seen her get this way before when she'd had too much champagne. John said some girls tried to act like old cabaret flirts when they were buzzed, and that the best thing to do was to wait it out and look the other way.

"My boss bought a bottle of Château Pétrus for the table," said Blond Haircut. "You guys want to try some?"

"It's the shit," said Swatch Haircut.

"I'd love a taste," said Monica Miller. "Sounds like a special wine." She drank from Blond Haircut's glass, then passed the glass to Charlie. He was going to refuse, but her lips had been where the Haircut's had been, and he needed to erase the intimacy.

"Senescent," said Charlie, handing Blond Haircut back his glass. It was what John said after tasting wine.

"We don't want to crash your date or anything," said Blond Haircut. "But you guys seem cool, and we're going to a loft party downtown if you want to join us."

"Loft party?" asked Monica Miller.

"Yeah. I mean, don't get me wrong, we're not a couple of creepy suits messing with your night, we just thought it was cool that here you were at an old man's bar drinking champagne on a weekday night."

"Thanks," said Charlie. "We're an old-fashioned couple."

"Where's the party?" asked Monica Miller.

"Down in Tribeca. Warren Street? I'm from California, still figuring this town out."

"Oh, really?" said Monica Miller. "My uncle's from San Diego. He took me to the zoo there when I was little."

A photo collage to that effect was in the Millers' kitchen. It looked like a hot day; Monica Miller's white shirt stained with something red. An Italian ice, most likely. Monica Miller and stained white shirt with giraffe. Monica Miller and stained white shirt with zebra. Being an only child meant redundant collages, Charlie had decided.

"The zoo. Cool, cool," Blond Haircut said, his California origins apparent in his mouth's inability to finish up a word with a consonant. "Coo, coo," was what it sounded like, but the rounded corners seemed to please Monica Miller.

"Love San Diego," said Blond Haircut, "but I'm from up north. Tree country."

"I guess, technically," said Charlie, gesticulating to the Adam's Rib bartender, in case he'd need corroboration, "everywhere is tree country."

"Not the redwoods, man."

"Oh my God, I've always wanted to see those," said Monica Miller.

"You totally should," said Blond Haircut.

Swatch Haircut flicked his adorned wrist and howled, "*Big-ass trees.*"

"Tell you what," said Blond Haircut, "I'll write down the address of the loft on the back of my card, and if you guys want to come, great. It's supposed to be wild. This guy at work throws one every summer."

"Last summer?" said Swatch Haircut. "The theme was James Bond. They gave all the girls vibrators shaped like golden bullets."

"Okay, then," said Blond Haircut, extinguishing his friend's creepiness with his redwoodsiness. "We'll catch you two later." He handed Monica Miller his card.

"Friends of yours?" asked the Adam's Rib bartender.

"No, absolutely not. We just met them," said Charlie.

"City slickers," sang the Adam's Rib bartender. "City slickers in the rain."

"They seemed nice, Charlie," said Monica Miller.

"Sure," said Charlie. "Blond Haircut was a handsome guy, don't you think?" This too was from the Book of John. Put out a fire by starting your own.

"Not my type," she said.

"Really? Huh. Interesting."

"So, you think we should go?" she asked.

"Go where?"

"To the party."

"*Barry*?" Charlie reminded her.

"Their party sounded really cool."

"Downtown loft parties are a little overrated."

"Have you ever been to one?"

"I don't do overrated things."

"Come on, Charlie *Bear*." She kissed his earlobe. He pounded the rest of the champagne, hoping to outrace an erection.

"I don't know."

"Well, I think I'm going," she said and readied another cigarette.

"Alone?" Mariella's Pizza loomed, but the thought of being in a room full of Haircuts, in a strange apartment, with a girl who had clearly developed a taste for older men over the summer? John would advise going to the party and letting Monica Miller roam the loft freely, separately. Sting sang "If You Love Somebody Set Them Free."

Nonsense, thought Charlie. He loved his navy-blue blazer but wouldn't dream of casting it up into the heavens on a windswept day in

Central Park. No, you put it on a hanger and sleep well, knowing where it is. If you love somebody, you hang them up in your closet.

"You're really thinking of going alone?" asked Charlie.

"I'm used to doing things alone."

"Well, I'm not going to leave a perfectly happy night at the Adam's Rib bar for a bunch of coked-out bankers and their overbearing watches."

"They're harmless, just boys dressed up like men. 'Haircuts,' as you insist on calling them, aren't my favorites, either, but I like meeting new types of people."

"I know, but I like meeting *you*. Over and over again."

"Thank you, but sometimes I need for you to be just a little more normal. A little more *eighteen*."

He could make out her bra underneath her silk blouse. He wished he could be normal for the bra, be normal for the blouse, for her whole grown-up outfit. She was probably wearing lingerie, too. An eighteen-year-old dressed like a thirty-year-old *woman*. He wondered if there was anything more enticing.

"How long would we have to stay for?" asked Charlie. She might never look as cute again. Just like John said, one or two long nights, and girls start to grow into their adult selves. Next thing you know, they're wearing pearls at breakfast, like his mother did on the weekends.

"We'll stay for a few hours, then we'll go to my place," said Monica Miller, staring down the length of her legs, admiring the gleaming shave.

John went to loft parties almost every weekend and described the atmosphere as progressively darker as the night became morning. Apparently, Haircuts after two o'clock on a Sunday morning grow desperate, snort a line of coke, and grab what they think is theirs. "It's actually not the worst training for a career in finance," John had said. "Doubling down is an art form. None of these guys ever want to go home alone."

"We can create our own loft atmosphere at your place," said Charlie. "I'll flicker the lights and read you my latest story. It's about a doorman I observed for many hours. Ironically, I depicted him as the least bored person in the world. He treats the building like his Rubik's Cube and is just waiting for the right moment when every apartment is empty at the exact same time, you know, uniformly, so he can—"

"It won't be the same at my place," said Monica Miller. "Feel how smooth my legs are, Mister Rubik's Cube."

"Smooth," said Charlie. "And shiny." She'd put cream on them, and to Charlie they felt cool, barely perfumed. Blond Haircut had spent some time looking at her legs. He had probably made some sort of Haircut bet with himself, that his hand would feel her thigh, even with Charlie sitting right there.

"What would you do if that Blond Haircut put his hand on your leg?" asked Charlie.

"I don't know," said Monica Miller. "It depends."

"On whether I go to the loft party?"

"No. Depends on my mood and how he did it. If he just wanted to see how smooth they felt, or if it was, you know, part of the conversation, then I'd probably be fine with it."

"What kind of conversation? About legs?"

"I don't know, crazy boy." She mussed his hair.

All day long, some part of him had believed he'd end up at Mariella's tonight, still a virgin. While getting ready, he was brave with that fate, but now it seemed so wrong. Home once again before midnight, pizza, and the *Times*. Maybe he *was* crazy, or at least not normal. A normal kid would go to the loft party and endure the night, even if it meant losing her to the Haircut's advance. Things like that turned kids into men, thought Charlie. You lose something young and shiny-legged to a junior analyst, or whatever the hell was printed on his card, and go home alone. Skip pizza. Just get into bed and sleep it all away. He pictured 10,000 bedrooms in the city where fully clothed kids dove face-first after a failed night, their hearts hardened but more muscular after losing their girlfriend in the Haircut den. He knew he should say, "Loft party? Why the hell not."

But he said, "I think I'd rather go to Mariella's than stand by while a Haircut touches your legs."

She smiled one of her thin-lipped smiles that occluded her plump lower lip. Her parents' smiles were similarly kindly but all-knowing, *pedantic*.

"Charlie, I probably won't let anyone touch my legs."

"I bought this Boodo Khan with you in mind."

"I so need a new Walkman."

"No. I mean, it's for tomorrow morning. I pictured us walking in the park at dawn. I made a tape for you. You'll listen to the Boodo Khan with my blazer draped over your shoulders. Imagine that scene: we're in love, with an hour left before college."

"In love?"

"If you say it, I'll say it back."

"That's not how it works. Listen, I've never been in love, and I doubt I'm going to start tonight."

"Maybe you will be in the morning? In fact, I know you will. If I'm wrong, you can keep my Walkman."

"What? No."

The bottle of Krug had been emptied for half an hour, and the Adam's Rib bartender was topping them off from some other bottle.

"Sorry, Monica, I'm a little buzzed," he said.

"Me too. Why don't we just go to the loft party and see what happens?"

"In the old days, a young couple such as us would make love the night before college, then never be apart."

"These are the new days, Charlie."

Even worse than that, thought Charlie, *these are the in-between days. Everyone knows the new days start on January 1, 1990, and the old days ended in 1969, when I was born.*

"Hey," he said, "let's order two Yorkshire puddings."

"I'd like to get out of here. The deer heads on the wall are giving me the creeps."

"Then stare at all the old trophies. I bet someone comes to polish them once a week, after closing. I wonder who he is? Let's talk about the mysterious trophy polisher and his amazing craft."

"No one earned those trophies. At least, no one here did."

"Angelina would like that. She calls earning things part of the *Dignidad.*"

"She's always mean to me."

"That's her way."

"Charlie, you can be so sweet, but you're putting too much pressure on everything. I sort of feel like going home now." She stood from the bar, wobbling a little in her mother's heels.

"I can't believe you're going to leave."

"I don't want to spend one of my last nights before college bickering like an old crazy couple at the steakhouse."

"Don't you remember what you wrote in July? That you could see us together for a long time? You bought lingerie. I bought a Walkman."

"It's September, Charlie. Your future starts tomorrow."

"I want the past. I want it with you."

"What time are you leaving tomorrow?"

"Early."

"Look, if you want to come over for a little bit—actually, maybe we should just call it a night, you know?"

So this was the end of their time together: five movie dates, six dinner dates, thirty-seven phone calls, and eight letter exchanges, the last four about sex. Sex tonight. She put on a layer of lip gloss, vaguely minty, and softly kissed him goodbye.

"So, are we broken up?" asked Charlie.

"No. I don't know. I just need to go."

"But not to the loft party, right?" Charlie asked after her, but she was gone.

Soon, she might be sharing her Krug champagne buzz, tingly lip gloss, and clean legs with another boy. *Future is just another word for pain*, he thought, and couldn't get to Mariella's quick enough, where he could claim two slices for himself and himself alone. At Mariella's, everyone had their own slice, and their own *New York Times*. There was no sharing. It was the old way, and it worked.

Chapter Three

"I DON'T UNDERSTAND WHAT exactly happened tonight," said Charlie to John. He'd called him as soon as he'd gotten home with his slice.

"She's probably still into you, but doesn't want a boyfriend right before freshman year," said John.

"I wish I could be normal for her."

"Just try to speak less. Girls like to fill in the blanks for the silent types."

"I always thought Monica Miller was eccentric, like me. She makes a point of wearing mismatched socks."

"What was her yearbook quote?"

"It was from a song," said Charlie. "The Grateful Dead."

"Uh-oh."

"She also had one by Kafka."

"Horrible combo: Grateful Dead and Kafka. She'll need some wild years, quite a few, probably, where she'll use philosophy nonsense to rationalize sloppy behavior. It's great to meet a girl who's in that phase on some random summer weekend, but anything more would be bad. You can tell a lot from yearbook quotes, especially with girls. It's their message in a bottle."

"I thought mine was good."

"Your French quotes and the depressing black-and-white photo of the Seine? Very Mom-and-Dad—and, to the outside eye, pretentious."

"You quoted Billy Joel."

"Yes, but as a joke. Ironically. I was making *fun* of yearbook quotes."

"Do you like the song 'These Dreams'?"

"By Heart? Girl song."

"Monica Miller and I like it."

"Then you're both girls."

"I miss her. I wish we were together in a cramped apartment with a small kitchen where she was making us a midnight snack."

"A girl like that won't hit the kitchen till she has kids. Kitchens are places she goes after sex, wearing the guy's dress shirt in search of a coffee saucer to use as an ashtray."

"I might pack my framed picture of her."

"I bet there's an industrial-grade container for those freshman-year girlfriend and boyfriend frames. Those pictures rarely make it past Thanksgiving."

"Maybe mine will stay out forever. Mom and Dad—"

"They weren't in college, they were in Europe, and it was a different time. You're too nostalgic for your age. It's going to be 1990 soon, and in the nineties, nostalgia will hold you back. Everyone I know on Wall Street's weaning themselves off. Look, I have to take my presleep shower. Have an amazing first day of college. It's going to be great."

John was good at life. Especially on Sundays. He made the day simple and light. A beer or two at lunch, a beer or two at dinner. Always with friends, always with girls. Laughter and a backward baseball cap. No shave, no shower, no problem.

Charlie couldn't relate. For him, every Sunday felt like lost love. Heavy, empty. At Camp Shining Star, he'd make an extra-big fire with the Very-Brown-Eyed Counselor and would be sure their conversation lasted until after midnight, until the sensibility of Monday. Nothing like killing a Sunday. His next Sunday would be at college. Girl-less. In the midst of an Indian summer. *The bright sun on my face will mock my empty insides*, thought Charlie. *I was supposed to fall in love tonight.*

Jee-Jee knocked and entered, carrying a snack tray. "We are happy you are safe at home for this last night, Charl." He sat where he always sat, in a lounge chair that Charlie never used, wearing one of his over-sized robes. "You care for some Nutella, Charl?"

"I have pizza."

Charlie watched him spread Nutella over toast, the knife working back and forth until each piece held a placid chocolate lake. He wished that for once the chocolate would resemble a choppy sea. Or that his father wouldn't eat chocolate every goddamn night. Charlie had seen pictures of Jee-Jee when he was young. Rail-thin and made of iron, now he was roly-poly. Jee-Jee and his Nutella.

"So, monsieur, what do you think about tomorrow?"

"Nothing, to be honest."

"We pulled many strings to get you into this wonderful school."

"I didn't ask you to."

"Practically gave away a Francis Bacon."

They owned two galleries, one in New York and the other in Paris. All of the paintings were stolen over a month of dangerous nights during the war by Charlie's maternal grandmother, who found them in a huge barn in northern France. The Nazis had taken them from the chateaus, from the ghettos, from museums. Charlie's grandmother took them back. She packed them in tarp, covered them in horse manure, buried them in the sod-lined basement of a ransacked synagogue, for retrieval after the war. Charlie's grandmother, five feet tall. They cast her shovel in gold and hung it above the Paris gallery's entrance. The number of times Rose Green had to say, "I'm so sorry, but my mother's shovel is not for sale."

"That doesn't really make me feel good about going to school," said Charlie.

"You're as smart as they come. If you did your homework, the world would be your oyster. Don't feel bad. Everyone uses their special connections. You'll figure this out soon enough."

Charlie's grandmother had written in her will that her two grand-sons, upon turning nineteen, would receive a painting or paintings worth the present value of two million dollars.

When he turned nineteen, John received a single Monet. He bor-rowed against its value in order to invest in the stock market. The results were dazzling, and now he owned a loft downtown with a ten-disc CD changer and a pasta-making machine, both of which he used to get women onto his futon.

"John didn't need any help getting in at Princeton," said Charlie.

"How can you be so sure?"

"He did?"

It always took Charlie's father extra effort to get out of the chair. "Who knows? Your mother makes these deals. I'm just the accountant."

"I should call John back."

"You and your brother, the two gossiping ladies."

He's taught me more than you ever have. "Maybe I should just take Amtrak tomorrow. We could have Nutella for breakfast here, and I could just go."

"Don't be silly, Charl. We can't wait to take you. We'll bring Nutella for the ride."

*

Angelina got up at five, to make sure the clothing in Charlie's duffel bag would be dryer-warm; her hope was that the warmth would make it to Philly, and that when he unpacked, he'd touch the clothing and remember her. She'd squeezed four cold oranges, one more than usual, and placed every cereal box, not just the unsweetened weekday brands, on the breakfast bar for Charlie to choose from. This would be Angelina's last breakfast service for Charlie. She'd been ready to retire and move back to Puerto Rico for over a year, but she stayed on to see Charlie to this very morning, and because the Greens made her a deal: stay until September '87 and own an apartment in the new condo development, with cable TV and maid service, rising above the ocean in new San Juan. She'd been asked not to break the news to Charlie until after he'd left for college. The Greens suggested a letter, but she couldn't do that to him, so she steeled herself against tears by praying over her eighty-five-year-old mother, a horse and carriage operator in old San Juan whose whipcrack was still the loudest.

"Time for juice and some chitchat," said Angelina to a bleary-eyed Charlie, still in bed. "I have good news. Next time we see each other will be on my island, just us two, like I promised since you were this high."

"Over Thanksgiving?"

"No. I am retiring. You're a big boy now, so I am going to be with my family there."

"You're joking, right?"

"No, my prince."

Charlie sat up in bed. Angelina cupped his head with her palm.

"But you were the first person I ever loved," he said. "Wait, is that true? I think it is."

"Is okay, *hijo*. Now drink your juice."

The doorbell rang a little after seven. Angelina hadn't been expecting any visitors. On this very important morning, she'd scheduled all domestic deliveries for the afternoon and couldn't hide her displeasure when she saw Monica Miller.

"I don't have enough oranges for you," said Angelina.

"That's okay, Angelina," she said. "I'll have a sip of Charlie's."

"He needs all of his juice. It's a big day for him. Why aren't you going to college?"

"I am, but here in New York."

"Charlie's in the kitchen." Angelina shook her head. The girl hadn't showered this morning and had rushed her makeup. There was a fresh bruise on her knee and the top button of her jean shorts was missing. Angelina wanted to point a finger and say, *Sexo*.

*

"You look cute in a robe," said Monica Miller to Charlie.

"What are you doing here?"

"I didn't like how last night ended."

She backed him up against the refrigerator and kissed him luxuriantly in and on his mouth. It was her best kiss ever, and he couldn't help but wonder if the Haircut from last night had taught her how to make best use of her parsimonious upper lip. The kiss was long, tinged with watermelon Bubble Yum and Marlboro Lights. *This is my first real kiss*, thought Charlie. It was slower and warmer than the others, and didn't end abruptly, like the rest. It didn't really end at all. Even when her head was against his chest, the kiss still existed.

"Call me tonight," said Monica Miller.

"Please don't go."

"I should let you be alone."

"That's the last thing I need. Angelina just told me she was retiring."

"Wow. How long has she been with you guys?"

"Since I was just a baby." *I wish I were still a baby and had another eighteen years before this terrible morning.*

She held Charlie by his bathrobe lapels and said, "Cheer up. Call me later. And have fun!"

"Wait. That was an amazing kiss."

"Yeah, it was nice."

"So are we, are we—"

"We are we. Call me tonight."

Charlie followed her out the front door and watched her jog east in her shorts toward Lexington Avenue, her brown hair bouncing off her back. He imagined her getting in a taxi and going downtown to the Haircut's apartment. He'd be getting ready for work about now, in the ritualistic and intense way that Haircuts did.

"Well, she has healthy hair," said Angelina, joining Charlie outside the front door to give him his juice, "but she shouldn't stop by so early."

"I can't believe you're leaving," said Charlie.

"Now there is work to do," said Angelina. "You do your work, and I do mine, and then for *siesta* we meet." It was what she had said, all these years, when *siesta* had meant juice and snack after school.

"But there won't be another siesta for us," said Charlie. "Not ever."

"Is okay," said Angelina, suppressing a sniffle, reminding herself that at this hour her mother was already perched in her carriage seat, awaiting the first wave of post-breakfast tourists. Unless Charlie came to Angelina's condo in Puerto Rico, she might never see him after this morning.

When the hand is too big to hold, it's time to go. She'd started babysitting children when she was thirteen, so after fifty-three years it was time to watch CNN on a color TV. There was a second room for her mother, but her mother would never leave her wooden house, broken by seven hurricanes, mended seven times—so many different patchworks of wood that in the proper morning light it seemed to hold all the colors of the rainbow.

Jee-Jee came out, toting Charlie's two large duffel bags. He'd worked one year as a bellhop at a four-star hotel in Marseilles and knew to bend his back and let his arms go limp. The Jaguar was already in front of the house. Jee-Jee had woken up especially early to secure the spot. He'd also had the car washed the day before. Charlie thought the car and its broad, gleaming grille had never looked better. He tried to use its brilliance as an antidote for his loneliness, but it only made his eyes sore.

"It is nice the girl came to say goodbye," said Jee-Jee, putting on his driving gloves, then closing the Jaguar's trunk. "But your Angelina did not approve."

"She wanted Charlie's juice," said Angelina.

"Charl, you can't go to school in a robe," said Jee-Jee. "Get showered so we can get on our way."

"I'm not feeling that great," said Charlie. "And my eyes feel weird from staring at the car."

"You need to become a man now," said Angelina. "You must shower even when you feel sad." She grabbed his face so she could press her wrinkly lips against his cheek one last time. "I am going on my shopping errands, and you are going to shower. *Adios.*"

"Maybe I could visit you in a few weeks?" asked Charlie. But Angelina was already on her way toward Madison Avenue.

*

More sad than manly, Charlie couldn't shower. Instead, he waited outside his mother's bedroom, waited to see her, bejeweled and perfumed. He was going to beg for Angelina to stay, beg for a last mother-son lunch instead of the ride to college, beg for one last night with Monica Miller, but when the door opened, Rose was in her cutoff sweatshirt. Bare, bony legs.

"I'm sick," she said, smelling of unoxidized wine.

"You're not going?" asked Charlie. They'd spoken about this morning for half a year.

"I'm sorry," said his mother.

"Is okay," said Charlie. Angelina was good at saying *Is okay*, and he wanted to be, too.

"I had a bad night."

"Is okay."

"We can have a wonderful phone call as soon as you get there. I want to know everything."

"I wish I was going to Paris instead of college," said Charlie, breathing in his mother's metallic breath.

"Philadelphia can be your Paris," she said, her words blanched of life. It was the sugar leaving her body. She once told Charlie about that awful feeling, about how it was the opposite of Paris. There, her skin never crawled, nor had sweat the audacity to collect on her face. There, stemless glassware with more sugar inside arrived in her hand at exactly the right moment.

"Go lie down," said Charlie. "I want to think of you having a great, fun New York day, after your nap."

"I love you, Charlie Bear," said Rose.

"I love you, too." Her eyes looked old this morning, like stale black coffee. *But she'll surely make a comeback*, thought Charlie. *Make a big sale at the gallery, and then the exposed capillaries will retreat. Maybe she'll sell the huge Picasso ceramic?*

He knew his mother. She was driven by hungover guilt. She'd positively embody Paris today, like the women she spoke of on bicycles after the war, the war widows who honored their husbands by filling the bicycle baskets with baguettes after sunrise. The women who no longer blinked. But before all that, she'd need a bath, a stiff vodka on the bathtub caddy.

*

John said there were always a few kids, freshman year, who didn't make it. That it started to get dark early in October, and then the ambulances came.

He had articles to prove it. Two of them were a month apart, during John's freshman year at Princeton. A kid jumped out his fifth-floor dorm window, bedsheets around his neck. Then another kid drank a bottle of Drano.

"Do you think college is lonely?" he asked Jee-Jee. They were speeding past Newark Airport, in tandem with the takeoff of a Federal Express plane that made the air crackle.

"Lonely? No, Charl, by tonight you'll have five, ten new friends. You'll be laughing with these new people. Tired and happy. A *fresh man*."

Charlie wished he could live up to Jee-Jee's forecast, show him the warm light of the future in his big brown eyes. He wanted to turn to his father and say, *Mais oui, Papa*, but he was looking out the window at the Federal Express plane, wondering if there were any humans in back, wondering if he'd have enough money to stay at a hotel tonight, ideally one near the Delaware River, where he'd heard about merchant marine captains who chose able-looking kids for adventures on the open seas.

Near the hotel he'd find a bar where people ate shrimp cocktail over shaved ice and told one another remarkable stories about leaving school on their very first day and falling in love with people who never leave you, despite how hard they, or you, try.

Ah, well, male lives begin when all the women are out of the picture.

Monica Miller, Mom, Angelina, the Very-Brown-Eyed Counselor. It sucked. And it hurt.

But it was necessary.

"I don't know if I'm going to make it," said Charlie.

His father laughed and popped in his beloved *Les Misérables* cassette. Charlie's response was to put on his Boodo Khan headphones. Jee-Jee looked over, disheartened. Charlie wished his father would grab the headphones and throw them out the window. That there would be an incident. A chance to pull the car over and cry hysterically about eighteen years of miscommunicated love, then go to a roadside diner and restart time.

"Come, Charl, remove the antlers."

"The Walkman's not even on."

"Then why wear them?"

"Did you know that the Delaware runs through Philly and empties out into the Atlantic Ocean?"

"Maman is so sorry she couldn't make it this morning. She had such a night, the baby leaving for college."

"She stunk of wine."

"Everyone has challenges."

"I think mine is girls."

"Let's sing *Les Miserables,* Charl."

"Dad—"

"You know, Charl, for me, these songs are about the Shoah."

While Jee-Jee thought of being liberated from the Nazis, Charlie imagined being free of Mariella's nights. Then panicked at the thought that Philly might not even have a Mariella's.

Chapter Four

CHARLIE AND HIS FATHER waited together in the lobby of High Rise South on an itchy, mustard-colored couch that also smelled like mustard, causing father and son to line their seat cushions with newspaper. Here Charlie filled out a final desperate request form for a single room. In March, in a happy, democratic mood after a joyous phone conversation with Monica Miller, he'd requested to have a roommate. It was two days after their first kiss, and Monica Miller said that she liked it when guys lived with other guys, that there was something cute but also masculine about it. He'd forgotten about his decision over the summer, somehow assuming that Monica Miller was going to be his roommate, not Francis Maglio of Haddonfield, New Jersey.

The manager of High Rise South told Charlie that singles were hard to come by, and that unless a series of inconceivable events unfolded over the next twenty-five minutes, a transfer would have to wait until the winter, and even then, another series of inconceivable events would have to unfold. Charlie watched his father handicap the first race at Philadelphia Park, a planned pit stop on the ride back home. For once, Charlie wished he was going with his dad to the track. An adult afternoon was what he needed. These kids with their posters and boom boxes—four years of them? Impossible.

Furthermore, Jee-Jee looked elegant, sitting there in his pow-der-blue three-piece suit and feathered cap. Other parents were inclined to point him out, a living symbol of the past on a futuristic day.

"Your father dresses like a gentleman," Charlie's mother had observed. He'd bought all of his suits in Paris, one morning in 1969.

"That was the last year Paris was Paris, Charl," Jee-Jee had reminded Charlie during the car ride to Penn. "Then, the bistros were black and white. Now they are gauche with colors."

"It's not fair that you got to live in the black-and-white times, and I get the colors," said Charlie.

"You'll find the shadows, Charl."

Not on the ground floor of High Rise South, where woolly carpets and Alpine furniture were covered in the colors of fake happiness. The decor wasn't dissimilar from the Contemplation Room at Camp Shining Star, where Charlie had counseled campers who'd gone astray with sugary contraband. In the Contemplation Room, there were glossies of celery growing and fish caught in a net. No photographs in the lobby of High Rise South, but rainbow murals welcoming the class of 1991, *probably made by schoolchildren*, thought Charlie, *or especially childlike members of the class of 1990.*

"Mom would hate this lobby," he said to Jee-Jee.

"She really tried to come, you know, but it was a hard night. Look, now!"

Jee-Jee pointed out a grandmother sunk in a chair, a box of pow-dered donuts in her lap, her nose tipped with powdered sugar. "What you think, Charl? We tell her to wipe her nose?"

"We're ready for the ninth floor," a megaphone voice announced.

"I thought we'd have more time," said Charlie.

Jee-Jee was already standing, the racing form tucked under his arm. "You sure you don't want me to come up with you? Mother said I should obey your wishes, but maybe you change your mind, no?"

"Is okay." Next to them, a father and son were engaged in a snif-fling bear hug, muffled I-love-yous spoken into their respective flannel shirts.

"I am not so good at making the beds, Maman will be the first to say, but maybe together we try?"

Charlie didn't respond. He wished the bear-huggers would stop.

"Okay." Jee-Jee clapped his hands, took Charlie by his shoulders, and kissed either cheek. "So! You'll study, not get into trouble, then we see you for Thanksgiving." Jee-Jee handed him an envelope that contained $2,000. "This must last you until Thanksgiving time, yes?"

"Oui," said Charlie.

Charlie watched his father hold open the door for a mother and daughter, smile his dimpled smile, and tip his cap like a kingly doorman before tugging his suit straight and wending his way out against the grain of Move-in Day.

*

John had told him to get to the room early, in order to claim the superior bed. He said he should make a friend, any friend. Ideally a pretty girl. Second-best would be an athlete. "Then, when the roommate's unpacking, bring the new friend into the room and speak with them as if you've known them your entire life. The roommate will feel second-rate and won't catch up until spring."

Charlie claimed the bed by the window, nearest the air-conditioning unit, a huge, yellowing Frigidaire. The beds were already made. All summer there had been talk of making the bed. It would have been more accurate to speak about remaking the bed and replacing the clean but iron-stained University of Pennsylvania sheets with the ones in his bag from Madison Avenue. His mother had packed the same sheets they had at home, a continuity that Charlie now found maudlin. He'd sleep in the standard issue, and the nice sheets would remain in plastic. "Fondee 1888," said the sheet store. High Rise South was *fondee* 1967. The housing unit reminded Charlie of the buildings near La Guardia Airport that always looked rained upon. Once, on the way back from a vacation, he'd asked Jee-Jee who lived there, and his response had been clear: "Poor people."

Charlie grew up respecting the people who lived near LaGuardia, and he hoped they would all make it to the airport one day. Or that their concrete slabs would grow contours and take off into the night sky, the residents cheering out of the tiny windows that they'd finally made it.

"There he is!" A stocky bald guy with a peace sign tattoo on his forearm grabbed Charlie's shoulder and spun him around. "Frank Maglio. Francis will be right up. His mom's buying him paper towels. That woman and her paper towels. Am I right? Hey, where's your folks? I wanna trade numbers with them."

"They already left. Just so you know, I put in an application for a transfer to a single room. No offense to Francis, it's just that I need a lot of quiet."

"Francis is a quiet kid. I see you're checking out my tat."

"I don't think I've ever seen one up close."

"My wife made me get it after I caused some trouble. Never caused any trouble again."

His hand was still on Charlie's shoulder. Then a second hand landed on Charlie's other shoulder.

"You do drugs?"

"No, sir."

"Well, neither does Francis. *Capiche*?"

"Peach."

If this man had a third hand, it would be on top of Charlie's head.

"You cook? Francis makes a mean lasagn."

"What's that?"

"Lasagn? You gotta be kidding me."

"Is it like lasagna?"

"You got it, you got it. *Lasagn*. It's the same thing. Us Italians drop the last part. You like pruh-shoot?"

"Huh?"

"There he is," said Mr. Maglio. "Francis Maglio. Ivy League, baby."

"Dad, did you remember me packing my protractor? I'm Francis," he said to Charlie. Their handshake was interrupted by Mr. Maglio's group hug.

"My kid's gotta loosen up. Am I right, Charlie, or what?"

"I actually don't mind unloose people," said Charlie, still in the huddle.

"Thank you," said Francis. "Dad, where's Mom?"

"Her and her freakin' paper towels."

"Here I am," sang Mrs. Maglio, hidden by a twelve-pack of Bounty towels. "You must be Charlie."

"Yes, ma'am."

"You be sure to help yourself to these towels. They have so many uses, and Bounty is the best brand by far."

Francis helped unburden his mother, then used his pocketknife to make a surgical incision in the Bounty towels' packaging. *What care*, thought Charlie, who had never seen such a small Swiss Army knife.

The Maglios stayed for close to an hour before taking their son to the Philadelphia Zoo, where, four years prior, Mr. Maglio had apparently predicted his son's enrollment.

"Right in front of the monkey cage, I told him he could do it. I says, 'Frank, you're going Ivy, baby.' I says, 'First day of school, while everyone's unpacking their books, we're gonna go tell the monkeys.'"

"My dad has lots of traditions," said Francis.

"Kid's got me dead to rights," said Mr. Maglio, offering his hands for cuffing. "What weird stuff does your family do?"

"Dad, not everyone's weird," said Francis.

"We don't have many traditions," said Charlie. "Maybe Chinese food on Sundays, but I guess that's over with. And we used to see a bunch of plays."

"The Great White Way," said Mr. Maglio.

"We used to all get dressed up. Angelina, too. But it's been a few years."

"Who's Angelina?" asked Mrs. Maglio, a happy, tired-looking woman with short free-flying hair. She tilted her head sympathetically, as if the answer might involve a chronically ill sibling.

"She's our governess." Charlie immediately regretted it. John had taught him to say *family friend*.

"How nice for your mother that she has some help," said Mrs. Maglio. Charlie watched her scan the four corners of the dorm room for dust bunnies. No dust, but one balled-up piece of paper. Charlie wanted to tell her the trash was not his, that he could be orderly without Angelina's chidings. Just not as orderly as Francis. He'd probably already made both a mental note and a Post-it Note about discarding the paper ball. Just look at him: everything unpacked, everything in its place, including a mini Dixie cup full of pushpins for his new corkboard.

Charlie hoped the Maglios weren't wary of their son's new friend, but this was what they were paying the big bucks for: an exotically brained rich kid with missing buttons on his blazer. They'd hope the New York kid would rub off on their son—not rub the Haddonfield, New Jersey, off the map of his life, but some ratio he could take back to Haddonfield for good measure. Ten percent New York was suitable—a little snobbery at the food court. *Maybe 15 percent*, thought Charlie— just enough so that Francis would stop shaving twice a day in preparation for his father's permanent five o'clock shadow.

"Charlie, are you working at Dining Commons, too?" asked Mrs. Maglio. "Francis's cafeteria uniform is real handsome."

"Mom," said Francis, "it's not that handsome." He couldn't suppress a little grin.

"Maybe. I hadn't thought about it, but why not?" said Charlie. He imagined a job as a late-night food taster, alone in a lab coat with vats of scrambled eggs, adding pinches of pepper.

"Francis likes his money." Mrs. Maglio put a roll of paper towels on Charlie's desk. "But who doesn't? Bounty towels aren't for free, you know."

"I forgot my scientific calculator," said Francis. "Damn."

"Your dad will drop it off, next time he's in town," said Mrs. Maglio.

"Damn," said Francis.

Mr. Maglio probably doesn't even know what a scientific calculator is, thought Charlie. *And he couldn't care less. God bless him. He's the type of man who'll get pennies pressed at the zoo. One for Francis and one for the family collection. The only thing my family collects is art. And it's all for sale.*

"Look at all those Post-its!" said Mr. Maglio. "Shit, son, you could slap a note on the caboose of every girl at Penn."

"*Frank,*" said Mrs. Maglio.

"Come here, you two college kids," said Mr. Maglio. "It's photo time."

Charlie liked Mr. Maglio's camera, a boxy Kodak Instamatic with a rainbow strap. He could see Mr. Maglio with that camera at the monkey cage, at graduation, at Francis's wedding.

"We should leave Charlie to unpack in peace," said Mrs. Maglio.

"Sure you don't want to see the animals?" asked Mr. Maglio.

"Angelina took me once. I remember the tiger cages, the way they smelled. I was too young at the time, but I think it was a mating smell."

"That brings up a good point, guys," said Mr. Maglio. "Protection, boys. For your wiener schnitzels."

"Dad, please."

"You got a girlfriend, Charlie?" asked Mr. Maglio. "Even if Francis had one, we wouldn't know. He tells us nothing."

"We should go," said Francis. "According to the map, it takes a while for the bus to get there and back."

"It was nice to meet you," Charlie said. "I hope I'll see you again one day."

"*One day,*" said Mr. Maglio. "We won't make ourselves a nuisance, but we'll be by once a month or so to make sure Francis is having some fun."

"They'll call before stopping by," said Francis. "We already agreed on that."

"So, *do* you have a girlfriend?" Mrs. Maglio asked Charlie.

"Yeah, *do* you?" asked her husband.

"Not everyone has one," said Francis, holding the missing calculator's power cord. Charlie watched the Maglios work in unison, making their son's bed, the synchronicity, the little nods when the top sheet was ready to be folded and creased.

"I dated a brunette girl named Monica Miller. We had a bad date last night, and I think she broke up with me, but then this morning, there she was. And we kissed." Charlie gulped, surprised at what he'd just told these people.

"Whoa," said Mr. Maglio. "Now this is getting interesting."

Francis sat with his parents, all three of them on the freshly made bed, his head bent. Mr. Maglio was right about his son. He was silent. And serious. He wore a necklace, almost certainly a cross. It went with the Dining Commons cap, the lightly pockmarked cheeks, and the short haircut, almost military issue. He had the torso of a wrestler. *He'll probably meet his wife here*, thought Charlie.

"Maybe Monica's got a friend for Francis?" asked Mrs. Maglio.

"Who knows when I'll see her again?" said Charlie.

"Trust me, she'll come around," said Mr. Maglio. "Just tell her to bring a friend."

"I might not like her friend," said Francis. "Or her friend might not like me. You don't have to ask her to bring a friend."

"She's probably a cute girl, and cute girls have cute friends. Am I right, or what?" Mr. Maglio asked Charlie.

"I never really met her friends," said Charlie. "We liked to be alone. At least I did."

"Romantic," said Mrs. Maglio.

"Can we please go now?" asked Francis.

"Kid's right," said Mr. Maglio. "Time for some real monkey business. Hug your new roommate and let's hit the zoo."

It was a brief but surprisingly tight hug. *Like we're brothers, or soldiers*, thought Charlie, examining Francis's brown bedsheets, with their hospital corners and a homemade quilt at the foot. Francis was done, his suitcases nowhere in sight. Books filled his bookshelf.

Charlie looked at his still-zipped duffel bags. He'd packed more for a vacation than a year of college. At least he had his composition book where he'd write more stories. One about Francis, for sure. And he had the Boodo Khan, and enough battery power to get him all the way to Monday. Labor Day. Stores would be closed.

Please last until Tuesday, Charlie told the batteries.

He wondered what other dorm rooms he might be in, had his parents not bought his way into Penn. UMass? Syracuse? Different monsters. Either way, he'd have the Boodo Khan, and his will to get the hell out of there.

*

A hairy student holding a clipboard peeked into Charlie's dorm room. "Green and Maglio?"

"I'm Green."

"Josh Feldman. I'm your RA, dude. Welcome to Penn."

"Thanks."

"Where's Mags?"

"Francis?"

"*Mags*. I'm great with nicknames. I can tell I'm going to call him Mags."

"He's still with his parents."

"That's so Frosh."

"What does RA mean?"

"Come on, Frosh. It's Resident Advisor."

He sat on Charlie's bed, plunked a backpack on the floor, and checked something off a list, his hairy, be-sandaled toes wriggling and snapping. "You allergic to anything, Chaplin? Any allergies?"

"Chaplin?"

"It's your nickname, Chaplin. Allergies?"

"Why do you need to know?"

Feldman produced a huge keychain and pointed at the air horn that was attached to it. "As you can see, I need to be prepared for anything."

"I'm allergic to oysters."

"You keep kosher?"

"I don't believe in that stuff." Charlie went to open the window, but it was bolted shut. "Why is it locked? Suicides, right?"

Feldman sat Charlie on his bed. "Look, once in a while, over the years, a few kids have had bad nights, and made some bad decisions. But you're not going to have to worry about any of that. Okay?"

"I hope not," said Charlie.

"Listen, first day of Frosh can be tough, but you'll never forget it, so try to chill out. Unpack. Make yourself at home. Tonight, we're doing a really cool meet-and-greet in the TV room. Totally hooking all you Frosh up with a flick and some popcorn. Give Mags this form to fill out. I'll need your forms before movie night. No form, no corn." He fingered Francis's art history book. "Fart history."

"Wow, you see the painting on the cover of the book—" Charlie stopped himself. It was the very same Maxfield Parrish that his grandmother had sold to the St. Regis Hotel for their barroom.

"You Frosh will change your minds about majors two dozen times before the end of the year. But if Mags is into fart history, we'll support him."

Charlie had sat beneath Parrish's *Old King Cole* at the King Cole Bar with Monica Miller on their fanciest date, which had hit a roadblock when when they'd forgotten to bring their fake IDs and couldn't get served a drink. Monica Miller had begged Charlie to use the Maxfield Parrish sale to sway the bartender, but Charlie couldn't. He'd been brought up not to brag about the art. It was a vestige of his grandmother's belief that theirs was an underground business. "What comes in the night can go in the night," she liked to remind her family. To throw off the scent, she even named her company Paris Home Supplies.

"My family has a couple of galleries, but we have nothing like this Maxfield Parrish," said Charlie to the RA.

"On my floor there are no poor Frosh or rich Frosh. There's just Frosh."

"The galleries are in so-so hotels, the kind that have a tour bus business in the lobby."

"Like I said, even if you came from a fleabag motel, we're all in dorm rooms now."

"So exactly when did they lock up the windows?"

Feldman tossed his clipboard on the bed and sat cross-legged on the floor. "Grab some carpet."

There wasn't much room to sit. Between Feldman, the desks, and the beds, two people sitting cross-legged would be uncomfortably close. But Feldman was persistent, telling Charlie that the carpet had been professionally vacuumed, and that he should enjoy it before the bugs started laying eggs.

"How are you feeling?" Feldman asked Charlie.

"Do you know any good places for lunch that are near the Delaware River?"

"I hear you, man. My first day? I wanted to go straight to the Wawa for a thing of ice cream, and it was *my* RA who set me straight. He said, 'Feldman, you don't want to ice cream yourself on your first day.'"

"I want today to be important. Maybe meet a girl whose light eyes understand me. I know that sounds weird." Charlie trusted Feldman. He probably used his own money to buy things like the clipboard and the popcorn.

"Okay, I hear you. And it can happen, it really can. But there's an order to things. First, you're going to need to unpack, you're going to need to attend the rooftop mixer for all the Highrise South Frosh, and you're going to need to stay on campus for a good few weeks. I didn't even make it down to the Delaware until the spring."

"I wish I was the sort of Frosh who would stick to the order of things, but between us, I'm not . . . normal." The way they were sitting, the soles of Charlie's penny loafers and Feldman's sandals touched. He'd sat that way with Angelina's stockinged feet. Human circuitry. Charlie was already happy for Feldman's eventual children, who would sit with their slouching dad, touching toes, completing the circuit. The kids would feel safe. Feldman's bag was open, and Charlie could see a Ziploc bag labeled AIDS gloves.

"You're premed." Charlie read it from his name tag.

"Parents like to know the RA's major."

"Wow, and you have AIDS gloves."

"If a Frosh pukes, and some of you will, I need to protect myself with the gloves. No offense, it's just that I don't know where you've been."

"I think you'll make a great doctor. Maybe one day down the road you can be my family doctor."

"Sounds good, except that I plan on being a surgeon. All right, good talk, my man. I have a bunch of trips planned for this week. I'll make sure you make it off campus. We'll probably hit the zoo first."

"That's where Mags went with his parents."

"Some parents like to use Move-in Day to sightsee, but they really shouldn't. If you don't do what you have to do on Move-in Day, the whole year could suck. You don't take advantage of Move-in Day, next thing you know, your GPA's down in the B range and you're asking every sophomore you know if they saved last year's notes. By the time you catch up it's graduation day, and while all of your buds are leaving stinking hot Philly for their cool new lives, the only job you can get is managing a sporting goods store in Center City."

"What nickname did your RA give you?" asked Charlie.

Feldman pointed to his name tag.

"But Feldman's your last name."

"Nicknames weren't a specialty of my RA. It was probably his only weakness. I'd love to sit and chat all day about life, but I have fifteen more Frosh to meet with. You only get your first day of college once."

"I couldn't agree more," said Charlie, shaking Feldman's hand, firmly and quickly, like the newsreel he'd seen of Babe Ruth meeting President Hoover. It was at a tiny movie theater in Palm Beach that still played old newsreels before the feature. It was a long time ago. He'd gone alone with John. It was the evening their grandmother was told about her lung cancer, and the adults needed to be together.

"Maybe I'll hit a movie today," said Charlie. "Then remove myself from the popcorn-scented darkness and step into my life."

"Poetic, Frosh, but I already got *Total Recall* and use of the popcorn machine. What you need to do is unpack and hit the Club Fair on Locust Walk."

A tube of cookie dough rolled past the door.

"I'm definitely getting myself a spoonful of that," said Feldman. "Later, man."

John had told him about raw cookie dough. He even speculated that the Soviets had created it to keep American college students down, saying, "After eating it, you don't care about anything else. Not classes, not girls. It's that good. Then the next day there's a zit on your forehead and you can't get out of bed."

A girl twirling a lacrosse stick, accompanied by an elderly man, knocked on Charlie's door.

"We're on the lookout for Grandpa's driving glasses," said the girl.

"I got confused," said the old man. "Thought this was her room. Sat right there at the desk for close to half an hour."

"Do you mind if we take a look around?" She introduced herself, but Charlie could only focus on the lacrosse stick she twirled from hand to hand. She had white teeth that she bared when repositioning the gum in her mouth, and muscles above her knees that made heart shapes when she'd crouch to look for the glasses. Charlie liked athletic girls. At least he liked watching them; they seemed unaware of their new muscles, unlike their male counterparts, who were always tensing and flexing. This lacrosse girl had short sandy hair and speckled gray-green eyes—*a color scheme that would look better on a canvas than on a human*, thought Charlie. But he could see how a regular person, someone like Francis, could find all he needed in eyes such as hers.

"I went to college in Philadelphia, too," said the old man. "Pharmacists' college. But there weren't dormitories like this, just the Armory Building down on Race Street. Paid for by Uncle Sam."

The old man was back at Charlie's desk chair. He was a big old guy, a gentle giant at home in smaller wooden chairs. He didn't cross his legs, but he hiked his trousers, revealing white socks.

"Grandpa's a World War Two vet," said the Lacrosse Girl. "It's okay to say that, right, Gramp?"

"Sure, honey. Nothing to be embarrassed about, there."

"Your back," Charlie said to the old man.

"Back? Why, I guess I came back in '46. They made you go through Hawaii, to delouse us."

"No, the glasses are on your back, under your shirt. I can see the frames through your shirt."

"Well, isn't that something," said the old man.

"You have no idea," said the Lacrosse Girl. "He needs them to drive home."

"Like I always say," said the old man, "the answer's right under your nose." He handed Charlie a bubble gum cigar.

"You're in good company," said the Lacrosse Girl. "Gramp gave the other cigar to the president of Penn."

"I came with three, and plan on leaving with none," the old man said, beaming, and with a two-fingered salute headed for the door.

"Tell Mom I'll be there in a second, Gramp," said the Lacrosse Girl.

"Take your own sweet time," he said, tap-dancing to avoid the tube of cookie dough that had apparently changed direction and gained speed.

"What a happy guy," said Charlie.

"You know, I never thought about it, but he is happy. Probably the happiest I know. You like cookie dough?"

"I've never tried it," said Charlie.

"I did, once. Really weird. Sort of too sweet and too salty, but also perfect."

"I may never try it."

"Isn't that what college is for? Trying new things? I'll probably have some, just not the roll that's been flying around." She was sitting on Francis's bed, resting her chin on the lacrosse stick.

"Were I you, I'd avoid the cookie dough altogether," said Charlie. "Unless you're the type of person who can stop at one spoonful, even if you want more. I'm not that way. If I love something, I can't stop."

She prodded him with her lacrosse stick to see if the utterance was alive with flirtation, but Charlie didn't squirm when the webbing brushed his jacket's vents.

"I wonder what Gramp would make of the whole raw cookie dough thing."

"He'd probably read the instructions, slice up the roll, and put it in the oven."

"Oh my God, that's so true. What is it with our fucked-up generation? Here we are, rebelling by eating uncooked dough, thinking it's so ironic to eat something that hasn't been in the oven, while the last generation risked imprisonment to protest a war. They ended Vietnam."

The Lacrosse Girl was smart. For a moment, Charlie had forgotten that he was at a college, a good one, where smart kids gave little speeches like that. He wondered if she'd given that exact same speech before, substituting something else for cookie dough.

He could see her using it in her valedictory address. Half the kids here were valedictorians. He'd read the stat but could have guessed as much. They all seemed to be on the verge of reciting the famous part of their valedictory address, where they railed against our supposedly fucked-up generation, or criticized the high school administration for firing a beloved French teacher.

"I for one don't think our generation is fucked-up, just a little nameless. We don't belong to anything. At least not yet. Where are you from?"

"Virginia," she said brightly, a good ambassador. "You're New York, right? I saw your dad's license plate when you were getting out. Nice car. Really shiny."

"He just washed it."

"Aw, that's sweet. He wanted the family car to look good on Move-in Day."

Charlie hadn't thought of the reason why the Jaguar gleamed, and now felt bad that he hadn't thanked his father.

"He's a good guy, for a French guy," said Charlie. "Did you see him?" He wondered what she would make of his old-fashioned suit.

"Your dad? I saw you two get out of the car. He looked like a dad to me. Where's your roommate from?" She was by Francis's desk, seeing if she could budge the suction-cupped pencil sharpener.

"He's from New Jersey. Installing that pencil sharpener was one of the first things he did when he got here. I think you'd like him."

He could tell that she preferred him to any possible desk-accessory-obsessed roommate. He wanted to tell her that she was great, truly, but that he didn't know what to do with all of her positive energy. *Lacrosse girls who live in their lacrosse shorts are beacons, day and night*, thought Charlie. He shielded his eyes.

"He's from Haddenfield," he said. "A high school wrestler." He opened Francis's closet and pointed out his varsity jacket. "He's organized. As you can see."

"That's a plus," she said. "I like my men clean."

"He's very clean."

"You're quite the matchmaker."

Charlie could see her and Francis together in the grocery store, or shopping for a Christmas tree. A healthy, practical couple, who met at a college in Pennsylvania. Theirs would be a love centered around errands, weekends, and sweatpants. They'd never speak about sex, and their inside jokes would be tedious, but they'd have healthy kids. Baseball gloves and ice skates would litter their mudroom.

"From the little I've seen," said Charlie, "I think you'd get along."

"Is he tall?" she asked, trying to decide for herself by examining one of his dress shirts. "His clothes smell like an old iron. I don't mind it."

"See, that's just it. Many girls would."

"High five," said the Lacrosse Girl.

"Why?"

"Why not?"

"Okay."

They produced a clean clap. Charlie believed she was plotting a kiss. Not today, but on some night over the next four years. To discourage her plans, Charlie leaned over his desk, like one of those pictures of

JFK during the Cuban Missile Crisis, and thought about this morning's Monica Miller kiss.

"You okay?" asked the Lacrosse Girl.

"Fine. Just thinking about someone."

"Girl back home, maybe?"

"Maybe."

"I only went to New York once. Museum of Natural History. I gave a speech about the American buffalo."

"I have buffalo nickels in my loafers."

"We have so much in common."

"Really?"

"I was joking. Sort of. So, the wrestler who smells like laundry. Why not?"

She'd actually made eye contact with Francis when he was leaving with his parents. He walked funny. Many wrestlers did. But he'd twisted his face into a childish smile during the eye contact, and it was endearing. "I should get back to parents' world. They've probably put everything away. I'll never find a single thing."

"I hope you're not insulted that I thought of you and my roommate," said Charlie, listening to a woman's high heels click in the courtyard below. "You're both dignified."

"How nice of you to say."

"It's something my family friend says. She's from Puerto Rico, where it's a real compliment."

"And are *you* dignified?"

"No. Not yet."

"Well, I guess I'll leave you alone. You seem deep in thought."

"*Pensive* was on the SATs," said Charlie, turning from the desk, the missile crisis safe in RFK's hands.

"Ugh, I was so sick that day."

"Hungover?" he asked.

"Flu. Well, enjoy your bubble gum cigar. See you at graduation."

He knew she was joking, but the thought of four years was daunting. Four years ago was ninth grade. What a terrible year that was: too old to be a child, too young to drink.

Chapter Five

SWEAT RAN DOWN CHARLIE'S back. Feldman must have turned off the wonderfully raucous AC. Or maybe Gramp. Old people didn't like the cold. Angelina said they were getting their bodies accustomed to heaven, where she assured Charlie that the balm of Hell rose up to heat the pearly clouds. Eighty-two degrees with a breeze. Entry to Heaven. Another reason to practice the *Dignidad*.

By now most of the parents had said their goodbyes, and the only people he saw passing his open door were groups of kids, hands in pockets, moving with a fake sense of purpose that reminded Charlie of *21 Jump Street*, the undercover cops and their endless high school year. A few looked in as they passed at Charlie by his desk with his Move-in Day folder. So many pamphlets, so many solicitations, so many schedules. But not one of them was mandatory. No asterisks, except to indicate an added cost, like tomorrow's Trivial Pursuit breakfast sponsored by the Law Club, or Friday night's bus ride to Camden for an outdoor screening of *Dirty Dancing*.

He was tempted to ditch the big dreams of running away from Move-in Day and just be Charlie Green, freshman. A kid stuck in the late eighties, figuring stuff out. Ditch the blazer for a Penn hoodie like everyone else.

Luxuriate in life's perfectly acceptable averageness. Prince's AIDS ballad "Sign o' the Times" was blaring down in the courtyard, and an entire roll of cookie dough was being passed around the floor. It would be easy to ask the Lacrosse Girl if she'd seen *Dirty Dancing*. But doing what was easy—normal kid stuff—did not come easy to him. It was effortless enough when he was very little. When he'd wait all morning on the bench outside his mother's room for their weekly walk in the park, for the ritual balloon purchase and a shared rainbow Italian ice. Those walks were euphoric for five-year-old Charlie. But when Angelina was hired, the walks ceased to be. For the first few months, Charlie continued to wait patiently outside his mother's bedroom and its shut door, until finally conceding one awful morning that he would never again take a walk in the park with his wine-cursed mother.

Normal kids do as they're told, the suckers. They sit on benches outside closed doors, for hours, just to end up heartbroken and alone. Life is a prison that needs to be escaped. He imagined a set of three skeleton keys, and named them Girls, Europe, and Vodka.

*

The name and number of his advisor, Victoria Pettibone, were written on his Move-in Day folder. They'd spoken on the phone, her voice young and bright. He'd thought about her since that conversation last month, from the telephone room at Camp Shining Star that doubled as the weigh-in center.

"Stop by anytime," Miss Pettibone had said.

"Including Move-in Day?"

"The door will be open. If you'd like to bring your parents, feel free."

"At my camp, the campers weigh themselves every Sunday, then call home. It can be a tough call."

"I'm sure you've been an excellent counselor. Maybe there's a sociology class that touches on your unique summer experience."

"I don't know about my classes."

"We do have you, by default, in four introductory classes, but they don't necessarily reflect *your—*"

"You should see how happy or sad some of the campers get when they step on the scale. It's like life and death."

"Hmm."

Even over the phone, Charlie could tell that Miss Pettibone said *Hmm* to great effect. Almost as well as the old dandy, now deceased, who'd frequented Adam's Rib and said *Hmm* after tasting wine to indicate that the bottle wasn't to his liking. Apparently he was a writer, famous for being gay and southern. Charlie didn't understand the appeal when his mother pointed him out, but then he overheard him saying *Hmm* to the coat check girl when she couldn't locate his scarf. By the time she found it rolled into the arm of another overcoat, the manager had bought him his dinner.

"Chaplin, they've moved the hacky sack mixer to College Green." Feldman had reappeared, leaning against the open door, taking notes on his clipboard. "Strongly recommend making an appearance. I met my pre-girlfriend there last year."

"I'm meeting my advisor," said Charlie, zipping up his book bag with exaggerated finality. He made certain his Walkman would play "With or Without You" when he hit campus. The song still reminded him of Monica Miller, but he'd turned a corner in his listening, making the song less about her and more about him, how it wasn't that easy being with Charlie Green, but things wouldn't be the same without him.

"Nice move, Chaplin, getting in to see the advisor on your first day. Head starts are what it's all about."

"What's a pre-girlfriend?"

"It's the girl you date before your real freshman girlfriend."

"Monica Miller's my pre-girlfriend. Well, was. Can a breakup end with a kiss?"

"You already got through your pre-girlfriend? Another head start, you could be RA material, Chaplin. As long as you get those ideas about partying on the river out of your head."

Charlie turned off the lights, casting Feldman in shadows. Feldman, undeterred by the surrounding blueness, kept using his clipboard. He'd raised a leg for added support, like Monica Miller did when she was trying to look seductive, and now it was more difficult for Charlie to leave his room cleanly.

"Let's be careful out there," said Feldman as Charlie inched his way past his knee. "You know that line? It's from *Hill Street Blues*. Great show."

"I don't watch TV."

He'd seen every episode.

*

Charlie had expected Miss Pettibone's waiting area in College Hall to be like his principal's reception area at high school, but there was no receptionist nor oil paintings, just a corridor of doors with numbers stenciled into cloudy glass. Some of the doors were open, on purpose, it would seem, so that adult voices could be heard down the marble corridor. "Goethe" and "ecclesiastical" echoed off the slabs, and the sound of electric typewriters. Pauses surrounded by torrents of letters.

Miss Pettibone's door was shut. Shadows moved behind the glass. He knocked and the shadows scattered, but there was no response, so he sat on the cold floor and waited. Charlie liked cold floors. He liked that things could be alive with coldness instead of warmth. He wondered if Miss Pettibone ever held her meetings out here, on the marble. He could picture the backs of Monica Miller's bare legs against the stone, but knew she'd ask to sit on his jacket, and that when he balked, she'd leave College Hall in search of a Haircut.

"Hi, did you just knock?" Victoria Pettibone was apparently unaware that her white blouse was open an extra button, and that part of her black lacy bra was exposed. "There's no one else here, so it must have been you. Do you mind waiting a minute more?" she asked through a tense smile. "I'm just finishing up a meeting."

"I don't mind waiting," said Charlie. "Really nice marble." A skinny bearded guy sneaked out of Miss Pettibone's office. He wore a back-pack and an open denim shirt, which revealed freakishly straight black chest hair.

"Oh," said Miss Pettibone, "you're leaving. I guess our meeting is over."

"I'll see you, Miss Pettibone," he said meaningfully, or sarcastically. It was hard for Charlie to tell.

"Okay," she half-yelled after him as he strode down the corridor, one hand clutching his book bag, the other in a fist. It would be a good time to crank "With or Without You," thought Charlie. This guy's walk was informed by the gravitas of that video, as was every walk away from a woman that involved a fisted hand.

"Hmm," said Miss Pettibone.

"Should we go in?" asked Charlie.

"Yes, of course."

Charlie couldn't tell if she was twenty-five or forty-five; at his age, all adults were still similarly dated. Her short spiky hair and citrusy perfume placed her in definitive adulthood, where skirt pleats battled with dangly gypsy earrings for the possession of her soul.

Miss Pettibone's office faced the interior and was starved of light. To make matters dimmer, her desk lamp was off. Charlie squinted at the window where, outside, the summer lived, but in here was like under the huge oak tree at Camp Shining Star, where campers would take naps at high noon.

"Should I be expecting your parents?" asked Miss Pettibone. "Traditionally, I meet the parents during Move-in Day appointments."

"My dad already left."

"I see." She was going to sit in her desk chair but now felt obliged to sit next to him. *Every year there's one who needs a mother*, she thought, finally buttoning up her blouse.

On Miss Pettibone's desk was a family photo: Miss Pettibone, a man with a gray ponytail, and a younger girl sitting in a canoe that wasn't on water but in the middle of a city street. It was a flattering shot of her, but the daughter's face was contorted from petulance, and the husband looked apple-faced or ill. Miss Pettibone shone by comparison. Charlie wondered if she were vain. She was pretty enough to be vain, though most of the prettiness came from her thinness and the way she wore professional clothing.

"Is that canoe on the street?" Charlie asked as she read his file.

"It was an art installation from last year." His file read GREEN, CHARLIE. A winning moniker, thought Miss Pettibone.

"Did it block traffic?"

"It was only up for a week."

"If I were driving home from work and got in a traffic jam because of a canoe in the middle of the street, I'd be upset. Not that I know how to drive."

"So, Charlie, what can we accomplish today?" she said, reclaiming her desk chair.

Green Charlie looks a little tired, she thought. Some pallor about the cheeks and forehead where his tan was fading. But the navy jacket was a nice touch. Miss Pettibone had married older, and she wanted the same for her daughter. Of course, not all older men were created equal; she'd chosen a professor who owned a beloved wok and wore hiking shoes with his dress suits.

"I've had my heart set on some sort of late lunch in the city," said Charlie, and Miss Pettibone nodded quick, birdlike nods that probably meant *no*. But Charlie continued. "To be honest, I sort of saw myself getting to Penn and having an adventure on the very first day. Things happen young to people in my family. At least with my parents and grandmother. The light in here seems to stop at the window, then just sort of dies."

"Now, when you say an adventure, what did you have in mind? Because along Locust Walk, today through Labor Day, is the club fair. It's where I would send you."

Some part of her didn't want Charlie to take the club fair bait. Lately, she knew about adventures. Real ones. Mournful guilt followed by new pangs of euphoria. She wouldn't wish all of that on a young heart. It was unsafe, if not unsavory, but her heart could handle it—ate it up, in fact. This was her sixteenth year at Penn, advising students. The only job she'd ever had. She'd gone to school here and never left, married her sociology professor and had little to no sense if her work at Penn had made any difference at all. She only received phone calls from ex-students when they were ready to apply to grad school and needed transcripts or a recommendation. All of her advice was geared toward the creation of a good—no, a great GPA. Which meant a good two-year job after college, then a good grad school, then a great job after grad school. Then a great salary, and from that great salary, great gifts for Penn.

Exhausting, thought Miss Pettibone, and pictured herself dancing with Green Charlie at her daughter's wedding. In ten years she'd be forty-eight, but knew her legs would still look good in stockings.

"My RA, Feldman, told me about the fair on Locust Walk," said Charlie, "but I'm interested in something else."

"What would your adventure look like?"

"It would happen near the Delaware River, at a restaurant, and there would be a bar."

"Charlie, it's my responsibility to let you know that the drinking age in Pennsylvania is twenty-one. What you've just said makes me think you might need some special sort of counseling. Have you had trouble with alcohol in the past?"

"No. I really like it."

"There are pretty strict rules at Penn," said Miss Pettibone. "I'd hate to see you get in any sort of trouble." Her perfume filled the small, dark office. She knew it was too much, but she didn't care. It was from a sampler she'd snatched months ago as she rushed through Wanamaker's department store after the first forbidden afternoon. She'd needed the overdose. Otherwise, her husband, with his wine bouquet snout, might have asked her why she smelled *nutty*.

"In most civilized countries throughout the world, I'd already be of drinking age."

"Well, Charlie, there's an excellent anthropology class that compares and contrasts world customs." That was her training: always bring it back to the course load.

"I like studying people. Especially ones at bars."

"I don't mind beginning our meeting with anecdotes about the adventures you have forecast for yourself. *However*, before this appointment is over, we do need to iron out your classes."

However. That was her husband's favorite word. Favorite flame-douser. *I love forecasting adventures*, thought Miss Pettibone. What else is there? Fuck *however*.

"So: courses. Because you hadn't chosen any, I've placed you in four freshman surveys. All good, but a little directionless. Tell me about you and museums."

"Museums?"

"You're from New York City. I'm sure your parents and teachers directed you toward your city's bounty of absolutely wonderful museums."

"I liked hanging out in museums, but not because of the artifacts, but because of how sound traveled, and how I could get lost in all that cold marble."

"Well, there's a course for freshmen about curating a museum, particularly ancient Egyptian art and artifacts. Taught in our very own world-class art museum."

Miss Pettibone liked to visit the college's museum minutes before closing, when it was all but empty, and pretend it was her palace.

"One of my summer job options was working at the gift store of the Met," said Charlie. "It was either that or Camp Shining Star. I didn't like the idea of selling people posters of great paintings. There's something wrong about a box of five hundred Monets."

"The museum course has only one opening. I think you'll love it."

"Okay," said Charlie. "I bet every girl thinks they're Cleopatra. I bet they go to the museum to find their old jewelry."

Miss Pettibone's department cocktail party had been held at the museum last spring. She drank too much and had to be picked up by her husband. But such fun. Young fun. She wandered off with her glass of wine, sought an obscure corner, and sat before a collection of jade jewelry. It was something Green Charlie might do, she imagined now— leave the main scene in search of a smaller scene all his own.

About that, she was always right. Finding the life inside of these kids. Of course, she wasn't encouraged to tap that force of energy. It was all about direction, helping these young men and women become people who would not wander off at the museum party, but stay in the center of things, listening to the speeches, clapping at the right parts, and drinking zero to one glass of wine. Adventures are what you read your kids at night.

"The museum's a special place. I think it's more in line with your sense of adventure," she said.

"I guess so," said Charlie, whistling a long, descending note that sounded like a bomb dropping, just as Jee-Jee did at the track after losing yet another horse race.

"Some students have visited Egypt in order to participate in a real excavation," said Miss Pettibone. "I actually had a student who had taken this very course, and he spent his junior year working at the Egyptian embassy in Washington, DC. Now he works for a private bank in New York, advising them about their Middle Eastern investments. It just goes to show you how one experience can lead to the next and so on."

"Hmm," said Charlie.

"I know it sounds overwhelming, but all of the pieces will fall into place. The key is to take it one piece at a time."

"It sounds like dominoes. My nanny wouldn't let me play, she thought it was a game the devil would play."

"Then think of it as building a foundation. Building something from the ground up. Something solid."

"Like a square box?"

"Sure. Rectangular. Solid—"

"Like a coffin," said Charlie.

She ran her fingers through her moussed hair and swiveled her chair to face the window. He was right about the light stopping where it did. At least the room was always a little cool. She'd refused an air conditioner on her very first day. Her pencil cup was precisely where she'd placed it on May 22, 1971, with the dangerously sharp letter opener she knew she'd never dare touch. The room was better suited for winter, but even in the summer, it was winter in here. Labor Day weekends were the worst, but it was Miss Pettibone's crunch time, so her daughter suffered a landlocked three days while her classmates held on to their summers, splashing in the ocean.

Tonight, though, Miss Pettibone was taking her daughter to see *Dirty Dancing*. All summer she'd asked to go. They'd bought her the soundtrack in June, but she'd played it so often that the tape came undone in her little pink cassette player.

"Were I you," said Miss Pettibone, "I'd avoid the bars near the Delaware today."

"I know that you'd rather have me on campus, but—"

"The lunches are cacophonous. Tables crammed together. And most of the old seafood places only have views of strangers in lobster bibs or those big glass balls in netting. The water is far away." Her husband liked to prey on the early bird dinners. Two lobster tails for $14.95. The sound of him licking his buttered fingers.

"Really? Please tell me more." Charlie leaned forward, his eyes wide and moist, to attract more details.

"There's a nice little place in Center City, with oyster plates on the walls and old wooden floors. Sawdust on the floors."

"Sawdust! Is it dark? I hope it is."

"It isn't really dark, but it's not offensively bright."

It was at the beginning of the summer that things had started falling apart, and other things started to come together. At the Sansom Street Oyster House, she confessed to having kissed another man; after many breathless *oh my Gods*, her best friend whisked her to a table in back for a debriefing. Miss Pettibone had chosen the Sansom Street Oyster House for its anonymity, but a colleague she never cared for had complained about its utter lack of modernity, its *sawdust* and *uninspired maleness*. People in her office made everything into a fucking book review. Same with the know-it-all husband at home.

"I think it's a charming place," said Miss Pettibone.

"It sounds that way. Were there any younger people? Not kids. Not college kids, but charming girls? A charming girl?"

"I was with my friend, talking, but there seemed to be some old salts at the bar."

Old salts. Charlie closed his eyes and smelled Coney Island on V-E Day. "Do you think, Miss Pettibone, that falling in love is a form of time travel?"

She had been about to mention the English department's Romantic Novel in Industrial America course, but instead she smiled. "Yes."

She was being generous, Charlie knew. Taking a big chance, sending a freshman to a bar.

"Thank you, Miss Pettibone. You might be the first adult who has ever treated me this way. I'm not sure if this is part of the advisory program, or maybe a new thing where you give students what they really want, regardless of the consequences, so they can learn some sort of a lesson. Whatever it is, I won't let you down. I'll definitely visit you again and tell you everything that happened at the—what was it called?"

"The Sansom Street Oyster House."

Nothing will happen, she thought. *But it's good that you'll feel free for a few moments. Two chardonnays and you'll get a big headache, and the adventure will end. You'll take a taxi back to campus with your tail between your legs, but all's forgiven. And I hope you'll forgive me when I put you back on track for, let's see, cum laude in economics? Sound good? Good.*

"It must have been cozy in there," said Charlie.

"At the Oyster House?"

"No, in the canoe, with your family. In the middle of the street."

"Not really. There was a line of people waiting to get in to have their photos snapped, so you couldn't get that comfortable."

"You can't tell any of that from the photo," said Charlie. "I didn't bring any photos to Penn."

"This year, you'll have plenty of new photo opportunities." Here she'd usually insert how Penn was his new family, and that this family, just like the one at home, lasts a lifetime. Even longer if you start gift-giving upon graduation. Twenty-five dollars a week was a more than reasonable start.

"This has been an unorthodox first meeting, Charlie," said Miss Pettibone, worried now about being fired for sending a student to a seafood bar. "Again, I must remind you of the drinking age in Pennsylvania, and urge you to remain on campus, but I am only your advisor, and your two legs will take you where they must."

My husband will want Indian food before the movie tonight, because it's cheap and he can smile knowingly at the sitar player. The definition of heaven is escaping hell, she thought. Or maybe the real, practical definition was enduring hell, accessorizing it with paisley scarves.

She'd moved in with her husband before they were married. It was tight, just the two of them, and now that the living room had become her daughter's space, there was little she could call her own, save for the corner in the bedroom where she had a standing desk and had draped a paisley scarf over the lampshade.

Charlie stood because Miss Pettibone was standing, looking out the window, rolling the eraser end of a pencil back and forth above her lip.

"Do you happen to know the address of the Oyster House?" he asked. "I saw on the map they gave us freshmen that the campus ends at Thirty-Second Street, then there seems to be a wasteland until Twenty-Third Street, when the city begins again."

"I'll write it down for you," she said. "As for that wasteland, there are some industrial stretches in Philly, but if you keep on walking, you'll get to some wonderful little neighborhoods. So, I've enrolled you in creative writing, European history, and chemistry, in addition to the museum course. Let's meet again in October and see how you're doing."

"If I'm still at Penn, of course."

You'll still be here, Green Charlie, thought Miss Pettibone. *But I'll miss the boy who stands before me today in his formal jacket, believing the world is knowing enough to know his dreams. If the dean asks, I'll tell him I sent Green Charlie into the city on an odyssey, that he was a fan of Homer's* Odyssey.

"Have you read *The Odyssey*?" she asked Charlie.

"I never got into myths."

There was a course called Myths and the Modern World; Wharton-ites took it to fulfill their one humanities credit, writing papers about how Morgan and Rockefeller were the only true descendants of Zeus. But this boy didn't want to wield 1987 lightning bolts. He wanted to hold 1937 stemware. Despite all his chatter, there was something humble about Green Charlie. Miss Pettibone watched him lick his thumb and buff his penny loafer. Something an older man might do. Not a great man, maybe even a wrecked man, thought Miss Pettibone.

Enough. He's only eighteen. He wants to get drunk at a grown-up bar.

"I bet if you encounter *The Odyssey* in your studies at Penn, you'll have a new appreciation, Charlie. I see some of that story in your desire to walk around today. It's all about a person wanting to go home, and whether that's even possible."

She gave him her home number, in case of an emergency. All of her students got it. Maybe he'd call during *Dirty Dancing*, she thought. Maybe he'd call and leave a long message from the crowded and happy bar where women just like her smiled with their husbands about how they'd make love once they were home. The lightest couple in the room. It was impossible to be light at the Indian buffet.

"Well, then, I should keep the office open for walk-ins. The parents get impatient if the door is closed for more than a couple of minutes.

Bon chance," said Miss Pettibone, throwing up her hands as her husband did when he felt he'd said all there was to say.

"*Merci,*" said Charlie.

There was no one waiting outside her door. There was no one in the hallway in either direction, just Charlie and the sound of typewriters. She took her time affixing the doorstop, making sure the worn brown triangle went all the way under the door. She'd just gotten a pedicure. She'd just had the soles of her feet kissed by red lips and their black beard. She'd just sent a kid to a bar.

Now I'll type up my notes about Green Charlie, she thought, *and my typing will join the other typing.*

Chapter Six

Club fair booths lined Locust Walk, students in costume barking about glee club and the Society for Creative Anachronism; the first dressed like Gatsby, the second like Dungeons & Dragons.

"SCA has the best kegs," John had told Charlie. "Amazing, imported stuff. Those D&D looking geeks know their beer."

One of them, a jester, was rapturously playing a flute, dancing in and out of the Locust Walk crowd with his pointed shoes. He was the only real *Odyssey*-like obstacle, and the worst he could do was poke you with his shoes. Miss Pettibone might be disappointed there weren't any real mythical dangers along the way, he thought, although a girl in the gay rights booth yelled "Are you gay?" at Charlie and everyone stared. But you didn't really come across that in the Greek myths. There was one beast toward the dregs of the fair, a boa constrictor draped around its owner's shoulders. It wasn't really an official college club, just a washed-out hippie who liked answering questions about his snake.

Across from him was the Hillel booth, with yarmulke'd kids in jeans.

"Are you Jewish?" they asked Charlie.

"Yes, but most people think I'm something else."

"I could tell a mile away."

"Most people think I'm European."

"European Jew."

"Initially, my ex-girlfriend thought I was Italian."

"That's why she's your ex. She never knew who you really were," said the smiling Jew with a razor-burned neck and corduroy pants that choked his fleshy thighs.

"She was Jewish, my ex," said Charlie.

If Monica Miller were here, he thought, *she'd grab my hand and walk us quickly out of the Club Fair; she'd want to see if there was any good shopping in the city center. She'd veto the Sansom Street Oyster House, unless shopping came first.*

"We have a shabbat prayer for ex-girlfriends," said the smiling Jew, wagging his finger. "It's sort of like, 'I wish you well, but I wish me a little better.' You should come to shabbat dinner tomorrow night. *Come,*" he said. "Come."

It made Charlie feel weird inside when his people repeated things like "Come." When younger Jews sounded like older Jews. "Maybe," he said, actually entertaining the idea.

"We have a brother who looks just like you. He'll be there tomorrow, and you can judge for yourself."

Charlie didn't care much for mirrors. He couldn't find his whole among the features. A mop of brown hair, big comic book circles for eyes, long limbs. He feared there just wasn't much to him; people were always pointing out his doppelgängers. He had been physically beautiful for a few winter months when he was fifteen. Even John had admitted as much. Charlie supposed the remnants of that lucky time were still about the face if you knew where to look. Otherwise, he was someone's cousin or brother. A tall boy with doe eyes. A brunette.

"People are always saying I look like someone else."

"Hey, it's all a shell anyway," said the smiling Jew, his arms open so that the whole world could get a glimpse of his perfectly imperfect shell.

Charlie wanted to tell him about the genetic magic that some girls saw. Monica Miller couldn't get enough face time, touching his mouth and cheekbones.

"When my mother was younger, she was beautiful," said Charlie to the smiling Jew.

"All mothers are beautiful." He said pretending to tip his tie-dyed yarmulke.

"No. Mine was truly gorgeous, and for a couple of years I looked just like her. I guess now I look like any other Jew."

"Hey, you're a cute guy, and with quite the sense of humor, I can tell. So, will we see you at shabbat dinner?"

"If I'm still around, sure."

"*Still around.* Will you listen to this guy?"

"I didn't think the rabbis would let you wear a reggae yarmulke," said Charlie.

"One of our Hillel brothers has the Rolling Stones tongue on his. You have to have some fun in life. Look at this." He pulled a yarmulke out of his back pocket. "The iron-on is the guys from New Order. Did you know that they're Jewish? It's true: the song 'Bizarre Love Triangle' is about three Jews. You want?"

"The yarmulke?"

"I was saving it for a dance party next month, but take it. It makes quite the statement."

Charlie tried to refuse, but the smiling Jew forced it into his blazer pocket; he was surprisingly strong, which was confirmed by their parting handshake. He was a good guy, thought Charlie. If the snake across the way were anti-Semitic and attacked him, Charlie would intercede, put his life on the line for him. The smiling Jew stood for something: he wouldn't care what people thought if he wore a New Order yarmulke. He'd just smile. He made Charlie smile inside, and he wished that he was a kindly Jewish kid with a killer handshake who believed in God. Kids like that needed a life-altering romance like they need a hole in the head. *It's us nonbelievers who seek out the oyster bars, looking for light eyes.*

The night after he first kissed Monica Miller, he walked home with a smile on his face just like this religious kid's. He wondered what it would be like to feel that way without needing a girl to get there. He'd read that antidepressants could do that. *If I don't leave college tonight, I'll write an essay comparing antidepressants to God and publish it in the school newspaper.* He could see the Hillel kid wagging his finger. "A pill is like the God of Israel? I don't know about that, my friend."

Charlie stood before the snake handler, wearing his new yarmulke. "You like?" he asked the dreadlocked white man, borrowing the Hillel kid's knowing smile.

"It likes mice," he said.

"That's a dangerous creature, that one is," said Charlie, wagging a finger.

"He's a sweetheart, man."

"Should be in a zoo, that one should."

"If you don't like my snake, you can buzz off, you know? It's a free campus, dude."

"Everything comes at a price, my friend." Charlie's finger wagged dangerously close to the man's nose.

The snake handler grabbed him by his T-shirt. "I think you should move on."

"Okay, okay. I was just joking."

"Whatever, dude. Have a better life."

Stupid white Jimi Hendrix, thought Charlie.

"I *will* have a better life," he shouted from a safe distance.

So many childhood predictions about that better life pointed to today, thought Charlie, leaving campus, yarmulke in hand. The bright scenes he'd dreamed up and counted on, the warm girl with whom he could feel forever at home, were nowhere in sight. On the corner of Thirty-Fourth and Walnut, where taxis waited, was a mini tornado of trash, and beyond that, where he was headed, were those famous Philly skies John had warned him about. "Polluted and depressing. The only thing that can survive in there are the pigeons, and they come out with broken wings."

*

Charlie cracked open the taxi window; the car smelled of overachieving air fresheners. Outside, however, was the scent of grease—block after block of spilled gravy. You'd think the city was one big diner that had caught fire, but the storefronts said SHOE REPAIR, LEATHER REPAIR, WATCH REPAIR, SHOE REPAIR TWO, USED BOOKS. And somewhere out there was the Liberty Bell. This city liked broken things. Maybe somewhere there was a huge cauldron of grease that was cracked, slowly leaking its roux into the streets.

"This city smells like lunch," Charlie said to the taxi driver.

"So."

"Hey, you think this diner up here has a phone booth?"

"You kids, these days, always needing to check your messages, needing to make sure someone gives a shit about you," said the driver. "Whoever invented the answering machine fucked with a whole generation."

Charlie believed he was beginning to understand Philly, the most unfriendly place on earth. He wanted to call Monica Miller, hear a friendly voice, then implore her to visit him so he could feel friendly skin. But as soon as she got here, she'd say *I'm hungry* and want to plant them at the diner where the specials would be written on a whiteboard, in plain view. Regardless, she'd still ask the waitress if there were any specials. An only child of two shrinks is brought up believing they are extra special; they believe that behind the specials board is an extra specials board. Maybe the city would make her feel as he did, that there was real danger in the air, danger you could drink your way out of. Drinks make dreams, and dreams kill danger. You can't get that done at a diner. But then Charlie pressed his nose to the diner window. He saw where they'd sit, at first across from one another, and then on the same side, shoulders touching. The heat of her shoulder blade. He went inside and called her.

"Hey, you," said Monica Miller. "How's college?"

"Not good."

"It's only been a few hours."

"I miss you."

"*Hey you*. We just saw each other."

"I miss our goodbye kiss."

"It was a good moment."

"You should come to Philly. This place can be full of good moments."

"I have to get ready for college."

"There's nothing to get ready for."

"I'm going to get a pedicure. Call me later, okay?"

Shit. Alone by a pay phone in a Philly diner. He decided to leave Miss Pettibone's notepaper with the address of the Oyster House atop a tray of wrapped corn muffins: DAY OLDS—25 CENTS.

I'll sniff the damn place out on my own. Miss Pettibone had mentioned little streets, and according to John, Philly's little city streets were the real deal. He'd mentioned unpredictable street numbers like 12½, and sneakers hanging in trees. Small Euro cars that looked like they'd been parked crooked by drunks. And music. Boom boxes on the fire escapes. The smell of cigarette smoke, and of course cobblestones. According to John, nothing beat cobblestones.

"Girls in heels will need to lock arms with you," he'd said. "Which means you're well on your way."

"To what?" Charlie had asked.

He followed a pint-sized sanitation truck that barely fit the alley where it brushed debris to the side. This alley was especially pungent with the grease smell. Turbines sprouted like mushrooms near handle-less iron doors. Charlie couldn't imagine what businesses fronted these doors. He thought of walking around to find out, but feared there would just be another alley, so he kept a respectful distance behind the garbage truck and kept at its sluggish pace.

In the myths, the gates to Hades are floral and pretty. That much he remembered from class. Then someone leans in to smell a flower and down they go. Conversely, when you walk through a place that looks like hell, there's a hidden passage to heaven. Maybe in one of these oil-slicked shadows? There were plenty of the glassy dark spots, and he tried to step in all of them. He decided to follow the truck a little longer and find some Odysseus in this dank alley with its roast beef gravy smell. Find some myth shit. *That's how Philadelphians talk*, he thought. *Myth shit in the alley. Sounds like Mike Schmidt in the alley. Great third baseman for the Phillies. Schmidty.*

"Schmidty!" Charlie howled, and the garbage man honked his horn, then put on the brakes, stuck his hand out the window, and waved.

"Hey," Charlie said, waving back, but it became clear that the man was talking to someone else, someone who'd been outside one back door or another. The width of the truck made it hard to see. He could hear the guy's voice: young, city-tough. Lots of *yeah*s and *ain't*s. Then a lighter voice. A girl's voice.

"Yep," said the girl, popping her P. Without looking, Charlie knew she had fleshy lips.

After the truck pulled away, there was a girl with long, very curly dirty-blonde hair, tied off in a ponytail. Tall, aproned, she was staring intently at her finger, where an eyelash had landed.

"I think there's a rule," she said, without looking up at Charlie. "If you don't make an eyelash wish immediately, the chance goes away." She looked up at Charlie with two Tiffany-blue eyes.

No, he thought. North Carolina basketball blue? Sistine Chapel sky blue? Charlie could only think to ask, "Do you know the garbageman?"

"I don't know his name, but sometimes I'll see him when I'm out here taking a break. If Cactus has gone through a lot of shells, I'll give him a few crates. He makes soup with them, I think."

"Cactus," said Charlie.

"It's only happened once, that I gave him the oyster shells, but it's all we really talk about, so—why? Do *you* know the garbageman?"

"No, not at all. I was trailing him down this alleyway. Weird place."

"This? Not really. It's just an alleyway. I like it. Sort of peaceful, behind the scenes." She was holding a pack of cigarettes and a lighter, and she saw that they had caught Charlie's eye.

"I don't smoke a lot," she said. "I should get back to work."

"Where do you work?"

"Here. The Oyster House."

"The Sansom Street Oyster House?"

"That's us."

"I'm going there!" said Charlie. "I mean, I knew I'd find it, and here I am. It's almost a miracle."

"I'd take you in through the kitchen, but you don't want to see that."

"So, the entrance is in the front?"

"Oh, I thought you'd been in before. You look familiar. Thought I might have served you and your parents or something. You meeting your parents?"

"No."

"Table for one. I like that. A man and his thoughts."

"I'm probably going to sit at the bar, with my Walkman."

"I wonder if it's bad luck to blow on an eyelash even after its wish has died. Well, not *died*, that's too dramatic."

She closed her eyes and blew a slow stream of air at her finger. Charlie watched her long lashes flutter while one of their own took flight.

"Welp, see you later," said the girl, twisting her mouth into a tiny, dissatisfied smile. She opened the door and walked past two flanks of trash into a kitchen where Spanish radio was playing. Knife clatter, loud Spanish voices, the brine of it all.

Charlie ran down the alley. He needed a drink and to see this girl again. The sting of vodka, the salve of blue. His throat and eyes couldn't make his legs move faster. He had to stop, panting, at the corner of Sansom. A little down the block was a wooden sign shaped like a long fish: Sansom Street Oyster House, Est. 1948.

He stood beneath the sign, making a Bono fist, petrified to enter but drawn, ineluctably. It was a word on the SATs. *Sometimes big words work.* He'd never really understood the word before, just memorized it, except maybe one summer on a high dive board when he'd surprised himself by climbing up and jumping off. Regardless, something other than him had begun to make his feet move when a sneering little man with white hair and a pen behind his ear popped his head out of a bar window.

"You're blocking the entrance to my fucking bar," said the man. "You in or out?"

"In," said Charlie.

Chapter Seven

"Applesauce, coleslaw, French fries, peppered hash, stewed beets," the bartender incanted.

"Um, sorry? What?"

"Applesauce, coleslaw, French fries, peppered hash, stewed beets."

"You'd better decide," sang the blue-eyed waitress. A lock of her twisty hair attached itself to Charlie Green's jacket sleeve. It was in the shape of a seahorse. He petted its head.

"Applesauce, coleslaw, French fries, peppered hash, stewed beets." The bartender moved his bifocals down on his nose to focus on Charlie and his unused menu.

"Listen," said the bartender, "order two sides, order a fish, order a drink, order more drinks. This is a fish house."

Charlie opened the menu, but it was upside down.

"*Applesauce, coleslaw, French fries, peppered hash, stewed beets.*"

The bartender smelled like coffee and cigarettes. He was a tiny wiry man with flaring nostrils that reminded Charlie of the dragons that guarded his family's Sunday Chinese.

"I think I'd just like a drink," said Charlie, producing his fake ID.

The bartender took one look at it and threw it back in Charlie's face.

"Listen kid, this is Philly. You got cash, a liver, and some hair on your balls, I'm not going to waste my time fiddling with my bifocals to look at your fake ID."

"Why do you think it's fake?"

"Give me a fucking break. And by the way, if you're not eating, you really need to order a drink every thirty minutes, or else relinquish the primo real estate you got for yourself near the girl and her service area."

"Okay. A vodka and tonic, and I'll definitely order more. sir."

"Vodka's just about the only way to keep that barstool. By the way, I'm Neil. *Sir*'s my dead father. God rest his evil fucking soul." A hundredth of a smile bunched up in the corner of his mouth, became a bead of coffee-stained spit, then dissipated into a tiny cloud that floated up to live forever on the antique tin ceiling of Philadelphia's oldest oyster bar.

"Sure you don't want any oysters with that vodka, kid?"

"I'm allergic."

"Fuck you," said Neil, drawing faint applause.

"That's Neil's way of saying 'Sorry to hear about your allergy,'" said the blonde girl. "God, happy hour bites today. It's weird that people need to be told when to be happy."

"I agree," said Charlie.

"But it's money."

"Exactly. This summer, I worked as a counselor at Camp Shining Star and spent almost all of it on this Walkman."

"I can never save, either."

"What color are your eyes?" he asked. He usually needed several drinks before he'd even speak to a girl like this, but with her things felt easy. Either she didn't know she was lovely or didn't care.

"Blue," she said.

"They're more than that," said Charlie. "They look like perfectly faded blue jeans."

"I've had the same pair since I was fifteen. I'll hold them up to the mirror when I get home tonight."

"I bet it'll be a match."

"I need new jeans for Christmas," she said, gazing down at her long legs.

"So do I."

"But yours look brand new."

"I mean I need to buy worn-in jeans for Christmas."

"You buy your own Christmas gifts?'

"No, of course not. By the way, we celebrate Christmas."

"Everyone does." She slapped her serving tray against her side, challenged by the idea that Christmas wasn't available to everyone.

"Yes, but we're Jewish. Not that you could tell."

"I could see it," said the waitress. "There was one in my school. He was serious, like you."

"I have a lighter side."

"Serious is good. When a stranger tells me 'Just smile,' or says 'It's not that bad,' I give them the finger. When I gave it up for Lent, I started using my pointer finger for F-you instead of the middle. It was like a girl's fuck-you. Softer but equally deadly."

Monica Miller never said *girl*. It was always *woman* or *female*. Never before had Charlie heard a girl fully embrace the word, embody it. *A girl who says girl has girl parts beneath her male-themed work clothes*, thought Charlie, happy he was a boy and hopeful that he exuded his gender as effortlessly as this girl did hers.

"I think if you flashed it quickly enough," said Charlie, "no one could tell the difference."

Simultaneously, they cursed one another with their second fingers.

"My boyfriend gave up empty promises for Lent."

"Boyfriend? That sucks."

John said that no pretty girls were single. And if they were, it was only for 180 minutes.

You'd need the Lord's timing.

"Excuse me?" asked the waitress. "What sucks?"

"Just his empty promises. They suck."

"Yeah, always promising the big trip to the old country. At least this time he got me this." She held up a fat Frommer's European guidebook, the 1984 edition. She flipped through the pages, fanning Charlie.

"It's used. Look at all these notes. I think it used to belong to an old lady. I hope she had a great trip. I hope she's alive. People who mark up books should leave their address." A lightning bolt of a curl bisected her face. "God, I need a haircut."

"No!" said Charlie.

"You're just like my boyfriend. What is it with guys and long hair?"

Charlie played with his Walkman's buttons and drank too quickly. *Of course she has a boyfriend. Why wouldn't she?*

"So, what's your boyfriend like?"

"Oh, I don't know. A guy. An Irish guy. My Irish guy. He has blue eyes, too. What's the big deal with eyes, anyway? They're closed when you kiss."

She said *kiss* so crisply, Charlie had to look away.

"I should check on my tables. Only an hour more to go."

"Then what?" asked Charlie

"Date," she said, teasing, challenging, tongue inside her cheek, hand on her hip.

Paula was being playful. Ordinarily she'd say *date*, then make an about-face and be done with it, but this boy, with his dress jacket and clunky Walkman? He had big, patient hands that rested on the bar when he spoke to her. He was gentle, that's what he was. In New Hope, Pennsylvania, where she'd spent all but the last fourteen months of her life, the only gentle men owned antiques stores and lived with other gentle men.

"Well, have a good date," said Charlie, feigning gravity about the ribbon peeking out from his Walkman's battery compartment.

"So, what are *you* doing tonight?" Paula was taught that a young man wearing a suit jacket was bound for the theater, or maybe even the opera, with a provincial girl he aimed to bed. These lessons came from her mother, who had a strict and (to her mind) irreproachable sense of the world and its secret meanings.

"I'm not sure. I sprung myself from college earlier today and came here to the Oyster House. This could be the beginning of something rather life-defining, or maybe—"

"I should check on those tables before I get sacked," said Paula. "That's what they say in Ireland instead of fired."

It's just as easy to fall in love with a rich boy, Paula's mother often preached. Although Paula didn't care for the way rich boys affected unhappiness in order to seem poorer and sexier. This one seemed well on his way to a big-time buzz, which was Neil's handiwork. She wondered if he'd end up in the gutter, or at a diner. Or maybe he'd take his buzz to a college bar and meet a nameless girl he could kiss in the dark. But by then, she'd be with Tommy, by his side at one bar or another, where he used to bartend. Now he worked at the Four Seasons Hotel, where employees weren't permitted to be customers.

"Sacked. I like that," said Charlie. "You know a lot of things."

"For a barmaid from New Hope?"

"No, for a person." Her cheek bones so sharp and her cheeks so red, he thought. A Vee softened by its own blood.

"That's definitely me, a person," she said, and left Charlie for the back room.

"Who wants dessert?" he heard her ask. She was in a good mood, and Charlie wanted to believe he was the cause, not only today, but every day. John had spoken about making a petulant girl smile, how it was a clear and glorious victory, but this girl wasn't petulant. Wintry? Maybe some weather inside.

"This drink is great, Neil," said Charlie. "And so is this place. This was almost exactly what I was wishing for this morning. You should have seen me this morning. I was a mess, driving to Philly with my dad."

"The shit customers do before they come in here and after they leave interests me about as much as my own life did before I was born and after I'm dead."

"Oh, sorry. I'm just happy. This day has become magical."

"Magic? It could be the four highballs I've been sneaking into your glass. Or the two twenties you had the good sense to plunk down. If it wasn't for those bills, you'd be banished to the shucker's bar, where Cactus the shucker is the prettiest thing going, and the booze tastes like frog juice."

"I'll keep the bills coming. My father gave me an envelope. I mean, I'm going to get a job soon, a real job, something using my hands, maybe a merchant marine, or maybe—"

"My father died last month," said Neil.

"I'm sorry," said Charlie.

"I hadn't spoken to him in twenty years, but he asked for me at the hospital, so I went because I had something to tell him."

"When my grandmother passed, or died—you're right, 'died' is better—"

"Kid, when I'm talking about my things, don't relate it to your things."

"Sorry."

"I had something important to tell my old man, okay?" said Neil, bearing down on Charlie.

"Okay, sure."

"Pop was short like me, so I wanted to thank him for giving me a big wiener."

"Oh," said Charlie. "Wow, that's—"

"Christ, here comes a Crumb."

"What's a Crumb?"

A large man in a tight terrycloth sweater-shirt sat next to Charlie. "Yo, Neil," he shouted and threw his money clip on the bar. "Neilly, Neilly," he said. "I'm thirsty thirsty."

"Shut up, Crumb," said Neil. "First of all, you're late. Second of all, that shirt makes you look like you have tits."

Neil called his worst and most loyal customers Crumbs. They nursed their drinks until closing, ordering labor-intensive dishes like ice cream sundaes. Having to shake a whipped cream canister and apply a cherry bedeviled Neil like nothing else. There was such a commingling of disgust and pity in Neil's heart for the lonely adulterers. Most of them were lawyers who'd been flung from their comfortable Main Line homes after getting caught. Now they lived in all-suite hotels, blocks from the beautician, the actress, the stewardess; blocks from the Oyster House, where they'd tell Neil about how they'd gifted gym memberships, Corvettes, and cases of champagne for a few weeks of young skin at the expense of a decade and a half of marriage.

"Don't mention that chick's name again, Crumb. Or I'll write it on your hand with your cigarette." Neil was no fan of cheaters. "I told you to start a porn collection years ago. Now look at you! Fuck it, no more ice cream, Crumb. Not ever."

"Hey, kid," the Crumb said to Charlie. "You know you're in my seat, right? Eh, don't worry about it. Just that I miss yapping with Paula is all."

"Her name's Paula?" asked Charlie.

"I actually call her Pauly, like the loser guy in *Rocky*, but that's just our little thing."

"Paw-La," said Charlie, the next time she was back at the service bar.

"Paw-*Lee*," said the Crumb, and laughed himself into a coughing fit.

"I like my middle name more. Katherine. But my mom wouldn't let me change it. I think I have seven ancestors named Paula."

"I'm Charlie. Charles Green. No one calls me Charles. My Dad's French and calls me 'Charl.'"

"I've never been. Maybe next summer." She placed her hand atop the Frommer's.

"I might be there," said Charlie.

"Really?" asked Paula, for a moment excited about seeing a familiar face in a foreign country. Then she heard her mother's voice in her head and bit her lower lip. Paula's mother had assured her that she would not be in an airplane this summer, that men promised many adventures for the five-minute adventure in your pants. Regardless,

Paula had invested in a set of Le Sac travel bags that she kept hidden under her bed.

"My mom has an art gallery in Paris," said Charlie. "But I've only been two times. At least to Paris. The other time, we stayed at my dad's childhood house in the country. You know? Up until this very moment I had little feeling for that old country house, but now I miss it."

"Paris, France," said the Crumb. "Where the ladies drop their pants."

"Is that so, Crumb?" asked Paula. "You think that's what ladies do in Paris?"

"Come on, Paula, you don't got to call me a Crumb, too."

"Neil says I should, and talking about girls' pants doesn't help. Well"—she turned to Charlie—"have fun in Europe at the gallery. Send us some postcards."

"I thought you said you were going to visit?"

"Maybe. Just a crazy plan. Maybe in two or three summers I'll visit your mom's store. I'll tell her I met her well-traveled son at the Oyster House. I was going to say 'well-heeled.' I like words like that."

"God," said Charlie.

"What?"

"Nothing, but I like those words, too, and so does my mom."

"Rich people words."

"I'm not rich, my parents are. I mean, they own two galleries, which really isn't a lot, compared to some other dealers."

"*Two galleries.*" Paula tried to sound sarcastic, but it came out reverential. "What sort of stuff is in these galleries?"

"The classics," said Charlie. "They sort of fell in our lap. My grandmother found them during the Second World War, and hid them from the Nazis, in the basement of a synagogue. When the war ended, she reclaimed them, hundreds of them, and most of them by the masters."

"Well excuse me, master *bates*," said the Crumb.

Two galleries full of old paintings is beautiful, Paula told herself, and hoped there were velvety couches where wealthy women drank tea and pointed at what they wanted.

"The Nazis were going to burn them," Charlie continued. "I think she stole them in the middle of the night. She was an intense woman. People compare her to me, except that she had green eyes. These famous green eyes everyone always talks about."

"You're really into eyes," said Paula. She gathered a trio of beers that seemed destined to overflow but did not. Charlie watched her disappear into the back dining room, certain she'd leave a few drops in her wake, but there was nothing, just a question mark of that caramel-colored hair snaking down her perfect back.

"You can sit here this time," said the Crumb. "But I like yapping with her, too. Don't get me wrong, I got a daughter her age. I guess she reminds me of my daughter. You know, the time my daughter came in here, Neil didn't call me Crumb. He called me 'Mister So-and-So.' I'll never forget that act of kindness."

"Neil's a great bartender. He might even be better than this bartender in New York who works at Adam's Rib. Have you ever—"

"Of course he's the best. He sat you in my seat, figuring you'd be all gaga over Paula, knowing you wouldn't stand a chance. That sort of stuff teaches you a lesson. A lesson about what is yours, and what isn't."

"Why wouldn't I stand a chance?" asked Charlie. "I think we got along. Actually, really well. It was weird, in fact."

"Hey, listen, she's Tommy's girl. Game, set, match."

"Who's Tommy?" asked Charlie.

"*Who's Tommy?* You ain't from these parts, are you kid? Hear that, Neil? *Who's Tommy.*"

"Shut up, Crumb," said Neil. "It's her boyfriend, kid."

"Oh. Well, what's he like?"

"Tell him, Crumb," said Neil.

"*What's he like?* He's a mick, you know, a bruiser, but he has a soft side, too, knows his poetry. Knows his Robert Frost, or whoever the mick version of Bobby Frost is. And the red hair on this guy's head, you'd think it could start a fire."

The Crumb told Charlie the story of Tommy. How he started as a teenager kicking bums out of his father's saloon in North Philly and made it all the way to Italy, where he apprenticed under the head barman at Harry's in Venice. "Tommy learned real class from the real I-talians. They're not like the ones we got here."

Talking about Tommy and Paula was something you did at the Sansom Street Oyster House, thought Charlie, just like talking about roast beef and Reagan was something you did at Adam's Rib.

"The key to Tommy is his broken nose," said the Crumb. "Don't you think, Neil?"

"I don't think about men's noses, Crumb."

"Well, chicks love a broken nose. That, and all he drinks are brown drinks. Some chicks like that, too."

"Paula doesn't seem like much of a drinker," said Charlie. "She looks healthy."

"Of course she's healthy," said Neil. "She's fucking young."

Tommy and Paula had apparently been together for almost a year, the relationship crowned by a recent trip to the Bahamas. The trip photos had been viewed right where Charlie sat.

"They were nice pictures," said Neil. "Couple like that in the water? Nice."

"And the bikini when she was on the Jet Ski? *Madone*," said the Crumb.

"But Paula can get Tommy to behave himself," said Neil. "Some girls like Tom's freckles and gym rat muscles exploding all over their lives, but not Paula, God bless her."

"So, what *does* Paula like?" asked Charlie.

"How the hell do I know?" said Neil. "You have to be on the inside to find out, kid."

"Here she is, Miss America," said the Crumb. "Hey Pauly, how much you say those Jet Skis cost you and Tommy for a half hour?"

"Twenty each," said Paula.

At one point, she leaned on Charlie's shoulder for balance while she slipped a finger inside her tennis shoe and scratched. She was five feet nine, Charlie knew. He'd memorized Monica Miller's height and John's height, and Paula was exactly in the middle. Almost twelve hours ago, Monica Miller's five feet seven frame had been against him in the kitchen. Now it seemed like such a modest height. A parody of being tall. In heels, sure, she shot up to five nine, but would talk about it all night, how she was practically six feet. Paula was probably the sort of girl who didn't know her height, or her weight, and would offer up a ballpark number, or say it didn't matter.

While Neil and the Crumb spoke about the Jet Ski racket, Charlie concentrated on the ball of her wrist, the little mound of bone, a tiny island, the down of her arms lapping against its shore. She'd play with her sleeves, trying to roll them up evenly, but get frustrated and let them find their own homes on her arms. All of the waitresses at the Sansom Street Oyster House wore white dress shirts, ties, and khaki pants. Paula's rolled-up sleeves, loose knot, cuffed pants—at Camp Shining Star, there was a deserted train car in which flowers seemed to have poked holes. Charlie had remarked to the Very-Brown-Eyed Counselor that the train car was no match for nature.

"Who says the train car is resisting?" she'd asked. "Who says the train car isn't nature, too?"

Watching Paula in her Oyster House uniform, Charlie agreed: he couldn't tell anymore where the girl began and the schoolboy getup ended. It was all her. All five feet nine of her. And her posture made her seem even taller. He'd once seen an egret on a golf course in Palm Beach; how could something so still also suggest a pirouette?

"Date night," Paula chirped and showed Neil her watch.

"You're free to go," said Neil.

"Let me just make sure my ladies at table twelve are okay with their coffee."

"See that?" said Neil, after she'd gone back into the restaurant. "You can't teach that. She's overqualified for this gig. There's nothing sadder than an overqualified barmaid."

"Pauly's the best," said the Crumb.

"I really like her uniform," said Charlie. "Is that weird?"

"Someone tied that tie for her on her first day, and she hasn't untied it since," said the Crumb. "Just slips it on and off."

"Who tied it for her?"

"Not you," said the Crumb. "It was Tommy. I saw it coming a mile away. Paula's nervous because it's her first day, and here comes Tommy with his Irish charm. Tell you what, if I'd seen Tommy tying my daughter's tie, I'd give him permission to take her out."

Neil had met the Crumb's daughter. She was sweet, but gene by gene resembled her father.

"Your daughter's a good kid," said Neil. "You don't want her to fall in love with Tommy just because he made nice with a necktie. Your daughter should marry the son of the baker, or the priest's boy."

"I buy my cakes and shit in the grocery store. I don't know who baked them," said the Crumb. "And the last time I saw a priest, it was in the mirror on Halloween."

Fucking Crumbs, thought Neil. *Every time you try to humanize the fat bastards, they crumble right in front of your face. Arrogant Crumbs who think Sinatra won't die during their lifetime.* He looked over at the kid in his blue jacket and stiff jeans. Rare to see a rich kid at a fish house. One or two came in each year. But that was one of the reasons fish houses existed, he figured—so the prettiest barmaids could get swallowed up by a vodka-happy loner in his five-hundred-dollar blazer.

"If Paula marries anyone, it should be someone like this kid," said Neil. "And as for Tommy, he's a bartender and a drunk. In time he'll be a drunk and a bartender. Then he'll lose his job. One of the neighborhood micks will take pity on him and give him a job bouncing at the local, but he'll drink, steal, or screw his way out of that, and then there will be a last bender. A monthlong bender that will erase him from the face of planet Earth."

"Yeah, my daughter will find a nice boy. No benders," said the Crumb.

"You really think I might marry her?" asked Charlie. "The crazy thing is, if someone said I had to marry her, I think I'd say yes. I know I'd say yes."

"Whatever," said Neil. "The future's bullshit, always running late. Like the milk train to Atlantic City. A 4:37 a.m. departure should mean 4:37 a.m., not fucking 4:49 a.m."

"What the hell's the difference, Neil?" asked the Crumb. "Hey, I'm out. Got to make the rounds."

"Tip me double today," said Neil.

"Why?"

"You don't have proper respect for the milk train, plus I had to talk serious with you just now about your daughter. Double it up, Crumb."

"Why not? It's only money, Neily. Are you staying, kid?"

Charlie's drink had risen two inches. Somewhere in between the marriage predictions, Neil had made a deposit, ice and all. Charlie turned to face the stairwell that led to the restrooms and the employees' locker room.

"Have you ever been in the employees' room?" Charlie asked the Crumb.

"I don't want to see that shit. The one time I saw Neil in his regular clothes, it freaked me out. It was just his Members Only jacket, but it didn't seem right."

"Do the employees have to exit up here, or is there a separate way?"

"Jesus, kid," said the Crumb, sidling his stool away from the bar an inch at a time until there was room for his girth to rise and turn. "Trust me, this way is better." He motioned to the front door. "When your time at the bar has ended, you get to go home, only a little poorer, and a little drunker. Bargain of the century: all this fun, pretty girls, Neil's bullshit and his Neilisms. You get all that and you never have to sign your name to anything or anyone, unless you pay by credit card. You know how you fuck up that deal? By marrying the waitress or buying the joint. As for me? My home is a suite at the Radisson. Right on Arch Street near the museum, above the new TGI Friday's. Probably stop in there for a last pop; they got a few cute girls working there. See, that's what I'm saying, you have to spread your wings. Girls like Paula, they're everywhere."

Charlie's attention was on the stairwell door. A faint red light emanated from below.

"Not like her," he said, watching the light.

"Yeah, she likes her nature, you know, *science* magazines, and some days she doesn't say too much, so those parts are different," said the Crumb, "but when you turn off the lights, they're all the same. Don't let Tommy break your nose. He notches his belt when he breaks a nose. Probably has ten notches in that belt of his. Just ask Neil. Fucking Neil," the Crumb said, and left.

Chapter Eight

THE HAPPY HOUR CRUMBS had all departed, and now only Charlie and the shucker remained. His dark face was fretted with flesh beads. People called him Cactus. While Neil was downstairs, counting his drawer, Cactus manned the main bar, his arms crossed in front of his chest while his only customer was a kid playing with his Walkman.

"Do you see that red light?" Charlie asked Cactus.

"Yeah, I see it."

"I think it's coming from the employees' locker room."

"When one of the girls grabs a smoke, they prop open the fire door and up comes the light."

"What's it like down there?"

"Lockers. An ashtray."

"Has to be more to it than just that."

"Not really."

There *is* more to it, thought Charlie, and wished to be on the *inside* of the Sansom Street Oyster House, downstairs, bathing with Paula in the red light. While Charlie daydreamed about the ambrosial contents of her locker, a rogue Crumb came in, asking for Neil.

"I don't like to bother Neil when he's downstairs after his shift," said Cactus.

"I have some news he'll want to hear," said the Crumb, who'd begun making a little pyramid with oyster crackers, using horseradish as cement.

"Neil's not going to like the statues you're making on the bar," said Cactus.

"When I tell him the news, we'll be all good."

This Crumb wore a summery beige suit that fit him better up top than in the trousers that were snug with leg meat.

"You know Neil?" the Crumb asked Charlie.

"Just met him."

"I've known him since 1975, when we both had beards. We also had these leather desk chairs, most comfortable chairs you could ever want. Went shopping for them at Robinson's Leather. Us and our macho beards went to Robinson's straight from here. Got two of the very same chairs for our rec rooms. Loved those freaking chairs. We were tight, me and Neil, but then, according to him, I became a Crumb."

"You seem more advanced than the last Crumb who was here," said Charlie.

"Thanks, kid."

"What did I tell you about making those things on my bar?" Neil appeared, wearing his tan Members Only jacket. Like the last Crumb had observed, it was disconcerting seeing him this way. He looked even smaller, constricted by all the zipped zippers.

"I got some news for you, Neil."

Neil slammed his disproportionately large fist on the zinc bar, toppling the Crumb's work. "Why am I up here talking to you after my shift?" asked Neil.

"Neil," said the Crumb, "Angie and I, we figured things out. I'm moving back in. We're a family again."

Neil looked deeply into the Crumb's eyes. The whites were clear. He'd been burned before by Crumbs and their declarations of reform. Crumbs couldn't really change. All they could do was cram the crumby parts of themselves into a lockbox. Then we pray they lose the key. But here was this Crumb, all suited up and smiling, despite the demolition of his stupid cracker house. The suit wasn't half-bad, either; it might not even have been part of a two-for-one. His legs still looked like over-stuffed sausages, though, which was why in his pre-Crumb life he was called Sausage Sam. But it was too much to ask—a diet on top of all this. The diet could come later, thought Neil. Next week.

"Okay," he said and went behind the bar to open one of the hard-to-reach corner refrigerated units, into which he had to crawl. There was frost on his Members Only lapels when he surfaced holding a glass bottle of Evian water. Charlie was familiar with bottled water; his parents had begun bringing home cases from France in the early eighties, but always plastic and always Vittel. Glass Evian was a rarer bird. A few of the modern Italian places on Third Avenue served it, but didn't always have it in stock, and when they did, they charged as much as a bottle of cheap wine. Charlie had always assumed it was a New York infatuation, something Haircuts ordered to convince girls they were pure. Still, here was Neil, in Philly, handling the bottle with two hands, using his bifocals to read the pink and white label's French words.

"Yessir," said the Crumb. "This beautiful bottle is what I came for."

"You're back with Angie?" asked Neil.

"Yessir. Back for good."

"You should lose some weight," said Neil.

"I'm already on it."

"And don't cheat again."

"Never."

"Then here you go." Neil handed the Crumb the bottle. "Don't fuck it up."

"I won't, Neil. We're in love again. This time for good. We'll have an Eve—wait, how do you say it?"

"Evian, Crumb."

"Eve-yawn toast to you tonight."

"How many more bottles of fancy water you got down there?" Cactus asked Neil. The Crumb had left while the leaving was good, before Neil spied dirt under his fingernails, or an untied shoelace, and wrenched away the prize.

"Got three more. Probably last me till 1999. If any more Crumbs want me, tell them to fuck off. I'm going to my chess lesson." Neil bused the Crumb's oyster cracker mess with his bare hands, placed it in Cactus's bare hands, and left through the kitchen. Charlie could hear Spanish voices saluting him, banging pots and pans in tribute. He hoped it was a daily ritual, and wished to become an expert about Neil, about oysters, and about the most charming waitress in all of Pennsylvania.

"What do you have to do to get an Evian?" Charlie asked Cactus.

"Be a good man. And if you're waiting for Paula, she takes the back way out."

"Who takes the back way out, Cactus? How you be? You seem just the same as the other day, which is a good thing, my man. We should buy you a drink in honor of your wonderful consistency."

Paula's boyfriend had climbed into the bar from the picture window that Cactus always left open at the end of his shift so that the place wouldn't be overwhelmed by fish smell. A fish house shouldn't smell like fish. It was rule number one, according to Cactus. If he had a second rule, it would be to flag drunk Irishmen, but Tommy and his brogue were too formidable. In addition to dating Paula, he helmed the Four Seasons Hotel bar, and because of that he outranked every server in the city but the mayor's butler.

"What are you having, Tommy?" asked Cactus.

"Quick Chivas before the wife comes up." He wore a black T-shirt, like Charlie's, but it didn't hang on his shoulders. Tommy's chest filled it. And he wore jeans, like Charlie did, but his were wildly torn and cinched with a rope belt. No navy-blue blazer, and no penny loafers, but sockless slipper shoes. The kind that Jee-Jee used to wear at the shore in New Jersey after seeing Sinatra wear them at a beach club in Nevada.

"So, who takes the back way out?" Tommy asked Cactus. "You were talking to the gent over there before I entered through the window like the mannerless Irishman I am."

"We were just talking about one of the Crumb's girlfriends," Cactus lied.

"Ah, those blasted Crumbs," Tommy said and turned to Charlie. "You been keeping the Crumb watch, gent? Buy the gent a pop on me, Cactus. He's been keeping watch and should be rewarded. Cheers, gent, cheers. Say, you wouldn't happen to be the well-to-do gent who's been chatting up the wife all day and filling her pretty head with thoughts of art pictures and trips to Europe? The wife called me asking for adventures in the old country."

"I didn't know she was married," said Charlie, standing now, stirring his drink, head bent, trying to appear dangerously contemplative.

"If you're feeling threatened at a bar, look like you're about to snap," John had recommended. "No one likes a snapper. It freaks out even the toughest guys."

"It's a playful figure of speech," said Tommy. "My father called my mother his girlfriend, you see?"

"I see," Charlie said, taking out his Boodo Khan so he could feel the weight of metal and hear the red Stop button click under the gentle pressure of his fingernail.

"So, what do you *think*?" Tommy asked Charlie.

"It's the best Walkman, really simple and solid."

"Not about the gizmo, gent, about my wife."

"Paula?" His voice cracked.

Tommy shook his head and ran his hand through his tight red curls. "You sound like wind chimes, gent. I hate the sound of wind chimes."

"I don't like wind chimes, either," said Charlie, loud and clear. "And your *wife*, she's, well, beautiful."

"Now you're talking like the rich boy you are."

"I'm really not all that wealthy," said Charlie. "My grandmother stole a bunch of paintings from the Nazis."

Tommy seemed to be listening less to Charlie and more to the toothpick he was twisting into a deep molar.

"My wife said you were rich. Don't get me wrong, the rich are my favorites. When I see a customer handle his fat money clip, it does my heart good. If only the rich were more committed to drinking. Two pops and they're off. I want to tell them to stay a while! Tell Tommy about the deal you got on the Rolex, and one for the missus to boot. Tell Tommy about the new condo in Vail. Stay a while, you pinot grigio superhero."

Charlie wanted to tell him about his mother, her collection of flasks hiding in her closet and her wineglasses full of tepid vodka, not pinot grigio. He wanted to tell him about rich people and their drinking. The morning Charlie spied his mother pouring vodka into a glass of cold milk. Funny how all of her flasks were monogrammed and yet she tried to hide them. All alcoholics not so secretly wish to get caught.

"I know rich people who pour vodka into their morning milk," Charlie told Tommy.

"Milky vodka? What a pisser." Tommy had the natty haircut of a Haircut, but this was no banker; both his elbows were on the bar, as if he were about to arm wrestle two people at once. Monica Miller said she could never date a redhead, that their freckles made them look dirty. His eyes were dark blue—an angry, piercing blue that belied his friendly little grin. *He and Paula have a blue-eyed club*, thought Charlie. But as the Very-Brown-Eyed Counselor had pointed out, it takes a brown-eyed person to truly appreciate a blue-eyed person. There were lines around Tommy's eyes from squinting, from the sarcastic grinning that must precede his freckled fist getting launched into the Philly night.

"You rich folks experimenting with the liquor cabinet. Leave it to the barman and tip them right. Another Chivas, Cactus."

"My parents are rich," said Charlie. "Not me."

"We know how that works. They'll get you the dough one way or another, then one day when you're older you'll look around the room and think you earned it yourself. There's my girl!"

Paula ascended the stairs in white chinos. No sooner could Charlie glean the beltless pants than Tommy's mitts were around her waist.

"Your girl doesn't like her man drinking before our date," said Paula, allowing Tommy to turn her this way and that by her belt loops.

"Couldn't help it, with this one down here talking about milk punch." Charlie raised his glass, a salute. *Something a Crumb might do.*

"I hope he didn't ruin your time," Paula said to Charlie.

"I'm fine," said Charlie, and mindlessly pressed Play. "These Dreams" blared from the huge headphones.

"Jesus, Mary, and Joseph," said Tommy. "That gizmo will make you deaf, gent. Say, Paula, what you say we have a quick pop for old time's sake, then go somewhere to visit with that travel book of yours? Cactus, can you manage two shots of the lady's choosing?"

"I thought we were going to a real dinner and then to the P&P?"

"It was a great plan, and one I'd love to see through to the end, but maybe next week instead. My cousin got into a mess, and this time, I fear—"

Paula sat a few stools away from Tommy and his excuses, closer to Charlie, her palm bent to support her chin, which was angled to view the usually unnoticeable corner of the barroom where they kept the baby seats. It struck Charlie as beautiful, her long neck turned to the side to see the worn plastic booster seats.

"I tell you what," said Tommy, "I'll set you up at the P&P tonight. Put you and your little Asiatic friend's drinks on my tab. It's the least I can do."

"It's a start," she said stoically, her long light-brown lashes blinking over the baby seats. The way she sat, Charlie could stare with impunity at how those lashes progressed to the light caramel of her eyebrows and then the light and dark honeys of her hairline. She wore her curls long. Like a sixth-grade school play about King Arthur and Guinevere. A time when curls meant virtue.

"You still owe me one, you jerk," she said to Tommy.

John believed that when people said *you owe me one* it meant oral sex. Maybe in the world of Haircuts, but not in the world of girls who could stare into the soul of a plastic baby seat.

"That I do," said Tommy. "Let's steal an hour at your place and we'll read from the travel tome."

"No. Tonight's over for us." Alone, she'd read the introduction to the book, written by Arthur Frommer himself, a gray-haired man who believed that 1984 would be the best year yet to visit Europe. But Paula wanted to ask him about 1988. She'd written him a letter and received a response from someone else in the Frommer family who advised her that the 1988 guidebook was already out and fifty-three pages longer than the 1987 guidebook.

"You're never lovelier than when I piss you off," said Tommy. "Your cheeks get wonderfully warm. The gadgety gent down there can't keep his eyes off you. Cheers, gent."

Paula knew Charlie had been gawking but didn't care. There were few men she trusted with staring. Tommy used his hands rather than his eyes. But he was thirty-two—an age, Paula's mother had warned, when men are done looking and only care about doing. Tommy liked to get to the bottom of things. Money, drinks, sex. Those were Tommy's things, and he was good at all of them. He worked out for two hours before every bar shift. A pro. A lion. Tommy and his big forearms that she loved to latch on to, late in the night. Those forearms would lead her home and no danger would befall her. *I'm yours because you know what to do. Now lead me out of the Philly night.*

"You may kiss me goodbye," she said to Tommy.

Charlie turned his head but wasn't spared the singular moist click. They knew how to kiss one another; their sound made that perfectly clear. *Monica Miller and I produce too many clicks, like the sound the Boodo Khan makes when a tape gets stuck.*

Tommy patted Charlie's shoulder on his way out. "I'll take the front door this time, gent. Although the window suits a savage such as me."

"Say, Paula?" asked Cactus. "Do me a favor and bring my shucker blades into the kitchen."

The knives were soaking in water that had been sitting all day. A mosquito swam on the surface.

"Time to make the donuts," she said to Charlie.

"Donuts?"

"You know the commercial?"

Everyone knew the commercial.

"No," he lied.

"It's a pretty famous Dunkin Donuts commercial. About work," she said.

"Do you think it's for work or against it?" asked Charlie.

"Neither really. Just about how it's necessary to be devoted even if it's something small like donuts."

"I will never take small things for granted again," said Charlie. "To think, until today I'd confused the black mussel shells of my young summers with *oysters*."

"Everyone I know, everyone I'm really close to, they work really hard, and take pride in what they do. Even when it's oysters." She looked down at the mosquito, who was lugging its wet wings up the side of the bin.

"You're great at what you do," said Charlie. "I mean, your shift ended, you were dressed for your date, and yet you're still here, dealing with the knives."

"I'd do anything for Cactus. He and Neil work harder than anyone, including Tommy."

"Where does Tommy work?"

"Four Seasons."

"Apparently that's the best hotel. My brother John went there for a wedding."

"Too clean for me. I like more rustic places. Like the P&P club."

"What's that like?"

"Dark. A little strange. You can get lost in there, in a good way." She undid her ponytail, bent her head, and let the jungle of dirty-blonde hair fall over her face. She rolled her head until the curls were clear, revealing the turquoise eyes of a panther. "Sometimes I'll bring a flashlight and just read in there. Have a couple of drinks. Hide."

"Wow."

"What?"

"You're different."

"Different?"

"The only different girl I've ever met."

"You should get out more."

"No, I mean you're . . . I don't know. Untouched."

She searched his face for sarcasm. The whites of his eyes were honest. Those long lashes.

"Hey, why don't you stop by the P&P later?"

"P&P?"

"It's called the Pen & Pencil. Lots of restaurant people go there after work and some journalists. Here, I'll write down the address. You should go."

"Really?" He stood too quickly, and she took a step back.

"Yeah, why not. I'll put your name on the list. Charlie, right?"

"That's what they tell me."

"Huh? Who?"

Shit, thought Charlie.

The mosquito was languishing on the side, its wings too heavy for flight. Paula tilted the bin so it would be engulfed in water, then watched it float motionless over the sunken knives.

"I don't want to be at this restaurant forever," she said.

Chapter Nine

THE WOMAN BEHIND THE bar at World of Wines had a Spanish accent and a beauty mark near her mouth.

"I'll have a chardonnay, please," Charlie said to the woman. He was drunk and needed only food. The Oyster House shuttered at nine and he'd had all of one and a half oyster crackers since first setting foot inside. His body repulsed the idea of another drink, but he could hear his brother's caveat, that at a place called World of Wines you can break the heart of the Spanish bartender by ordering water.

Charlie had been directed here by Cactus, who advised, "The owner, she's not all there, so I stay away."

"You like *jamón*?" She had a nice lopsided smile, but there was lipstick on her teeth.

"Sure. Who doesn't?" said Charlie, pretty sure it was ham. "But I think I need a steak."

"First I will give you the *jamón* and the wine."

She opened a bottle. It wasn't chardonnay. Ordinarily, Charlie would have been offended that someone had edited his life, but he'd only asked for a glass and now there was an entire skinny bottle of Spanish red with black gothic script on the label.

"Tell me your story," said the woman.

"Well—"

"This life," she said, smiling, covering her face with her hands. "Okay, Iñez is in love," she said and poured wine for them both.

"Who's Iñez?"

"She is me."

"I could really use some food," said Charlie.

"This life," she said again, and hid her smiling face again.

"Maybe some bread?"

She took her time slicing a baguette, stopping more than once to smile her love smile. Sometimes Europeans could be infuriatingly European, Charlie thought. She only placed three baguette slices in the basket but had produced a ramekin of soft butter and a plate of dark, lacquered ham. Just when you want to hate Europeans, they make little miracles, and all is forgiven.

"Really good bread," said Charlie.

"When you are in love, the bread tastes better."

Charlie could picture her on the back of a moped with scarves wrapped around her head, holding onto the flanks of an older Spanish guy. Charlie's mother had a friend like Iñez from when Charlie was very little. Raspy smoker's voice and a freckly chest. Iñez smoked her cigarette like his mother's friend, looking down at her Camel Light as if it were a snowflake melting on her hand. Another customer came in singing her name and speaking Spanish.

"You ever been somewhere and be so lost? So, so lost?" Iñez asked Charlie.

"There was a corn maze field trip at fat camp."

"You should let yourself get lost one day," she said. "In a place that's huge—the forest, the beach. Get lost with your love. You fall asleep and you don't care if you wake up. That is how we fall in love in my country. We don't care if we die. If we are in love, death is not a problem."

Charlie had been a single head spin away from needing the toilet, but now he felt calm and stationary. The sandwiches had righted him:

more and he might be asleep, less and he might be passed out. *Sneaky brilliant Europeans.*

"I don't even think I need the steak anymore," he said.

"What steak?" asked Iñez.

She had short chestnut-brown hair that fell over her face. Acne-scarred olive skin born of a thousand days at the beach. Charlie could imagine her running in the sand. He wasn't sure if Spain allowed top-less bathing.

"Certain girls are so impressive naked that they permanently change your life just by untying a bikini string in the light of day," John had warned. Iñez had beautiful breasts. It was her best feature. She wore a boy's white V-neck T-shirt, no bra.

"What are you looking at?" she asked Charlie.

"This red wine, you served it slightly chilled. It's interesting." John would have said *your chest* and been either slapped or kissed. In John's stories, he was always getting slapped or kissed.

"You know this guy?" she asked, referring to the Spaniard at the other end of the bar.

"Nope," said Charlie, popping the P just like Paula.

"You should come over and drink with the guy, such a funny guy."

"Thanks for the invitation. I have a lot on my mind."

"I know," said Iñez. "*Que vida, que vida.* What a life. You guys be okay a few minutes?" she asked Charlie and the Spanish friend.

Charlie nodded and the Spaniard hunched his shoulders. "*Quizas.* Maybe, Iñez. Maybe."

"You so silly," said Iñez, as she made sure the ten unoccupied bar seats were angled to face the front door. It was an economical place: a long zinc bar, a tiny kitchen, and above the kitchen a curtain-covered loft accessed by a rolling library ladder. She knew her way on that ladder, Charlie could tell, skipping every other rung. He wasn't sure if the loft was for storage or sleeping until she peeked her head behind the curtain, laughed at something, then disappeared, up and over.

"*Iyee,*" said the Spaniard.

"Where did she go?" asked Charlie.

"There is a man in there, and she asks *us* if *we* will be okay for a few minutes. The question she should ask is if *she* will be okay for a few minutes. A few minutes behind a red curtain can ruin your *vida*."

There was probably a futon up there; it made the most sense, given the space. John was a big proponent. He'd told Charlie that almost every pretty girl owned one. "They treat it like a flying carpet. They're obsessed. It's weird. They think it makes them seem more grounded, but also sexually aloft. Girls are really into their own paradoxes."

The Spaniard approached Charlie and pointed at the plate of ham. "Iñez knows the good *jamón*. She knows the good *vino tinto*. Then why she don't know which is the good man, and which is the bad?"

"The bad man is up there with her?"

"He doesn't like me, and I don't like him," he whispered, and wagged a cautionary finger at the red curtain. Sometimes it would flutter and Charlie could make out a cigarette glow. It was dark up there, and dark in the restaurant as well, just the light of many votive candles. There was a huge candelabra at the end of the bar, from which flowed decades of multicolored wax. But its candles were frozen in time, stuck on some other night.

"They should light these candles," Charlie said to the Spaniard.

"It's a mess, this place. I tell her to open a video store. Easy money. You buy *Gandhi* once, and rent it to everyone a hundred times."

They were both watching when the red curtain parted, and the man backed his way down the ladder. Barefooted and plodding, his weight made the ladder creak.

"What wine did you say?" he called up to Iñez.

"Whatever you want, darling," said Iñez.

The man paused on the ladder, swung himself around, and jumped down, landing on both feet like a gymnast. His shoulders slowly rose.

"Tommy?" asked Charlie. "What are you doing here? Wait, you were up there? Wow." An amazingly good turn of events, thought Charlie. His heart's divided. Like a Crumb's cheating heart.

"Holy shit," said Tommy. "You're the gent from Oyster House. Shit."

"Listen, Mister Tomas," said the Spaniard. "We are paying customers, and this is not your bar. This is not the Four Seasons, this is the World of Wine, and you have no right—"

"Your drinks are on me, gent," he said to the Spaniard, his eyes on Charlie, who picked nervously at a candle-wax scab. "How you be, gent?" he asked Charlie, then said something about being there to repair the refrigeration units. He sat elegantly, gentlemanly, at the bar, legs crossed at a feminine angle, and scratched his head. "How you be, gent?"

"Good," said Charlie.

"Iñez and I are old friends."

"*Old friends*. Please," yelled the red curtain.

"She's very nice," said Charlie. "Very European."

"That's right, gent. We bummed around Europe a while back."

"*Bum around*. How can you?" yelled the red curtain.

"Are you coming down, Iñez?" yelled the Spaniard. "If not, I have to get my own wine. I tell you, open a video store. Buy one of *Gandhi* and rent it to the people a thousand time."

"You know where the wine is," yelled the red curtain. "And if you want to give people a hundred *Gandhi, you* open the store."

"You know I don't have the time to make my own drinks," said the Spaniard, grudgingly making his way behind the bar.

"Tell him, Tomas," yelled the red curtain. "Tell this boy about the Black Forest. Tell him about our camping. Tell him it wasn't just bum around. Tell him that my refrigerator is not broken. Tell him that this bed smells like our love. Tell him that I cry when I have to wash these sheet. Tell him about the Black Forest, Tomas."

"It was a good time, gent. That's for certain. It's just that not everyone appreciates hearing these yarns about the camping trip, if you understand what I'm telling you." Tommy mouthed "Paula" and Charlie nodded.

"Who wouldn't love these story, Tomas?" yelled the red curtain. "Whoever it is, they don't have a heart."

"I won't tell her," said Charlie.

"What he say?" yelled the red curtain.

"He say," yelled the Spaniard, "that he won't tell it to Paula."

The red curtain grew silent, and Tommy bent his head.

"You know that Paula's just a kid," yelled Tommy. "She's just a friend." The red curtain said nothing in return.

Two-timing was exhausting, thought Tommy, at least if you did it at all well and drank with both of them, not just with one or the other. It should be an Olympic sport. Iñez had followed him to Philly after their summer in Europe—a wealthy Spaniard with a world-class chest. She was two years older and didn't want kids. She'd told him he could name his own salary if only he'd work at World of Wines and live with her in the loft. He'd agreed and then he'd met Paula, who kissed his fingers. Iñez who bit and sucked his fingers. Paula who folded all of her clothing into these perfect little piles. Iñez whose jeans were either on her naked ass or somewhere in the sheets. The home fire in Paula's eyes, the bonfires in Iñez's.

"Go tell Paula whatever you want," Tommy said to Charlie. He was tired of lying. Only shots of Jameson could numb the guilt, and on more than one occasion he drank himself to the verge of making things right. Telling Iñez no. No more. But then he'd see the busty Spaniard and remind himself that dancing around the bonfire with a bottle in hand was his wheelhouse, not spooning or holding hands. His life couldn't wear tenderness, much as he tried with Paula.

"I'm not going to tell anyone anything," said Charlie, unsure if he believed it. It would be so easy, now, to strike this monster down. *Guess who I saw tonight, Paula?*

"Is there a pay phone in here?" Charlie needed to speak with John about how to proceed.

"Who you calling, gent?"

"What do you care?" Iñez had been sauntering up to the bar, taking her time. The slow rotation of her hips. "We make the Black Forest blush. Remember, Tomas?"

Tommy had said as much after thirty-six hours of extraordinary, interactive nudity that ran parallel to a hashish fog, a wine fog, and an endless bag of homemade beef jerky, whose smokiness was the anthem of their blush-making.

On the contrary, his and Paula's vacation had been pure. They read books by the pool. She taught him—a nineteen-year-old girl taught him—how to be on vacation. Early to bed, early to rise. The smell of Coppertone.

"I could use the pay phone outside," said Charlie.

"Use the house phone," said Iñez. She sat in Tommy's lap, grinding her hips into his belt, his ribs. "Call the curly-hair blonde girl."

Tommy sat there nodding, trancelike. He wasn't ready to lose Paula. He wasn't ready to go back up the loft ladder and into the Black Forest. He could tell from how Iñez moved in his lap that she was wet.

"Fuck it all," said Tommy.

"I'm sorry," said Charlie. He actually was. Tommy looked stuck, with that woman sitting on him, a bottle in one hand, the other hand barely free enough to scratch his nose.

"Why are you sorry, gent? There's all the wine in the world here, and a beautiful ass in my lap."

They all drank to that, Tommy from the bottle. Charlie could see the wine pass behind his Adam's apple. His throat was thick and venous, a drinking muscle.

"I should probably make that call," said Charlie.

"Sounds urgent," said Tommy.

"Let him call her, Tomas. Let him find his own messy sweetness." Messy sweetness. Charlie could relate. His lips were dehydrated from the day of drinking, chapped red and wine-stung. He'd nervously picked a hangnail, at the Oyster House, and now it bled. Sweat had baked and then cooled his T-shirt, like those birth-of-a-planet movies when the lava finally starts to steam off. This was a birth, he decided, and dipped his hangnail into the wine.

"Get your finger out of your Rioja," said the Spaniard. "No polite, *chico*."

When? Charlie wondered. When exactly did it happen? It was probably when she said that she'd hold up her blue jeans next to her eyes that he fell in love, because he believed that she would do just that. He could see and feel her doing it. He felt her doing it right then, even though she was nowhere in sight. He felt her when the wine entered his cut. He felt her before, when his gums itched with hunger, and felt her again when he tasted Iñez's salty ham sandwich. He didn't even wonder if she was feeling him; it was irrelevant. If he never saw her again? Irrelevant. This was the scene well after the lava had cooled, when the oceans teem with sperm-like fish, and one of them has the audacity to step out onto a rock. The ultimate leap of faith that gills will turn into lungs and that air is real; that these thoughts about a girl will turn into the girl herself.

"The house phone is in the back of the restaurant," said Iñez.

"Have a good call, then," Tommy said and toasted with his bottle, then expertly flicked his wrist, shattering the vessel against the bar. Iñez bore the brunt of the crimson splatter, her T-shirt soaked through, her hair, her legs. But all she could do was laugh, "*Bueno*, Tomas. *Bueno*, darling."

Tommy was expressionless. He held the broken bottle by the neck, glass stalactites pointing at Charlie.

"Really, I was just going to call my brother," said Charlie. "I don't even have her number."

The lurid, laughing woman stained in red. The Spaniard and his high-pitched *iyee*s. Tommy's eyes, the driest eyes Charlie had ever seen; he wouldn't have been surprised if they popped out of his head and bounced on the floor like marbles. It was a dark scene, these thirtysomethings and their thirty generations of glassware.

"You should go, *chico*," said the Spaniard.

"I didn't pay."

"Go," implored Iñez. "Go and leave me with my own messy sweetness."

Fuck these crazy old people. "I'm going," he said, taking on Tommy's eyes. *One whisper in her ear. One whisper, gent.*

Chapter Ten

A TAXI DROPPED CHARLIE in front of what looked like a condemned complex of brownstones complete with yellowing notices about pesticides and an imminent wrecking ball, scheduled for next Thursday, 1978. The driver assured him the Pen & Pencil Club was "somewhere inside the bullshit." They were in a warehouse district. No people, no stores, few cars, just the smell of steam. Waiting for a sign of club life, he felt as if a silent animal were watching him in the distance; he remembered a Crumb's vague threat about the foothills of the Appalachian Mountains, where living, breathing mountain lions, in view of the skyline, sharpened their claws against petrified tree trunks, making sparks in the night. If the wildcats pounced, he'd yell up in the direction of the building's upper floors; he'd yell that Paula should know that Tommy was with Iñez. Time permitting, he'd also yell that he loved her.

"You help us settle a bet?" From his blind side appeared two Crumbs, but not the Falstaffian version. These Crumbs were younger, scruffier, caught perhaps in a botched becoming.

"Me?" asked Charlie.

"Yeah, unless you're too good to settle a bet for us."

One wore an army jacket and camouflage pants, the other a 1950s bowling shirt and slicked-back hair. Man-children of a mean-spirited Halloween.

"How can I help?" asked Charlie in his Jee-Jee voice. How his father's arms would open so wide when a stranger would ask him for directions or for a dollar.

"This guy says that you're only carrying twenty dollars, and I say you're carrying a hundred dollars."

Charlie started to reach for his inside pocket to show them his cash envelope and help decide on a winner, but he had the good sense to stop, his hand frozen like Napoleon's. A pose that fascinated Jee-Jee, who often tried to copy it but looked less like an emperor and more like a heart attack victim. *Napoleon's heart probably never beat this fast.*

"So, which one of us got lucky?" asked the army jacket.

"Yeah, who won the bet?" asked the bowling shirt.

"I don't have a lot of money, so I think neither of you won or we could say that you both won."

"Aw, see, we're gonna need verification of who won the bet, just because we gotta be sure," said the army jacket.

There was still a small chance that the bet was real, thought Charlie. Maybe this ratlike strain of Crumb is especially fascinated by amounts.

"Okay," said Charlie. "Around nineteen hundred dollars."

The army jacket smiled wide. "We gotta take that to the lab to verify it isn't counterfeit, 'cause if it's counterfeit we gotta make a citizen's arrest on you."

"It's not counterfeit," said Charlie. "It's mine."

The smile was gone. "They got trash bins around here cops don't even know exist. Throw a kid in there. Padlock it shut. You'll become a skeleton they'll find in 2001."

"We can share my money. Please. I don't want to be a 2001 skeleton. Not tonight. I'm in love."

"Get on your knees, Romeo."

"Please," said Charlie, kneeling. "You can take it all."

"That's more like it, but we're still gonna give you a new home in the trash bin. Got my padlock right here."

From behind, Charlie felt a hand like a meat hook under his armpit. It hoisted him upright. In Neil's other hand were two bottles of White Horse whisky, one of which he gave Charlie to hold.

"Oh, hey, Neil," said the army jacket.

"Oh, hey," Neil replied, then hit him with the bottle over the side of his head at an angle, across the eye and nose. The army jacket dropped, holding his face, blood and whisky pooling around him.

"Give me that other bottle," Neil said to Charlie, approaching the bowling shirt.

"What the fuck? We were just having fun, Neil."

"I'm not going to waste a second bottle of White Horse, but the next time I see you, I'm going to crack you. So, if I were you, I'd start hiding right now."

"Fuck, Neil," the bowling shirt said. He skulked away after examining the army jacket, who was out cold, his cuts sopping up the White Horse.

"I told you," said Neil to the comatose man, "you should have never sold me your World Series ring. Assistant equipment manager for the '80 Phils," he told Charlie. "Bought the ring off him summer of '82, down at the shore. Nine hundred bucks. I told him the moment he sells me that ring, bad things will start to happen. And they have. Just look at him."

"Should we leave him there?"

"I have to finish my chess lesson. Just went out to the car to get my private stash. Lucky thing, they would've taken your wallet, maybe roughed you up. Come with me."

"Should we call an ambulance?" asked Charlie.

"Nah, he'll wrap his face in his camouflage jacket and stumble home. It's good that jacket will get some blood on it. He's been lying about 'Nam for years."

Entering the Pen & Pencil Club involved climbing up a fire escape to a first-floor landing, then going down a hall. Neil moved as if it were his own home, whistling as they went, flipping the White Horse bottle. Once inside, they parted ways, leaving Charlie to the inky darkness—a purple darkness, interrupted by crooked lampshades and their weak bulbs. He couldn't decide whether it was decrepit or cozy until he sank into an old loveseat that was right by the front door and waited for his eyes to adjust. This was a comfortable place, he thought, until he saw a very old woman rolling a mop bucket.

"Next time they kick the hot dog crock over, they can clean it up themselves," she barked.

Indeed, the club smelled like hot dog water. He could hear the *phtt* of cork in the distance, a dartboard in a faraway room. Sound didn't travel well here, like on an airplane, deep into a transatlantic flight; you could be sitting next to speaking lips and still only hear the white noise. On Charlie's first trip to Europe, he'd boarded the plane with a slight fever, but by the time the stewardess pulled the plug on the night and put up the window shades, he'd been cured. Charlie considered it medicinal, the air inside a Paris-bound cabin, a blanket of powdery aspirin covering everything and everyone.

"What the fuck? Thought you were here to see my chess lesson." Neil was back, carrying a rook instead of whisky.

"I'm actually here to see Paula," said Charlie. "She said I should stop by."

"She's in the back with her Chi-knee friend. If you want to learn some chess, I'm in the bar room with Slutsky, bald Russian. Uses his forehead like I used my bottle of White Horse."

Paula was standing near the jukebox, smoking a cigarette. Her friend, a squat girl of vaguely Pacific origins, Hawaii, maybe Tahiti, was gyrating around Paula's long legs.

"Hey you," said Paula. "Most people get dropped off here and turn right around."

"It was a little dicey outside, but Neil and I took care of it."

To see white bra straps beneath her black tank top. To see black-and-white straps carried by her shoulders, her curls even curlier from sweat. She wore her pants low, and in the jukebox light Charlie could make out the hairless pores of her abdomen.

"Good man," she said, sounding less like herself and more like Tommy. *At least she didn't call me* gent.

"This is Jazz," she said. "My roommate, Jasmine."

"Night-blooming jasmine is one of my favorite smells," said Charlie.

"Good for you," said Jazz.

"Be nice, Jazz," said Paula.

"Penn guys can be such assholes," said Jasmine.

"Charlie's different. He's a gentleman."

"I'm going to do a dance," said Jazz. "Don't watch me, Penn boy." She slunk away in her combat boots, laced almost to the knee. They were half her person.

"What is it with this city? Everyone's pissed off."

"She's just making a statement," said Paula. "Let's sit. I'm buzzed." She seemed so happy, but Charlie could tell that her happiness was not due to him, nor really the buzz. *To be with a girl whose smile belongs to another guy is awful*, he thought. She chose a sofa, ripped, like all the seating at the Pen & Pencil, and sank in, the smile growing as the couch became her bed. "Night-blooming jasmine, huh?"

"It's a great smell," Charlie said, trying to move closer to her hair in order to smell her last shower.

"It's a wonderful flower," said Paula. "I know all about it. I study plants and animals that function at night."

"Owls?"

"Especially owls. Fireflies. The night is a better world. I'd hate to see this club in the daylight, it would ruin everything. When he was first starting out, Tommy used to mop down the place in the morning. He said it was pretty disgusting in the light."

"Tommy," said Charlie.

"I know he comes across a little rough. It's the whole Irish thing. But there's a poet inside of him. How about you? You have a girlfriend? Someone you can smell the jasmine with?"

"I dated someone this summer, but things are strange now."

"I can relate."

"Are things strange between you and Tommy?"

"Of course, but then I'll—forget it. It's stupid."

"No, tell me."

"I don't think you'll want to know."

"I do want to know. I want to know everything about you."

"I can be so mad at him, but then I'll smell his neck."

"His neck?"

"It has this sweet *man* smell. He uses Old Spice, just a drop, and probably forgets half the time. I could float away with that smell. I told you, you didn't want to know."

She was right. *Sorry, Tommy*, he thought. But enough's enough. Her pink lips on your odorous neck? *No mas, Tomas.*

"I saw Tommy again tonight," said Charlie.

"You did?"

"At World of Wines."

"No, you probably saw him at the Irish bars in the old neighborhood, with his cousin. Look, I know he'll tell me one thing, then end up at the Irish bars. He just works so hard that he needs to let off some steam, and he doesn't want me to worry. Like I tell everyone, there's another side to him. Did you know that some Sunday mornings he drops off boxes of pastries at the church? They're a little stale, but still."

She put a cushion over her head.

"Are you okay?" asked Charlie. "Can you breathe in there?"

"Are you sure it wasn't an Irish bar?" Paula spoke through the cushion.

"It wasn't an Irish bar," said Charlie. "It's more of a European place, just a couple of blocks from the Oyster House—"

"I know where it is," she said, sitting up. "Tommy doesn't go there anymore."

She scoured the room for proof that he was anywhere but with that Spanish woman. "What was he doing there?" she asked Charlie. Iñez

had an aunt who sometimes worked there. A nice older woman. There
was a chance Tommy saw the aunt in the window and stopped in for a
friendly chat, even though he swore on his life, and the afterlife of his
deceased mother, that he would never go in there again.

"He was hanging out," said Charlie.

Paula tossed the cushion to the floor. Her face had turned white, aside
from the red stars on her cheeks that looked as if they had burst and were
bleeding. Her lips were parted, paralyzed in a state of pre-trembling.

"Was he drinking?" she asked. "You're an idiot, Paula. Of course
he was."

"He was having a little wine," said Charlie.

"That means bottles. Was she there?"

"I know that he likes you so much, and you like him, so maybe—"

"Was she there?"

"You mean was Iñez there?"

"I don't want to hear her name, please."

"She was there."

"Were they—to your eyes, did it seem that they were a couple?
Were they doing couple things?"

"It was a little hard to tell. Maybe I have everything mixed up." Hurting
this girl felt wrong. *My life is allergic to hurting her*, thought Charlie.

"Yeah, maybe you mixed it up," said Paula. "But that's okay. Look,
just—um—tell me . . . tell me all about your girlfriend." She righted
herself on the couch. A fresh start. Boys have girlfriends, and girls have
boyfriends. Loyalty rules the Earth, and no one needs to suffer.

"She's going to NYU next week, and she and I are probably broken
up, or in some limbo she's created so she can be effectively young. I
might have cared this morning, but tonight?" He twisted his mouth
into a question mark signifying comedic indifference.

"I understand her. I haven't felt young—I haven't felt young since
I was thirteen. Sorry, but that's what boys do. They fast-forward your
life." She gestured to Charlie's Walkman.

"Sorry, I should stop fiddling with this thing."

"A Walkman, a beach chair, a book; for a girl who likes things simple, my life always seems fucked up."

"With Monica Miller, nothing came easy. I think I overthought everything."

"Well, join the club. As far as I'm concerned, 90 percent of a love affair is in the head, right in here." She grabbed a fistful of Charlie's hair. "God only knows if the other 10 percent is anything at all." Paula released her grip: "Fuck it," she said. "I want to know all the facts."

"About what?" He knew what she meant.

"Tommy. What you saw."

"I was pretty buzzed."

"I can take it. Talk."

Charlie watched her friend Jasmine on the dance floor, turning round and round like a broken robot.

"Well, she was sitting on Tommy's lap—"

"And?"

"He broke a wine bottle."

"That's normal for him. And?"

"They were together in the restaurant loft."

"The loft. The loft that he told me disgusted him. The loft that he told me he'd never fuck in again."

I have to lie, thought Charlie. *Right now, say that Tommy was going on and on about how much he loved his Paula. That Tommy was there on a mission of celebratory love.*

"Not really sure about what's in the loft," said Charlie.

"A futon," said Paula. "A dirty futon with one sheet that she never washes."

The bad man who fucks a madwoman on a dirty bed should not be with this earnest girl and her downy cheeks.

"Did it seem like they had sex?"

"I don't know."

"There's a gun to your head: yes or no."

"I don't know."

"Okay then, Charlie. Let's say there's a gun to my head. They're going to kill me, and you'll never see me again if you lie. Yes, or no?"

"Yes. *Yes*."

"Can you please buy me a shot of Jack Daniel's?" She held out a five-dollar bill.

"It's on me," said Charlie. When he returned with the shot, she'd already been bought another shot. *When Paula becomes single, the line forms quickly*, Charlie thought, wondering if he'd lost his place in that line. But then she downed both shots and took Charlie by the hand into the darkest corner of the club.

"I thought he was getting better," said Paula. "I'm such a fucking idiot." She leaned against his shoulder. "Your neck doesn't smell like Tommy's. No one's does." She was crying. *Oh, to be a tear running down that face.*

"I'll buy Old Spice," he said.

"I haven't not had a boyfriend since I was thirteen. And don't think I'm going to all of a sudden be your girlfriend. I'm not this thing to be passed around."

"I would never think that."

"Boys always say the right things in the beginning. Always."

"I'm not like the other boys."

"What makes you so special?"

"I'm different. You can ask anyone."

"Who am I going to ask?"

"I feel things intensely. You and your life, this hangnail that I soaked in wine, the red light down the stairs at the Oyster—"

"You don't know my life. You're just a kid. You're eighteen."

"So are you."

"I'm nineteen. An old nineteen and getting older by the minute. Thanks for the drink." She pushed herself away from Charlie and vanished into the gloom of the P&P. Charlie knew not to follow her; John would agree. Although he would not have approved of the Tommy revelation. "Don't make girls cry," was one of his top rules. "If you can make them cry, you've gotten too close. You've gone too deep."

Chapter Eleven

"I'M HUNGOVER," CHARLIE TOLD John. Francis had gotten dressed for his breakfast shift at six, and Charlie hadn't been able to fall back asleep. He'd been awake for five hours in bed, his heart racing to clean his blood.

"Okay, here's what you do: go to the Wawa and buy a carton of orange juice. Drink it all in one sitting, then ask around about a health club. Buy a one-day membership and take a sixty-minute steam, followed by a cold shower."

"Then what?"

"What the fuck do you mean, 'Then what?' Then you breathe air, live your Penn life, date the waitress on weekends, whatever. Listen, I should go. Shannon Chang just called me into her office. You ever meet Shannon?"

"When would I have met her?"

"Hottest Asian chick on Wall Street. Older than me, outearns me. Amazing, six-figure Shannon Chang."

Stupid Haircut affectations about liking exotic women, thought Charlie.

"Do you like Asian girls? I forget," asked John.

"I like only one girl," said Charlie.

"What about Monica whatshername?"

"Monica Miller? I never loved her."

Outside the campus was ninety-one degrees at eleven in the morning. Kids in the courtyard shouting inanities. Nine floors up, everything sounded like a taunt. *No wonder the windows are bolted shut.* There was a campus Wawa on Feldman's friendly cartoon map of Penn, but killing this professional hangover wasn't something Charlie wanted to do in front of amateurs. Reborn thanks to John's advice, he jumped out of bed, splashed his face with water, added shoes, and got into the first taxi he saw, having avoided saying a single word to any fellow student.

"I think I'm gonna hit the Wawa," said Charlie to the taxi driver.

"Which one?" asked the driver.

"The one away from here."

"Fifteenth and Chestnut."

"Perfect. How are you doing today? Me, I'm a little hungover."

"I hear you, boss. Join the club."

There had been anecdotes, not only from John but from others as well, that Philly was a hungover town. A family friend had spoken about the gray and green faces that populated Philadelphia mornings. Jee-Jee worried it would deter Charlie from attending Penn, but it had the opposite effect. Waking up numb and stung felt more like a romance between him and the world than a disconnect between him and his body.

But those were high school hangovers. This was a Philly hangover, and the Wawa was air-conditioned. Weapons-grade; the employees wore hoodies.

Charlie bought and consumed a tall carton of orange juice while watching the early lunch crowd order their sandwiches. The Wawa customers, particularly the businessmen, sweated even in the winter of that store. To a man, they carried handkerchiefs to wipe it away, then more would drip from their foreheads and temples, and out would come the hanky. The heat of their lunch orders—cheesesteaks, only cheesesteaks—hastened more sweat. Charlie wondered who had to wash and iron the handkerchiefs. He felt bad for some feminine form waiting by the window for nightfall and the arrival of the unctuous square of fabric.

"Excuse me," he said to one of the businessmen. "Do you know a good gym around here?"

"Do I look like I know a good gym?" The man was obese with a childlike face, his handkerchief dotted with light-blue baby seals. "I'm just giving you a poke in the ribs, kid. Gyms. Okay, gyms, let's see. If you want boxing and stuff like that you have to go South Street, but I don't know where exactly. And if you want the fancy stuff, the pools and shit, your best bet is the Bellevue on Broad. Hell, I'm a member there, Christmas gift from the wife, and I've been, what? Two times? Nice try, Denise!"

Philly, thought Charlie on his way to Broad Street, where more businessmen huddled around lunch carts, tapping their feet in time to the spatula's chatter. *I hate being a snob. Paula's not a snob. So what if these guys are fat and curse a lot and sweat gravy? I bet they're happy. Men destroyed by the night before. They have all day to mount a comeback. What a life, of course they're happy. Plus, they own beautiful handkerchiefs with baby seals on them, and they appreciate the rhythm of the cheesesteak man. Screw it: I'll be happy, too, and find jazz in the spatula.*

And Charlie was happy, for many moments, until he remembered Tommy, who was out there somewhere, perhaps hiding behind a cheesesteak cart. God only knew how *his* morning was going.

Maybe he'd be in the steam room. Yes, that's where he'd be. Contrite. Shaking Charlie's hand. "No hard feelings, gent. She's all yours. Stop by my bar, one of these days, and I'll buy you a pop."

In the light of day, the hungover class were nothing if not peaceful. After all, the streets ran dark with grease, not blood.

*

Jee-Jee was a steam room aficionado and would freeze the *New York Times* prior to his epic stays in the Harmonie Club's tiled spritz palace. An hour later, the paper would be a mushy ball, and Jee-Jee would emerge grinning ear to ear, slapping fellow members on the back. The Bellevue's facility was much smaller than the Harmonie Club's expansive if not endless steam room; Charlie could never count all the senators. In here, however, there was just one man in front of him, ooh-ing and ahh-ing about the heat. He wore no towel to protect Charlie from the sight of his seventy-something body.

"When I was your age," said the naked old man, "I'd put shaving cream on before the steam. Those shaves were like butter."

"I bet," said Charlie.

"But these days, I'm closer to my last shave than my first."

Charlie wanted to shave, even though he had little hair on his face. Just enough that the Afta would sting. John called it shaving's orgasm.

"I might actually lather up," said Charlie to the man.

"Well, hell, I might join you."

They walked together out of the steam room to the sinks. The man was tall, taller than Charlie even when hunched over, with a bulging middle and long, stringy testicles that swayed as he moved. Walking with him from the sinks back into the steam room was like walking with a prehistoric creature, but a friendly one who was proud of his species.

"What are you going to do with your close shave?" the man asked Charlie.

"I'm going to show it to the girl I love," said Charlie.

"Ah, that's the best. Now all you need is a box of candies, and she'll be yours."

"Really?"

"Absolutely. Candy and a close shave. I don't care who she is or what year it is, girls like soft skin and a big box of chocolates."

It would be a bold move, thought Charlie, but this was a wise dinosaur.

"I think I might take you up on that advice," said Charlie.

"Try Marone's on Seventeenth. They have good candy and all these stuffed animals in the window. Maybe I'll see you next year and you'll tell me how it went."

"Maybe sooner," said Charlie. "I'd join this club just for the steam room."

"I have a flight out of Dodge tonight. Florida until May. My wife passed away, and there isn't much for me here in the city."

"Sorry about your wife."

"We had a great run."

"I hope you have lots of close shaves in Florida," said Charlie.

"My close-shave days are over, and yours have just begun. That's how it goes. Then one day you'll be the old man in the steam room."

*

Marone Chocolates was run by a man in a sweater-shirt that clung to his soft torso, much like the Crumbs from last night. Philly was big on man blouses. Jee-Jee wore them, but could pull it off due to his stoutness, his chest remembering the chores of his French youth. The chocolatier wore many bracelets that clanked against the candy case, and he exhaled, bothered. Each and every time, he had to reach into the case with his gloved hand.

"Like I said before, the premade boxes are just the same."

"My friend Angelina always insisted that her candy come right from the case," said Charlie.

"Well, if Angelina says so."

While Charlie watched the man pluck sweets, he held on to the neck of a lifelike baby giraffe. A corner of the store was dedicated to stuffed animals, and it was the perfect place to be while the effects of the steam bath finally settled over his muscles, and the vitamin C from the orange juice slaked his blood.

"What's it like to have a mustache?" Charlie asked the chocolatier.

"What's it like not to have one?"

Charlie generally got along with gay men. Angelina had a very good gay friend who would come over to watch *Fantasy Island* and gossip about Ricardo Montalban's gayness. He was the first person any of them had known who'd come down with AIDS. Regardless, young Charlie had let him hug hello and goodbye.

"I like your bracelets," said Charlie.

"They just seem to get in the way," said the chocolatier, fussing over an unwieldy bonbon and its place in a compartment.

"They should make larger spaces for the bigger chocolates," said Charlie.

"Well, they don't, and I just have to figure it out for my little ol' self."

When it came time to pay, the chocolatier noticed that Charlie had dented the giraffe's neck.

"Look what you did," said the chocolatier. "No one wants a giraffe with a broken neck. Now you're going to have to pony up."

"I suppose I could give her the giraffe, too. Probably get my ass kicked by Neil for bringing in a stuffed animal."

"Now you listen to me," said the chocolatier. "If someone gets in your face because you're carrying this beautiful toy, you don't think twice, you go for the balls. Grab them and squeeze them like you're wringing out a wet towel, and don't let go until he's down." The chocolatier composed himself and finished the box by airdropping two mint thins that slipped perfectly into their assigned slots. "There," he said. "The forty-eight-piece assortment."

"It's amazing," said Charlie.

"Now, I like to tell people, so they don't get all crazy, that the plush animals are $129."

"But I thought you said I had to buy it no matter what?"

"Yes, but you should still know the price."

"Okay, thanks. God, I hope today doesn't suck. Sorry just thinking out loud."

"How old are you?" the chocolatier asked.

"Eighteen."

"Then the world is your oyster."

Charlie wanted to tell the chocolatier about the Oyster House and his unwitting pun, but the man was elsewhere.

"When I was your age, I was at Parris Island," he said.

"Paris?" asked Charlie.

"No, not Paris. Boot camp. Go for his fucking balls."

*

Neil had allowed the Crumbs in for lunch. They were usually forbidden until happy hour, but the gossip about Paula and Tommy had spread like wildfire, which meant heavy-drinking Crumbs, and devotional tips in honor of youth and heartbreak.

"My friend's been with Tommy all morning," said a Crumb. "They've been hitting every bar in town. Fucking Tommy. God bless."

"It's a sad day, Crumb. Breakups bring me down," said Neil, fixing Charlie a vodka and tonic. "People should stick together."

"Thanks again for last night," said Charlie.

"I don't remember last night," said Neil.

"The bottle? That guy?"

"Like I said, I don't remember. Only thing I remember are what you Crumbs drink."

"I'm not a Crumb."

"Not yet."

It was another half hour before Paula came in from the dining room. She was working the back bar. It was an easier gig. One of the other waitresses had switched with her, given the circumstances.

"I need a corkscrew," she said to Neil.

Charlie watched her forearms work the tool. They were beautiful. Little muscles born of summer jobs: ice cream scooper, lawn mower, babysitter. *Thank you, New Hope, Pennsylvania*, thought Charlie, *thank you for her tendons*.

"Hi," said Charlie. "Remember me?"

"Yep," she said, the P un-popped.

"I have something for you."

"I'm fine, thanks. I just want to get through this day."

"Chocolates, and a giraffe."

She stopped what she was doing to take in the giraffe. It was different from the usual offerings. She'd received her share of candy boxes, usually from boys who'd fallen in love. Unrequited. She never had the heart to open those boxes; she'd give them to her mother, who piled the empties next to the fireplace. The column almost reached the mantel. Paula hated it when her mother would brag to a friend, "What a heartbreaker. Will you look at all the Russell Stovers."

"I like giraffes," said Paula. "They're the tallest living ground animal."

"And this is a forty-eight-piece assortment from Marone's."

"They're preyed on by lions. You probably shouldn't be here."

"Why?"

"Tommy's under the impression that you told me about him and that woman."

"I did."

"I told him it was feminine intuition, which is partially true, but he didn't believe me. He wants to kill you."

"I'm not afraid."

Here he is, buzzed again, thought Paula. She returned to opening the bottle of wine.

"Suit yourself."

"You suit me," said Charlie.

She stopped with the bottle, the corkscrew stuck mid-handstand, and closed her eyes.

"Please, Charlie, I just want this day to be over. You don't know me, and I don't know you." Her eyes remained shut until two tears raced down her cheeks. Paper streamers. They were too fast for Charlie to dab them with a bar nap.

A Crumb tumbled into the barroom, spilling popcorn. "Tommy's coming. Tommy's coming and he's ripped."

Cactus placed his shucker's knife on the cutting board. "We don't need this shit, Neil."

The Crumbs had been chattering about a fight, a once-in-a-lifetime ass-whupping. They had located an area, out in the back alley, where it would go down. Crumbs loved fights, especially when they were over a girl. Especially ones over Paula Katherine Henderson, the best-looking girl ever to work at the Sansom Street Oyster House. Sure, it wasn't saying much, but she had that wild long curly hair, and white teeth always glistening from an imperceptible layer of spit. Features that made Crumbs lusty. Watching men fight over her was a cause for hope; perhaps there would be a double knockout and she'd allow room in her heart for a Crumb.

"He'll kill that boy," Cactus said to Neil.

"These things are never as one-sided as you think they'll be, Cactus."

Paula had seen Tommy drunk dozens of times, really drunk, unable to walk, other than in a circle around himself, winding himself down for a final collapse. While he'd never laid a hand on her, she'd watched him pick a man up by his throat and toss him across a back alley into a row of steel garbage cans. That was in the beginning, when Tommy's feats of chivalrous rage widened her blue eyes. The man he'd bowled into the trash had been fresh with her. Tommy told the man that an apology would spare him harm. Instead, he called Paula a whore, then into the air he flew.

Growing up in New Hope, there had been a few fights over her, but they'd been inconclusive scraps: shirts over heads and bloody noses. More often than not, Paula would end up drinking beer with both fighters, slightly offended by their burgeoning friendship. Charlie and Tommy wouldn't end up friends, she thought, and then believed there was a chance, and dreaded the thought of them leaving her alone at the Oyster House for reconciliatory drinks elsewhere.

"If Tommy comes in, I'll do my best to calm him down," Paula said to Charlie. "But if I were you, I'd go back to school."

He knew that if he left, she would never take him seriously.

"I'm staying," said Charlie. "I'm not going to leave you alone with that guy."

He'd never been punched in the face, and actually wanted to get it over with. No harm in losing a fight to an older guy, a famous Irish bartender who used the gym for more than a steam.

Paula ran her finger down the giraffe's neck where it was dented. "Okay. Thanks for staying."

She wondered how his lip would look fattened. They were already nicely plump. He'd probably never been in a fight. No scars, nothing. Mom would say not to go with a boy who'd never been in a scrap. Mom would call him soft. She thought again about the fat lip, about tending to it with her first aid kit, while he read to her from the 1984 Frommer's. Something her boyfriend never seemed to get around to.

When Tommy entered, it was with little fanfare. Trailed by a single Crumb, he walked slowly, smirking. His movements were stiff and mechanized, as if every fiber of muscle was working on the same virtually impossible project: to not seem drunk.

"What's hot, Neil?" he asked, full brogue.

"Nothing much, Tom," said Neil, who'd had his share of poundings at the hands of plastered Irishmen. It was in their DNA. Like how a Rottweiler won't unclench its jaw until it—or its prey—is dead. If he tried to break up the fight, Tommy would send him crashing to the floor. *Too old for another broken bone*, thought Neil.

"I think I'm going to take my break," he said.

"You're going?" asked Charlie.

"Good luck, kid."

The warmth of the steam room left him. He'd been secretly counting on Neil, should Tommy not be satisfied with only a knockout.

"There's the gent," said Tommy. "The gent and my girl. The girl and my gent. Gossipy gent, am I right?"

"Stop it, Tommy," said Paula. "He has nothing to do with this. He's eighteen, just leave him alone."

"When I was his age, I spent hundred-hour weeks cleaning the shitters in Germantown. Go with my Clorox from one bar to the next.

Makes a man understand other men. Makes a man hate other men. Ah, you brought her chocolates, like a good gossipy fag gent?" Tommy grabbed the satiny box and flung it across the room.

"Holy shit, those are Marone's," said a Crumb, thinking better of crawling after the still-racing pieces and into a war zone.

"Would a fag gent do this?" asked Charlie. He fumbled in his duffel bag, found the New Order yarmulke, and put it on his head.

"What the fuck is that thing?"

Charlie was standing, smiling, Paula's hands now on his shoulders. Jee-Jee always said try to make the other guy laugh—the best way to end a fight before it ever starts. But Tommy didn't see the humor.

"Are you mocking me?" he asked.

"No, I just thought it was funny."

Tommy snatched the giraffe, tore open its neck with his teeth, and spat out its white filling. Now they were nose to nose, Tommy's nostrils heavy with snot. Charlie felt Paula's hands slip away from his back. It had an effect like being pushed into a ring. Ideally, the blow would come right now, he thought. But Tommy needed to work himself into a lather. The heavy breathing, the fist-making, the proximity of his face to Charlie's. This was as close to fighting as two people could get without actually fighting.

"Have a seat and a drink, Tommy," said Cactus.

A hot, freckled hand collared Charlie's neck, just above the Adam's apple. Then a knee to the gut and down he went, into the sawdust, where Tommy straddled him and began slapping his face with one hand, the other tight around the throat.

"You're a woman, is what you are," yelled Tommy. "A gossipy bitch. I'll slap you like one."

"Enough," said Paula, trying to pull Tommy away by his shirt, then by his hair. But he had indeed become a Rottweiler, tone deaf to mercy.

This is real. Breathing no longer works.

This is what it's like not to breathe. You try but can't. Then try harder but can't even more. Then you stop trying. There was sawdust in Charlie's eyes and nose, his cheeks a fiery pink. Cactus, Paula, and a

Crumb rode Tommy's back, trying to wrench the beast away. Through the sawdust, Charlie could make out a chocolate truffle dusted brown. *What a beautiful thing*, he thought, and remembered the chocolatier. Charlie thanked the man for his patience and said goodbye. He was about to say goodbye to his mother, his family, and Paula, when he saw the rip near Tommy's crotch and the light-blue boxer shorts. He went for that splash of blue.

Not Paris. Parris Island.

At first there was just thigh meat until he scraped his way into the fly, feeling for two soft mounds. And when he found them, he squeezed them. Like he was wringing a wet towel. He squeezed and squeezed and didn't stop even when it was Charlie who now straddled Tommy. He didn't stop for Tommy's soprano shrieking, nor when he felt his hands wet with blood. Or was it urine? Now Charlie was the Rottweiler. He couldn't care less about bodily fluids.

It took three Crumbs to remove him. They sat him in a barstool, where he watched Tommy squirm on the floor. It looked like the embarrassing breakdancing intensive Charlie's eighth-grade class was made to take, twenty-nine white kids rolling around on gym mats. Paula knelt by Tommy, unwilling to touch his hair, as she ordinarily might.

"Gent got the better of me," said Tommy through a crazy grimace. "Smart gent to aim for the onions."

"Well, you should ice them," said Paula.

"I was just defending myself," said Charlie. "I couldn't breathe, and he wouldn't stop." He hoped the ring around his neck might elicit her sympathy.

"I told you to go. Now look at him. Look at both of you."

"I was defending *us*," said Charlie, proud of the sawdust stuck to his face, and grateful for the cold vodka shots getting bought for him by the Crumbs. *I'm the new Tommy*, he thought.

"I would have died for us, Paula."

"Fucking men," said Paula.

Men.

Neil returned and examined both Tommy and Charlie with medical curiosity. He took stock of the scene and tried to kick the sawdust back into place.

"Okay, you're banned for life, O'Leary," he told Tommy. "The kitchen boys'll take you out the back. The kid's banned for six months. Would've been a year, but I hear you went for the snappers. Got to like a man who goes for the snappers. And as for Paula, sorry, honey, but I have to can you. It's the owner's rules. He hates the Romeo and Juliet bullshit in his bar, and he happened to be in the back having scrod when the shit hit the fan. Fucking scrod. He could have anything off the menu, including lobster."

"I'm fired?"

"You're meant for better things than sawdust and seaweed."

"Like what?"

Neil raised his eyebrows at Charlie. "You should help her box up her locker."

"I should? I mean, of course I will."

Paula watched two busboys drag Tommy by his feet back into the kitchen. He looked euphoric, laughing at the ceiling, or maybe crying. Regardless, Paula knew he wouldn't miss work tonight. He'd ice himself and un-wreck himself.

"His last name's O'Leary?" asked Charlie, proud that he'd felled a man named Tommy O'Leary.

"I need to find a job," said Paula, smoothing over Tommy's sawdust tracks.

"I'll help you look," said Charlie. "In the meantime, I have some money."

"You should go wash your face."

"Am I bleeding?" He hoped to God he was. He hoped as well that amid all the slapping he'd actually been punched.

"There's a first aid kit downstairs."

Paula had expected her tenure at the Oyster House to end with a champagne toast and a hundred shouts of "Bon voyage!" Engagement party, college graduation, something—just not this. She led the way down the stairs, toward the red light, for the last time. *One of the girls must be smoking a cigarette*, she thought. *I'll smoke one, too. How many times can a girl press reset on her life?*

"I like the sticker on your locker," said Charlie.

"*My Little Pony*," said Paula.

"I love it."

"It was there when I got here. And will be here for the next girl, and the one after that. Maybe the next ten girls. Neil says that new waitresses last about two years, tops. So that's twenty years."

"We could come and visit it in twenty years," said Charlie, using his hands to beckon the red light of the open fire door into his heart.

An older waitress had been smoking. Gray hair, granny glasses. She hugged Paula, gave her a cigarette, and headed back upstairs. "My dogs are barking, Paul," she said during her ascent. "Need new sneakers, had these since well before you started."

"She called you Paul," said Charlie.

"Just something the older girls do. It's a Philly thing." Paula lipped the cigarette by the fire door but didn't light it. "So many daydreams out here during break. Guess I'm a sucker for alleyways."

Charlie watched her squat like a catcher, bounce on her haunches, then spring up.

"Dammit," she yelled.

"Sorry you have to say goodbye to this place," said Charlie.

"Just thought some good things were finally happening."

"Maybe Neil will change his mind. Maybe—"

"Nah, I'll never see *My Little Pony* again for as long as I live." She put the cigarette behind her ear, shouldered her pocketbook, and ascended.

"*Vamos*," she said.

So unsentimental, marveled Charlie, tasting his own blood. *We're a* tough *couple.*

Chapter Twelve

WHEN THEY CAME BACK upstairs there was no sign of the conflict, except for a debate among Crumbs about the virtues of wearing a jockstrap in everyday life. Paula was disconcerted to see the new young waitress that Neil was already equipping. A stack of guest checks, a box of pens, a wine key, and a Sansom Street Oyster House baseball cap, which Paula knew would remain in her locker until this girl's version of today.

"Where'd *she* come from?" asked Paula.

"Owner just sent her my way," said Neil. "Katya, this is Paula. Paula, Katya." Paula gave Katya a once-over, and for the first time ever a small wrinkle, a faint tilde, appeared on Paula's forehead.

"How old are you?" Paula asked the girl.

"Eighteens," she said.

"Great accent, Neilly," chimed a Crumb. "Like that fucking Elton John video. What's the name of that video with the hot Russkie?"

"'Nikita,' Crumb."

"I was even younger than you when I started," said Paula. "Good luck here."

"Thanking you," said Katya.

Neil and Cactus had seen many a barmaid exit that front door, their boyfriend holding a box.

"Don't be a stranger," said Neil. It was what he always said, and nine times out of ten it was the last thing they ever heard him say.

"Can't believe this is it," said Paula.

"How long you been here, anyway?" asked Neil. "Five seconds?"

"Almost two years."

"Years are bullshit," said Neil. "Decades are what matters."

"Years aren't bullshit to me. I learned a lot here."

"By the time you hit Broad Street, you'll be saying to yourself, 'Neil who? Oyster what?'"

"I for one will never forget this place," said Charlie.

"No shit. Most people leave with a few oyster crackers in their jacket pocket, maybe a mint and a toothpick. Look at what you got." Neil chortled.

"Bye, Pauly," said a Crumb. "Whaddya say we do a goodbye smooch?"

She blew him a kiss.

"I'll take it," said the Crumb. "Adios! Hey Katya, you a Commie or what?"

They walked in silence, Charlie a little behind Paula, the weight of her boxed personal items testing his fight-weary arms.

"She was pretty," said Paula. "Don't you think?"

"Who?"

"You know who. My replacement."

"Not my type," said Charlie.

"Yeah, right. If she was the first girl you met at the Oyster House, I wouldn't be your type."

"That's not true."

"It's been a long day."

Charlie wanted to say *ditto*. He felt unmoored, in a part of his life that he didn't recognize, and all he wanted was to lie down next to Paula and acclimate to this strange new place.

"Are we going to your apartment?" asked Charlie.

"I guess you can come up for a little bit." She hoped he wouldn't try to kiss her. She'd be obliged to kiss him back. He'd won the fight, and it was the right thing to do. Besides, she didn't want to go to sleep alone. She'd ask him to wait, to watch her fall asleep, and then he could leave. Most guys would try for more, but this Charlie was safe. Obedient, even. And then she heard her mother: *All boys are the same, Paula.*

"I'm usually not like I was today," said Charlie. "I mean, you have nothing to worry about. I'm not a violent person. Not at all."

She was going to say how weird it was that they'd both touched the same part of Tommy's body but thought better of it.

"I'm not worried. I've been with lots of tough guys, and they all want the same thing."

"I don't want that."

"You don't want love?"

"I thought you were going to say something else."

"So, you don't want sex?"

"No, of course I do."

"Well, it's not happening tonight, I'll tell you that much. So, here we are. This is my apartment building."

"Wow, so stately. I thought it would be different. More modern."

"It's nothing special."

It was smallish, eight stories, maybe nine, "1922" etched in the stone above the entrance. A little piece of Manhattan in the Philly streets.

She lived on the sixth floor and the elevator was broken.

"The elevator's always broken," she said. "The pizza guy makes us meet him halfway." Charlie watched her bounce up the stairs. The golden brownish corkscrews of hair—ten question marks? Twenty? It was hard to count.

Her apartment was larger and cleaner than he'd envisioned. There were flowers on her bureau, another dozen on the coffee table in the living room, and a third set in the kitchen.

"Lots of flowers," said Charlie.

"From Tommy. He sent them this morning."

"I'm surprised you kept them."

"The flowers don't know where they came from."

She believes in things, he thought as he watched her put away her work stuff. She had, she said, about $150 to her name and no clear plan for adding to that. Rent was due on the fifteenth, and Jasmine's name was on the lease.

"Jazz would do anything for me, but when it comes to the rent, she becomes a different person."

Charlie sat on her bed, not a futon but a four-poster antique. Apparently it had belonged to her mother. There was a story about how it ended up in Paula's possession, but Charlie wasn't listening. He was watching her put away her jewelry and choose a CD.

"I have to get out of these pants," she said.

"Should I close my eyes?"

Before he could look away, she'd removed the khakis.

"It's just like a bathing suit, and I don't ask every boy at the beach to shut their eyes. They're just my legs. Everyone's got 'em."

Not like these. The only other girl legs he'd seen, live and up close, were born of diets and lotions, cleverly chosen shorts and muted lighting. Paula's had no bad moments, no detritus behind the knees, no overworked calves or pillowy thighs. Legs are composed of lots of little parts, but hers had exactly two, thought Charlie, as he watched her fold her pants into an improbably small rectangle.

"Is that you?" he asked, nodding at a framed advertisement hanging above the bed. A slightly younger Paula, wearing a soccer outfit, drank a sports drink after a game, her foot on the ball, her curls soaked.

"God, don't I look sweaty?"

"No, not really."

"It was for this drink called Frucor. Hence the big 'Frucor' on the bottom. It's an Australian drink, but they shot it in Ireland."

"I didn't know you modeled. I'm not surprised."

"I'm not a model. *Please.* I only really did that one gig. Summer after junior year. Better than selling ice cream, and I loved Ireland, even though I was only there for a week. I was supposed to stay a month, but then this boy gave me a bracelet, and when I gave it back to him, he accused me of stealing it. Irish boys sure are interesting."

"You look a little Irish. Maybe something in your cheeks?"

"My dad's side, his cheeks are always red. Booze." She held out three CDs. "Okay, you're the guest, so you get to choose. But if I start to fall asleep, you have to go." They were all by Chet Baker. "Isn't he beautiful?"

"His voice?"

"Everything." She put on men's boxers over her underwear. For sure they were Tommy's.

"Can I wash my hands?" asked Charlie. "I probably should—after, you know, the fight."

She was already in a Chet Baker trance, so he helped himself to her bathroom, the mothership of all her smells, while "My Funny Valentine" played and she hummed along from her bed. She fell asleep one song later, during "Like Someone in Love," rolled over, and made the bed creak. He felt privileged to hear these sounds, but knew others had heard them, too. Worse—they'd contributed, masculine weight testing the old wood. He hovered over the bed. There were no chairs in the room, just the antique bed and its four posts. His mother hung hats from her bedposts, but Paula's posts were clear, a clarity that would have spoken to Angelina's *Dignidad*. Multipurposed furnishings offended Angelina. She had once called her sister a peasant for keeping a box of tissues atop the television.

"I guess I should go," whispered Charlie, but there was no response. She was out, breathing deeply, occasionally making a clicking noise, but not snoring. Lips barely parted, eyelashes fluttering. He touched the feathery blanket that was touching her, rolled an edge of the comforter between his thumb and forefinger.

"I'm going to turn off Chet Baker," he whispered. After the CD player stopped whirring, she changed positions. Now she was an S taking up most of the bed; the notion that he might join her was reduced to impossibility.

He tried to memorize the scene. He wanted to own the Frucor poster. That her advertisement was not above all the beds of his future seemed wrong and crazy. He also wanted to pop open a bottle of champagne, slip into a lounger, like the ones they had at Adam's Rib when your table wasn't ready, and have a conversation with himself about her.

And then she took off her pants right in front of me and folded them so carefully. And in her bathroom was this pink razor blade with its plastic cap. Unbelievable princess of small things.

"Hey," said Paula, her eyes still shut.

"Hey."

"Thank you for everything. For telling me the truth, last night, about Tommy, and for my giraffe, and just—for wearing that—um—Jewish hat."

"Yarmulke?" asked Charlie.

"Yeah. And for noticing the *My Little Pony* sticker."

"Always," said Charlie, moving closer to the bed, but she was out again. Protective of the sleeping girl, he ended his own loitering and showed himself the door.

Chapter Thirteen

When the phone on Francis's desk rang, his alarm clock glowed an icy blue 7:38 a.m. "It's for you," said Francis. "It's a girl."

Paula was downstairs, on a pay phone in the lobby of High Rise South. She'd sat in the lounge near the security desk, pretending to be a Penn kid, reading a flyer about used textbooks. Because of the early hour, only a few kids had passed by. To Paula's eyes, they all looked young, untested. These boys didn't manage to look at her, and it worried her that her magnitude was diminished in an Ivy League lobby. Usually, even on an early morning, Paula could attract boys. But these Penn kids, breaking in their book bags. "Smart boys are smart enough to avoid the stallions, Paula," her mother had said.

Paula worried that she'd see Charlie exit the elevator with a non-stallion—one he didn't have to fight for, one who had spent the night. Perhaps asking him to leave had been wrong. He'd left so quietly. No kisses, just the click of the door, and when she woke at six, after ten hours of the deepest sleep, she missed him. His big sympathetic brown eyes and still hands. So patient for a kid. She would have been happy had he sneaked into bed. She needed a hug upon waking. *Hugging boys can be better than hugging men*, she thought, watching two boys with backpacks on their way to breakfast. *Men hug tight.*

Tight and fast. Boys still hugged like little boys. Tommy hugged her in a mock squeezing-the-life-out-of-you way that did nothing for her.

"Hi," said Paula.

"Hi."

"I'm downstairs."

"At your apartment?"

"No, silly. At your dorm. Is this a bad time?"

"No. I mean—I just woke up."

"Want to have a breakfast picnic?"

"You're downstairs?"

"Yes. I'm feeling so much better. Bring a blanket for the picnic. I'll wait for you outside. This lobby is creepy."

There was a quilt on Francis's already made bed. A family quilt organized by squares, each square occupied by an arcane farm tool.

"Mind if I borrow your quilt for the day?"

"Feldman was asking about you," said Francis.

"What did you say?"

"I said you were at the library studying."

"Thank you. And thank you for the quilt?"

"I don't know," said Francis.

"Otherwise it'll just sit on your bed. Quilts like this need stories to tell."

"It's sort of a family heirloom."

"I understand," said Charlie. "My family sells all of its family heirlooms to strangers. If I had one, I'd be protective as well. I just want to bring it to a picnic."

"Is the picnic with that waitress?"

"Yes, with Paula. Ex-waitress, in fact. She's downstairs."

"Can I meet her? I like meeting the actual people after I hear stories about them."

"Sure, you can meet her. I'm not sure if I did her justice last night."

Charlie had needed last night's retreat to college life. He'd needed sleep and the soundlessness of Francis's hygienic slumber. College had proven to be a decent home base. Certainly not a home; home was her four-poster bed. Still, he'd been happy to de-girl himself, regroup in High Rise South, and tell Francis the story, but now he dressed nervously, hesitantly. She was in the building. Saturday 7:45 a-fucking-m. A time too attached to yesterday's battle, too close to last night's bed-hovering, and he felt incapable of humanity as he and Francis rode the elevator down to the lobby.

"What the hell do people say to girls so early in the morning?" he asked Francis, who had draped the quilt over his shoulders and looked like an absurd, folksy superhero.

"I don't know. I guess I would talk about breakfast, but after that, I'm not really sure. Maybe something about the sunrise."

"She was just on this phone," said Charlie as they passed the lobby pay phone. Francis gulped. "Maybe I should just give you the quilt and leave you two alone."

"No. I need you out there. Why would any reasonable person engage in a morning date? I mean what could possibly be the point?"

"I like breakfast," said Francis. "I like bacon."

Paula was sitting in the grass, in a triangular micropark bordered by the backs of three benches. Charlie had picnics with Angelina when he was little but couldn't get along with all of the bagged sandwiches and plastic containers. Invariably, something chocolate melted and systemic sloppiness ensued: a brownie-stained frisbee, brownie-stained lips, a dusty Saturday afternoon.

"This is my roommate, Francis."

"The quilt's a keepsake," said Francis.

"It's beautiful," said Paula.

"Thank you," said Francis and presented her with the quilt. "Well, bye, then."

"Wait," said Paula. "You can join us, if you want."

Charlie whipped his head around for his roommate's response. The ice had been broken; the quilt delivered. Francis was more than welcome to leave.

"No," said Francis. "I have to work at nine."

"Rats," said Paula. "Maybe next time."

"Well, have a good picnic. Nice sunrise." With that, he did a military about-face and walked back to High Rise South.

"He's so sweet," said Paula.

"He's good-natured."

"Does he have a girlfriend?"

"No, but he likes this girl on our floor, I think. Hard to get too much out of him."

"Be nice to him."

"I *am*," said Charlie sounding like a twelve-year-old shopping with his Angelina. He prayed it didn't make her miss Tommy's brogue.

"Help me up," said Paula.

They were face-to-face. She closed her eyes; she wanted to be kissed. Charlie's racing heart understood, but Charlie did not. On came her sunglasses.

"Wait," said Charlie, "was I just supposed to—"

"It's okay. Come on. Let's go to the bus stop."

"Guess I'm still a little groggy," said Charlie.

"Not a problem." She fished two tokens from her change purse and dropped one in his palm.

"I like your sunglasses," said Charlie.

To date it was perhaps the only truly boring thing he'd said to her. She rewarded the banality with a false smile.

*

Breakfast was a takeout order of coffee and rolls from a tiny aluminum food cart that marked the entrance to Fairmount Park.

"It's a bit of a walk," said Paula.

"So where are we going?"

"Just this little place. It's actually sort of famous because there's a palm tree. People like to pretend they're in Florida, or something, but it won't be crowded this early in the day."

That there was enough of the South in the Philly sun to support a palm tree excited Charlie. He could speak to her about Palm Beach, where he'd gone as a child when his grandmother was still alive, and about the sound of toy poodles on her marble floor.

"We used to go to Florida every winter," said Charlie. "Yet another amazing 1980s tradition. I love this decade. I hope it never ends."

"I don't know. It'll be refreshing when Reagan steps down."

Charlie actually dreaded that day. Reagan was safe ground. Who knew what lunatic would come after?

"I'll miss him. Changes aren't easy for me."

Charlie was happy he had the cardboard tray to carry, otherwise there would be handholding urgencies.

"I don't think changes are easy for anyone," said Paula. "My mom is still adjusting to the divorce, and it's been, like, nine years. I don't know why she can't just move on. My dad totally cheated on her, and he still lies about it. I used to see him every Thanksgiving, but now it's just a weekly phone call. Sundays."

"I hate Sundays," said Charlie.

"Me too. They're such heavy days. Long afternoons. My mom's spooky grandfather clock. Not to mention that Tommy was always so hungover. Ugh."

"I've had my share of Sunday hangovers, too."

"I shut down on Sundays, just so you know. I like all my friends to know, so they don't take it personally."

"Friends?" asked Charlie.

She took him by the shoulders and backed him up against a tree. "We're just having a picnic, you know?"

"I know," he said, his voice cracking.

*

They lay the quilt in a bowl-shaped meadow and sat a mile from where the bus had deposited them. Only during the last few minutes of their trek had the highway noises receded. Dandelions grew next to crushed beer cans; patches of weedy grass gave way to bald spots of glittery dust. In Central Park, the city ended, but here the city was hard to shake. She'd said that five or ten miles further afield it was completely rural.

"I even think there are farms," she said. "Do you see the palm tree?"

It was a dwarf, barely taller than Paula. In order to grow here, it looked like it had sacrificed its identity.

"It's really small and stubby," he said.

"Well, it's been on TV, mister big shot."

She buttered his roll for him, then buttered her own, licked the plastic knife, and laughed. "My mom hates it when I lick knives. She thinks I'll cut my tongue." A warm wind picked up, and a Hawaiian Punch can trundled by.

"What would you do if I cut my tongue?" she asked.

"How badly?"

"Just a little cut."

"Well, let's see now."

"What comes to mind?" she asked.

"I would—"

"Listen, this picnic is going to suck unless you kiss me."

With Monica Miller, he'd offer himself ongoing coverage of the kiss, and predictions about when it would end and who would end it. An accounting of tooth collisions. This kiss, however, cleared his mind. He didn't have a mind, just a body. With Monica Miller, he only felt the kiss in his mouth. Now he felt it everywhere and forgot his species. Or that humans also used their mouths for speech.

"Mm," said Paula. "Now there won't be any weird *we haven't kissed* stuff."

"I should have kissed you before."

"Yep."

"So, we're more than friends?"

"I don't know. We are what we are."

"You sound like Monica Miller," said Charlie.

"Who's that?"

"My ex."

"I forgot that you had one. I guess everyone has one. The world is full of exes. No wonder people need happy hours. I have to start looking for a job," she said, yawning. "But I don't want to think about that right now. Lie down and fall asleep with me."

"I still have most of my allowance. Maybe we can figure something out? Maybe *I* can get a job? I can work really hard, for us."

"Sh."

Charlie didn't think he could sleep, but soon enough they were both out. A deer walked right by their picnic, stopping to bless the young couple with a sniff of its rubbery nose.

Chapter Fourteen

THE DEER INCIDENT WAS absorbed by Charlie as a dream about Tommy looming above, and he woke in a panic, sweating from a brown sky and its oppressive midday heat. Paula said it was typical of Philly. "You just sweat and sweat and get a zit, but you don't even care because everyone else is sweaty and has a zit."

"I've never fallen asleep outdoors," said Charlie. "Is it a brave thing to do?"

"It requires trust," said Paula. "Animals do it all the time."

"Do I have a zit?"

"No, you're clean. Me?"

"Clean."

They left the park holding hands. Francis's heirloom flung over Charlie's shoulder. *Odd*, he thought. *Fall asleep and wake up with a girlfriend.*

"Do you want to come over, or something?" she asked.

"Sure." It wasn't even noon on a Saturday. What do you do with that? It was too bright, and he was too sober to lose his virginity in a room without an air conditioner. A full eight hours till moonlight; more Chet Baker would be a mistake. Kissing under the Frucor poster would be good, but it might lead to daylit nudity, which would be bad;

he wasn't ready to show all of himself to her. She was right about falling asleep outdoors. It took courage, a contract of sorts. He wasn't ready to sign a similar contract with Paula. Maybe tonight he would sign? But he suspected that contracts between boys and girls were signed behind your back, by your better or worse selves, and the next thing you know, you're walking around the kitchen naked or sharing a credit card.

"So, what should we do today?" he asked.

"You probably have schoolwork, don't you?"

"Classes don't start till next Wednesday, and frankly the thought of taking notes in a classroom full of kids seems ridiculous."

"I was never good at paying attention in school. Daydreams were my specialty. So, listen, I thought we could have a talk."

"A talk? About what?" *Talks never end well. My last talk was with Angelina, and then she left.*

"I think I'm going to go back home to New Hope. I had a long phone call with my mom this morning, and I think I'm going back to regroup."

"When?"

"This afternoon, I think."

"But we were just getting to know each other."

"I know. Which is why I thought you could come with me, for the weekend. Would that be weird? I told my mom about you, about how you stood up for me and everything. She'd like to meet you. She'll do your laundry, if you have any."

"Wait, are you going to be in New Hope permanently? I mean, how will this work?"

"I don't know. So, you'll come home with me for the weekend?"

"Yes. Of course."

*

The plan was to go back to her place, pack, say so long to Jasmine, and go to High Rise South so he could get his things together. She wanted to see the inside of an Ivy League dorm room.

It took her only an hour to stuff her life into a bulging suitcase. She had Charlie take down the Frucor poster and agreed with Jasmine to leave the bed until some future day when she had a place of her own. She also left the CD player, a lamp, and her bicycle. It was only fair, Paula thought. When she'd moved in, she'd inherited the bike from the last girl, in addition to a garbage bag full of books and magazines. *It's what girls my age do. We leave each other things. Maybe it would be best to leave Charlie to the new roommate.*

But she needed him this weekend, and wanted his big brown eyes searching for hers. Going back home was a defeat, she knew. She'd try to get back her waitress job at Martine's. She'd try to avoid dating Gary for the fourth time. She'd try to save enough to move out of her mom's house before Christmas, then save enough to visit Mr. Frommer's Europe next summer or, more realistically, the summer after. As for Charlie: an instant boyfriend was dangerous, but so was being alone in New Hope.

Jasmine had already called in an ad to the *City Paper* for a new roommate. She sat on the floor while Paula finished packing, Charlie bouncing on the now-stripped bed.

"You're really high up when you're on this thing," said Charlie.

"Everyone loves this bed," said Paula.

"I'll miss you, man," said Jasmine. "Shit me."

"Everything will be fine."

Everyone loves this bed. How many other boys had loved it? The *Dignidad* must surely forbid ever asking such a thing.

"I'll mail you the security deposit after I go over your room," said Jasmine.

"I'm a clean girl," said Paula. "You know me."

"Yeah. I'll miss you. Shit me."

In the taxi to Penn, Charlie asked if Jasmine was a lesbian.

"I don't really know," she said. "I think maybe."

"What does 'shit me' mean?"

"I don't know, she just started saying it."

Charlie thought they were best friends and assumed Paula would know everything about her. Perhaps John was right, that a politeness separated girl friendships, and that they used the friendships as flotillas before reaching the landfall of marriage.

"I thought you guys were best friends?" asked Charlie.

"No, not really, we just hang out a lot. I've never really had a best friend. Lots of good friends. My mom's probably my best friend. Does that sound sad?"

"No, not at all. I wish I knew my mom better, or at all. We seem to keep a healthy distance, but after today I find distances awful." He found her hand as they drove by the university's football stadium, where they could hear a marching band.

"Sounds like fun," said Paula.

He kissed the hot center of her palm. *Crashing cymbals are for freshmen*, he thought.

*

"If you guys want to do it, I can go to the TV room," said Francis.

Now Paula was jumping up and down on Charlie's bed, kicking the tires of dorm room life.

"Don't be silly," said Paula.

"I have studying to do, anyway. One of my professors mailed us the syllabus over the summer."

"You're getting straight As, aren't you?" asked Paula.

"An A-minus average is my goal."

"We'll both be working for you, one day."

"Francis works in Dining Commons," said Charlie. "Our industrious friend is up every morning at six thirty."

"Six," Francis corrected. "But I only work four days out of the week. Still, I get up at the same time every day, that way I'm used to it."

"Makes sense, fellow hash slinger. Actually, I guess I'm now an ex–hash slinger."

"It's a good job," said Francis. "On top of the salary, I eat for free. Well, have a good weekend in the country."

"He's so cute," Paula said after he'd left.

"Really? You think?"

"Not cute like you're cute, just nice and a little strange."

"You don't really think that we'll work for him, right?"

"I don't know. Who's to say?"

"I've been keeping a secret from you: I'm rich."

"Come here," she said, and whispered in his ear, "No shit."

"How do you know?"

"Oh, because of everything."

"Well, I'm not rich yet. As poor as anyone, except for the cash in my wallet, which has to last me till Thanksgiving. But when I turn nineteen—"

"Don't blink," she said.

"Why shouldn't I?"

"It's what my mom says. 'Blink, and the next thing you know, you're thirty-five.'"

"I wish we were thirty-five already," said Charlie, blinking, holding a stack of his underwear imprinted with tiny tennis rackets and tiny tennis balls.

"I know you're rich because there are tennis rackets on your Polo boxers, and you have long, rich eyelashes that blink all the time. I like the boxers and will probably end up stealing a pair from you and wearing them tonight, and I like the lashes because they're sexy, but I don't really care about the money, because it's not mine, and even if it were, there's nothing much I need, except love and honesty. Lots and lots of honesty."

She rolled over in his bed, and over again.

"When you come back here after this weekend, you'll smell me on your sheets. Now, come lie down next to me and say pretty things about my eyes before we have to catch the bus."

"I thought we'd take a cab," said Charlie, looking for space amid the S she'd made.

"Too expensive, and the bus stop is right near here."

"Move over," he said.

"Make me."

He shoved her gently, but she sprang back into place, panting, laughing. He pinned her down and she didn't resist, just laughed; in her eyes, Charlie saw the blue skies of New Hope, the bus stop near the river, ugly luggage in the green grass. He searched her face for her eyes, found them every time.

"Butterfly me," she said.

"What's that?"

"With your lashes, butterfly my lashes."

He did, and it made him shiver.

"God," he said.

"This is the best, when it's just starting."

"I know," he said. But he didn't know. This was new. The start of Monica Miller felt more like the middle of things. He'd wanted so much more from Monica Miller, and he'd called the wanting *love*. The having, he thought—the having is love. Charlie faced Paula in bed and went to kiss her neck. She lifted her chin and let him in.

"I hope you like New Hope," she said, while his lips brushed the barely tangible cilia that guarded her skin.

"I already love it."

Chapter Fifteen

MRS. HENDERSON WAS A big blonde polar bear of a woman. When they got off the bus she was leaning against her Buick, smiling. "Hi, you guys."

She shook Charlie's hand, then said screw it and gave him a hug. She had Paula's eyes and a weak chin; semicircles of rouge were smeared over the age avalanches of her cheeks. Paula had said she used to be a real looker, but then came divorce, and now the ultraclean blue jeans of middle age contained her formidable caboose.

"You sit in back, Charlie, where there's more room. I'm making Paula's favorite for dinner tonight, Chicken Paprikash. Hope that's okay. *So.* What's the gossip, you two? You mind if we stop by Simple Pleasures? I bought this beautiful blouse, but it doesn't fit. Miss Cipriano was asking about you, Paula. So, Charlie, your parents live in New York City? My husband used to take me. Mr. Asshole. We'd always go to the Russian Tea Room. Will you look: this new girl did my nails, but she was rushing, and now look at them."

Charlie sat in the back, the Frucor poster by his side. They took River Road, stopping at a landing where Paula had learned to swim. Above the river were green hills with huge old Tudor homes and, below, the boathouses that belonged to them.

Charlie didn't like the superior attitude of the homes, glaring down on his middle-class girl who probably had to trespass in order to learn to swim.

"She was a real good swimmer," Mrs. Henderson narrated from the car window. "Her coach said she could've swimmed in college, but she never practiced. She was afraid she'd swim better than this boy she liked."

"Mom, that's simply not true."

"The things boys do to get a girl, and the things girls do to keep a boy," said Mrs. Henderson.

"What's Simple Pleasures?" asked Charlie.

"It's the cutest store," said Mrs. Henderson. "I have to say, Charlie, I'm happy to see Paula with a boy her age who wears a nice suit jacket."

"Mom wasn't such a Tommy fan."

They stopped at several stores just like Simple Pleasures. Grand Designs. Elegant Lawns. The stores were new to Charlie. Creaky with old wood. Set pieces for a western, with hitching posts and weathervanes. Everyone knew the Hendersons. Everyone was a version of Mrs. Henderson, broadcasting their own incessant radio station about their life. The chatter was comforting. It reminded him of when Angelina would get on a roll, complaining about Jimmy Carter wearing jeans in the White House, complaining about the price of 1979 milk.

"Did Paula tell you the Chicken Paprikash story?" asked Mrs. Henderson.

"Mom became pen pals with an inmate—"

"Death row, Charlie."

"A death row guy who would send her recipes, and the chicken dish—"

"Chicken Paprikash, Paula."

"The Chicken Paprikash was the last recipe he wrote her before they executed him."

"Poor guy," said Mrs. Henderson.

"Dad used to call it electrocuted chicken."

"Mr. Asshole."

Mrs. Henderson had set Charlie up in the study, on a foldout couch by a window that looked out on a hummingbird feeder, but Paula insisted that he sleep above the garage on a bed whose top sheet was populated by a collection of grasshoppers dressed in tails for a grasshopper wedding.

"Suit yourself, Paula," said Mrs. Henderson. "That room doesn't have any pictures and whatnot. It's so sterile up there. We always had plans to make it into an arts and crafts room. But you know what happens to all those plans, don't you, Charlie?"

"They go away?"

"*Exactamundo.*"

*

"Your mom's great," said Charlie. "So *real.*"

"As opposed to what?" Paula asked, removing the grasshoppers from the bed. On every surface there were lace doilies under teacups or miniature animals.

"What's the deal with the flag outside the front door?"

"The garden flag? It's a garden flag. My mom bought a set a while back. She's supposed to change them every season, but I think the one that's there has been there since I was in high school."

"I like stuff like that. I mean, I've never really seen things like that."

"Well, we have lots of stuff like that here."

"And the stone bunnies and turtles all over the yard."

"You're easily impressed, Charlie Green."

"I could spend a year on this grasshopper bed, reading old *TV Weeks* and watching the hummingbirds. I'd learn more about life than any college could teach me."

"Oh, no," said Paula. "You're going back to school after the weekend. Someone should have a college degree."

"But what will you do?"

"Get a job serving beer to guys who have known me since I was twelve."

"I don't want to leave you to that. Classes don't start till Wednesday anyway. Maybe we could have a long weekend?"

"Maybe," she said. At that instant, she felt hollow, and wished Charlie were elsewhere so she could cry. She heard her mother's garden flag flapping in the weekday afternoons of her future, the phone ringing and going unanswered, Charlie from outside a classroom. She'd boy-friended him too quickly. A way out would be to take him into town and get drunk. She'd run into a half-dozen exes, some of whom still interested her, but only when she was a little wasted in New Hope. Any other place in the world, she'd never consider them.

Charlie was different—the type of boy you marry for his genes and soul. For his brown eyes that would always glow with love. For now, though, she wanted a shot of tequila, and needed him to just be her drinking buddy. Maybe score a joint from an ex and smoke it with both the ex and Charlie, sitting on the river rocks, both boys wanting her, while she'd only want to know the secrets of the river, its ancient tur-tles and unruffled swans.

"Do you want to go to Martine's with me?" she asked. "It's a really cute little bar I used to work at. It used to be part of an old salt mine. I feel like getting a beer or something. Sometimes being home can be depressing."

*

Gary, a perennially shirtless ex-boyfriend of Paula's, made huge sculp-tures out of found metal and had recently sold one to Andy Warhol, according to the *New Hope Free Press*, the area's free newspaper that seemed to be in everyone's hands at Martine's. There, on the front page, was a photo of shirtless Gary standing next to Warhol and his small, shocked eyes. After reading the news for herself, Paula hugged Gary long and hard.

"I always knew you'd be famous," she told him.

Bushy underarms, hairless otherwise, and feminine, pointy nipples: Gary smelled like sweat. To Charlie, he smelled like the Paris metro in the summer. North Africans *sans* deodorant. Italians *sans* deodorant. The heroic melting pot of the metro; there was a depth to the sweat that suggested soil, rather than cities.

"So how do you know Paula?" Charlie asked Gary, while Paula went upstairs with Martine to speak about a job.

"We go way back," Gary said, downing a tequila.

The bar had a good fireplace smell, even in the summer. Something briny. *Must be the old salt.* Despite Gary's brooding, half-naked presence, Charlie could see himself making Martine's a mainstay. The bartender, apparently another ex but a more manageable one than Gary, sang along to the Smiths.

"You know, I actually might like the Smiths," said Charlie to the bartender. He'd avoided them because John had said a girl would bolt if she snooped out a Smiths CD in your collection. She might as well find makeup in your medicine chest, he'd said. But tonight, in this sleepy little bar, where beer cost a dollar and he could sometimes hear Paula's voice upstairs, he felt unabashed about what he did and did not like.

Gary made a face. "Smiths were good for only one year."

"Bull," said the bartender.

"Nineteen eighty-five," said Gary. "That was their year. Paula and I used to listen to them on my boom box. Winter of '85. Great winter in front of the Franklin stove. That's when the Smiths were good. In front of *that* stove. What's your name, again?"

"Charlie."

"Charlie. Right. She likes simple things, Charlie."

"I know," he said, annoyed with the world of ex-boyfriends.

"Hey," said Gary. "None of my business anymore. Just be careful with that girl. She can change your life."

"I hope she does."

"I mean, she can mess it up. Haven't felt like myself since she left me. Hell, I haven't worn a shirt since she left me."

Gary put a small felt pouch in Charlie's hand. "Give this to her. She said she wanted a J."

"Panic on the streets of London," the Smiths bartender sang. "Panic on the streets of Birmingham."

"Hang the DJ," said Gary, smiling. "Ah, maybe the Smiths are more than just 1985 after all. Night, folks." He was barefoot as well. Only a pair of splattered painter's pants separated him from nudity.

"What was Gary saying about Paula?" asked the Smiths bartender.

"That she could mess up your life," said Charlie.

"Yeah, I guess I could see that; she's so freaking smart. We only dated for, like, three days, but I knew she was way too smart for me. Just wish I'd been into the Smiths back then."

Chapter Sixteen

PAULA HAD BEEN HIRED by Martine and was starting next week. At first she was proud to be welcomed back so quickly, but then as she and Charlie walked along the banks of the Delaware River, she thought about the farewell party Martine had thrown for her two years earlier. The excellent predictions about her new life in Philly. Something about coming back in eight years, a veterinarian. Dr. Henderson?

The morning after that party, Gary had driven her to Philly in his pickup. It was early summer. She remembered seeing Jasmine for the very first time, outside the apartment, waiting to give her the keys. Jasmine had painted Paula's room. White paint, what a promising smell, Paula had thought.

"Do you get high?" Paula asked Charlie, lighting the tightly rolled joint.

"Not on those things," he said. "My poison comes in glasses."

"I guess I'm feeling a little weird about everything," she said, inhaling.

Charlie kissed her cheek. He decided that girls who mess up your life don't have such warm faces, made warmer by the four o'clock sun.

"This river's the real deal," said Charlie. "Like a river Twain would write about. An American river. New York City rivers look like international waters, indiscriminately green or gray. This one is brown, with Colonial mud."

"Like your eyes," she said, exhaling in peace.

There were swans asleep on the rocks, their heads tucked away. So many clean white feathers. Docked pontoon boats rocked in the current. Church steeples across the river in New Jersey. Charlie was used to the East River, watching for cruise ships with Angelina. The imagined luxuries aboard the *Sea Princess II* were nothing compared to this, as ducks quacked somewhere far away.

"Washington crossed it just a few miles up there," said Paula. "Our claim to fame."

"If we were at the crossing, I'd collect a water sample, put a flower in it, and put it by your bed."

"I guess, growing up here, you take it for granted." She pictured waking to a wilted dandelion and took a deep drag. *I want to hitchhike to a new country. One where there's no one I know, nothing I've seen before, and no chance of return.*

Charlie had sat by, once, while Monica Miller got high on her fire escape. There was nothing to do but watch her. It was emasculating to be at the mercy of a girl's pot rhythm.

"Look up. Crazy clear skies," said Charlie.

"Too clear," said Paula. "I always expect to see a nuclear mushroom cloud when the sky is like this."

"There'll never be one here," said Charlie. "Not on the banks of General Washington's river."

She extinguished her joint and turned to face him, made sure he hadn't just been sarcastic about her river, then hugged him with all her might. He wished that things like handholding and pre-thermonuclear-war hugs didn't make him so easily hard. He hoped she didn't notice, but John had said that girls know. "They just know."

"Thank you for coming home with me," she said.

"You're my home," said Charlie, then he lost his erection, and Paula ended the hug.

John had made it perfectly clear: Hallmark Cards were the enemy of boners.

*

Dinner was all Chicken Paprikash, all the time.

"If your mom wants the recipe, Charlie, just let me know," said Mrs. Henderson. "It's not as complicated as I've made it sound."

"They have a cook, Mom," said Paula, anxious for dinner to end so she could sit outside by her favorite tree, where a tin was buried that contained childhood jewelry, her father's Zippo, and the pendant necklace Gary had made for her, metal pounded into the shape of a dented heart.

"Well, that makes sense," said Mrs. Henderson.

"She was more like a family member," said Charlie.

"Can we do the dishes later?" asked Paula.

"*We* don't have a maid, Paula," said Mrs. Henderson, then wagged a finger at Charlie. "You tell your cook that the key to the chicken dish is the paprika. She has to get the paprika fresh, there's just no two ways."

"Angelina got everything fresh. I'm sure my mom will do the same."

There had been two aprons hanging by the sink, because there were two girls in the Henderson household. The logic appealed to him. He wondered if that made him a male chauvinist, but decided it made him an American male, so he sat back in his seat like the man of the house. Paula had changed into denim shorts for dinner. How wonderful to watch the backs of her legs, apron strings dangling down her rear, drying dishes while her mother bubbled over with paprika caveats. In the Green household, his mother made the money but didn't do the dishes. Angelina lived in an apron, and both of his parents wore pants. In the Hendersons' world, there were pants or aprons. The pink and blue order of things.

"You want to dry, Charlie, and be next to Paula?"

"He doesn't have to, Mom."

"Some boys like to help."

Paula threw a towel at Charlie that landed on his head, over his eyes, tenting him from the scene, and for a moment he was nine again, pretending to be a ghost while Angelina cleaned up after dinner. He preferred tonight's checkered dish towel specter. A middle-class American ghost in a middle-class American kitchen.

"Take that rag off your head, Charlie," said Paula. "You look ridiculous."

"Be nice to him," said Mrs. Henderson, before sitting back at the table and sighing. "Paula can be a little rough. She's a bit of a tomboy, Charlie."

"No, I'm not."

"Well, she used to be. These girls are always changing. One day she's a punker, the next she's a princess. Hard to keep track of."

"We're going to finish the dishes later, Mom, okay?"

"Okay, you two go have fun. I'll finish up. These dishes and I go back twenty years, Charlie."

*

They sat beneath the tree of Paula's childhood, replete with rope swing and the remains of a treehouse. There she dug up a metal box advertising French lavender soap.

"*Savon lavande*," said Charlie.

"Wow. There's a joint in here," said Paula. She lit it and took a deep hit. Charlie's pronunciation made Europe seem just down the driveway. It temporarily liberated her from what was coming after the weekend, another tour of duty at Martine's. Gary and his friends would be at the bar, not only on her first day but every day she worked. He'd try to wear her down. Propose marriage again with another homemade ring.

"Do you smoke a lot of pot?" he asked.

"No, only when I'm back home, but this might be my last. Such a townie thing to do."

Charlie dipped his fingers in her tin box, feeling the necklaces and rings of her preadolescence. He felt bad that they had to live with a joint and fantasized about replacing it with an airplane-sized bottle of Smirnoff. "Do you have anything to drink around here?"

She took Charlie by the wrist, inside the house, to the liquor cabinet. He'd never seen a plastic bottle of alcohol, nor a liquor cabinet underneath a Zenith Ellipse IV Chromacolor II television.

"My mom's not a drinker at all. These bottles are probably from the seventies."

"There's something weirdly classy about old plastic jugs of nameless vodka from 1974, or some other faded year."

"You're weird. Make your drink, then let's go up to your room."

My room, thought Charlie.

"We'd probably be better off if we didn't drink or smoke or do anything," said Paula. "I tried it one summer. I miss that summer. I slept so well and laughed so easily."

"You know what, I should do that, too. The *Dignidad* is no fan of overindulgence of any kind."

"What's the *Dignidad*?"

"Oh, sorry. It was my governess's philosophy. A life of sacrifices and good behavior. A simple life."

He toasted her water glass.

There was nothing that simple about it, she thought. He had poured himself a milkshake glass full of ice and Gordon's vodka. Men always laid out their best plans for the simple life from the safety of a buzz.

*

She turned off the lights, but the shade-less room looked movie-lit because of the nearly full moon.

In bed, they kissed and intertwined and untwined their hands.

"Our hands are dancing," said Paula.

John was spot-on about this: he'd warned Charlie that at night girls become pretentious about body parts, saying things like *Our legs are heroes*, or *My arms will be your heart's crutches*.

There was an hour when they didn't kiss or hand-dance. They stared, spooned, and almost slept. Well, he must have slept, because when she woke him, his tennis racket boxers were by his side. For so many years, Charlie's nakedness had been famous, a rapt audience of one, every night a sellout, and now it was famous for someone else. It was in her hand. How had she gotten his shorts off without waking him? How could one part of him have been awake while the rest slept? How was she naked, too? He went to touch her between her legs. It was the newest thing he'd ever felt. Astonishing, that girls had hair there. *Were they imitating us? Were we imitating them?*

"I'm so wet," she said.

Charlie couldn't believe people actually said that.

"I am, too," he said.

"What?"

"Nothing."

"Take off your shirt."

I wish I had gone to the gym more. Pale and soft, his chest hadn't really evolved since puberty, but she didn't seem to mind. She pounced on top of him, pinned his arms, and bent her head so that her blonde tendrils would tickle his stomach. He wanted to tell her to stop, that it was too much, too good.

"Are you clean?" she asked.

"I think so. I shower every day."

"I mean, AIDS and things like that."

"Definitely."

"How do you know?"

"Well, I haven't really—"

"Are you a virgin?"

"Technically. I mean, define 'virgin'?"

"That means you are. I'm clean, too. Just so you know, my gynecologist said I can't have kids unless I get this procedure done. Something with the tubes. Still, you should wear a condom at the end."

"Of course. That's what I'm used to, anyway." His abs trembled as she put him inside of her. "My thing," he said.

"It's a nice thing." She was moving slowly, shallowly on top of him. "My thing feels very good."

"Good."

"Too good."

"Good." She placed his hands on her hips, showed him how to move her.

He wanted to ask her to stop, to dismount so that he could calm down, rewind, maybe go to Martine's for a nightcap. It hadn't even been a minute, and he was awfully close to the end. This was never how it was at home, in bed. There he was masterful. A stop-and-start artist. A prodigy.

"I don't want it to end, Paula."

"Let's not talk about that stuff now. Let's just enjoy this."

"No, I mean what we're doing right now."

"Sh."

He wanted to ask her what exactly he should do with her hips. Her lesson hadn't stuck. His hands were along for the ride, just sitting there on her flanks. *Now* was it over a minute? He wished to Holy God that it was at least over a minute. He tried to buy time by thinking about his grandmother and her funeral. What her decomposed body might look like. But his mind kept going back to the warmth on top of him. The click of her elixir. How does anyone last a minute?

"Kiss my breasts," she said. "They're sensitive, so start softly."

He'd been to the rodeo once, at Madison Square Garden, and would watch the clock. He knew how long 8.6 seconds could be when roping a calf or riding a bull. What a motionless bull he was, a single buck away from disaster.

"Let's do it in every position," she said. She ground herself deeply into him, mining the depths.

"Maybe we could stop for a second?" asked Charlie.

"God made sex feel so good," said Paula.

"God." Charlie slammed his eyes shut, jerked his head to the side, into the pillow, trying not to be a spectator to his own horribly early ecstasy.

"Oh," she said. "Oh, wow. Are you—"

"I—"

She remained on top of him, moved her hips a couple of times, a futile attempt at revival.

"I just wish you would have told me. You weren't wearing a condom."

She was still on top of him, looking away. He'd slipped out, and she didn't want to embarrass him.

"We could try again later," said Charlie, wishing she'd dismount so he could cover up the mess.

"Do you know where my robe is?" she asked.

He didn't know there had been a robe. He didn't know anything. She found it in the sheets and dressed with her back turned to him, everything mercilessly luminous. *Shitty full moon*, he thought, bringing the bedsheets up to his chin.

She paused at the door. "Well, I guess I'll see you in the morning. Night."

"*Night*." He tried to make the word an apology, but it sounded more like *Leave*, which she did.

Chapter Seventeen

HE THOUGHT IF HE didn't move, he could erase what had happened, or downgrade it to a nightmare. But it had happened. There was evidence: the unopened condom, and that thing, useless, glued to his body.

It took all of Charlie's will to get out of bed, clean himself off, put on his boxers. He picked out a *TV Week*, one from 1984 with the cast of *Fantasy Island* on the cover. When the show got canceled, Angelina blamed the yuppies for accumulating enough money to be able to afford their own real-life fantasies. "Señor Roarke had so much more to give," she'd said. "The yuppies with their cufflinks, they ruined it."

Haircuts probably lasted twenty minutes in bed, he thought. They went about their business mechanically, secretly using the act to strengthen whatever muscles give buttocks dimples. He remembered reading about an author who'd had a problem with endurance but convinced his wife that it was virile to cut to the chase, that true men explode when they explode. The rest of it, the before stuff and all the pumping, was for Haircuts doused in Polo cologne. But the world was dominated by Haircuts and Tommys, who grabbed the girls they wanted, then lasted the length of an entire rodeo. They said goodnight to their women like they owned the moon and said good morning to them like they owned the sun. While Charlie practiced saying *Night* to a grasshopper bride, Paula knocked on the door and asked to come in.

"No one's good their first time," she said, sitting by him in bed. "I wasn't. God, I wasn't."

"I just didn't think I would be that quick."

"Sometimes quick is good. We'll work on it." She patted his chest and kissed his forehead goodnight. That's what the quick ones get, thought Charlie, a motherly kiss on the head.

"Where are you going?" he asked.

"To bed."

"You should stay up here with me."

"Guys like to be left alone after sex."

He didn't want to be left, not by her, not ever, but he was a guy, who had indeed had sex, so he found the *TV Week* in the sheets, shrugged, and read. Paula paused at the door, tightened her robe, and wondered if there were enough moonlight in the room for him to read. She felt no regret about what they'd done, not yet. It could come in the morning and then she'd need him to go back to school so she could clean the slate before starting work again. Go through her things and sort out her life. *Maybe I'll paint my bedroom*, she thought, looking blankly at the curly hair on his legs. She'd painted her room red after high school.

"Maybe you could help me paint my room tomorrow?" she asked.

"That would be great." Charlie sat up in bed.

"What color, you think?"

"Maybe red?"

"But that's what it already is." She thought of Sunday at CVS, spending the last of her cash on beauty supplies. She'd be sure to look great for Tuesday night at Martine's. The tips would come. Next thing I know, I'll be in Europe, she thought. Next summer. Next summer is so far away.

A whole year in a red room, her mom complaining about Mr. Asshole while the kitchen reeked of Chicken Paprikash. She bum-rushed the bed, jumped in, pushed him back down, and lobbed a leg over his chest.

"Let's go to New York," said Paula. "I don't want to be at CVS tomorrow."

"Tomorrow?"

"Screw CVS, I'm going to use the last of my money to buy something in New York City," she harrumphed, her leg advancing across Charlie's torso.

Exquisite bodies must weigh more, he thought. They must be made of denser material than regular bodies. He reminded himself to ask John about it. John would have an opinion. He thought about when they were seven and thirteen and lived together at home, watching Spanish soaps with Angelina, flipping baseball cards. *My childhood is over.*

"So, what exactly did the doctor say about your tubes?"

"Don't worry, I'm not pregnant."

Charlie wanted to rise out of bed and pace the room, but her leg locked him in place. He had to urinate as well, but knew he had to stay put, maybe deep into the night. There was nothing between himself and this other person. His naked chest wore her limb. That was all there was. He missed home. Mariella's and Angelina. *I've bitten off more than I can chew.*

"I'm not sure about New York," he said.

"K," she said, her leg finding even more of his chest. She is living on me, thought Charlie. I'm her home. Why can't she be mine? So he removed her leg and turned her so they were chest-to-robe. *Is this what love is? Two people needing each other at the same moment?* It felt more like math than love, but the feeling permitted him to smell her hair, run his hand along her thigh, lift her downy arm, and show the moon its staticky blonde hair.

"Actually, maybe we *should* go to New York," said Charlie.

She placed herself directly on top of him. All 122 pounds of her. Cheek to cheek, sealed with sweat.

"Good," she said.

I've never been closer to another human being, he thought, the word *good* still tickling his cheek. She probably wanted more, so he lifted her robe and held the places where the spine becomes sex.

"I wonder what I'll wear tomorrow," she vibrated into Charlie's jaw.

*

Sunday morning in the Henderson household: hairdryer sounds, Mrs. Henderson and her muffin tins, flashes of Paula wearing a pink towel. Charlie and Paula, going to the big city.

"Now, don't forget my bagels, you two. And it's better to get them just before you leave rather than when you first get there, so they stay nice and warm. Now, it might rain later, so just keep that in mind. New York City," said Mrs. Henderson, shaking her head.

The happy drowning sounds of the Hendersons' coffeemaker made Charlie feel sleepy and in need of a mug. In the Green household, there was only espresso. This would be his first regular cup of coffee. His mug read LOVE.

"You want coffee, Paula?" hollered Mrs. Henderson.

Through a toothbrush she yelled back that she did.

"Make her a cup, will you, Charlie? Watch, she'll brush again after breakfast. Why not do it only once? I've been telling her this for years. She likes a little more milk in hers. You can go bring it to her in the bathroom."

Paula was leaning into the bathroom mirror, casting spells on her face with tiny brushes. A single blue vein ran up her leg and disappeared under the pink towel.

"I missed you this morning," he told her. He'd woken to an empty bed, a little after sunrise. They'd forgotten to lower the shade, but even if they hadn't, the papery barrier would have turned translucent by seven.

"Couldn't sleep," she said.

"Last night was pretty magical. I mean, after the initial bad part. The quick part. Things like last night don't happen to me every day. I've never spent a whole night with anyone but myself."

"Lots of firsts," she said, sticking out her hand for the mug.

"Although it felt like we've been bedmates forever."

"Ha!"

"What?"

"Just, *Ha!*"

The bathroom was still steamy from her shower, nebulas of wonderful girl smells in the air. Charlie couldn't help but kiss away a drop of shower water from her shoulder blade. Nothing smelled better than a freshly showered girl, he thought, and wished to God she'd remove the towel and turn around to face him in the bathroom light.

"We have to get bagels for Mom," said Paula.

"I know, she told me. Get them later rather than before."

"But we'll go shopping first, okay?

"Sure."

"Are we meeting your parents?"

"Parents? No. I hadn't planned on that at all."

"Why? Are you ashamed of me?"

"Of course not. We can meet them if you want. I just thought it should be just us."

"I like meeting parents. Lots of girls don't, but I do. It tells you a lot about the guy."

"My parents won't tell you anything about me," said Charlie, seated on the toilet's fuzzy pink lid.

"Um, let's see: your mom's rich from stolen paintings and drinks a lot, and your dad's a European guy who doesn't have to work. I think that tells me something about you. Now shoo, so I can finish putting on my face."

*

Mrs. Henderson had set up breakfast outside, three chairs in front of the hummingbird feeder. It had the feel of a photo op, or an interview: Mrs. Henderson overdressed for muffins and coffee, wearing a large, floppy hat and sunglasses, every sentence starting the same. "So, Charlie, tell me . . ."

He told her about the town house and its wonderful proximity to Adam's Rib and Central Park.

"Is Bonwit's close to you?" she asked.

He wasn't sure, but said it wasn't too far away.

"I used to collect shopping bags from Bonwit's," said Mrs. Henderson. "I loved their shopping bags with the purple violets, but I sold them all at my yard sale, and for two bucks, who would've thought? But you know, Charlie, you get divorced and you just have to move on. Just look at that hummingbird! Don't you just want to hold on to its little tail and fly away?"

The hummingbird's next stop was almost certainly the future, where Charlie would have a good read on his new love, what made her cheeks go red, what made them turn white, and why her curly hair and turquoise eyes were alive with primordial energy. In the future, everything and everyone would be as comfortable as Mrs. Henderson, spreading margarine on a steaming muffin.

"I have a feeling," said Mrs. Henderson, "that one day we'll look back on this weekend as the first time we met Charlie Green. Just a feeling I have."

"I hope so."

"It's not easy being young, I know. You hang in there, Charlie."

"Thank you, Mrs. Henderson."

"Thank *you*, Charlie."

By the time Paula was ready, breakfast had ended. Mrs. Henderson rose to applaud her barefooted daughter, who was holding her sandals and twirling in her sundress, a string of clunky pearls ruining the simplicity of her neckline.

"The pearls are just perfect," said Mrs. Henderson. "You want a muffin, honey bunny?"

"I don't think we have time. Could you pack it in my lunchbox? Can Charlie have your lunchbox?"

"Of course he can," said Mrs. Henderson.

"No, really, that's okay. I actually thought we could have lunch out."

"The lunchboxes are for the train ride, Charlie," said Mrs. Henderson. "You know, in case you get hungry."

"Well," said Charlie. "Amtrak does have a really amazing little snack car."

Charlie loved Amtrak. The faintly Indian red and white seat covers. Screwdrivers and M&Ms from the amazing little snack car, placed on the amazing little foldout tray by the window, little houses whirring by. There was a real place in his heart for home after home, where, he imagined, young lovers separated by mowed lawns used their flashlights to say goodnight.

"I love Amtrak," said Charlie.

"Their bathrooms are sort of gross," said Paula. "Mom, are you sure the pearls aren't too much?"

"Pearls too much. Just listen to you. I'm going to pack two lunchboxes just in case," said Mrs. Henderson, carrying the breakfast tray back into the kitchen with just one hand. Tray dexterity must be inherited, thought Charlie, imagining their own daughter practicing with dollhouse beer steins.

"You look great," said Charlie.

"Really? Thanks. Figure, why not get dressed up. It'll be jeans and T-shirts for God knows how long."

"We can talk about the future on Amtrak. The train rhythm and a screwdriver go a long way toward problem solving."

"Oh, I don't drink on Sundays. At least not till later."

"My parents drink champagne for breakfast every Sunday, but that's just because they're French."

"I guess if I were French, I might, too, but as you can see, I'm just a Pennsy girl in her mother's pearls."

"You're more than that. Absolutely zero reason for you to feel insecure."

"Insecure?" She took a step back so he could take all of her in. So he'd be reminded of all the men, and boys, including Charlie Green, who got their lifelines in a tangle just to hold her hand. "I don't feel insecure. Do I look insecure?"

She'd somehow made her curls especially tight, her teeth especially white from the Hendersons' commercial-strength Gleem. She was right: what insecure person had turquoise eyes? Charlie did want to tell her about the comical irrelevance of mascara near those eyes, but John had decreed: you don't say a damn thing after the makeup's on.

Chapter Eighteen

MRS. HENDERSON DROPPED THEM off at the Trenton train station thirty minutes early. Paula made a beeline to the newsstand to buy gum and a magazine, *National Geographic* with "The Secret Life of Hummingbirds" on the cover.

"For your mom?" asked Charlie.

"For me."

She'd been mostly silent during the ride, except for one- or two-word deflections of Charlie's New York City jingoism.

"Paula's a little cranky on Sundays, Charlie," Mrs. Henderson had said. "But I packed you both vanilla pudding so that should take care of that."

Shadowless, the Sunday sun bore down on the tracks, baking the coals, activating their creosote. For Charlie, the odor was a tonic against the church-dressed family who fussed with bagged sandwiches. The kids in matching blue suits, the parents with their hands on their knees, making the station benches into pews.

"Don't you love the smell of train tracks?" he asked his gum-smacking date.

"Yep-p." At least she was still popping her P's, he thought.

She became more talkative in Newark, after Charlie dug into his vanilla pudding. There were hints of power in the way he tore off the foil cap and thrust his plastic spoon. Some pudding on the side of his mouth. There was something about hungry men. She rewarded his pudding swagger with a head on his shoulder.

"Someone told me that the TGI Friday's at Penn Station is the first TGI Friday's," said Paula. "Is that true? If so, I'd like to see it."

The original Friday's was elsewhere, he knew, but if it meant an end to her Sunday prohibition, he'd treat it like the Louvre.

"We can definitely visit that Friday's," said Charlie.

"Then Bonwit's."

"Then I figure we could say hi to my parents."

"It's Jee-Jee, right? I never met anyone whose parents had an accent."

"He'll probably be at the track, but after you meet my mom, we can have lunch at the Plaza."

They'd spoken about the hotel yesterday, when she was high. She'd said, "If I lived in New York, I'd get buck naked, and at 4:00 a.m. I'd roll around the floor of the Plaza Hotel. All of this gold dust would attach itself to my skin and I'd be able to walk around the city glittering like a superhero."

Monica Miller never humored Charlie's Plaza love and had shot down his idea of staying over on their final Adam's Rib night. She thought the place was stuffy and, despite the army of maids and their cleanings, permanently dirty.

"Yes," Paula had said, "I'll have lunch with you at the Plaza Hotel."

Friday's, Bonwit's, champagne with Mrs. Green, then the Plaza Hotel? She rushed for the Amtrak bathroom. In anticipation of the most glamorous day of her life, it seemed to her not gross at all, but a beautiful little room in which to check her makeup. *Charlie's right*, she thought, *Amtrak is amazing. Lunchboxes are for tourists.*

*

"Don't you love all the things on the wall?" Paula was admiring a Sunoco sign, gesticulating with her Amstel Light. "Where do you think they get all this stuff?"

Charlie couldn't decide if her appreciation of the TGI Friday's junk was cute or insane, but from the swarthy Friday's bar he enjoyed watching her give herself a tour, stopping to curl a finger around her upper lip and ponder the nostalgia of 5¢ LEMONADE.

"There must be a Friday's near New Hope, right?" asked Charlie.

"Not like this one. Pennsylvania Friday's are too new. These New York City Friday's are way more authentic."

The obese Friday's bartender couldn't take his eyes off of her.

"That your girl?" he asked, chewing on a straw.

"I believe she is," said Charlie.

"Hot stuff. Better keep her close by." The bartender knocked on the bar. "Next round's on me. Welcome to New York."

It tickled Charlie that, by association with his Friday's-obsessed girl, he'd been relegated to *visitor*. He wondered if Paula was no good in the city. He'd met people who could only really function in certain places and were hopeless anywhere else. Like how the Adam's Rib bartender must only feel like himself when he was behind the Adam's Rib bar, or how a French cousin of Charlie's had spent his one week in America hiding in a closet.

They had a second round of drinks in front of the bartender; Paula asked him about King Kong atop the Empire State Building and the famous King Tut exhibit at the Met.

"Yeah, they got all sorts of museums in this crazy town," said the bartender. "And, yeah, Kong was up there a few years back, but he was hard to see unless you got up real close."

Paula asked the bartender to take their picture. Charlie took one of her beneath the Sunoco sign. She explained that the first part of the roll was left over from her Bahamian vacation with Tommy.

"I remember Neil talking about that trip," said Charlie. "It made me jealous."

"It shouldn't have."

It actually hadn't made Charlie jealous. At the time, he'd have done anything to see a photo of her in a bathing suit. Now he'd seen much more and would do anything to avoid an image of her and Tommy in the water. Everyone knew what a wet bathing suit really was. At least John did. He'd taken a girlfriend to Barbados, and the sex, he'd said, was so continuous that he returned home tired and chafed, his bathing suit in tatters.

"If you guys like Kong," said the bartender, "then you'll probably like the Circle Line. Just a thought." He handed them each a brochure. "I wrote my number in there in case you need anything while you're in town."

"That's sweet of you," said Paula.

There was no phone number in Charlie's Circle Line brochure.

*

At Bonwit Teller, after an hour of trials, she bought a dress. Charlie sat in the seats where men sat and watched their wives. *The dullest living room in the world,* he thought. Copies of *GQ* nearby, mocking his gender. He used the house phone to call his mother and say he was bringing a friend by.

"A classmate?" asked Mrs. Green.

"No, not really, although she's already taught me so much, and I can't say the same for any Penn classmate I've met."

"Well, she's more than welcome. Does she go to school?"

"She's between jobs. She goes to *life.*"

"How interesting."

Charlie believed his mother would rush a couple of glasses and be at a pinnacle of white grape optimism when she opened the front door. And he was right.

"Paula, welcome," she said when they arrived. "You have the most gorgeous curly hair. That's it. I've decided to grow mine long and wild, just like Paula."

Paula hadn't been expecting a backyard but was happy to see one. Backyards she understood, but the rest of the house, at least the first-floor parts that Charlie showed her, were alien. Everything was in its place. Paintings were everywhere, including in Charlie's room, which had no signs of boyhood, except for a stack of baseball cards on an antique desk. He asked her to sit on his bed and told her she was the first girl who ever had; Monica Miller's bedbug phobia forbade her from getting any closer than the rug.

"Your bed is so tightly made."

"My mother's a neat freak. So was Angelina. If I hadn't met you, I might be on a plane to Puerto Rico. Amazing that Angelina goes away, and in her place, you appear."

"I'm not the reincarnation of your maid, Charlie." For a second, she wondered if the Greens would ask her to put on an apron and start dusting.

"Of course not. I just couldn't have expected this."

"God works in mysterious ways," said Paula, and allowed her hand to glide over the cool and silky top sheet. "Should we join your mom outside? I think she's drinking champagne."

"Just as I told you, every Sunday," said Charlie. "And sometimes Monday, too." *Monday, too*, thought Paula.

She hadn't expected to enjoy the town house this much. In fact, she had been prepared to find it drab or pretentious. She pictured it gray and cold, like something from Dickens. Instead, she found everything fantastic and superior—the order of things, the solidity of all the furniture, the square corners. The carpets were thick. She liked the way her sandals sank into them, liked that she didn't have to take her shoes off at the front door. How much did a town house cost, she wondered. A million? Ten million? Must be more. She wanted to know about this world. Wanted to be an instant expert, so she could laugh with Mrs. Green about how the old Paula thought a town house cost a mere million. Charlie's mom was the opposite of her mother: easy, graceful, slowly reclining into her wicker lounger. She didn't pelt her with questions but asked her opinion.

"Jee-Jee and I have been discussing the space shuttle. He thinks it's a good use of our tax dollars, even after the accident, but I say, feed someone or educate someone, there's nothing in space but space. What do you say, Paula? Pour yourself a glass and set us straight, darling."

She said that she agreed with Mr. Green. That nothing was more important than exploration, even if it disrupted some lives along the way. Mrs. Green applauded her honesty and topped off her champagne. Charlie was stunned. His mother seemed so human, so charming. He'd warned Paula about his erratic mother and her bouts of Bette Davis, but that was nowhere to be found on this summery day. Instead, here was the queen of hospitality. She'd transformed, in all of three days.

"Shall I get the strawberries?" asked Mrs. Green. "They're from Fraser Morris, dipped in white chocolate, just as you like them, Charlie Bear."

"That's John who likes them that way," said Charlie.

"No, it's always been you. He's very particular, Paula."

"I don't know, Mom," said Charlie. "I'm not sure if you get me anymore."

"Does your mother get *you*, Paula?"

"Sometimes. When I open up."

"Then you have a special relationship with her."

"We should probably get going," said Charlie. He'd been sitting in the grass, like all those years with the worms and ants, with Paula and his mother, the adults, above him.

"Before we go, I'd love to try a strawberry," said Paula. "And I want to show your mom my new dress from Bonwit Teller's."

"I haven't been there in years," said Mrs. Green. "I'd heard they'd gone a little downhill."

"Oh, they have," said Paula.

*

They left hours later with a parting prize, an emerald ring from Mrs. Green's jewelry box that sat heavily and loosely on Paula's finger.

Rose was on her fourth glass, showing the wide-eyed girl the second and third floors, when Paula pointed out the ring on the dresser. Not in a million years would Paula expect it, and not in a million years could she take it. Paula liked saying "not in a million years." It was how the rich spoke, for only the rich understood what kind of number a million was.

"I have so much jewelry, and besides, I think it's a costume piece. A very good costume piece, mind you. Oh, you know what? This one might be real. I just don't remember."

"I couldn't take this, not in a million years."

"We'll have no use for rings in a million years, sweetheart."

"This is the most beautiful thing I have ever seen. If you ever, *ever*, want it back, I'll drop what I'm doing and bring it right to you."

*

In the taxi, Charlie watched Paula turn the ring, her head turning with it. He wished his mother had asked his permission. He would have told her no. Not yet, and not your ring. But there was Paula, engaged to Rose Green, having made it to the big leagues of dress-up.

"I bet my ring will look particularly amazing inside the Plaza Hotel," said Paula. "Are we close?"

"Next block," said Charlie.

"I still can't believe she just gave this to me. Crazy."

"I told you she was crazy."

"I mean, crazy-generous. Oh, my goodness, the hotel is so gorgeous," said Paula, her head fully outside the taxicab window.

"The side entrance," Charlie told the driver.

"*Please?*" prompted Paula.

"Please," said Charlie.

They entered the hotel holding hands, bounding up the carpeted stairs. *She's a natural*, Charlie thought. Especially in the Oak Room, where she chose their table, catty-corner seating in a commodious booth in New York's wooden cathedral to chateaubriand.

"Look at how the dust particles float up to the rafters," said Paula. "It's like we're underwater and they're not dust but bubbles. The wood-work—oh my God."

"They don't carve wood like that anymore."

"Well, they should."

"I'll learn how. I'll build us a house."

"Of course you will," Paula said, and toasted to that.

Charlie wondered if they were pretending to be a couple. Their patter followed an old-fashioned but unearned rhythm. Was it the ring? Was the ring an upper-crust curse?

"I can't believe we're here," said Charlie.

"Here we are."

"Everything happened so quickly."

"You're not getting freaked out, are you?" asked Paula. "If anyone should be freaked out, it's me."

"Are you?"

"Maybe a little. Going back home from this world is going to suck, but like my mom always says, fairy tales never last."

"Let's stay here tonight," said Charlie.

"Don't be silly."

"Why not?"

"One, it's probably insanely expensive, and I have no money. Two, I didn't pack any of my things. And three, I have to start work."

"Tomorrow's Labor Day, and you don't start till Tuesday. Also, my mom gave me the emergency credit card and encouraged us to have fun, remember?"

"My mom would be so jealous, but I don't know, Charlie." She had already decided to say yes, and while Charlie went on about the gift store's extraordinary inventory, designed to accommodate the lost luggage of princesses, she observed that there was something stronger about his jawline. Right angles had grown overnight. Sex could do that. Before, his cheeks had seemed girlishly round, but not today, even when he flopped around in the grass in front of his mother. Somehow, he got an American Express card out of the champagne and strawberry morning. Shrewd family of handsome Jews, thought Paula. I want to be Jewish. I hate Martine's.

"Okay," said Paula.

"So you'll stay?"

"But I have to call my mom when we get to the room."

"Of course."

"Listen, and I'll pay you back, but is there any way I could get a Plaza robe?"

"I'd love to buy you a Plaza robe."

She scooted over to his side of the booth and kissed him. Just once on the lips. Paula's mother would say to enjoy it while it lasts, while you're the only princess in the world for him. One day he'll fall for a real princess, and then all you'll have are memories and a Plaza Hotel robe. You'll give back the ring, paint your room green in memoriam, or brown, like his eyes, and start over.

"Let's never be any different than we are right now," said Paula.

He wasn't accustomed to seeing her vulnerable. Something had shifted in their relationship, and he wasn't sure if the new order suited him.

"Who knows what the future will bring? For now, it's baked Alaska and the gift shop."

"Funny how guys want you to be in their future, then when you accept the offer, they pull at their shirt collars for air."

"I didn't pull my shirt."

"You did, it's okay. Don't worry, I've seen it before. If this weekend's been too much and you're starting to panic, maybe I shouldn't stay over."

The old order was back, and he kissed the length of her arms up to the shoulders.

"I promise we'll never be any different than we are right now," he said.

*

Their luggage was Charlie's duffel bag, Paula's purse, and her Bonwit's shopping bag, the last added to the luggage trolley by the bellman to help create the illusion of a longer stay. The bellman was old and made plaintive noises even when pushing the light, well-oiled trolley.

"What a beautiful luggage cart," said Paula, making conversation while they waited for the elevator.

"We polish them all right. Few times a day. The brass attracts fingerprints like flies to honey." The bellman showed them his white-gloved hands.

"Well, it shows, the work you do," said Paula.

"Would you mind pressing twenty-seven for us, Mr. Green?" asked the bellman, trapped behind the trolley.

The elevator buttons were long, glowing bars. They made a heavenly bell sound when pressed, then filled with angelic vanilla light. Charlie wanted to touch more of them, like with Angelina at St. Patrick's, when he'd want to light another votive candle. He'd extinguish the yardstick of a match in the container of sand, watch for the barest trickle of smoke, then beg Angelina to let him save another soul.

"You're in good company," said the bellman. "The Beatles were on twenty-seven. Brought them up myself." He showed them his gloves again.

The trolley made a churning sound as it passed over a city block's worth of carpeting. "These carpets remind me of your house," Paula said to Charlie, deciding that New York was a profoundly well-carpeted town.

"What's the room number?" Charlie asked the bellman, wanting to walk ahead. The way they were configured now, in a single file, was funerary, led by the brass hearse.

"It'll be just up here," said the bellman and kept on pushing.

Charlie understood the coyness. Were he a luggage person, he would wait until the very last second to relinquish his hotel to strangers.

"Help him push," whispered Paula.

"You're not supposed to," Charlie whispered back.

"So what? He's old."

"I think it would offend him."

"Do you need any help, sir?" asked Paula.

"No, thank you, Mrs. Green. These trolleys and I have been rolling along together for many years. Sometimes I think they're guiding *me* to the room."

At the door, the bellman fumbled purposefully for the room key. "It's in here somewhere."

Some guests paid a kill fee to have him out of their hair, while other guests rewarded efficiency. It wasn't always easy to figure out which were which, but in the case of these two? The young man probably wanted to get to nailing blondie. He found the key in his very own gloved palm.

"Got a nice room here," he said, kneeling on the floor to deploy the door stop. "If you work here long enough, they give you a weekend stay as a retirement gift. This is the sort of room I'd want. The suites are too big."

"It's great they let you stay here," said Charlie.

"Oh, yes, sir."

In reality, the hotel offered employees with at least twenty-five years of service a two-night stay or four hundred dollars. To date, not a single employee had taken the room. The bellman knew he'd also take the money and run, but the anecdote had the effect of loosing bills from guests' wallets for reasons he decided he'd rather not comprehend.

"Now, we have five restaurants in the hotel, and I'll go over the dress code and hours with you."

"That's okay," said Charlie, "I'm sure it's all in the hotel guest book."

"Now you got your minibar over there, chockful of goodies, and of course there's room service."

"I love room service," said Paula. "I mean, the one time I had it in the Bahamas."

"Twenty-four hours," the bellman said. "Seven days out of the week. They'd serve it twenty-five hours and eight days, if God had made things that way. I can show you how the shower and tub function, if you'd like. Maybe I should, they have the European spray and it takes some getting used to. Lots of our guests are from Europe and they get cross if they don't see their spray."

"We'll figure it out," said Charlie, shaking the man's hand with a twenty-dollar bill.

"I'm sure you will, sir," said the bellman, bending down once again to release the door.

"Thank you for your help," said Paula.

"The pleasure was all mine," said the bellman, his back cracking on the way up from the floor.

"There must be a better way to keep the door open," said Paula.

"If there is, they're keeping it from me," said the bellman. "Enjoy yourselves."

"You had room service with Tommy?" asked Charlie, once the door was closed.

"Yes, but the hotel was nothing like this. Oh my God, I'm *so* putting on my robe!"

She kicked off her shoes and unzipped her dress. In two seconds, she was down to just her underwear. He planted himself in a chair and wondered about all the guys who had dreamed of seeing Paula Katherine Henderson in her bra and panties. All the flowers and candy, notes and phone calls, just to get a glimpse. *It's so simple,* he thought, *when a girl wants to take off her clothes in front of you, it happens just like that, in an instant. Otherwise, they stay on forever, and there's nothing you can do.*

"Don't just sit there watching me," she said, about to unclasp her bra. "Here, read this."

She tossed him the Guest Informat, which had on its cover a picture of a Checker taxi parked near a hot dog stand, the cabbie about to bite into a dog. His jaw muscles must hurt from having to smile and eat a dog all at once. The Guest Informat's New York was a city Charlie had never visited: there were only shiny Checker cabs, the cast of *Cats* roamed the streets, and doormen dressed like ancient submarine captains happily balanced dozens of gift boxes while holding open the doors for angular women and their enormous hats. When Charlie looked up, Paula was naked, biting the tags off her new robe, the bathtub filling with water.

"I think I'm going to take a long bath," she said, her arms finding the sleeves, the belt still unfastened. There was a line of tiny birthmarks just beneath her navel, maybe even smaller than beauty marks. Freckles? Confetti? A celebration. He looked closer and could see more of this genetic stardust on her body. Tiny bronze celebrations of her thighs, shoulders. She went over to him, stood before him, slapped his leg with her belt. "You could join me."

"I'm not that into baths, I'm more of a shower person."

He was, in fact, a bath person, who cherished slipping underwater and listening to the infinite hollowness of this safest ocean, but by no means could his anatomy compete with hers. *By no means should our nakedness share the same ocean.* He knew he'd be sophomorically hard or shriveled into an infinitesimal button. Either way, he'd shiver.

"So, what are you going to do?" she asked.

"Maybe I'll go to Trader Vic's. There's a Trader Vic's in the basement. You could join me, after your bath."

"This is how it's going to be? Me in the tub, you at the bar? I get it: men like their bar time while their girl gets all pretty upstairs. Just don't cheat on me with a Trader Vic's waitress."

"They only employ Hawaiian-looking men, and I would never cheat on you."

"I believe you. For now."

He went to kiss her goodbye, and she insisted he wait until she was submerged in the tub. She said it was something from childhood, that once she'd slipped getting in and hurt herself.

"Stitches, unconscious and everything. Mom says it turned me into the weirdo you know and love. Well, not love."

Charlie sat in the bathroom's makeup chair and watched her become submerged. The V between her legs, which in the light of day was the very particular color of cloudy honey, was now plainly dark.

It was disconcerting to Charlie, as if there were two girls, not one. He preferred the honey one.

"What is Trader Vic's, anyway?" she asked.

"It's a dark, tropical bar where you drink out of coconuts. I'm sure you did that in the Bahamas. Although Trader Vic's is a pretty classic place, and I'm not sure if wherever you two stayed had something like that."

Why am I picking a fight with her? Charlie wondered.

"Oh, it had a bunch of bars."

"Yeah, but I'm sure it was one of those all-inclusive places."

"So what?"

"That's just not what Trader Vic's or the Plaza is all about."

Paula suddenly felt naked and slid down into the soapy water. "I know what the Plaza is about. I read about it this morning in the encyclopedia. That's why I left your room so early, to look up the Plaza Hotel, so I wouldn't seem like a fool."

"You're not a—"

"Opened on October 1, 1907. Designed by Henry Janeway Hardenbergh. On opening day, rooms were two dollars and fifty cents. The statue in the fountain outside is of Pomona, the Roman goddess of orchards. We had lunch in the Oak Room, but the Edwardian Room is where the big shots go. Oh, and the Plaza is the setting for the Eloise books, about a little girl who lives at the Plaza. My mother wouldn't let me read those books, she didn't want me to have fancy thoughts, and for that I'm not sharing my robe with her."

"I'm impressed."

"If I could, I'd spend my whole life reading. Only really Gary understood that about me. Hopefully, the next one will understand."

"The next one?"

"Go enjoy your coconut drink, Charlie."

He went to kiss her, but she was under the water, her palm above the surface, a stop sign.

Chapter Nineteen

"WHAT BRINGS YOU TO Trader's?" a middle-aged man with a southern drawl called over to Charlie.

"*We* go every Labor Day weekend, for the boat and camper show," said the man's wife. "Are you here for the boat and camper show?"

"No, can't say that I am. I'm here with my girlfriend. While she's in the tub, I figured I'd cool my heels at Trader's." Charlie was trying to approximate their southernness.

"I hear you, partner," said the man and raised a ceramic coconut. "I remember Bea's first soak in the Plaza tub. Came out looking like Grace Kelly."

"It was Jayne Mansfield," said Bea. "You never get that story right."

"Well, okay. Jayne Mansfield? Okay then."

"I think I'm getting the egg rolls," said Bea.

"Good choice, Bea."

"We hail from Virginia," said Bea. "Where are you from?"

"Oh, we hail from Pennsylvania. New Hope."

The couple looked at one another, pleased with the young man's choice of a verb.

"Originally, Bea hailed from Florida, and I hailed from Buffalo."

They introduced themselves as the Mussens but garbled their surname. *The Messes*, thought Charlie.

"This is our fifteenth year making this trip," said Mr. Mussen. "Every year we hit the trailer show, then spend the last night in the lap of luxury at the Plaza."

"Although, I must say, it gets a little less luxurious each and every year," said Bea.

"Women," said Mr. Mussen. "Sure are hard to please."

"This year, I started taking little knickknacks," said Bea. "Like the swizzle sticks and the slippers, just in case the hotel goes under. Those things will be worth something, you know."

"Plaza ain't going nowhere, Bea, but if you want to take the souvenirs, help yourself."

"It's the Jews," Bea continued. "The Jews in this town want to own everything. Turn everything into an office building or a mall."

"Well, she has a point there," said Mr. Mussen.

Charlie laughed nervously and looked into his Scorpion cocktail.

"Your table is ready, Mister and Missus," said a grinning tiki statue of a man.

"Don Ho!" said Mr. Mussen. "We call him Don Ho."

"Nice talking with you," said Bea to Charlie. "Try the egg rolls, they're divine."

Don Ho led the couple into the bowels of the restaurant. Charlie could hear a faint drumbeat. He hoped that Don Ho would throw the Mussens into the mouth of a smoldering volcano. Once, at a diner with his brother and father, two beer drunkards in the booth behind went on about *the fucking Jews*. Jee-Jee turned around to face them and said that he was Jewish and so were his children, and that they should stop the way they were talking, or he would take them outside and break their jaws.

"Another Scorpion?" the bartender asked Charlie.

"Yes, please," he said. "You know, I'm Jewish."

"Not to worry. At Trader Vic's, everyone is from the islands."

*

She was in her robe, asleep on the bed, under the full blast of lamp and chandelier light. There were six light switches by the door. It took Charlie a minute to figure out how to turn off all but the reading light on his side. The bartender had promised, "The Scorpion will sting you now, but you won't feel it till later." Later was now, as he fumbled with the switches. It stirred Paula, and she spoke from her dream, "Twice struck by lightning."

Charlie got on top of the bedcovers in his jacket and shoes. It was what you did here, he thought. You sleep in your blazer and shoes with the Toblerone bar, the Guest Informat, and the Trader Vic's Scorpion buzz, next to the girl in the white robe. He bit off a Toblerone tooth and began reading. After every article, he'd check on her. Eventually, during a sidebar about Little Italy, he looked over and her eyes were open.

"I fell asleep," she said.

"I know."

"What time is it?"

"Still early. Barely seven."

"How was Trader Vic's?"

"I almost got into a fight with an anti-Semitic couple."

"Screw them."

"It's not that great of a place, after all. The egg rolls suck."

"I'd still like to go there tonight."

"Or we could order room service, and just be in bed together. I'm a little tired, all of a sudden."

"I'll revitalize you."

She threw the Guest Informat off his lap and turned off the light. She took off his shoes and socks, his pants and underpants, then there was the sensation of cold, perfumed lotion.

"I'm definitely stealing all these little creams," she said. "Is it too cold?"

"No," he whispered. His eyes adjusted to the darkness. The drapes were slightly parted, and some city light had found its way up to the chandelier and its light-trapping crystals. He wondered how many other men had been in this position, in this bed. The thought wasn't helpful; she needed to work in more lotion, but then she brought her lips to his ear and shared her breath. Charlie couldn't tell whether she was mimicking rapture or was excited herself. Regardless, the sensation was pure heat.

"Did you get it on my robe?" It was a rhetorical question. She darted to the bathroom and shut the door.

He felt dirty in his navy-blue blazer, naked from the waist down, and surveyed the room for the downhill signs that Bea Mussen had foretold. Charlie had overheard Don Ho tell another customer that Donald Trump was going to buy the Plaza and infuse it with cash, but the customer didn't believe it. The customer said he liked the hotel just as it was: time-bleached and worn, which was just how Charlie felt. The moisturizer she'd used had made it onto his lapel and would leave a little white cloud there forever. The Scorpion buzz was ending. Drowsy, flaccid, stained, he got dressed and needed to get under the covers. It was cold enough to be an early winter's night.

"Are you awake?" asked Paula from the bathroom door.

He pretended to be asleep.

"Men," she said. She regretted having bathed instead of going down with him to Trader Vic's. To have spent her only night at the Plaza stuck in the room made her sad. *Mom's right, I'm no Eloise*, she thought, and considered throwing the emerald ring out the window into the streets.

"What are you doing up there?" asked Charlie, exiting his pretend sleep with a yawn.

"Gosh, the AC goes all the way down to forty-nine," said Paula.

"It's really cold in here."

"Nothing I do is right."

"That's not true, you do a lot of things right."

"Like hand jobs?"

"*No.*"

"Let's go out. Let's leave the room, come on."

This was his third bed in four days. Four drinking days and his tank was empty. His body craved Mariella's slices and the deep and certain sleep that only the salt and starch of Mariella's could deliver.

"I thought we were going to order room service," he said.

"If you want to keep me up here as some sort of, I don't know, hand job slave, well, you're with the wrong girl."

"You're being silly. Why don't we just relax for a little bit and see how we feel, okay?" It was something an adult would have said to him over the years. Oh, how he wanted his Mariella's slices and his own bedroom. *Adulthood is lonely—a sentry who can never sleep, never retreat to Mariella's heaven, in case the girl wants to go down to Trader Vic's.*

"Okay," she said. "But if we feel like going out, we will."

She plopped down heavily on the bed with her *National Geographic*. "I wish my dad had bought me a microscope when I was little. That could have changed everything."

She proceeded to lament her single-parent upbringing, particularly her mother's nonintellectual life. Her father had left Mrs. Henderson for his secretary, a bottle blonde with an astounding body and a cracked tooth that made her whistle when she spoke. Paula saw them once a year, usually for Easter in Pittsburgh, where he worked as a stockbroker.

"Just thinking about that whistling bimbo makes me so mad." She tossed the magazine off the bed, then rose to retrieve it.

Charlie liked that she picked up after herself. Monica Miller would have left it there, while Paula put it back atop the Plaza's house magazines.

"I can't believe these walls are lined with fabric," said Paula. "I think we should go out. I'll get dressed, okay?"

"Okay," said Charlie. "Or we could order Mariella's."

"What's that, sweetie?" she asked from the bathroom. "I'm going to wear new perfume. I hope you like it."

"I hope it's pizza-scented," said Charlie.

"I can't hear you, honey."

Sweetie and *honey*. Screw it, he'd fill the empty tank with Scorpion juice and the scent of her neck.

*

They drank from lava troughs for two and fought when her hair got coated with Scorpion blood.

"Don't just sit there! Ask the waiter for a wet towel. I'm not some girl with a drink in her hair."

"You actually are a girl with a drink in her hair."

But they made up and made out in the gloom of the Trader Vic's cocktail lounge, then fought again about whether Hawaiians originally came from China, or if emeralds were green diamonds.

They closed the place down, Don Ho's huge hands on their shoulders, grinning maniacally, showing them the bamboo gates. Charlie had never been part of a sloppy couple. Famous drunks who can't walk straight. It was exhilarating: Paula asking an old European lady what the hell she was looking at; Paula using the men's room; Paula asking the doormen for their autographs. All along the sloppy ride, his hand was placed squarely just above her rear.

In the room, they ordered an unquantifiable amount of room service and made love for hours. The Scorpion haze had numbed Charlie, and he was able to remove himself from the sex and therefore last. They'd take breaks to feed on the room service carts, until the lovemaking and the eating blended, then a third ingredient of near sleep was added. In the moments before dawn all three happened at once, but they passed out just before recognizing the achievement.

When Charlie awoke, he could hear her in the shower.

The room service carts were two warring cities, both destroyed. One had bled ketchup, the other ice cream. He walked around the battlefield, looking for his clothes.

She emerged dressed, unscathed by the night except for the slightest circles under her eyes.

"I was thinking of getting some breakfast," she said. "And I found a credit card in my purse with a little something on it, so I might go to the Gap." She was moving quickly, folding things, packing a shopping bag.

"Quite a night," she said in passing, tapping his shoulder on her way to retrieve her sandals. She'd thrown them at the curtain, attempting to trigger something on the wall that might make them close.

"I could meet you for breakfast, after I check out," said Charlie. "Even though I thought we could have an early lunch, before possibly hitting—"

"I just really need to get out of this room," she said, embarrassed to be so proximal to the bed. When they had checked in, it had been so well-made, so lovingly tight. Now she blamed her New Hope self for the tangle of sheets, the food stains, the pillows without their pillowcases. "Should we make the bed?"

"No, they have maids who will come in the second we check out."

"I might write them an apology."

"Okay, well, we could meet a little later? How about the St. Moritz? It's another hotel, not as nice as this, but it's close by and has this incredibly well-air-conditioned room that's based on a place in Paris called the Café St. Moritz. We took Angelina there on a special—"

"*Really* have to get something in my stomach."

"Okay, but the St. Moritz is on Fifty-Ninth and Sixth. Here, I'll write it down. Maybe at noon? Are you okay? I, for one, loved last night. No regrets. I know it was a little on the drunken side, but when you're young and at the—"

"I'm just really tired," she said, holding back tears. "I guess I feel out of my league or something. You ever just need to be home in your bed, and cry?"

"This bed was our home. Wasn't it?"

"I'll never forget yesterday, but now I need to get back to New Hope and get prepared for work tomorrow."

"I could come with you."

"You go back to school and learn things for us both."

"When will we see each other again?"

"You know where I'll be." She kissed him somewhere near his mouth and left.

The room buzzed with silence. Charlie hated silent rooms and their minuscule insects, gossiping about what was wrong with the blonde girl with the long kinetic curls, which today were imprisoned in a strictest ponytail. *Everything's fine*, he told the room's din, then flopped face-first into the bed, wallowing in her clean, girly scent. How could a few drops of L'Oréal shampoo—$1.99, he'd read on the bottle—blossom into acres of flowers? *She was just here, and now she's not. Beds aren't homes, people are.*

Chapter Twenty

PAULA'S FIRST WEEK AT Martine's had gone smoothly, aided by her resolution to shelve things. Shelve Tommy, whom she hadn't properly mourned; shelve Charlie and the Plaza, an experience she couldn't yet categorize as either magical or filthy; shelve her life's digression back into her childhood bed. It was a skill she had, dumping everything in a barrel, hammering it shut, then rolling it down the hill and into the river, where it would bob with the current and maybe find her again one day. Then she'd pry it open, shocked that the contents were intact and dry. She'd resolved to get lost at Martine's, make some drinks, make some money, have some fun, just be a girl in New Hope for a spell. During slow shifts, she'd read her magazines, read *National Geographic*. She finally got to the article about hummingbirds.

Tomorrow I'll tell the lunch tourists about the hummingbirds. I can read it once and remember almost all of it, but put a school test in front of Paula Henderson? Her GPA was 2.0.

"So, it's average," her mother had once said. "Which means you're doing what you're supposed to. Nothing wrong with that."

"Hummingbirds are the only birds who can fly backward," she told two girlfriends from high school who stopped in for dinner. They'd both gotten engaged that summer and could only speak about weddings. They toted huge three-ring binders they called their workbooks, full of wish lists and magazine clippings. Paula told them if they ever had a big wedding, it should be at the Plaza Hotel in New York City.

"And be sure to stay on the twenty-seventh floor, where the Beatles once stayed, and be sure to go to Trader Vic's for Scorpions. The bubble baths are wonderful, as is the room service." She held out her hand, into which she wanted her emerald ring deposited. Over the last two hours, everyone had worn it but her.

Charlie had waited a full day after the Plaza to call her. She appreciated the self-control, but he'd called Martine's every afternoon since, and she found it difficult to speak with him from the house phone by the beer taps.

Martine's was home to so many banalities: *Gonna snow before you know it. You see Gary's new Honda? The Fall Happy Hour at Karla's is gonna be three-for-two.*

Charlie, however, wanted to speak with her about the Plaza Hotel on Labor Day morning, one of the most depressing mornings of his life. How it took all of his willpower not to fill the emptiness with vodka. How he filled it with more emptiness until the barren spaces became muscles. No Boodo Khan, no love notes, no bar car. How when he arrived at 30th Street Station in Philadelphia, he pretended to march like the new soldier he'd become, but tripped over his own feet, landing on his face. He let his cheek rest against the station dust for an extra moment, so he could watch a Plaza Hotel pillow mint roll away from him and then roll back to him, settling like a coin in front of his bloody nose. Someone dropped several tissues, which fell about him like parachuted rations. He sat up and pressed them to his nose, unsure which midday commuter had made the donation. Probably an older lady like Angelina, fussing through her purse for Kleenex.

Angelina was always doing stuff like that. It was part of the *Dignidad*, helping strangers. "This is what people did," she'd say, "when my island was an island, and not a slum. Horse and buggies, and old San Juan always clean. It was beautiful, my island, even if you are poor. Because if you are poor, people will help you, treat you with *Dignidad*. Some fruit, maybe a bed. And in return you will work their little garden or fish for them. But you will not overstay your welcome. Then, when you make some money, the first thing you do is go back to the people who helped you, bring them gifts of thanks. *Dignidad*."

He told Paula how he'd scooted himself up against the base of the train station's soaring statue, depicting an angel taking a mortally wounded soldier up to heaven. It was a famous memorial, and last spring, during pre-freshman orientation, the guy from the Admissions Department spoke about it, saying that one day you'd come back to Penn from a break, see the statue, and know you were home.

"I realize now that beds aren't homes, girls aren't homes, homes aren't even homes," he told Paula over the phone. "Missing you is my home. Loving you is my home."

I should really go, was on the tip of her tongue, but nothing came out. She teased her hair around a finger. "I like your *Dignidad*," she said, watching Gary lip a cigarette and scratch at a lottery ticket. "Tell me more."

*

Two weeks into the semester, folding chairs had been placed outside Miss Pettibone's office to facilitate the overflow of students. Still, Charlie chose the cold marble floor of College Hall. He'd been waiting for close to an hour; ahead of him was an already famous freshman girl who'd been on the cover of *Seventeen* this summer and had a pretty name, Nicoletta. Had she been less attractive, Charlie was certain people wouldn't invest the four syllables; instead, they'd call her Nicki. He'd heard about her from the Lacrosse Girl and Francis.

"Nicoletta's already dating a senior," said Francis.

"But they broke up because he was too flashy for her," said the Lacrosse Girl. "She's actually really down to earth."

She did have a cool name, Charlie thought, staring up at her from where he sat.

"You have Miss Pettibone, too?" asked Nicoletta.

She had different-colored eyes, one blue and one hazel. "Nicoletta, right? Interesting name. And interesting eyes."

"It's called heterochromia. David Bowie has it, too."

They spoke easily for many minutes. He told her his new girlfriend, Paula, had a lovely case of homochromia, which seemed to put Nicoletta even more at ease. Charlie's heart was elsewhere, despite her conflicting irises, lanky body, and long, lanky name.

"I'm thinking prelaw," she said while they waited. "Do you have a major?"

"A major life doesn't have a major, or a minor," he said, and she laughed. "It was something my brother said, but of course he had a major, economics, and now he's on Wall Street."

"Yuppie?"

"Haircut."

"What's that?"

"It's like a yuppie, but worse."

He wished Paula had a more interesting name. Weird-eyed girls should have weird names. The rest of Nicoletta he was mostly immune to. There was a conventional friendliness to her, and she was quick to smile. Paula's smiles were all earned. They were surprising. Once, Paula smiled just because a bird ducked its head into the Delaware River. Nicoletta's wacky eyes would have surely missed the bird moment. And even if Nicoletta were more complex and unpredictable, he couldn't imagine non-Paula skin against his own. Although, when she was done with her Miss Pettibone session, Nicoletta half-hugged him, and he could feel the great bones of her jaw.

"I'm so happy we met," she said to Charlie. "Maybe we could have dinner or something, one of these nights?"

"Maybe."

"I'm in the Quad."

He hadn't been there yet, but according to Francis it looked like Oxford or Cambridge, and the kids who lived there were generally more *open* than the Highrise South kids: barefoot hacky sack players, versus—well, Francis. Charlie wondered if he'd ever make it to the Quad or even see Nicoletta again. Today he was to ask Miss Pettibone about an open-ended sabbatical.

"Well," said Miss Pettibone, opening a window in her office, "you made quite an impression on Nicoletta."

"It's easy to impress beautiful girls when you're in love with someone else. I guess it's the only thing that really impresses them, that you don't love them."

"She thought you were fascinating, and you'll probably become more fascinating if you don't miss so many of your classes."

"I'm having a hard time concentrating. I'm usually with my girl-friend, and when I'm not with her I'd rather be alone and walk around Philly. By the way, I can't thank you enough for sending me to the Oyster House. It's where I met Paula. It's where my life began."

Shit, thought Miss Pettibone.

"I'd forgotten about your odyssey."

"It turned into a real-life one, complete with monsters, one of which I battled and won. It happened right at the Oyster House. I'm banned from the place for six months but left with Paula. She got fired."

Because of me, a poor girl lost her job, thought Miss Pettibone. She'd told her husband about her affair and he'd left to stay on a col-league's couch. That Labor Day weekend was one long, wonderful exhale. She opened all the windows, baked a cake with her daughter, threw out old clothes, left old textbooks on the curb. Her husband had called her selfish and weak, a destroyer of worlds, and a slut. Perhaps he was right. She only directed Green Charlie to the bar as an act of rebellion against her own job, her own life, neither of which she'd had the courage to change, until now.

"I'm so sorry she got fired. I must say I feel responsible."

"She already has another job, in New Hope, this amazing town by the river."

"Well, that makes me feel better. But let's get back to your classes."

"I've been writing my short stories. Lots of things to write about in New Hope. Paula reads every one of them. She's an avid reader."

"Have you been once to your creative writing course?"

"Being with a girl like Paula, a real girl who lives in a real place like New Hope, is incredibly educational. Classes couldn't possibly teach me all I've learned."

"Balancing a social life with classwork is tricky at first."

"Life is a war. Philly taught me that. So did Paula. About strength."

"College is such a wonderful—"

"I guess it was really what Angelina was speaking about all those years: the strength to do things. The strength not to do things."

"Very philosophical. Think how much more insight you might have should you decide to *major* in—"

"Only Paula makes me happy. I'm dedicating my life to chasing that feeling. To do something like that, you have to be all in. Devoted, as if your life depended on it."

"Why don't we give it a week, so you can think things over? One week of classes."

"All I'd do is stare out the window. Have you ever been able to be with someone who's not present, just by staring out a window?"

"No," said Miss Pettibone.

She'd spoken just yesterday with her lover about a trip. Key West, they'd decided, where she would drink tequila under the sun and walk the old streets barefoot, dancing to Jimmy Buffett and wearing shells around her neck. She wanted to tell Charlie the only real happiness is the one derived from freedom; that being happy during a marriage is like a caged gorilla's playtime with its rubber tire. But he'd probably say that for him and his Oyster House waitress it would be different, that what they had now would never wear off. *That's the right attitude*, she thought. *Ride it for as long as you can, ride it even when the wheels have come off and the track has disappeared into the underbrush. Ride it until you need to feel twenty-one again, in Margaritaville.*

"We can, perhaps, freeze your enrollment—"

"Freeze away." He had to stop himself from blowing Miss Pettibone a congratulatory kiss for possessing the power to benumb time.

"But I want you to talk things over with your parents."

"I don't know," said Charlie. "When they were my age, they pretty much froze their lives, too."

Miss Pettibone was prepared for a back-and-forth. She was prepared to argue all the reasonable arguments, but instead leaned back in her chair.

"Okay. What's she like?"

"She has all this long, curly hair, honey blonde, but sometimes even darker, and in some places lighter! And full lips that I swear are pink without any makeup. That's the Swedish part of her, that mouth. Oh, and a face that grows scarlet when she's flustered. Or excited. And these eyes. These weird eyes that are like the color of a Tiffany's box, but maybe even lighter. You know that Tiffany blue?"

Of course I know that color. All girls know that color, and I'm still a girl. My lover is only nine years older than you, Green Charlie.

"But the best things about her are indescribable. Little things she does. Little things she doesn't do. Silences. Ever meet someone like that?"

No, she thought. Maybe in high school, but it was unrequited, and life goes on.

"How do you think your parents will feel?" asked Miss Pettibone.

"About her? My mom already met her and loves her."

"No, Charlie, about leaving school."

"It depends on my mom's wine mood. Jee-Jee won't like it, but he'll side with what my mom wants. Plus, the Frenchman in him will appreciate the things I'll learn about New Hope life: fishing, chopping wood. Those things matter as well."

So true. She thought about her husband and about the thousands of young men she'd met in this very office. How soft and impractical most of them were. They'd never go to war, or work on a farm, or chop wood. A bicep-less race. Useless.

"You're paid through the end of the year, so I'm not sure if we could refund your room and board. I could have someone from the registrar's office visit with us. Let's see if she's available. She's just down the hall."

Sylvie Blaustein was Miss Pettibone's only work friend. They weren't social outside of College Hall but shared the same arch watercooler disposition about the student body. They were about the same age, owned the same blouses and dangly earrings, and moved about their days holding mugs of flavored room-temperature coffee that looked almost as white as milk.

"Hey, Sylvie, thanks for popping in."

"Hey, Vic. Who do we have here?"

"Here is Charlie Green."

"Hello, Charlie Green."

The two women leaned their rears against either desk corner, winking at each other and sipping coffee, loudly, then licking away the residue from their upper lips.

"Charlie wants to defer enrollment," said Miss Pettibone.

"I *see*. What's the story, Charlie?"

"I met someone."

"Charlie's a very bright and *certain* young man," said Miss Pettibone.

"I can see that. Listen, Charlie, have you talked this through with your folks?"

"I think he's deliberating on that, Syl."

"Uh-huh, uh-huh," said Syl, staring deeply into Miss Pettibone's dark eyes. After she got what she needed, she turned to Charlie.

"Looks like you want out."

"Looks that way," said Charlie, angry that the sanctity of his Miss Pettibone time had been ruined by this coffee slurper.

"Then I suppose the next step is the paperwork," said Sylvie, rolling up her sleeves. "We do need a signoff by the parents, Charlie."

"I'm eighteen, they can't force me to stay in school."

"Uh-huh, uh-huh," said Sylvie. "I see where you're coming from. Can we have a moment, Charlie? Would you mind waiting outside for a moment?"

"Nope," he said, popping the P.

"You can leave your bag in here, Charlie," said Miss Pettibone. "I'm sure we'll be just a minute."

There were a few kids in chairs, and Charlie was happy to sit below them on the marble floor, cross-legged and hunched over, rocking like an old Jew while his fate got decided. He considered donning the New Order yarmulke to complete the picture, but the other kids were deep inside course guides and wouldn't even notice.

The typewriter sounds made eavesdropping impossible. What was there to talk about, anyway? He hoped the second lady wouldn't extinguish Miss Pettibone's youthful inner light. He could see it in her eyes when they spoke. *Adults look nothing short of adorable when they slip out of their adult lives.* Thank God it was Miss Pettibone and not the second lady who invited Charlie back in.

"We think we've found a compromise that might suit all parties," she told him.

"You're lucky Victoria believes in you, Mr. Green," said Sylvie. "There's an awful lot of students who are on a waiting list to join your freshman class."

"We think you should enroll part-time, take two courses," said Miss Pettibone. "Just two, then ease your way into things. Stay active in the community. That way, there's no chance your enrollment will be revoked."

"Suppose I say no?"

"At least continue with one course, Charlie," said Miss Pettibone.

She was being sweet, and he could see the light in her eyes. *She's in love, too; we're in the same club, age be damned.*

"I'll do the museum one." That place had marble floors as well.

"Mr. Green, you're not doing us any favors," said Sylvie. Both women sipped from their mugs. Charlie hoped Miss Pettibone didn't have bad breath, but was certain this other woman did, and that the tepid, treacly coffee, which was supposed to disguise the stink, actually caused it.

"It meets on Tuesdays and Thursdays," said Miss Pettibone.

"That's a rather short workweek, Mr. Green," said Sylvie. "Okay, Vic, looks like we're going out on a limb with this one. I'll get the paperwork rolling."

"Yes," said Charlie, batting his long lashes at her until she saw in his face the preeminence of youth.

"Good luck Mr. Green."

He was going to tell her that he didn't need luck, but instead slipped her a wink, just like Jee-Jee did every day, everywhere, to men and women alike. He was great at it, and Charlie had inherited the skill.

"Oh, boy," said Sylvie, and left.

"Today's a busy day for me, Charlie, so I'm going to have to end our meeting, okay?"

Miss Pettibone's next student was in an automated wheelchair that she operated with her toes, because her hands were malformed and stumpy.

"If you're seeing Miss Pettibone, you're with the best," Charlie told her.

"Thank you for the endorsement, Charlie," Miss Pettibone said as the wheelchair whirred past them into the office.

He wondered if she could have sex, the wheelchair girl. He felt bad for her and wished he could clone himself and instruct his clone to fall in love with her the way he loved Paula. *Wait, am I a narcissist?* He examined his soul for goodness, found some, then willed the wheelchair girl a life of real and surprising happiness even if it meant he'd die young or have to sacrifice something important. Just not Paula. Not Paula.

*

Charlie visited New Hope on Sundays, her day off. He slept in the room above the garage with the wedding grasshoppers, the *TV Week* collection, and the magical late-night visitations from his Plaza-robed lover.

These were sixteen-hour dates, long enough to make parting painful for them both. Charlie would return to college, to his wide-open week and another countdown until the next date; and Paula to Martine's, where she'd slowly twist her emerald ring around and around while she watched the beer tap fill mug after mug. They made a rule not to speak on the phone more than once during the week, and then only to plan the logistics of their next meeting. And there were letters. Long letters from her that smelled like her hair, written from her bedroom or from Martine's, describing her day, her heart. She wasn't accustomed to having a long-distance boyfriend; they'd all been in her face. Even though she was lonely during the workweek, she liked how Charlie called their segregation "literal lovemaking." He'd mail her his short stories, about how Francis cleaned the frozen yogurt machine in Dining Commons, or about the sound Miss Pettibone's heels made in the hallway outside her office. He'd written one about Nicoletta but did not send it. Mrs. Henderson had just about convinced her daughter that there were too many temptations at an Ivy League school such as Penn, and that Charlie wouldn't be able to help himself. He'd leave her for "an intellectual."

"You'd tell me if you ever had a change of heart about us, right?" she had asked Charlie.

"Impossible."

"What is?"

"Impossible that my heart will change."

"You could just say 'yes,' that you would tell me."

"Impossible."

In the middle of October, Charlie asked to cancel their date, because he and Francis had been invited to a wildly popular fraternity party. He did not want to be hungover in front of her the next day, an assured side effect of Sigma Alpha Mu's "Sammy Fest."

"Then don't drink that much at the party," said Paula.

"They make freshmen do shots in order to enter."

"Doesn't sound like your type of party."

It wasn't, but Francis, a Sammy pledge, had to work at Dining Commons late into that Saturday night, doing inventory, and had asked Charlie to escort the Lacrosse Girl, now his girlfriend.

"It's the only thing he's ever asked me to do," said Charlie. "And I've asked him to do so many things. Most have been in the name of you."

Paula understood, but when she woke up that Saturday morning, her stomach was knotted.

"You shouldn't let him go to the party, Paula," said Mrs. Henderson, stuffing her fanny pack for her weekly group walk along the river. "You might never hear from him again. Boys get a taste of those parties and get hooked on the action. Have you seen my Gator Gum?"

Paula's knotted stomach wasn't reassured by her pre-dinner-shift phone call to Charlie.

"Have fun tonight," she said, "but be careful, you know?"

"Frat Haircuts don't scare me. Not even Tommy scared me. Remember him?"

She did remember him, especially after a difficult phone call with Charlie. Tommy was so much simpler than Charlie. Irish drinks, Irish jokes. Somehow, Tommy's infidelities were easier to deal with. They were simple. The thought of Charlie cheating—

"Just be good, okay?" she told Charlie. "I trust you."

The knots were gone by the time her dinner shift was in full swing, but something else, something worse, was in their place. With Tommy, there was a limit to the pain he could make her feel. There was something superficial about it. She wore it on the outside of her body and brushed it off before the next date. Tonight's discomfort was deep inside. If it got any worse, she'd need to lie down, but it lingered just below that threshold. Weapons-grade jealousy? True love? She wasn't sure. But it felt like a new organ that hated its new home.

Chapter Twenty-one

SIGMA ALPHA MU, OR Sammy, had a plastic Santa on the front lawn. The brothers referred to him as Sammy Claus and did whatever they could to have freshman girls pose topless with him. A Sammy Claus album got passed down from class to class. Next to Sammy Claus was a punch station. There were many punch stations at Sammy parties, but none more elaborate than the one next to Sammy Claus: three trash cans filled with red, redder, and reddest punch. In order for a freshman to set foot in Sammy, they had to drink a cup of the reddest punch. An ancient thirtysomething Sammy alum manned the punch station, persuading people to have second and third cups. Girls who had three cups almost always posed with Sammy Clause, then made their way into the frat house, where there was darkness, a pounding bassline, more punch stations, and Sammys grinning knowingly in the dark, for only they could see how the night would unfold.

"Are my lips red?" Charlie asked the Lacrosse Girl. Francis had asked Charlie to make sure that she drank no more than 1.5 glasses of punch. He'd calculated the formula based on her weight and his inside knowledge of the ingredients.

"Yes," she said. "Are mine?"

"Really red," said Charlie.

Everyone's lips were red. One of Charlie's favorite stories growing up was his mother's about a costume ball in Paris and the absinthe zombies roaming the steps of the Opera House, falling and laughing.

"Ever wonder what blood has to do with beauty?" asked the Lacrosse Girl. "I mean, isn't that the point of makeup? To show a guy that there's blood in your face?"

He thought about the little capillary blossoms that would appear on Paula's cheeks. She'd called just before he left for Sammy and said she was going on a midnight river cruise after work. She said she had a weird feeling inside and needed to be out on the water. Tonight, during their weekly Saturday call, John had confirmed that promiscuity was a given on a cruise ship. That the rhythm of the water made people insatiably horny.

"The subliminal message is, 'You're going to drown, so go and pro-create before the end.'"

"You really think she'll be promiscuous?"

"A single, healthy, nineteen-year-old girl on a party boat after midnight?"

"I never said she was single."

"Every human being is single."

Charlie wished human beings would act less human, but according to John, resisting nature was futile. At the Sammy Claus punch station, a skinny girl with brown nipples kissed Santa's cheek as camera flashes went off.

"I'm getting another punch," Charlie told the Lacrosse Girl.

"Get me another?"

"Do you mind if I get you a half?"

"Just get me a full one."

"Francis was very specific about 1.5 punches."

"I just want to have some fun."

Me too, he thought, spotting Nicoletta at the far end of the lawn. Her hair was up, and she'd fully embraced her height by wearing heels. Charlie had seen her magazine cover. The headline was "Summer Love." Nicoletta wore a sundress and threw her hands up in the air in celebration of summer love, although, according to the Lacrosse Girl, Nicoletta was single, and they shot the cover in early March. Elsewhere in the issue, there was a Q&A with the cover girl.

"What does it feel like to be an Ivy League model?"

She said she didn't consider herself a model, and that school came first.

"Any summer crushes you'd like to share with us?"

She said she didn't kiss and tell.

"What's something no one knows about you?"

She said she had nothing to hide.

"There's Nicoletta," Charlie said, handing the Lacrosse Girl her full cup of punch.

"You should say hi to her. You like her, I can tell."

"I like that she's not embarrassed to be six feet in heels and that she wore her hair back exactly like the magazine cover, but she's not my future, that much I know. My future is on a midnight cruise along the Delaware. I just hope she remembers that I'm *her* future. Cruise ship rhythms can mess with important facts."

"Maybe Nicoletta's your fact tonight? Paula sounds great, but Francis and I fear that she's aging you. You worry so much. We're young, Charlie. It's sort of our job to be youthful." The Lacrosse Girl finished her second cup and grabbed a third. "Let's go inside. I want to dance."

She grabbed his hand and walked them past the entrance, which was teeming with Sammys in togas and backward baseball caps, stomping their feet and bobbing their heads.

In his mother's story about the party at the Paris Opera House and the longest night the world had ever known, the sun didn't seem to rise for two whole days. People got lost in there, some forever. The end of the world was in an antechamber's antechamber, where absinthe filled the holy water fonts and a man in a mask in a birdcage rattled the bars like a furious chimpanzee.

*

By the time he reached the third floor, the sweat of at least ten strangers was on his person. Charlie counted himself among the drenched and red-mouthed, a people whose voices could not be heard above the bassline, while their masters, the Sammys, whispered in the shadows. He was alone now, on the top floor of the frat house. The Lacrosse Girl had gotten sucked into a centrifugal group of dancing Sammys, who wore pink wigs and swigged peach schnapps. Charlie tried to reel her in, but it was too late. Within moments a wig had been placed over her short, sandy hair. They put her in a chair and told her to throw back her head, so the schnapps would have an easy trip down. Charlie wondered if the Sammys had missed on purpose; only some of the schnapps made it down her throat. The rest was on her shirt and shorts. They laughed about it; the Lacrosse Girl laughed, too. Regardless, tomorrow she'd stink of peach. *Francis won't be happy. He's the sort of kid who freaks out about food stains and their associated smells.*

"In here," someone said. "I'm here," she said. "In *here*."

Here was a dark room, some sort of repository for expired furniture. Blocky wooden chairs were piled high, and in the back of the room was a naked mattress, on which sat Nicoletta.

"Hey," she said. "We both sought out the top floor."

"My brother advised this tactic at college parties."

"Smart guy."

"Sometimes."

Her punch cup was empty. She was smiling. *She's always smiling. Maybe it's a modeling habit that can't be unlearned.*

"This room smells so old," she said.

"Like wooden ghosts," said Charlie.

"I like that."

"I just made it up."

"Want to sit down?"

"I guess so." She pulled him down and he tumbled over her. In the seconds before she kissed him, he knew he'd be kissed and felt panic, a hot piece of lead going through his middle. *Guilt smolders just below the rib cage.* He hated the feeling, and decided he needed the moisture of her mouth to put out the heat.

She was a subtler kisser than Paula. She'd probably kissed less and was still developing her lip muscles.

"I'm sort of seeing someone," said Charlie.

"Oh, right, Miss Blue Eyes. I have one of those. How *sort of?*"

He looked at her different-colored eyes. They were hard to pass up, especially the hazel one. He wished he could request which color their next kiss would taste like. There would be another kiss, he decided. John would bet good money that Paula would kiss someone on the cruise. Maybe it was unwritten that couples kiss other people when they're apart. No real harm. As Paula had once asked, "What is kissing, anyway?"

Make this one taste like the greenish one, Charlie wished, and kissed her again, then again and again, dousing the guilt until it was extinguished for good, leaving him in a limbo. "I feel like a forest after a massive fire," he said.

"Are you okay?"

"Confused." *While cheating, one can be so honest.*

"I know what you mean."

"Have you ever heard of Frucor? It's an Australian sports drink. My girlfriend was a model for them."

"Oh, wow! Which agency?"

He kissed her again, blaming Paula for not belonging to an agency.

"Do you think this mattress is dirty?" she asked.

"Yes," said Charlie, again using his cheater's honesty.

"I don't care." She got out of her long blue jeans.

"How tall are you?" asked Charlie.

"Tall. Here." She put his hand between her legs, showed him what to do.

The cheater's honesty allowed him to take a clinical interest in it. He told himself that he was practicing for future Paula reference. Sometimes Nicoletta would stop him and remind his hand how to move, other times she'd moan, and Charlie would smile. It was an amazing game, the prize at the end, her fists pounding the mattress.

"Do you want me to do something for you?" she asked, tugging at his pants.

"No, I'm fine. Like I said, I'm sort of seeing someone, so, you know."

"Well, Charlie, we just like, you know?"

"Of course, but does that really count in terms of . . . future things?"

"It doesn't mean that we're girlfriend and boyfriend, but it does mean something. I mean, I've never let a non-boyfriend do that."

Fuck, he thought.

"Let's sleep on it," she said. "But you have to spoon me after touching me."

Charlie complied. Two young, skinny bodies forming a crescent over a wet spot.

*

He woke to a dry mouth and a pain in his forehead, a vein full of punch worming its way around his skull. On the wall was a poster of Mike Schmidt winning the 1980 World Series, jumping for joy.

"Schmidty," said Charlie. Nicoletta's back was turned to him, but he could tell from her breathing that she was awake.

"I had his baseball card from that year," he said, fingers under nostrils.

"I should get out of here," said Nicoletta. "Will you walk out of here with me?"

Her morning voice was delicate. *Only two years ago, she was sixteen*, thought Charlie. And that was how she sounded now, like a sixteen-year-old girl.

"Sure, I'll walk out with you."

"Do you know where the bathroom is? Don't worry, I'll find it."

She wasn't afraid of what was outside the door in the Sunday-morning corridors of Sammy, while Charlie lay paralyzed in bed looking at Schmidty and smelling the new smell. But it wasn't entirely new. He'd had this on his fingers before, though not from Paula. She smelled of flowers. This scent almost certainly smelled like a food, but which one? Not that nonsense about girls and fish. This was a rich, heady, almost spicy scent of scents. He vowed not to wash his hand until he figured out its secrets.

"Looks like my friend also crashed here, so I'm going to go have breakfast with her," said Nicoletta, back from the bathroom where she'd wet her face. She was back to smiling, but this morning Charlie didn't mind, as long as the smile meant taking last night lightly.

"Last night," she said. "I don't know, I guess last night was last night." She went back to the mattress to kiss him goodbye. Her breath was minty.

"Did you use mouthwash?"

"Yeah, I found some Scope in the bathroom. Didn't want to smell for our goodbye kiss."

"Does my breath smell?" asked Charlie.

"No, not really. I think we're still at an age when our breath doesn't really smell in the morning."

"Hmm."

"What does that mean?" asked Nicoletta.

"It's just something I do."

"You're cute. I like you, Charlie, but please stop smelling your fingers, it's making me feel self-conscious."

"Oh, sorry, it just smells so good."

"Oh. Okay. I guess that's sweet."

"And spicy."

They kissed goodbye, and when she left the room, he missed her. He didn't have to explain the feeling to himself, he just let it be. *We had fun. She's nice. I'm nice. We're still at an age when our morning breath is sweet. And I don't really miss her, I miss the room having held two people instead of just me. And Schmidty. By the way, Schmidty, stop jumping for joy. It's not 1980 anymore, it's 1987. Christ, Schmidty, why did I do those things with that tall girl? And that smell? What is it, Schmidty? And my headache. I need food, Schmidty. Stop jumping for joy. I'm such an idiot.*

Chapter Twenty-two

"HOW WAS THE PARTY?" asked Paula from her bed.

"How was the river cruise? I hear those things can get pretty wild."

"Oh, I didn't go."

"What?"

"I still feel weird inside."

"Shit."

Charlie was calling from a pay phone outside Sammy. In the light of day, the punch station was nothing more than three trash cans. Last night, the place had seemed like a *place*. An Asian kid had curled himself around one of the cans. He was asleep, hugging his baseball cap in lieu of a teddy bear. *If I could get him a pillow and drape a blanket over him, last night would be erased.*

"So how was your frat thing?" asked Paula.

"Weird."

"How so?"

"Nothing happened."

"What happened?"

"Nothing. Just drank too much punch and ran into this girl. Nothing really happened."

And then there was a dial tone. She'd hung up and Charlie had no more quarters. Mrs. Henderson had been very clear about her strict collect-calling policy. It was forbidden, unless it was from a hospital or police station. Charlie thought of waking the Asian kid and asking him for change, but he hadn't the heart. The anesthetic of sleep should wear off naturally, and the horror of having passed out at the Sammy punch station should be experienced alone, with no one watching.

Sammy loomed in the distance. There was probably change in there. On the dance floor? Beneath the mattress where they'd slept? He needed to call Paula. To confess it all. Or deny it. John preached the latter: that a man should always deny it. Always. Neil had told a Crumb that the truth comes out one way or another. Don't waste another moment, tell her all the crumby things you've ever done.

Sammys must be experienced with infidelities. Perhaps they knew the safest way out. He entered the fraternity house, climbed the stairs, and found the bathroom Nicoletta had used. His bladder was full, and he wanted his mouth to be minty, too, but there in the doorless stall squatted a Sammy.

"Jesus," said Charlie.

"Making some room for an aigle," said the defecating Sammy.

"What's that?

"An aigle? You gotta be shittin' me, bro. It's the best sandwich in the world. Aigle time, aigle time!" sang the Sammy. "Aigle, aigle, aigle time!"

"I'm really hungry," said Charlie.

"Then let's do it, dude. Let's aigle out. Hey, toss me some TP."

A block from Sammy was a greasy spoon whose livelihood relied on the hangovers of Sammys. On Saturday and Sunday mornings, the owner manned the griddle, making the house specialty: fried egg atop a slightly burnt, buttered bagel, slathered with brown gravy. He made each one to order, some Sammys asking for *beaucoup* gravy, or extra-burnt, or double eggs, or "Mario, melt me some cheese on that aigle, bro."

"One aigle, two aigle, three aigles," Mario sang, happily collecting crumpled bills, some pulled from socks, others from punch-stained palms.

"I hear you never had an aigle before," a Sammy said to Charlie. "Dudes, this is his first aigle. First aigle alert!"

Charlie was last in line, the only non-Sammy. The conversations were about aigles, taking a post-aigle dump, and who'd gotten lucky.

"She wasn't *that* wasted," said a Sammy. He had probably graduated just last year. Still in his suit and wearing a backward baseball cap, he probably took the amazing Amtrak down last night from New York. Haircut Sammys. The worst.

"Love those sports chicks," said Haircut Sammy.

"Tight," said a Sammy.

"Flexible," said Haircut Sammy.

"You do her?" asked a Sammy.

"There was some pen, there was definitely some pen."

"Full pen?"

"*Some* pen, okay?" The skinny part of Haircut Sammy's tie was longer than the fat part. When he became agitated, he'd pull at it, making matters worse. "If I say *some* pen, that's what I mean."

"Yeah, that's cool," the Sammy conceded. "Fuck it, I'm getting two aigles."

"What's pen?" Charlie asked a Sammy.

"What's pen? *Dude*, it's when you do it. It's when you put it in."

Haircut Sammy turned to face them. "Dudes, you don't talk about pen on the aigle line." Disgusted, he tugged at his tie.

"Was the girl you penned—did she play lacrosse?" asked Charlie.

"This is the last I'm gonna talk about pen. You don't talk about pen on the aigle line. You don't talk about pen when my man Mario's making beaucoup aigles. But yeah, I think she played stick."

Charlie pictured the Lacrosse Girl crying into Francis's shoulder after a confession, stoic Francis willing to absorb her sobbing but unable to hug her back.

"Since it's your first aigle, it's on me," Haircut Sammy told Charlie. "You want beaucoup gravy on it?"

"Yes," said Charlie.

"Yeah!" a Sammy cheered. "That's the best way to get it. You bite in, and the egg yolk and gravy drip down your face. Beaucoup gravy aigles rule. Dude, why you keep sniffing your fingers? You get finger pen last night? Dudes, this dude got finger pen!"

"You can talk about finger pen on the aigle line, just not real pen," said Haircut Sammy. "It's disrespectful to Mario, but finger pen is okay."

"Oh my God," said Charlie, unable to remove his finger from under his nose. "That's it, that's what it is. Cool Ranch Doritos. It's a new flavor. I had it over the summer."

"Dude. Chill," said Haircut Sammy.

"If you fooled around with a girl, would you tell your girlfriend?" asked Charlie.

"I don't have a girlfriend, and if I did, I wouldn't cheat," said Haircut Sammy.

"Yeah, cheating is for losers," said a Sammy.

*

Mario gave Charlie two dollars' worth of quarters. "Call your mama, tell her about my famous aigles," said Mario.

"I'm actually calling my girlfriend."

"One aigle, two aigle, three aigle."

Charlie had decided to tell Paula the truth. He couldn't live knowing he was morally inferior to Haircut Sammy, but the Hendersons' phone just rang and rang. He called for close to an hour, sniffing his fingers, praying to hear Paula's voice. He was going to trade the sin for an admission of eternal love, maybe even a proposal. "It made me realize how much I love you. Not *during* the finger pen, but *after* the shameful finger pen. Will you marry me?"

John said that being in love was the least-efficient mode of existence, like going through life with a piano on your back. That was
how it felt at the pay phone. The guilt, the hangover, the desultory
Sunday of the post-Sammy party perimeter. The Asian kid had vanished, leaving behind his baseball cap. *You can love someone's essence
purely by what they leave behind*, thought Charlie, and remembered
the Dentyne Paula had left behind at the Plaza. A slick of hot aigle
grease ran down Charlie's shirtsleeve. He punished the sandwich by
taking an enormous bite. It was unspeakably rich. A pill the size of a
brick, it dissolved in his stomach, its nutrients attaching themselves
to un-oxygenated punch. The Sammys had warned Charlie about the
aftereffects: narcolepsy, bowel stimulation, a deep, almost deathly sat-
isfaction. Nihilism. They'd told him of the time a Sammy had fallen
asleep and shat himself.

"You'll want to fall asleep, but don't. Don't until you've evacuated
the aigle from your body."

When the greasy brown bag was a ball crumpled in Charlie's hand,
he was, as the Sammys had said, capable of hibernation. But he used
his cool ranch fingers as smelling salts, undeterred by the looks he
received as he made his way to the Wawa, where he found a bag of
Doritos. He brought the chips to a bench on Locust Walk and poured
them over his palms in hope of permanence, but he lost the more delicate scent, the Doritos scattered about his loafers.

While Charlie sniffed in vain, Francis sat next to him, smoothing
down the creases of his freshly ironed Dining Commons smock.

"What's the deal with the chips?" asked Francis.

"I spilled them," said Charlie.

"How was last night? Must have been pretty good if you didn't
sleep in your own bed. Was it a wild night?"

"Not really."

"Did you see my girlfriend?"

"Just in the beginning, when we were outside with Sammy Claus."

"She didn't get her picture taken or anything? I mean topless."

"No, not at all."

"I stopped by, after midnight, but it was too crowded to even get inside."

After midnight, thought Charlie, the nimble Lacrosse Girl was getting penned.

"Did something weird happen at Sammy?" asked Francis. "She was acting weird this morning. Probably just girl stuff."

"Probably. She really likes you. I can tell."

"Thanks."

Pen, pen, pen, pen.

"And couples should stay together," said Charlie, "despite all the temptations to cheat."

"I agree."

"That fraternity house is a bad place."

"All I know is, Sammy brothers essentially run Wall Street." Francis picked a feather off his apron. It wafted down to the Doritos pile, but veered away at the last second. "I'm definitely going to pledge."

"Don't."

"Why?"

"You're better than the Sammys."

"You really think so?"

"By comparison, you're way classier. Although they're against cheating, just like us."

"My dad says I'm middle class."

"Maybe so but saying you're middle class is upper class."

"Thanks. I should get to work."

"I could help you today, if you want."

"You'd need twenty-five hours of safety and CPR training, and a uniform."

"Right," said Charlie. He wanted the proximity of a hot stove so he could work off his sin and was tempted to ask Mario if he could become his apprentice, but Mario's sandwich had begun to make itself known to Charlie's small intestine, at first in subtle ways and then more bluntly, squeezing and kneading; he had to hold his stomach as he bum-rushed

Wharton's men's room. During his many minutes of relief, a custodian whistled his way in and began mopping. Charlie wished there were a polite way to ask for privacy; even though he was winning the war against the aigle, the battle was noisy and involved, and the song in the air was "Amazing Grace." Ordinarily, Charlie would flush along the way, but he didn't want to give the custodian the impression that he was finished, for fear of a barge-in, so he waited till the very end to flush. It was a mistake. The whistling stopped as soon as the water gurgled and rose.

"All I did was flush," said Charlie as he backed his way out of the stall, the contents of the toilet spilling out and sliding along the floor. He and the custodian watched the solid waste make its way, a life-giving stream of toilet water allowing it to settle all the way behind the sinks.

The custodian threw down the mop and withdrew his holstered plunger. He rolled up his pantlegs and positioned himself above the overflowing toilet. There was white in his afro; his bare calves looked dry and scaly.

"I'm really sorry," said Charlie. "You shouldn't have to do this."

"*Shouldn't have to*? Thirty-five years, this is my job."

With both hands he plunged, violently disturbing the toilet water. Miraculously, it receded, sucking itself back into its hole.

"Wow," said Charlie.

"Now for the death blow." With both hands he raised the plunger high above the toilet, brought it down with all his might, then yanked it clear away like a dragon-slaying knight. The toilet belched once, again, then a third time, farting sewage, splattering the custodian's face. Thirty-five years of undigested aigles must have been waiting in there for this poor man.

"Fuck me," said the custodian.

"I'll help you clean up this mess," said Charlie. "Just tell me what to do, and I'll do it."

"You want to clean up these turds?"

"Yes. Some of them are mine."

The custodian removed his shirt; like Jee-Jee, he wore an undershirt, probably the same ribbed Jockey Classic A-shirt. Francis wore one, too.

"I should wear an undershirt," said Charlie.

"Say what?" The custodian was at the sink, scrubbing his face and hair with soap and hot water.

"I like your undershirt."

"You a fairy?"

"No, not at all. I just appreciate this type of shirt. The best people I know wear one, and I should, too. A *Dignidad* shirt, if there ever was one. So, please, tell me how to clean the turds."

"Well, you're going to want to put on those big yellow gloves before you go fetch the turds, and you're also going to want to take off that suit jacket."

There were many steps to the process, all of which the custodian orated from the sink, atop which he sat directing Charlie. "Remember, nothing's clean until the mop water runs clean."

Charlie must have gone over the bathroom floor fifteen times before he could wring the mop of clean water. Only the last few passes involved disinfectant.

"You've got to set the stage for the soap," said the custodian. "If you put it on too soon, the soap won't work."

He taught Charlie to save one sink for last, because that was where he'd pour out the dirty water. "That last sink's your sewer. It gets the bucket water. But you can't leave that poor sink coated with bucket water. You have to clean that one the best of all. That's your signature sink, your mark. At least that's the nonsense I tell myself to make it through the day."

When the last sink gleamed, the custodian hopped down and shook Charlie's hand.

"Nice job."

"Thanks. And thanks for letting me. It was exactly what I needed today. I did something bad last night, and now I feel better."

"You Wharton students are crazy, but you're industrious. Know how I know?"

"How?"

"My son goes here. MBA. My only rule is that he has to take a shit elsewhere."

He was in his undershirt and had thrown the soiled overshirt in the trash.

"Hey, want my jacket? You can have it. Brooks Brothers."

The custodian tried it on—a perfect fit—then rolled his mop and bucket toward the ladies' room, whistling "Amazing Grace."

*

"Hi, Mrs. Henderson. It's Charlie. May I please speak with Paula?"

"We're watching *60 Minutes*. You should know better, Charlie."

"Can I call after the show?"

"Can he call you, Paula? She's shaking her head no."

"Shit."

"Language, Charlie."

"Sorry. Tell her that I love her and that I'm sorry."

"He says he loves you, Paula. She's just staring at the TV. She's not feeling so hot, Charlie. What is he sorry for, Paula? She doesn't tell me anything. The commercials are almost over. I haven't missed *60 Minutes* since Paula was a little girl."

"Just tell her I'll stop at Martine's tomorrow to see her."

"She's going to the doctor's tomorrow, hon."

"I can go with her."

"I'm going with her, Charlie."

*

Most Monday mornings, Charlie would be on a bus back from New Hope, his lips still moist with their goodbye kiss. On this Monday, he found himself in the lobby of High Rise South, watching students put up Halloween decorations. He wondered who would volunteer to do such a thing, and why it was never him.

"Need any help?" he asked.

"We're good," said a girl at the base of a ladder, holding a small, warped broom.

"Everything looks very festive."

"We've been at it all morning."

"I could help, really. These are the sorts of things I never do, but should, you know?"

"It's just that we sort of have a system going," said the girl.

"I like the bales of hay. And I've never seen a pumpkin that big."

"It's the Pennsylvania soil," she said, then ran up a ladder so the broom could join its green-faced witch. *I could watch this all day,* thought Charlie. A finger tapped his shoulder.

"Hi," said Paula. Today was the first truly cool fall day, and she wore a pink turtleneck sweater and white jean jacket, clothes Charlie hadn't ever seen. She was smiling, too—beaming brightly. "I went to the doctor."

Her smile proscribed anything but a white lie. He was going to say that he fell asleep in the vicinity of a homely girl, and that was that.

"So, you're all right?" asked Charlie.

"There's nothing wrong with me."

"That's great. Listen, about the frat party—"

"It doesn't matter. I don't care. I don't want to know."

"Good, because there's nothing to tell."

"Do you want to sit somewhere?"

"Sure. We could have lunch, too. I don't have class today."

"My mom's waiting in the car. Let's sit outside."

Paula pointed to a wooden bench outside a small chapel about a hundred yards away from High Rise South. It chimed every hour, just a single chime, and Charlie was comforted that he often didn't know the time. Especially at night. It could be midnight; it could be four.

"I've never sat here," said Charlie.

"First I need a hug."

"I'm so happy to see you. I'm so happy to hug you."

"So, the doctor told me some pretty incredible news."

He thought about the ladder the girl had climbed to reach the witch, and the smell of hay in the lobby.

The smell of hay. They would be the last words to sound inside his skull before he found himself in the back of Mrs. Henderson's car, the top down, on the way to New Hope. Mrs. Henderson lecturing Paula about womanhood, the wind lecturing Charlie's boyish locks about manhood.

Mrs. Henderson had made sure to break out a value pack of Kleenex, placing each and every packet in strategic locations throughout the house, including one right in Charlie's lap. He sank into the couch and watched Mrs. Henderson shake her big proud head. He watched Paula's pink sweater sleeves, stretched ridiculously, flopping at her sides. Odd, thought Charlie, finding yourself places. Like when he found himself at Disney World, next to Angelina, in the admirable darkness of Peter Pan's Flight. He didn't ask how he got there, or try to recall the airplane to Florida, or checking into the hotel. He squeezed Angelina's hand and thanked all the stars over London that life-bookmarks whisk you away to happy scenes.

Now he tried to avoid looking at the crucifix that Mrs. Henderson wore for the occasion.

"We're very Catholic, Charlie," said Mrs. Henderson. "There are certain things we just won't do. Your mother will understand."

It had been decided that they would all go to New York tomorrow to meet with Mr. and Mrs. Green.

"This is a family decision," said Mrs. Henderson. "Some people try their whole lives to have a baby. The doctor told my honey bunny that she couldn't, unless she had surgery, so I guess this is some sort of a miracle. Your mother will understand, Charlie. Mothers just understand."

He'd called home earlier, from the Henderson household, which was awash in paprika smells and Christmas music, the soundtrack for *keeping it*. He wanted to ask his mother if she might adopt the child, so that he could indeed resume being young, but instead just babbled something about a freshman field trip.

"You sound funny, Charlie Bear," Mrs. Green had said.

"Just don't like field trips. They treat you like a baby."

"Suppose I don't want it?" he'd asked Paula while Mrs. Henderson set the table.

"You heard my mom, it's like a miracle. I don't know if I can give it up."

"It could kill my youth. I mean really ruin my life."

"If you don't want to have anything to do with this child, fine. We never have to see one another again. You can go right now."

"No. I want to stay."

"Let's just take it a day at a time," said Paula, lifting her sweater and bringing Charlie's hand to her warm belly. "That doesn't feel like a ruined life, does it?"

He'd been hoping for at least a glass of wine, but there was a glass of milk in front of his plate, just as there was in front of Paula's and Mrs. Henderson's. They'd held hands before dinner, and Mrs. Henderson had asked God to bless them all, including baby.

"When Paula was little, she got the flu real bad, slipped in the tub, and cracked open her skull. We all held hands that night, and prayed around the table, just like we're doing now."

There was a cartoon that Charlie watched when *he* was first flu-stricken: a bunny tries to shove a lion into a bowling ball's finger holes. His feverish mind kept telling him that turn of events was impossible. So, so impossible.

Chapter Twenty-three

"EVERYTHING'S GOING TO CHANGE for you two. You got to grow up real fast now," said Mrs. Henderson to the backseat passengers of her Buick Regal. "Hon, do you remember the cocktail dress that was in the window at Grand Designs?"

"No, Mom."

"Look at you two, back there like a couple of grumps. You should lighten up. So serious. Sheesh."

"This *is* serious, Mrs. Henderson." It was the first time he'd snapped at the rosy-cheeked polar bear.

"You kids don't know from serious. Going to Vietnam is serious. Having a baby is joyous. You have to grow up and know the difference, Charlie."

But this felt like war to him, like the movies he'd seen of young recruits swimming in their newly issued uniforms. He didn't know how to wear this. Nor where the flares might be on his utility belt. Everything was dark, external to the light of his childhood. Adult. Stomach-sickening. *No wonder they all take Tums.*

"We're almost at the Greens'. Don't worry. I'll wait in the car, like I promised, so you two can have your moment with Charlie's folks."

"I don't care if you come in," said Charlie.

"No, you have big news to say, and listen, you two, from here on in, if you want to share the bed with Paula, be my guest. You don't have to sneak around the house anymore. At this point, what's the difference? Ooh, a parking space."

Charlie and Paula stood at the door. Deep inhalations.

"You want to be the one to ring the doorbell?" asked Charlie.

"No, not really."

"Me neither."

"Fine, I'll ring it," said Paula.

"No, I'll do it. We'll both do it at the same time. She'll be out back, which gives us a little more time. Maybe we can ease into stuff, you know?"

"Yes," said Paula. "We can begin by speaking about Mother Nature."

Rose Green needed only to look at their faces.

"She's pregnant."

"Well," said Charlie. "Technically, she is."

"Oh my God! Come in, come in, let's go in the kitchen and tell your father."

They stood around the kitchen island, everyone in autumnal sweaters, except for Charlie, whose college uniform, less the custodian's blazer, was reduced to just a black T-shirt and jeans. *Well, the uniform sure got me laid.* He thought it would take hours for his parents to digest the news, but it took minutes, everyone smiling, including Paula, whose emerald ring was being cleaned by Rose Green.

"I respect that you want to have this baby," said Mrs. Green to Paula.

"I went to the doctor's positive he'd tell me I was going to die," said Paula.

"*L'chaim*," said Jee-Jee. "What a pleasure to meet you, and for the record, you are the opposite of death, my dear."

"We'd love to meet your mother, dear," said Mrs. Green.

"She's in the car. Parked around the corner. I know she'd like to say hi."

"Go get her, Charlie," said Mrs. Green. "I'll get the foie gras."

"Yes, Charl," said Jee-Jee. "I must teach you the secrets of treating the mother-in-law so well. A lost art, my boy."

I'm not the fucking messenger, Charlie thought, and decided he'd take his time. He stopped by the pay phone at the corner of Seventy-First and Second Avenue and called Monica Miller. There was a time when that was the only number, aside from his own, that he knew by heart.

"I was just out the door to the gym," said Monica Miller. "It's good to hear your voice."

"I'm in town."

"No school?"

"Have some personal things going on."

"Are your parents okay?"

"They're fine."

"You sound weird."

"You wanna meet up?"

"When?"

"Now. We could go to Mariella's."

"I really have to go to the gym. And I'm sort of seeing someone, just so you know."

"Who?"

"He's actually a teaching assistant at NYU. You'd like him, I think. He's English. He says 'feck' instead of 'fuck.' He looks like William Hurt. So, what's going on with you?"

"I should go."

"Look, call me later. I'm sorry we didn't feck the night before you went off to school. We probably should have just fecked, then we'd always have this thing between us. Friends?"

"Sure, why not." He wished they'd fecked as well. *Now I'll only know one fecking girl.*

Forever.

When Charlie went to retrieve Mrs. Henderson, the car was empty. She'd retrieved herself. *Self-retrieving adults. The worst.* But he'd never seen the kitchen so lively. The birth of a new family necessarily begins with all the optimism in the world. Bottles were uncorked and popped. Mrs. Henderson heaped liver paté onto cracker after cracker.

"Your accent is divine," she told Jee-Jee. "And Rose, you have to tell me who does your toes. My girl never gets it right. *A la familia*," she toasted.

Charlie drank heartily and silently while Paula sat on the couch, looking through the family albums. He stood over her, away from the adults and their knowing corroborations about prams and teething pain.

"I might take a walk," said Charlie, playing with her curls. "Might just buy a pack of baseball cards and a quarter pound of fruit slices, for old time's sake. Maybe even a *Playboy*. Those three purchases meant the world to me. Three years ago."

"You can still do things like that. Just because I'm pregnant doesn't mean you can't be eighteen. Men act like boys their whole lives anyway."

"I don't feel eighteen. I feel as old as death."

"Look, no one's putting a gun to your head. I'm telling you right now, if you want out, it's okay. I don't care what my mom says, I can do this alone."

"But you'd rather do it with me?"

"Well, yeah."

"So, we're like a family now, you and me? And it?"

"Yes, Charlie." She arched her caramel eyebrows.

A family. Go to hell, Monica Miller. We are as solid as the steel casing of my Boodo Khan. He thought about going to Adam's Rib to toast his new status but hadn't the muscle to leave her. A wave of protectiveness washed over him. He surveilled the four corners of the living room for danger.

"I still might buy some candy. You can come with me. I can show you all my spots on Lexington Avenue. It's just a block or so away. We can even go to Mariella's."

"Your haven," said Paula.

"It used to be a lonely haven, but now it has no power over me. It's just a pizza parlor. A *family* place."

They didn't bother to say goodbye to the parents. *They* were parents, now, and could come and go as they saw fit. What a comfortable pace, he thought as they strolled, swaying their held hands.

"I used to walk ahead of my parents. Like a dog," said Charlie.

"I like it when men walk slowly."

"Did Tommy walk slowly?"

"Actually, he did. God," she said. "So much, so soon. I haven't even told him."

"Told who what? I hate Tommy."

"Then go hit him in the balls again. Is this your pizza place? It smells amazing. I'm so hungry."

"Why would you bring up the ex, you idiot?" said John. Charlie had called him in a panic from one of the worst pay phones in the world, the one that was stuck on the wall of the Mariella's men's room.

"I'm not sure why. I sort of felt like Tommy, the way we were walking. I was in control."

"Well, shit. Here's what you've got to do, bring up that smelly tall chick you fingered at the frat."

"She wasn't smelly."

"Tell Paula that you get it, that you both have a past with other people. Sit back and revel in your indiscreet night of smelly fingers."

"It was a great smell."

"It sounded grotesque. Real women shower twice a day. Once before work and once before a date. The girls at work shower three times. Four on the weekends."

"I can't believe I'm going to be a dad."

"No one can. The key is not spending too much time with the kid, otherwise they'll get sick of you."

"I guess. Dad didn't spend too much time with us."

"He's French. What did you expect?"

"I'm not going to be that way. I should get back to Paula."

"Look, some chicks have exes they just can't shake. When's the wedding?"

"What?"

"You need to hurry up and close the deal."

"Marriage?"

"Of course marriage. Maybe in ten or twelve years, when the dust has settled, and the kid is mature, it wouldn't be the worst thing to have a discreet affair."

"I hadn't thought about marriage."

"She's thinking about it. Trust me. Just ask her."

She'd gone through a slice and a half and was now jotting something down in her Mead composition notebook. On its cover, in purple glitter ink: SENIOR YEAR.

"So, what did you think of the pizza?" asked Charlie.

"Good. I was really hungry."

For her, this is just a restaurant. "Listen, we haven't really spoken about the future."

"Back at your parents', you said we were a family." She'd stopped writing, her eyes on the notebook page.

"We are. We are, but what does that mean?"

"What do you want it to mean?" Now she capped her pen, closed SENIOR YEAR, and raised her chin imperiously, bravely, ready for anything this boy had to say.

Charlie was accustomed to his future being an adventure, something that would be young for many decades. Fifty years of being eighteen, then maybe ten of being an old man, then another twenty of being an eccentric, boyish old man, one who buys baseball cards and fruit slices and *Playboy*, as a salute to the beginning. Clearly that was not how it worked; he saw that in her eyes. If he said the wrong thing, she'd leave him at Mariella's and go it alone. Then he'd be stuck forever in between: no longer Charlie the freshman, and never to become Charlie the adult. A pizza parlor mutation.

She saves her composition books. He'd seen the junior and freshman ones, full of thoughts and dreams written in a beautiful girlish pen hand. No hearts dotting i's, just lots of hopeful, loopy letters, and no cross-outs, either. Honesty needs no edits. It showed in her posture, how she wore her shoulders. He'd stolen a glance at one of her composition book's aphorisms: *Love your fate, even if it sucks.*

Heroic, dirty-blonde genius with lightning bolts as locks. *She's stronger than me. And smarter. Add the wacky blue eyes, and we're talking about a sort of superhero. A girl who can lead us into 1990 like Washington led his men across the Delaware. Face forward.*

"We should get married," said Charlie. "I've been thinking about things the wrong way. This is the best thing that ever happened to me, not the worst."

"Kiss me."

He hoped the pizza man was watching while his loneliest Saturday-night customer held the warm cheeks of a *woman* and made a life pact with sauce-tinged lips.

I want my own, I want my own, he'd wail at night as a child. He often wondered what his infant self had meant, but it wasn't until this moment that he understood.

Chapter Twenty-four

A HORSE AND CARRIAGE and a driver in her top hat waited outside the New Hope courthouse. It was parked here on weekdays, in the hope that there might be newlyweds and they might want a ride. Paula had grown up feeding the horse, and they'd already decided to ride the carriage to the Logan Inn after the ceremony.

It was a warm November morning in New Hope, Pennsylvania. Charlie was comfortable in his suit; he only needed it and a cashmere Burberry's scarf that had been Jee-Jee's, one of many hand-me-down wedding gifts that had been bestowed on them by the Greens. A weathered (but still intact) set of Louis Vuitton luggage. A fur stole for Paula.

They'd decided to limit today's festivities to two witnesses, Rose Green and Mrs. Henderson, and have a real celebration with family in the summer after the baby arrived. Charlie and Paula had slept separately the night before, Charlie at the Logan Inn, in their wedding room. A restless night atop the sheets. He'd expected to be hungover on the morning of his wedding. That was always the story he told himself. After being at a bar in New York with John. So many toasts. So much advice. Champagne deep into the night. Instead, he'd had orange juice and a burger in his room and watched *The Honeymooners*: the brassy big-band intro while fireworks go off in the background; the camera panning up to a starry night; Jackie Gleason's face, superimposed on the moon. Charlie could barely keep his eyes open while he watched a live audience on a Saturday night in 1955 applaud Norton's entrance.

"They think he is a fool, Charl, but Norton? He is the wisest of them all," Jee-Jee had said. "In fact, he reminds me of you. A skinny genius. A true compliment, no?"

Charlie watched the good-natured sewer worker with vaudevillian elbows yell for his best friend to come out: "Ralphie boy!"

While Norton waits, he looks at his watch, puts it to his ear, frowns, then bangs it once, just so, against the breakfast table. He puts it back up to his ear, turns to the camera, and smiles.

Jackie Gleason was probably grabbing a drink, thought Charlie, and Norton was forced to improvise.

People can be so selfish. I hope my mom isn't drunk tomorrow.

*

Charlie waited across from the courthouse, red and yellow leaves drifting over his new shoes. Now would be a good time to be a smoker, he thought, watching a guy in a jean jacket light up in the distance. The guy looked Charlie's way, then darted into an antiques store. *The shopkeeper won't like that. He and his cigarette will be out in no time*—but even after many minutes, nothing. Smokers have all the luck, he thought, stamping out a pretend cigarette. *I want to see my wife-to-be. I hope she shows.*

Paula had bought a new white dress for the occasion, not a wedding dress, just a white dress. When she tried it on for him, she looked more like an old-fashioned nurse than a bride. It fit so cleanly over her imperceptibly swollen belly.

I need to unzip that dress soon, he thought, though John had said that wedding night sex was the most overrated sex a man could have. "No drama. Might as well go right to the room service menu and pay-per-view."

Charlie wasn't sure what they would do with the hours in between the courthouse and bedtime. Paula didn't want a photographer, or a big lunch. The flowers came from Mrs. Henderson's garden. The dress she paid for on her own. They'd considered spending the day looking for a house to rent, but the Realtor refused to bother them on their special day.

"We could get drunk and have day sex," Charlie had suggested on the phone, the night before.

"Maybe," said Paula. "Don't worry. You're definitely getting lucky."

"Not too much drama there."

"I'm tired of drama, aren't you?"

"I guess."

"You *are* showing up tomorrow, right?" she asked.

He'd said *Of course*, but she had her doubts. Her mother said it was fifty-fifty, as it is at all weddings. So Paula called Tommy in an irrational panic. She told him to wait by the phone the next morning, in case she got jilted and needed his chest to cry on.

"I'll help you bring up the baby, if the gent doesn't do right by you," Tommy had said.

In the morning, she came to her senses and tried to call him, to tell him not to worry, but there was no answer. While Mrs. Henderson brushed her hair, she left a message on his machine: "Listen, Tommy, I overreacted last night. I just—I *know* you, and I really hope you don't do anything rash. I feel guilty enough that you came over for coffee. I love Charlie, and I know he loves me."

He'd begged for the coffee date, a chance to apologize. Some closure. So while Charlie was in Philly, shopping for a suit, they met in Mrs. Henderson's noontime living room, the emptiest room in the world; against open windows, gossamer curtains sounded like sailboats a million miles away. The scene suited Tommy, who'd sobered up, lost his muscles, broken things off with Iñez. He'd seemed refreshingly mortal to Paula. Gentle, like an old, sweet Irishman slurping his tea through missing teeth. But after hanging up the phone on her wedding morning, Paula was sure he was skulking nearby. Drunk, chainsmoking, dangerous.

"Mom, if you see Tommy, don't be all flirty. Tell him he has to go."

"I don't flirt, Paula."

"I'm serious."

*

The wedding chapel was a converted courtroom. Streamers and plastic flowers lined the aisle, whose carpet was fifty years removed from showing its pattern. And all of that bunting from an ancient Fourth of July. Mrs. Henderson blubbered in the front row, while Rose sat a few rows back. She said it was to give her camera better perspective, but Charlie saw something in her purse: a plastic bottle of Tropicana orange juice that was no doubt a stiff screwdriver. After a slug, he saw his mother's face. The human face can't suppress a booze cringe.

Charlie's voice didn't crack when he said *I do*, and their kiss was as tender as the very first one. *Man and wife.* Nothing ever sounded better to Charlie. He wanted to carry his wife to the inn, throw her on the bed, and rip off her dress.

"This is amazing," he said to Paula as they ran down the aisle, then down the stairs.

"Husband," she yelled in the stairwell.

"Wife," Charlie yelled back.

They could hear their mothers' applause trailing them down the stairs.

"Screw it," said Charlie. "We should really celebrate. Let's take the horse and buggy to New York." He slapped open the courthouse doors and raced down the steps. There, holding the bridle, wasn't the Dickensian costumed woman, but Tommy.

"You got a nice steed here, Paula," said Tommy, lipping a cigarette.

"What is he doing here?" asked Charlie.

"He's doing nothing," said Paula.

"Looks like I'm too late," said Tommy. "Ah, well. Take good care of her, gent." He dropped his cigarette dangerously close to a hoof, then lit another. "Was up all night. Guess I'll be a day boarder and sleep it off. Enjoy the nuptial bliss."

"I left a message that you shouldn't be here, Tommy," said Paula, hugging her new husband from behind. Tommy popped the collar of his jean jacket and jogged down Main Street, lipping his cigarette.

"Even on her wedding day, they're still lining up," said Mrs. Henderson, who had just come outside with Charlie's mother.

"You handled that well, Charlie Bear," said Rose.

"I didn't do anything."

"Which was the right thing to do."

"I defeated him, and he still shows up? That's not fair. And how did he know it was today?"

"We'll talk later," said Paula.

"I have to live with that memory forever."

"Charlie Bear, just enjoy the moment," said Rose, closing her eyes and inhaling the air. "You can really smell the river in the air. Just like the Seine."

"This isn't the Seine, Mom."

"All rivers are sisters, sweetheart."

She's buzzed, thought Charlie. Probably started around nine this morning.

"Tommy looked like he lost some weight," said Mrs. Henderson. "It suited him."

"Jesus," said Charlie. "I can't believe we're talking about him on our wedding day."

"You have Paula," said Mrs. Henderson. "Tommy doesn't have much."

"How did he know today was the day?" Charlie asked Paula.

"I called him. It's a long, boring story. Let's get in our carriage and go to the inn."

"Listen to your wife, Charlie," said Rose. "You'll look back on this day and only remember the good."

He wanted to sink her then and there, destroy her croissant-and-Chablis vision of the world. Call her an orange juice drunk and a senseless romantic, even if it meant taking his own old, romantic soul down with the ship. But he saw sadness in her eyes. He saw an old woman for the very first time, the whites of her eyes lubricated in pain, a hardened face connected by a network of tiny purple capillaries. The November daylight of New Hope was such an honest light. Not even Le Bon Marché makeup could hide her from it. She'd been a beautiful woman. All those nights with the two of them touching shoulders on the couch, luxuriating over black-and-white photos of young Paris Rose.

Charlie made a wish that his mother would never, not for a single moment, lose her 1950s joie de vivre even if it meant having always to drink her way back there.

"Listen, you two, said Mrs. Henderson, "Get in that buggy, go to the inn, make whoopie, and stop with all the Tommy nonsense. The two moms are going to Martine's to tie one on and cry about our babies."

The tears came early, as the moms watched the horse slowly pull its cargo down a carless Main Street. The clomping of hooves was the only sound in the air.

There was silence in the cab, too. While Paula clung tightly to Charlie, he couldn't help but scour the streets for any sign of the Irishman.

*

In homage to their wild Plaza night, they ordered room service, two colonial wedding luncheon platters. Oxtail stew and pot roast, straight from the inn's famous rathskeller, where Washington's faithful drank and prayed in December 1776. History's meat stunk up the wedding suite. They had to open all the windows.

"You realize that Tommy could be staying in this very building."

"We could find out. I could ask him to go. He'll listen to me."

"I don't want you speaking with him. Not ever again."

"He's just a friend. An old guy with lots of problems."

"A *friend*? I have friends, too. Remember that frat party I told you about?"

"I don't care. I don't want to know. Did you have sex?"

"Define 'sex.'"

"Gross. I'm going for a walk."

"Wait. No. You can't. Alone on your wedding day?"

"Who was she?"

"She's a girl in my class. We were drunk, you were on the river cruise. Well, you were supposed to be on the river cruise. I'm sorry. We've both made mistakes."

"*I* didn't have oral sex with anyone."

"We didn't have oral sex or any sex. No, Paula, please don't go."

She slammed the door behind her so definitively that the slam subsumed its own echo. *My wife sure knows how to slam doors*, thought Charlie. *My wife.* He opened the door in the same spirit it had been closed and ran after her. He was prepared to run for miles, tackle Tommy, and carry her back across the threshold, but there she was in the lobby, slumped in a chair in her white dress.

"He's not staying here," said Paula. "And if he were, we'd go to another inn."

"Thank you. I'm sorry I brought up my frat night."

"If you ever cheat on me, I just don't want to know. Lie, and lie well. And don't cheat in New Hope. It's a small town. Everyone's slept with everyone, and bad news travels fast."

"Have you slept with everyone?"

"I've had a lot of boyfriends. There's really not a lot else to do here. So just don't let me catch you."

"Paula, I have zero interest—"

"Shh. Let's go upstairs."

They had soft, soundless afternoon sex in the woodsy room. It seemed more a demonstration of sex than sex itself. Two instructors teaching a class on the missionary position.

"Married sex," said Charlie.

"It was cute." She usually kissed him before disappearing into the bathroom but didn't today.

"I don't think I should wear my wedding dress all day," she said over running water. "If you want to go to the rathskeller for a drink, I'll meet you there."

"I'm going to wait for you," said Charlie. "We shouldn't be apart today, not even for a second."

There was no response. After a minute, Charlie got out of bed and pressed an ear to the door. "Are you all right?" he said, finally. "Are you crying? You miss him, don't you?"

"I miss my mom," she sobbed. "I miss my fairytale wedding. The soap in this bathroom is so tiny and skinny. Why did they even bother to wrap it?"

"Let's get the hell out of here," said Charlie.

"Not the rathskeller. It smells like wet deer."

"No. Fuck the rathskeller. Let's have a real honeymoon, like my parents did. In Paris. At the George Cinq. It's like the Plaza, but a million times better. My mom already offered us a honeymoon."

The bathroom door opened to a bright face. "Paris?"

"I should have thought of it before, but you said you didn't want to make a big deal out of this."

"I know, but today I realized it is a big deal."

"Let's go find my mom. She'll be well-buzzed and will write me a check."

"We shouldn't take advantage of her. We can save up and go in the summer."

"She drank vodka at our ceremony. Paying for our honeymoon will help with her guilt, and besides, by the summer I'll already have inherited my paintings. Our honeymoon should start tomorrow."

"I need time to buy clothes. I have to go to Philly to buy Paris clothes."

"Sweetheart, you buy Paris clothes in Paris."

"Oh my God!" She jumped into Charlie's arms. His knees buckled, but he held on. "I can't wait to tell Mr. Frommer that I'm going to make it."

Chapter Twenty-five

ROSE AND JEE-JEE SPOKE with Miss Pettibone and they agreed to defer Charlie's education for at least the semester.

"You only honeymoon once in this life, ideally," Rose had said to Miss Pettibone.

"Ideally," said Miss Pettibone, who could not help but envy the young marrieds. Her honeymoon had been three nights in the Poconos. Lots of reading in bed. Lots of silences.

"Charl will find his way back to you," Jee-Jee said to Miss Pettibone.

"I'll be right here if he does," said Miss Pettibone, then made a wish that she would never see Charlie at college again. That he would escape College Hall for them both.

*

They flew first class out of JFK. Ten nights at the George Cinq, whose monstrous gilded mirrors and muted, white-gloved staff permitted the children in and sat them in a divan while their room was being readied.

"Do you think people were staring at us?" asked Paula. "We're so young to have all your parents' leather luggage. People must think we're waiting for the real adults. I'm happy I'm turning twenty this trip."

"We're wearing wedding rings, and Europeans applaud young marrieds. They don't snicker like Americans, who always assume there must be a pregnancy."

"But there is."

During the flight he'd forgotten. He'd fallen asleep in the dark cabin, over the dark Atlantic, his wedding ring finally numb to his sleeping skin. He awoke to the smell of coffee, so happy to be going on the date of a lifetime. But when he looked over, she was chatting up the stewardess about where to find maternity clothes on the Left Bank.

They'd agreed that she could have one glass of champagne each day. It was at Charlie's urging; he didn't want to drink alone. But Paula said her body craved healthy things. So there they were in the hotel lobby, Paula aglow with her plate of fruit and glimmering bottle of Vittel water, and Charlie raccoon-eyed with his second vodka and *jus d'orange*, his fingers stained from the *pain au chocolat*. Just like Jee-Jee's were, after Nutella.

"Sometimes I forget you're pregnant," said Charlie.

"Well, I don't have that luxury," said Paula. "We should wait till our last day to get Mom's napoleons, don't you think?"

"Your mom can get those things in New Hope."

"Just look at my cranky husband."

"Do you like saying 'husband'?"

"I do."

"We haven't said the other thing. At least you didn't say it back."

"You know I love you." Paula kissed Charlie's cheek. But she hadn't actually said it yet. She'd said, *Me too*, or *I feel the same way*.

"I'm probably the only married guy whose wife hasn't said it to him."

"I bet there are plenty of girls who say it and don't mean it. In fact, I know there are."

"I'd even downgrade us from a suite to a traditional room just to hear you say it."

"Let's just stop talking about it. It'll happen when it happens."

"So, it'll definitely happen?"

"Listen, I've never said it to anyone. My mom told me to wait as long as possible, and that's what I'm going to do. A girl has to protect herself."

A pantsuited French woman appeared from behind the divan to announce that their room was ready for occupancy, that their luggage had been unpacked for them, and that she could confirm today's lunch reservation at the horribly expensive restaurant inside the Eiffel Tower. It was where Charlie's parents had eaten on the first day of their honeymoon and was one of a hundred immutable plans he'd made. Paula had tried to warn him against such rigid days, but he'd been planning this trip his whole life. *Mr. Frommer had other plans for me*, thought Paula. *Backpack, Eurail Pass, three summer months in the same pair of shorts.*

"Did you have a nice trip in, Mr. and Mrs. Blue?" asked the woman.

"It's actually 'Green,'" said Charlie.

"Oh, of course, so sorry. Mr. and Mrs. Green, of course."

She reminded Charlie of Miss Pettibone. The perfume, the exposed neckline, the short stiff hair. "A honeymoon, I understand?"

"Yes," said Paula. *I can't believe I'm Mrs. Green. I can't believe my last name is a color. Forgive me, Viking ancestors.*

"We have you for ten nights in one of our nicest suites," said the woman. "Just this way."

The key fob was hoary with tassels and heavy with brass.

"The key's gigantic," said Paula. "Do we each get one? I'm happy I brought my bigger purse."

"You leave it at the front desk," said Charlie.

"Yes," said the woman. "It's better this way, so your bag isn't so heavy while you explore. *Voilà*. Your room, Mr. and Mrs. Blue."

The woman marched the length of the room and opened French doors that led to a balcony overlooking the hotel's marble courtyard below, where breakfast waiters palmed trays of coffee.

"This is what I love," said Charlie. "When you first get to Paris and it's still breakfast time. Everything's ahead of you."

"Yes," said the woman. "The beginning of the honeymoon is, um, magic, yes?"

Paula saw that her fingers were ringless and for a moment envied her freedom. She wished the French woman were her friend. Having only a husband in Paris was starting to feel isolated. Or maybe it was the jet lag? She'd been warned by Charlie about a dark surreality that comes with that first time change.

"I will leave you to the magic," said the French woman.

Don't go, thought Paula, but she did, leaving them to the sounds of breakfast winding down, Charlie worshipping from the balcony. "I love how noise carries in a French courtyard."

"Let's get undressed and go to bed and watch French cartoons and fall asleep together," said Paula.

"I thought we could do that on our second-to-last full day. Also, you don't want to fall asleep in the middle of your first day in Paris. You'll wake up, it'll be dark out, and you'll feel really lost. Trust me."

"Okay, I guess you're the boss," said Paula. She found her makeup bag and the master bathroom.

Down below, Charlie spied an older gentleman reading the newspaper. Trousers hiked from his crossed legs revealed green socks and a bare shin. Gray Hitlerian mustache. His was the only table set for one. He sat, amid families and couples, at the center of the butter and jam carnival.

Wealthy and lonely, thought Charlie. He wondered what the man would do after breakfast. Where would he take his little mustache? Probably to lunch, where there would be another table for one. Then the evening edition and dinner for one? The old man would read a paragraph, look up at nothing in particular, and make certain his demitasse cup was in its saucer, or marvel at his table's wealth of sugar cubes.

Charlie promised himself, then and there, that he would never become the lonely old man. That he'd do everything in his power not to let Paula down. *Women leave men all the time, and the men don't see it coming. And once they leave you, there's nothing you can do except roll the sugar cubes like dice, but every time they will come up fortuneless. As blank as your future when your love vacates your life. The old man must pray night and day that death is soon and dreamless. How many times, before going mad, can you ask only yourself, "Remember when she kept calling us Mr. and Mrs. Blue?"*

Charlie shut the French doors and drew the curtains, there and in the bedroom, and turned off the lights. He got undressed and found Canal+ on the color TV. *Golden Girls* in French.

"What are you doing?" asked Paula. She opened the bathroom door just enough that he could see a bare shoulder. "I was going to take a shower."

"Come here. We're going to do what you said. I don't want a stuffy lunch on our first day. I just want you to be happy. Forget about all my plans. I'm not the boss."

She turned off the light and got in bed.

"Oh my God, these sheets. So crisp. Hold me. I hope it's a *Golden Girls* marathon."

"Me too," said Charlie. They embraced under the sheets, the only people in the world, except for the bilingual Golden Girls.

"Hey," said Charlie. "Remember when the lady said Mr. and Mrs. Blue?"

*

It was under black and blue clouds that the Greens waited in line at the Louvre, sandwiched between two gaggles of Japanese tourists.

"French skies are so pretty," said Paula. "So low and moody. Maybe we should've brought an umbrella?"

"It's not going to rain on us. It wouldn't dare."

They'd spent the majority of their first three days in bed, really only leaving the room so the maids could clean. Now they held hands easily, their fingers intertwining with a consciousness all their own, and when they kissed it was as if they accessed a second chamber of warmth, a fantastically balmy one they hadn't known could exist. They carried on this way amid the Japanese, shrouded by the foreign chatter. Kissing your wife on your honeymoon was probably the greatest home field advantage a man could have, thought Charlie. Hold hands, advance in line, kiss. Repeat.

"I'm happy," said Charlie. "Really, really happy."

"Me too. I wasn't sure I would be."

"I could tell when we checked in."

"When did we become *us*?" asked Paula, finding new comfort in the brownness of his eyes. Today, despite the murky sky, they were rich with light. And the whites so clear. They'd eaten well, slept long, and had tender sex. Washed one another in the shower. They brought chairs out to the balcony so Charlie could show Paula the old man.

"I don't know when we became us," said Charlie.

"It's magic," said Paula. "Like the hotel lady said, and to think I was jealous of her ringless fingers, even for a second."

They kissed while the Japanese throng cascaded by them, reminding Charlie of the schools of fish that had circumvented his boyhood raft ten summers before. That used to be his safest memory, but it had become trite. *True love has no use for the past. Its fuel is* now. If only they could explain that to the nostalgic old breakfasting bastard and the croissant crumbs in his stubby mustache. After the longest kiss of their lives, they entered the museum, where Paula and her disposable camera made a beeline for the *Mona Lisa*.

"Whatever you do, don't photograph it," Charlie called after her. "It's supposed to be bad luck."

"Frommer's says it's the most photographed painting in the world, and we haven't even taken a single picture yet."

"Okay, but slow down."

"I don't want to miss it."

"It's not going anywhere."

"My mother says nothing is guaranteed."

"We're skipping over so many great paintings," said Charlie, trying to catch up.

"Okay, well, maybe it'll be the only shot of the trip. I used to think there'd be this famous honeymoon album. Maybe we'll just remember everything and remind each other all the time."

With that, she stopped in her tracks and waited for him to reach her, for him to hug her from behind, which she knew he'd do. Take her hands and raise them angelically, barely kiss the vein on her neck. With every touch, his education grew more and more complete. He was learning her, and she was falling in love.

I'm going to wait to say it, though, thought Paula. *Wait until it bursts out of me.*

Chapter Twenty-six

BY THE ONE-WEEK MARK of their honeymoon, they had gotten into an impressive vacation rhythm: long athletic mornings walking the city; lazy afternoons in one park or another; and nights spent at the hotel restaurant, at the same table reserved for Mr. and Mrs. Green, bedecked with candles and flowers. Charlie had expected the trip to be a boozy affair, a farewell to his youth before fatherhood via a bottle per meal, including breakfast. Instead, he drank little more than Paula and got high on their togetherness, on the narcotic ether of their little world that traveled so floatingly about the old city. Like Cézanne dreamers.

"We must walk ten miles every day, but my feet feel nothing," said Charlie.

He didn't even need for her to say it any longer; others were saying it for them. *Just look at those two, so in love.* The oblivious poster children for honeymoons in Paris. Even the woman who'd checked them in was compelled to pick fresh flowers from her own garden to adorn their dinner table.

"I bet she expected honeymooning Haircuts, who come to Paris to hoard magnums and dabble in gout," Charlie had said. "I could tell she had her doubts about us."

"I thought I'd need to befriend her while you left me for the cafés," said Paula.

"That was sort of my plan, which now seems crazy."

*

"3.14159265358 . . ." Paula knew pi. She'd memorized five new digits on the trip and would sing the number while getting ready in the morning, Charlie at the balcony, checking on his mustachioed man. But on the morning of their seventh day, the math song ended: "Three-point-one-four."

"You know the rest," said Charlie, watching the man complain about an overdone poached egg.

"Blood," said Paula. "*Blood,*" she yelled. It echoed in the courtyard, where the old man's wide, outraged eyes found Charlie's. Charlie used the split second to psychically apologize for the *petit déjeuner* interruption before whipping around. Paula's mouth agape, a crimson spot on the carpet, her newly acquired slip bunched between her legs.

"What happened?" asked Charlie "What did you do?"

"I didn't do anything." She crumpled to the carpet, spread herself over the dark spot. "It's over. It's over. Now you can be free of me."

"Nothing's over," said Charlie, joining her on the floor.

"Call the front desk, ask for an ambulance. It's over."

"My wife is bleeding from her private parts," said Charlie. He was on the phone with *monsieur*, who asked him to kindly hold so that his colleague, *madame*, could better assist. "Sanitary napkin? Hold on one second. Paula, do you want—"

"Ambulance, sweetheart."

Just this past summer, Charlie had told the Very-Brown-Eyed Counselor about waking up in Paris to that famous ambulance sound. How it was more of a serenade than an alarm. Now he was inside of that sound with his sobbing wife. In a Citroën ambulance. Such a weird shape, like an eclair, and the EMT guys in robin's-egg-blue aprons and cafeteria hats. Only one of them had some English. "Your wife, she is with a baby?"

"Yes. She's pregnant."

"For how long?"

"Eleven weeks, maybe twelve."

"*Oui*," he said, but it sounded like "way." "Your stomach, *madame*?"

"Cramps," said Paula through a pink oxygen mask. *The French and their fucking pastels*, thought Charlie, while the EMT guy placed the hearing end of his stethoscope uncomfortably close to Paula's barely hidden nipple.

"Way," said the EMT guy.

"Way what?" asked Charlie, brushing away the stethoscope.

The man wrinkled his lips. "Eh, the doctor, eh, will show you, eh."

The doctor was sparrow-like and bespectacled. A tiny, immaculate human being who did not smile and did not blink.

"Your wife will be fine," he told Charlie in the waiting room. "As you might know, there was a complication with the pregnancy. I am sorry, but she has lost the baby. These things happen, but she is young. For now, she is resting. We gave her a sedative. She should stay here tonight, then see her doctor in the States when you return."

"We should return tomorrow?"

"It's not necessary, if you wish to finish your trip."

"Can I see her?"

"Soon, not yet. She asked that you phone her mother."

"Me?"

"Of course. The phones are this way. Come."

He walked quickly for a small man. Hospital employees got out of his way. *He's a good doctor. He's despised. I'll write a story about him tonight. No, I'll get very, very drunk tonight. Sit in the George Cinq courtyard at the old man's breakfast table and order a bottle. I wonder if they cleaned the rug.*

"I told Paula, no collect calls unless there's an emergency," said Mrs. Henderson. "Is everyone okay?"

"Paula's okay. But we're in the hospital."

"Oh my God, I knew it."

"Paula had an accident and lost the baby."

"Oh, no. Oh, no, my poor baby," Mrs. Henderson cried.

"She's still with the doctor, who said that everything—"

"Thank God I knew to get my passport renewed. Mothers can sniff out trouble a mile away. I'm coming there, Charlie. I'm calling your mother. You stay with her, honey, you hear? Tell her I'll be there as soon as possible. Mama's coming."

Charlie sat in the waiting room. The French waited differently. More like Angelina at the beauty parlor, with curlers in her hair and a magazine. Not anxious. Resigned to a fate, while Charlie sat, hunched over, wringing his hands. He thought of *The Day After*, the TV special about nuclear war in which Midwesterners dropped their rakes to watch mushroom clouds appear over the farmlands of Indiana. They didn't know exactly how their lives would change from that moment on, but they knew that everything would be different and much, much worse.

*

The doctor announced that Paula was ready to be seen by tapping Charlie's head with his clipboard. "Come," he said.

Charlie had never before been nervous to see her, except for that very first day at the Oyster House, when his legs and heart did what his brain could not.

"Hi," he whispered, forcing a smile. It was how people were supposed to enter hospital rooms. He saw his mom do it many times, visiting his grandmother. Hushed tones and prepared smiles.

"I'm sorry, Charlie."

"Shh."

"We lost the baby," said Paula.

"It's okay."

"Once we get back home, you can do what you want, I just don't want to fly alone."

"I called your mom, and she's coming."

"She is?"

"Yeah."

She looked so peaceful. Was it the drugs? Or maybe when something dies inside of you, the body is secretly relieved that its workload is lessened.

"Thank you for calling her. Oh, you look so handsome right now."

The doctor raised his eyebrows at Charlie, insinuating that it might be the sedative talking; he looked like a wreck. It was close to dusk. Eight hours since she began to say pi.

"You can come back tomorrow," said the doctor. "And if all is well, you can take her home."

"I'll be fine," said Paula, her eyes closed. "You should have fun tonight. I guess this isn't the honeymoon you always dreamed of."

"It's exactly what I dreamed of."

"I love you," she said, before drifting off to sleep.

"*Honeymoon*," said the doctor. "Un-y-moon."

*

The hotel had sent flowers to their suite, wishing Mrs. Green a speedy recovery, but despite the best efforts of housekeeping, the carpet stain was still visible.

"They'll probably replace the entire carpet, once you leave," said John.

"That stain is all we have left," said Charlie.

"It's not like it was a person. It was around the size of a sesame seed."

"I wish I could cut out the piece of carpet."

"Then they'll charge you for the whole thing. Look, what happened sucks, but it gives you a chance to just be eighteen."

"I want to be older right now."

"That's so stupid."

"You're stupid."

"Look, you have a free night in Paris. Consider it a gift from the sesame seed. Live out your Hemingway fantasies. Go to a strip club. Wake up on the steps of Montmartre with a stripper and a bottle of Veuve."

"Veuve is for Haircuts."

"Girls love that orange label."

"I'm not interested in girls, and Paris fantasies don't exist. Hemingway was a liar."

Charlie spent the night huddled around the stain with four minibar bottles of Absolut. "Minibar Absoluts are the Veuve Clicquot of real life," he'd told John.

He fell asleep around the tiny patch of discolored wool, surrounding it fetally, dreaming that it sprouted limbs and organs and emerged as a carpet-covered baby that danced around its father while he slept. He awoke stiff-backed, a minibar bag of French Cheetos in his fist. Its absurd mascot was a toucan wearing a beret and sunglasses.

Ordinarily he wouldn't have thought twice about the cartoonish bird, but now he sobbed that his child would never get to giggle at a beret-wearing toucan. And what of a future child? He'd saved baseball cards. Even written the child a letter from his pre-wedding night at the Logan Inn about the value of nonconformity. *She's not fertile.* He threw the Cheetos bag out the French doors, watched it float down to everyone's fertile Sunday breakfast paradise. The mustachioed man was nowhere to be seen. *The real French go straight to lunch on Sundays*, thought Charlie. *And so shall I. Down a bottle and toast my carpet baby.*

*

Outside the hotel, a barrage of ambulance sirens chased him down the tiny Rue Marbeuf and into a bistro where a harpist played. Little was open, save for places with harpists. The hotel had one, too.

"Do you have a table away from the harp?" asked Charlie, but the maître d' couldn't understand why anyone wouldn't want to be near the precious instrument. So he left the tuxedoed man and wandered down the surprisingly familiar little street. *Of course it's familiar*, he thought. Next to the Résidence Hotel, boasting two stars, was his family's gallery. Closed on Sundays and the store window gated, a prototypical Miro, black dots and red sticks, was asking 110,000 francs. As a child, he had helped his grandmother slide the golden numbers into a placard, always beginning with F. A trio of duck-footed French Haircuts sporting sweaters across their shoulders jabbed fingers at the storefront's price tags, particularly *A Bust of a Man in a Gorget and Cap* by Rembrandt Harmenszoon van Rijn. *F12,000,000.*

"It's a steal," said Charlie.

"Voof," said the French Haircuts.

"You should buy it. Ask your parents to buy it for you."

"*Va te faire foutre.*" But even to Charlie's trained Franco ear it all sounded like "voof." French Haircuts spent all day with their starched polo collars flipped up, telling American tourists to go fuck themselves.

"No, really, you should buy it. If you do, my grandmother will reward me for the sale by protecting the soul of my dead child. Come back tomorrow when the gallery opens. Now I'm going to find a bottle of Chablis and steak tartare and raise a glass to you pussified French fucks."

Chapter Twenty-seven

"CHARLIE'S MOM WANTED YOU to have this envelope, honey," Mrs. Henderson said to Paula while they waited for room service. They'd decided to remain in Paris for the final nights of the honeymoon. Paula and Mrs. Henderson were to share the king bed. Charlie would sleep on the couch.

"What is it?" asked Paula. It was Monday, dusk. Their flight home was on Wednesday morning. One precious day left, thought Charlie. One last chance to undo the trip's deathly turn. But with Mrs. Henderson taking over cheerleader duties, Paris was reduced to its clichés.

"Well, open it and find out," said Mrs. Henderson. "Can you believe I'm going to have frogs' legs tonight after all these years? I was always curious what the fuss was. Go on, honey bunny, open it."

Since the hospital, Paula mostly slept, and Charlie mostly drank. She'd wake up, tell him *I love you*, then fall back asleep.

He spent the last two afternoons reading their Frommer's and writing letters to Francis and Miss Pettibone on hotel stationery. At first, he didn't have the heart to ruin his perfect tale of autumn in Paris but couldn't help but add the postscript: *Paula lost the baby. We're fine.*

He sent a postcard to Neil, c/o the Sansom Street Oyster House: a photo of Hemingway at the Ritz Bar. *The original Crumb*, wrote Charlie. *PS Paula lost the baby. We're fine.*

"You open it, Charlie," said Paula.

"Well, someone should," said Mrs. Henderson. "All Rose said was that it's just a little something for Paula that can be all her own."

His mother's envelope smelled like her bedroom. Lilies of the valley. Overpowering. "It's a note," said Charlie. "And a check."

Dearest Paula,
I wanted you to have something for a rainy day so you can treat yourself.
We love you and are so sorry about what happened.
Rose & Jee-Jee

"Wow," said Charlie. "Twenty-five thousand dollars."

"What, that's crazy," Paula said from the bed.

"Oh my God," said Mrs. Henderson. "We need to buy her something. Maybe a box of napoleons."

"I can't accept this," said Paula.

"It would be rude to turn this down," said Mrs. Henderson. "She'll insist anyway, honey bunny."

"Well, then I should call her," said Paula. "Do you mind if I call her from the room? And I really don't want to call her collect."

"No, of course. Use the phone," said Charlie. He wasn't sure if he was proud of the ease with which his family could cut checks with all those zeros, or if he felt betrayed that his mother had, at least temporarily, made his wife the wealthier spouse.

*

On their final day, Paula felt well enough to go outside. Mrs. Henderson led the charge. Despite Charlie's request that the day unfold easily and slowly, they were among the first tourists emptying out onto the Eiffel Tower's observation deck.

"What a world," said Mrs. Henderson from behind the coin-operated lookout binoculars, and Paula smiled for the first time in days.

"My mom's not afraid to be happy," she said.

It was precisely what the young couple needed to see, a survivor. Their last-day leader's will to see it all and do it all was a shot in the arm for Charlie and Paula, who happily followed, happily listened to her tour book narrations about the City of Lights, until they came upon a group of college students on the Left Bank, laughing and flirting by a fountain. It was Paula who let go of Charlie's hand, as if urging him to join his truest peers and reclaim his place as a freshman.

"Why'd we stop?" asked Mrs. Henderson. "I think I want crêpes for lunch."

"Just give us a minute, Mom."

"What is it?" asked Charlie.

"You know," said Paula. "Those kids."

They had, of course, caught his eye. Their vitality. White teeth and happy voices.

French Lacrosse Girls. French Francises. And a French Charlie in the mix as well.

"What about them?" asked Charlie.

"Maybe you should go back to college. I could live with Mom; you could visit me when you want. Lead a normal life. Now that the baby isn't, well, here, there's no rush to move in together."

He envied the French students' lightness, but he'd always envied the lightness of others. The kids who didn't overthink every blasted thing. Who didn't worry and want, but played, while Charlie sat with Angelina on a park bench, wondering when his life would start.

My life has started, thought Charlie. He grabbed his wife's hand. "Crêpes it will be, Mrs. Henderson."

"Charlie, look at me," said Paula.

"No, you look at me. As soon as we get back, we'll look for a place to rent in New Hope. I'm going to borrow money from John that I'll pay back when I get my inheritance in the spring, plus I'm going to get a job."

"We could use the money your mom gave me."

"No. That's yours."

Paula held his face. "I've always wanted someone to grow up with. Really grow up with. Watch me become a woman, while I watch him become a man."

*

They rented an old farm keeper's cottage, restored as a one-bedroom duplex, with a backyard that sloped down to the river. A mere half-mile from Martine's, where Charlie had started working as a waiter. He'd trail the Smiths bartender some nights, in the hope of one day becoming the head barman. Paula worked part-time at Grand Designs, selling scented candles and wispy scarves to her mother's friends, and in her free time she was the homemaker. She wanted to impress Charlie with her young womanhood, her wife skills. *If I can't give him a baby, I'll give him a home*, she thought. *Anything to keep him near and happy.*

But it didn't come naturally to her. Her mom was a pro. Mrs. Henderson didn't need five rolls of paper towels to clean the tub, or need an hour to sew a button on Charlie's shirt. And when she'd fail, she'd curl up in bed and pray to God that Charlie would forgive her, not leave her because of an under-seasoned meat loaf or another sexless week. Since the miscarriage, lovemaking was physically painful and just plain sad. All she wanted at night was her head on his chest, the banality of TV, a clean goodnight kiss.

"It's fine," he'd said. "We have our whole lives to sleep together."

But her mother had warned her that when things go cold under the sheets, the party's over.

Charlie wasn't at all frustrated. He was fully invested in his Martine's job, making practice drinks at home, his red Mr. Boston's cocktail book always at his side. At work he'd all but befriended Gary, no longer wary of any man who'd inhabited Paula's past. It was clear: Charlie and only Charlie was married to the most coveted girl in town, and it came with privileges. If they were late returning a video, no late fee. The manager of Blockbuster had a crush.

"How's that wife of yours?" the guy at the wine store asked, throwing in a free corkscrew.

The weeks were deeply patterned. Movie night. Mrs. Henderson night. Groceries on Saturday and yard work on Sunday. Contentment sped up time. No sex, but no fights, either. And little on the horizon except for the late April day, Charlie's birthday, and the delivery of a John Singer Sargent portrait of four daughters playing in the shadows. As per his grandmother's wishes, it had a present value of just over two million dollars. When it came, they decided not to immediately sell it; they replaced Paula's Frucor ad above their bed. It was a dim painting. A nineteenth-century doll lay lifeless at one of the girl's feet.

"I could ask my mom for a different one," Charlie had said to Paula, but she'd become attached to the little dolly.

"I love it. It reminds me of the strength you need to leave the dolls of childhood behind."

She saw a therapist every other week and was on a drug called Prozac, which dulled her a little, a film of translucent bubble gum between her and the world. A subtle difference, but Charlie noticed. Or perhaps it wasn't the drugs, but the serene marriage, the hand-me-down silverware that didn't match? He found it all quaint and interesting. Collecting coupons and raking leaves.

"Weird existence for a nineteen-year-old millionaire," John had said during a visit to Martine's. "A Blockbuster drop-off box shouldn't make you so happy."

"But it does, participating in the *Dignidad*."

"Angelina meant *sacrifice*; she didn't mean talking to a bar customer about the durability of Weber grills while overthinking a Harvey Wallbanger."

"It was a White Russian. You and I are different, John."

"Look, Paula's a sweetheart. And yes, she's not bad-looking, but in ten years, when your friend Francis is fresh off his honeymoon and expecting a kid and making somewhere around—"

"Paula probably can't have kids."

"I just want you to know there are many fish in the sea who can."

"Paula's not a fish."

"Listen, I have something for you." Lying in both his palms was a black square with a belt clip.

"What is it?" asked Charlie, paranoid it was some sort of recording device. John could be merciless with Charlie's intimate details.

"Are you serious? It's my beeper."

"I didn't know you had a beeper."

"Of course I had a fucking beeper. Everyone on Wall Street has one, but now I have a car phone, runs me $750 a month, but your beeper? Paid through for life."

"Why do I need a beeper?"

"Look, that wife of yours should always be able to reach you. Mom and Dad agreed with me. When she—I mean if she gets in trouble—all she has to do is dial the number on the back, and it'll beep, and show you where she's calling from."

John demonstrated, but instead of a beep, there were the low-techno notes to a song, a Christmas song.

"'I'll Be Home for Christmas'?"

"It came preprogrammed that way. One day you'll thank me."

"I don't want your creepy Haircut pals calling me."

"No, idiot, it's a new number; it's written on the back. My old number is attached to the bomb. That's what sweet six-figure Shannon Chang calls my car phone."

"Thanks, John," said Charlie, clipping the device to his belt, certain he'd wear it every day of his life.

*

In August, the Smiths bartender left Martine's for nursing school and Charlie was given all of his shifts. He made his commute along the towpath, which he could join from his front door. The perfect icebreaker for tourists.

"You know that path that mirrors the river?" Charlie would say. "Well, mules used to tow barges all the way to Philadelphia. Barges full of supplies that helped us win the Revolutionary War."

The towpath's canal was usually filled with water, but this summer it had been sapped by the sun and barely on the fragrant side of putrid. The sunflowers that exceeded Charlie, the scraps of metal that glimmered as he walked by; the towpath is helping me win my *evolutionary* war, he thought. He'd gained muscle over the months, doing yard work, and didn't want the summer to end. Behind the bar, he felt competent, in charge; the same was true at home, despite their infrequent lovemaking. The man of the house had grown some scruff on his face and was supporting them in every way. He'd all but stepped into manhood, in work boots, at the age of nineteen, his penny loafers on the furthest closet shelf. The Boodo Khan? Dead batteries for half a year, now.

*

Topless, Gary skulked in on a slow Saturday afternoon. "Look at that little beard you're trying to sprout," he said, rubbing Charlie's chin.

"Don't touch the bartender. Never touch the bartender."

"You and all your rules."

"You're lucky I don't make you wear a shirt, Crumb."

"I'm not a Crumb, dude."

In walked a girl in a short summer dress wearing glasses, strands of her brown hair dyed technicolor. She stopped before the bar, placed her hands on her hips, and rolled her tongue against her cheek.

"Bet you don't recognize me," she said to Charlie.

"I remember customers by their drinks. White wine spritzer? No, that's someone else."

Monica Miller was the only real brunette he knew, and this girl shared little. Shorter and bustier, and her navel, exposed by a knotted T-shirt, was tight, athletic. Monica Miller's navel was buttressed by a mound of baby fat that Charlie had once found quintessentially femi-nine, and Paula had neither fat nor an athlete's muscle, just soft white skin.

"The last time you saw me, I was a chubby little Madonna freak, sobbing because you didn't like girls with brown eyes."

"The barkeep, here," said Gary, "has made quite a splash in our little town."

"I looked for you at Penn, and your roommate said you left for here. What happened?"

"It's a long story. And a good one," said Charlie. "Brown eyes. Oh my God, you're the Very-Brown-Eyed Counselor!"

"It's Lucia, Charlie. Remember? Rhymes with fuchsia?"

"Right, of course. Wow, you look different."

"I joined Stanford crew. We're Division I, by the way. No rowboats, like at camp."

"*Lucia*. God, what a great name."

"It's all I know, and slightly less demeaning than the Very-Brown-Eyed Counselor."

"Charlie here likes names," said Gary. "Names and eyes. What did he say about Paula? 'Colors like places in the Caribbean where God kicked over the inkwells.' Can't he just say *blue*?"

"I know, I know, *light eyes*," said Lucia. "You know, you really got under my skin with that whole eye obsession. I got colored contact lenses and they scratched the shit out of my retinas, and now I'm stuck with glasses forever, but a lot of guys at Stanford like a girl in glasses."

"I'm so sorry, Lucia." What a tight little tummy, thought Charlie. Good for her. "So, what brings you to New Hope?"

"Eventually," said Gary, "everyone stops here, and then they get the hell out. Well, most of them. Cheers, Lucia."

"So, what happened at school?" asked Lucia

"I'm on an open-ended life break."

"Jeez."

"At first, we all thought he was playing townie with the town princess," said Gary, standing to stretch and show the bespectacled girl the tangle of his armpits, "but he hasn't missed a day of work."

"Why aren't you wearing a shirt?" she asked.

"Ah, a fine question—"

"Actually, whatever, I don't really care. It's just sort of gross."

"It's really good to see you. I miss that summer."

"You mean last summer?"

"So much can happen, freshman year," said Charlie, wiping down a brass beer tap for effect.

"Can I have a beer or something?" asked Lucia.

"I should probably ask for ID, but we're old friends, so—"

"He carded me on his first day," said Gary, "and I'm ancient. My name's Gary, by the way."

"Lucia, well, by now you know. Rhymes with—"

"That really is a beautiful name," said Charlie. He wished he'd known it better last summer. Everything could have been different. Rowing crew, he thought. Of course. Something like crew was all she needed. And her eyes, more honey brown than mud brown, sparkling behind those big lenses.

"Well, Charlie, I was always a fan of your colorful surname."

"We should hang out," said Charlie. "My shift's almost over."

"Sure," she said. "I didn't come all the way here to see Mr. Smelly Pits."

"Deodorant is for phonies," said Gary.

"Is Charlie a phony?"

"Charlie? Nah. He's a romantic."

"Reformed romantic," said Charlie.

"Bullshit," said Gary.

Chapter Twenty-eight

THEY SAT ON A dock adjacent to Martine's, where Paula had first taken Charlie.

Lucia was pointing her chin at the sun, talking and sunbathing at once. "Hey, mind if I take off my clothes?"

"What?" In a panic, Charlie felt for his ring, then remembered Martine's edict about men's wedding bands clanking against glassware. The sound annoyed her. No rings.

"You're going to get naked? Here?"

"No, silly, I have a bathing suit underneath. And the sun feels so good."

"Oh." He was going to add that it was a free country, then turn his head. Instead, he watched her strip down. There was a tattoo of the Apple computer logo that disappeared under her bikini bottom. *Why can't I tell her about Paula?* he wondered.

"Guess what I have?" she asked.

"A tattoo?"

"That's not what I was going to say, but yeah. Do you like it?"

He nodded, one too many times. *In her mind I'm eligible. How I've missed that feeling.*

"It didn't hurt," she said.

"What didn't? Life didn't? It shouldn't when we're young, right?"

"What? What the hell are you talking about? I meant the tattoo didn't hurt. Anyway, what I brought is—well, I'll give you a hint: it's silver and has your mother's initials on it."

"No clue," said Charlie.

"The flask, Charlie. Remember the last day of camp?" She found it in her bag and handed it to him.

"I'd forgotten about that thing. Still full, too."

"Oh, trust me, it's been emptied many times over the year. I always think of you when I take a sip. We could take a sip now. It was sort of a dream of mine that we'd meet up one day and do that."

They passed the flask back and forth, the Very-Brown-Eyed Counselor smiling wide, now that her flask dream had come to pass.

"Well, you seem really happy," said Charlie, trying not to stare at the tattoo and where the bottom of the apple lived.

"I am now. I mean, *right now,* being with you. Just brings back good memories. Not really memories, because camp wasn't the happiest time for me. More like, I've sort of thought about you a lot over the school year. God, feel that sun."

The sun did feel good, and he shut his eyes so he could face it. "Good old late-summer sun. It tries so hard to stay warm for us."

She wasn't speaking, but he could feel her breath on his neck. *She's staring at me. Or maybe her eyes are shut, too, and she doesn't know how close we're sitting.*

"*Us,*" said the Very-Brown-Eyed Counselor. "I love hearing you say that pronoun."

Charlie heard her take a deep swig from the flask. "I have to tell you something important, okay?"

"Okay." His eyes were still shut. He'd heard her say *something important* before, and it usually preceded a proclamation about a new diet or some gossip about an ex-boyfriend. Charlie was utterly comfortable in her company, especially with his eyelids receiving heat. So much young, soft talk around the campfire. *Maybe she's engaged?* He hoped she was, so he could spill his secret, then hoped she wasn't so that he could bask in her flirtatious heat. This teenaged girl, smelling of suntan lotion, and the September sun—he was becoming aroused.

"I can't wait anymore." Her mouth was over his. Charlie kept his eyes closed. He was paralyzed. If he pushed her away, she could fall in the river. So he allowed it. Just sat there, letting her wash him with her lips, her tongue.

"I'm sorry," she said. "But I had to do it. I've been in love with you, and it's been killing me inside.

"Listen, Lucia, I have to tell you. Listen, Martine doesn't let the bartenders wear wedding rings at work. She was jilted, I think, or something."

"Huh?" Now she stood up.

"Uh, I got married."

"Why the hell didn't you tell me before I made a fool of myself? You haven't changed."

"I should have said something, but I—"

"Whatever, it's fine, really," she said, hurriedly dressing. "I mean, congratulations, right? Marriage, wow!" Now she'd taken off her glasses and was furiously rubbing her eyes, rubbing her face. "Well, look, I'm going to go. It was nice to see you. Oh, and here's your flask back. Have a good life, Charlie Green."

*

Girls, he thought, slowly making his way back to Martine's. *Girls are a little bit crazy, but that's okay, they grow out of it. Women are awesome. Lucia is a girl and Paula is a woman.* He thought of throwing the flask in the river but didn't feel the need for the gesture. Stuff like that comes after a young drama, and there was no drama just then. Only a kiss, perhaps his last non-Paula kiss ever. *And that's just fine.*

"What's that?" Charlie asked Gary, his eyes adjusting to the bar's old salt mine roots. "God, I love this bar's darkness. Bad things can happen under the sun."

"Lemon squares."

"What?"

"Paula and her mom just dropped off a basket for you. Don't worry, I haven't had one yet. They said it was your favorite. Lucky man."

"They were here?"

"Yeah, you didn't see them? I told them you were outside with that wacky chick." There was a red and white cloth towel from their kitchen lining the basket. Odd to see something from the kitchen out in the world. Out of place. *It misses home.*

"Did they say anything about Lucia? Did they see her? Us?"

"Nope. Just said they worked all day on getting your lemon squares right."

He ran outside, ran to the dock, then ran out to the street and looked both ways. Back to the dock to see if there were any remnants, anything. Then back into the salt mine darkness.

"Fuck," said Charlie, reaching to feel the soft terry cloth towel.

"What is it?"

"Probably nothing. I have to go," he said, grabbing the basket.

"Hey, can I have a lemon square?"

"No."

*

When he got back home, the front door was wide open. Charlie's gait changed from a jog to something comically ginger. An inept 1950s TV detective.

"I'm home," he said in a weak singsong voice, from the front porch.

This is stupid, he thought and marched right in. "I'm home!"

There were no bad signs in the kitchen. Perhaps it was conspicuously clean, but if Mrs. Henderson had assisted with the day's baking it made sense. He placed the basket on the kitchen counter and shouted upstairs, "Thank you for my treats."

Their key basket was empty except for the car keys. She'd taken her house keys. Which meant she still had use for them. A good sign. They owned Mrs. Henderson's second car, a 1981 Buick Regal. It was still in the driveway, which meant she was either upstairs or with Mrs. Henderson, together in her primary car, a 1985 Buick Regal. Charlie decided she was home. She was upstairs, getting ready for their Saturday date night. He sat on the couch, crossed his legs, and reached for the *New Hope Free Press*.

"Just occurred to me that your mom only buys Buick Regals. She probably thinks all that dashboard wood is real. How was your day? The lemon squares look amazing. Work was slow. Old friend from camp came in. Nice to see her. She lost a lot of weight. I hope she finds the right guy. So where are we going tonight?"

He lay down on the couch, shut his eyes, and *willed* that he would feel her weight over his body, but it was exhausting, this telekinesis, and he fell asleep. He awoke to nighttime, the lemon squares precisely where he'd left them. It was a little after nine. *A three-hour nap. The longest of my life.*

"I think I fell asleep," he shouted upstairs. "People say that naps are refreshing. This one made me feel dead. Maybe I'll see if the answering machine is blinking. Maybe I'll fix myself a drink and make my way upstairs. Maybe you left a note."

*

He left twelve messages on Mrs. Henderson's machine, the last one at three in the morning.

I don't know if you saw something today, but things aren't always how they seem. I love you so much.

Her clothes were still in their drawers, her green Samsonite World Traveler in the closet. Her valuables, however—her birth certificate, her passport, and her Pennsylvania Savings & Loan passbook—were missing. She hadn't spent a dime of Rose Green's $25,000 gift. In fact, with interest, it was worth $25,177, an appreciation that delighted her.

"Interest is like magic," she'd said. "Maybe one day, when we're old, it'll be worth double. Then I'll take *you* on a vacation." She'd held her head so high.

Okay, so something is definitely *off*, thought Charlie. I won't say *wrong*. Not yet. He hadn't closed the blinds, nor gotten under the covers. He hadn't the heart to concede it would turn morning without her, but it had. The birds were chirping, light pouring in, and he was alone, in yesterday's work clothes, the same he'd worn when he'd been kissed. He hadn't even taken off his boots.

I'll shower, change, throw away the clothes from the kiss. Maybe burn them outside. Then I'll buy flowers, go to Mrs. Henderson's. No, no flowers. It'll make me seem guilty. I'll pick sunflowers from the towpath. I won't even bring them to Mrs. Henderson's, I'll just put them in a vase here. Next to the basket of lemon squares. The kitchen counter will look like a painting, and its yellowness will lure her back home.

*

The Hendersons' driveway was empty, the front door locked. Charlie looked in every window, but nothing seemed out of the ordinary. No signs of distress or a changed life. The garden flag flapped in the wind. Charlie waited for hours, pacing, practicing speeches. Some were angry.

You shouldn't just leave. Even if you're upset, you should give me the benefit of the doubt. You should give me the chance to explain.

Some were desperate.

Without you, my life is a horrible mistake.

Every hour, he would hear the Sunday peal of bells, a sound he'd never noticed. A grotesque sound for the internally desolate. God didn't rest on Sunday; he used the day to practice torture.

The bedroom above the garage was unlocked. He'd stashed away a shot glass and the Hendersons' ageless and endless plastic liter and a half of Gordon's vodka that he used for post-lovemaking nightcaps. Today, he needed some protection from the hourly bells: an empty stomach buzz. He also needed to be with the pile of *TV Weeks*, which he ordered chronologically. *Bonanza* to *ALF*. That they ended abruptly in 1986, with the fall TV preview, sat heavily with Charlie. It was probably when Paula moved out of the house to Philly that Mrs. Henderson stopped adding to the collection. He could just see her waving goodbye in the driveway. Paula's tears, Mrs. Henderson's tears, Gary waiting patiently in his admirably beaten pickup. That was a beginning for Paula, and now Charlie wondered if today she might be experiencing an end.

"Where's my love?" he pleaded with ALF. "Where's my heart?"

He brought the vodka downstairs and sat outside, against the garage door. A slumped-over sad sack.

"Girls forgive sad sacks," John had said. "It's a rule for them."

*

"Come on, Charlie, let's go inside," said Mrs. Henderson, snickering and shaking her head. "Just look at you."

"Where is she?"

"I'll explain everything inside."

She'd pulled into the driveway at dusk. Charlie had closed his eyes, hoping to hear the sounds of two car doors, but there was just the one.

"You went to the airport?" Mrs. Henderson held the handles of a Philadelphia International Airport Duty Free shopping bag.

"You really hurt her this time, Charlie. Now you come sit down at the table, I'll heat up some pasta."

"I did nothing wrong."

"Necking with an almost-naked girl right under her nose? I thought she would faint."

"Where is she? *Please*, Mrs. Henderson."

"Charlie, she asked me not to say. She needs time. I'm not even sure what she'll settle on."

"What do you mean?"

"Which country."

"Country? But she didn't take her suitcase. Her clothes."

"Well, today she withdrew your mother's magnificent gift and we bought all-new. Then to the American Express office for her traveler's checks. Never saw her sign so many things. Think her hand got cramped, poor thing."

"She can't withdraw from a bank on a Sunday."

"She grew up with the banker's son, and they made an exception. She's beloved, that girl of mine, and you treated her like a dog. I'd usually heat up the pasta on the stove, but it's been a long day, so I'm going to cheat and use the microwave. You know all about cheating, don't you, Charlie?"

"*Listen*, Mrs. Henderson—"

"Watch your tone with me, Charlie. I spent all yesterday and today trying to pick up the pieces of my daughter's broken heart. It took all the strength I had to put her on that plane."

"Okay, fine. When is she coming back?"

"It was a one-way ticket, Charlie. I insisted it be that way."

"This can't be happening to me."

"She's always thinking about what other people need. What you need, what her boyfriends needed, never about herself. Now this is her time."

Charlie's chin was on the dining room table, his arms lifeless at his sides. He looked into the convex glint of the Parmesan cheese spoon. *If I can just focus on that light forever. Mrs. Henderson can feed me through a tube. Then eventually I'll expire, and the emptiness will be gone.*

"Chin up, Charlie. If it's meant to be, you'll find each other again. But Paula has very strict rules when it comes to cheating. She got that from me. One and done. I was the same way with her father,

Mr. Asshole. I always told her that you men are just no good when it comes to fidelity. And as much as we both cared for you, it's the truth. 'Men cheat, women weep.' Well, excuse my French, Charlie, but that's bullshit. How about 'Men cheat, women go to Europe.'"

"What? No but I didn't really—"

"I've said too much. Now eat some pasta, you'll feel better. Come on, Charlie, take that chin off the table, hon. Charlie?"

Chapter Twenty-nine

CHARLIE HELPED FRANCIS AND the Lacrosse Girl move into their off-campus two-bedroom apartment, sophomore year. It meant a day off of work for Charlie, on an early September Tuesday.

"She'll come back, Charlie," said the Lacrosse Girl. "Eventually."

"Should we separate the refrigerator into two zones?" asked Francis.

Francis had told Charlie about their agreement: she was allowed to date other boys while Francis would remain faithful only to her. There were ground rules, however: the Lacrosse Girl vowed never to bring a date back to their new apartment, and Francis got a weekly sleepover.

Charlie had no time for modern arrangements. "You two should live as one," he said. "Create something beautiful and indivisible."

"Maybe one day," said the Lacrosse Girl.

"Maybe next semester," said Francis.

"I wish I knew where she was," said Charlie. "I'd leave tonight. But Mrs. Henderson might not even know where she is, and if she did, she probably wouldn't tell me."

"Some girls like to be rescued," said the Lacrosse Girl, peeling away Francis's dividing line of fridge tape. "But from everything you've said,

Paula doesn't seem that way. She has her own sense of timing. Perfect, like a wild animal. When the time is right, she'll know what to do."

John had a darker perspective. "Europe gobbles up American girls, and most can't find their way out of the belly of the beast. They sleep with married men. Usually butchers, fishmongers, ugly men with big hands. They get lost in lives not their own, turn into an old, bent-over Frenchwoman some tourist will point out in five decades. 'Look at that poor old thing.'"

Charlie tried not to despair. *She'll realize that she overreacted*, he reassured himself. *Get the Frommer's out of her system. She'll miss me and call the beeper in the middle of the night: I'll be home for Christmas.* But there wasn't a peep from her, nor a beep. Just the clothes she left behind, which Charlie would check on every night, just in case they'd been moved or altered. Her pile of underwear. If only she'd come home while Charlie was at work and unfold one, maybe throw it on the bed. A clear symbol of her return. Forgiveness. Lovemaking to follow.

"Maybe you should go back to school," said the Lacrosse Girl. "You could crash on our couch."

"Yeah," said Francis. "Might as well get a degree while you wait for her, but it's not a sleeper sofa."

He'd entertained it for all of two seconds, but what if word ever got to her that he'd also abandoned ship for college—Nicoletta's college? In novels, word always reached one of the estranged lovers. *Maybe word will get to me first*, he thought. *All is forgiven, but I live in Marseille with my husband, the oyster shucker.*

"I need to stay put, in New Hope, and just wait for her," said Charlie.

"That's romantic," said the Lacrosse Girl.

"For me, it's a matter of survival."

"Well," said Francis, "I hope you'll come and visit us. You shouldn't be alone all the time."

"I will visit, but you should know I'm not lonely. Missing someone is a way of being with them. A horrible way, but a way, nonetheless."

*

Francis and the Lacrosse Girl walked Charlie out. Moving had made them hungry, and there was a Hoagie Heaven right beneath their apartment. There was also a Hoagie Heaven right next to the Oyster House, where Charlie hadn't set foot since before the wedding. He planned on walking there today in search of any news from Paula. Maybe she'd sent Cactus and Neil a postcard or confided something in a letter. Or maybe just stepping into the first temple of their togetherness would inspire the gods, and the young couple would be allowed to pass into the future together.

Charlie hugged Francis and the Lacrosse Girl. They told him to stop by later and see their apartment in its finished state, and he said sure, but the hug felt like a terminal goodbye. He watched them through the store window, holding hands in line and looking at the menu board, each of them pointing at their desired hoagie. Charlie wished they would turn around and point at him, the pariah who should exit their world at once, for their hearts were still developing. Theirs were minor muscles, while Charlie's was tested; it had become a world-class muscle. *My heart has turned pro*, he thought, and touched his chest.

I will always remember them like this. Next in line at Hoagie Heaven. They will forget me, as they should; I'll be a footnote on graduation day.

"Whatever happened to that kid?"

Better yet, I'll be a small part of Francis's smile when he throws his cap high in the air. Oh my brawny heart.

*

There was, in fact, a postcard behind Neil's left shoulder. The Colosseum. Italy, of course. It was pinned over the one he'd sent from Paris. And behind that, dozens more. He could make out a pastel drawing of the Everglades, and perhaps an ancient one of Mt. Rushmore. Mailmen must love postcards. Or maybe it breaks their hearts. Surely postcards are little cries for help. Rescue me.

"Rome," said Charlie.

"What about it?" asked Neil.

"The postcard."

"Just got it yesterday. Didn't think he was the postcard type."

"He?"

"Tommy. Up and quit his job out of nowhere, the schmuck. Now he lives in fucking Italy."

The tunnels beneath the Colosseum where the lions waited. The elaborate cages and tunnels that led to the arena. The lions teased into ferocity with cow bones and pig's blood.

"What did he write?" asked Charlie. "Did he say anything about Paula?"

"I don't really read those things. I just like the pictures."

"Shit," said Charlie. "He's trying to pick up her scent. Could I have a martini, please?"

"Listen, kid. When I started working here as a busboy, there was a barmaid who looked like Liz Taylor. Took me a while, but we became a thing. Then a ritzy customer came in wearing a suit and tie. A sophisticate is what he was. Brought her flowers. Took her to see a show. He stole Sandra from right under me. Here's your bowl of vodka."

"I didn't steal Paula from Tommy."

"Sure you did, but that's how things work. In fact, that's one of the best reasons bars exist, so that sophisticates can steal the prettiest barmaids. Make them their own. Took me a while to realize that. But even to this day, I think she'll walk back in here. Frankly, it's the only reason I've stuck it out this long. Could have retired to AC a decade ago."

"AC?"

"Atlantic City, asshole. It's the Europe of Philly."

"I just wish she would come back so I could explain."

"What? You cheat on her?"

"Not exactly. I was kissed, and she—it doesn't matter."

"You really want her back?" asked Neil.

"Of course I do."

"Cactus, watch the bar for me."

Neil tossed his apron aside and made a beeline for the kitchen.

"Am I supposed to follow him?" Charlie asked Cactus.

"Yes," said Cactus. "You'll find him out back, in the trash alley."

Neil was seated on a stack of wooden oyster crates branded KUMAMOTO, RASPBERRY POINT, NONESUCH. *Why can't life be as magical as the names of oysters?* Charlie wondered while Neil smoked a cigarette with three fingers, as if the Pall Mall were a dart.

"So, Sandra, the love of my life gets snatched up by a sophisticate. So what does Neil do? He saves up every penny and buys the fucking joint. I put the business in Sandra's name and mine so that if she comes back, she'll know I'm in it for the long haul. That I mean business."

"You bought the Oyster House? You own this?"

"Sandra and I own it, but don't tell anyone. Only Cactus and a few other people know. Crumbs find out, they'll stop tipping. Plus, I blame this make-believe owner schmuck for all sorts of shit."

"But she hasn't come back, right?"

"Not yet. I have a feeling the sophisticate one-upped me and bought her a boat. She loves to fish."

"I'm sorry."

"Who knows," said Neil. "Maybe she'll get tired of island-hopping with the sophisticate and come through those doors during happy hour. Or maybe tomorrow afternoon, while the Crumbs are sucking down their scotch and sodas. You know, one of these days."

"I hope Paula doesn't meet a sophisticate."

"Nah, she doesn't care about boats and things like that."

"You think Tommy went to Europe to find her? Should I go to Europe to find her?"

"What's the name of the place you bartend at?"

"Martine's."

"Buy it." Neil flicked his cigarette at a bucket of sand but missed. "Zilch for eleven this week. Got to get back to the bar, or *the owner* might get pissed." Neil cackled, patted Charlie's shoulder, and made his way past the oyster crates into the kitchen. "Que paso, banditos?" Charlie heard him yell.

He retrieved Neil's errant cigarette and sat where he had sat. A flick of two fingers and it sailed right into the bucket. A bull's-eye.

Kumamoto, Raspberry Point, Nonesuch.

Life *is* magic, he thought.

*

"I'm so sorry, Charlie, but the restaurant is not for sale," Martine told Charlie.

"I think I could get close to two million dollars for my painting, maybe even more."

"I don't have any kids. I don't have a husband. All I have is this place, and I love watching young people like you and Paula get your feet wet at Martine's before moving on to do wonderful things."

Martine was a tall woman with high cheekbones. There was something Native American about her. Paula had said that she was part Sioux. There was a serenity about her that Charlie hadn't the heart to plead against.

"Well, would you mind if I put our honeymoon picture on the mirror, behind the bar?" he asked.

"That would be just fine." Martine smiled sympathetically and patted Charlie's shoulder.

Why does everyone pat my shoulder these days?

*

Six weeks to the day after he was kissed by the Very-Brown-Eyed Counselor, there appeared in Charlie's mailbox a beautifully wispy Par Avion envelope. How it crinkled in his trembling hands. The postmark: Aix-en-Provence.

Dear Charlie,

First, I owe you an apology. I had a breakdown on the flight over and if it wasn't for this girl I sat next to, I don't know how I would have made it through that flight, through customs, through everything. So, I should have called you, or been in touch, and I'm sorry I didn't, but I didn't have the power to do much of anything until recently.

I have had lots of time to think. The girl I sat next to, she took me in. She and her family live in Aix, and I help them around the house and work at the local café.

I do not think I left you and New Hope because I saw you kissing some girl. That put me over the top for sure. (Who was she by the way? Are you still with her?) Until now, my life has been distant from me. Boys, boys, bars, bars, Tommy, you, shotgun wedding, miscarriage, all before 21. I haven't lived. I feel as if life has lived me.

Things feel different and better here in France. Maybe it's the new language? Maybe it's the distance from anything and anyone I know? I don't know, but I feel at peace. Maybe a little wiser. And grateful. That's the word. I feel grateful for so many little things each day.

I'm not sure what the future will bring. I'm taking this new life day by day. I have to ask you not to come and try to bring me back home. I know that's what you'll want to do, and I'm trusting you with my address in case you want to write me back, but please let me be. I don't think I've digested all that happened to me and us, perhaps one day when I'm sitting in my favorite lavender field (you should see it, so beautiful, Charlie) it will all come rushing back, and I'll miss you. For now, I'm like Pink Floyd said, comfortably numb.
xo, p

*

"I scoured our memories for Pink Floyd and just couldn't find anything," Charlie said to John.

"I bet it's the French girl from the plane. The French have the shittiest taste in music. Even when they like a great song, it's for the wrong reasons. I bet she planted her headphones on Paula while she was having her meltdown, and on came 'Comfortably Numb.'"

Charlie was halfway through a bottle of chardonnay, the letter ironed flat from the continual passing of his hand.

"She always signed our letters 'xo, p,' so that's good."

"Look, she wouldn't have told you her address unless she actually wanted you to rescue her. What you need to do is call the travel agent, book a one-way, first-class ticket on Swiss Air—which is superior to Air France and their shitty Folger's coffee, by the way—then you'll want to spend a night or two in Paris to acclimate, then take the Eurorail to Aix. Book a room there for three nights in their best hotel. If it's available, choose the honeymoon suite. Show up at her farm, or wherever the hell she is, at dusk, not the morning. Bring wine. And a single flower. Bring the letter and wave it at her."

"She said not to go, John." Charlie poured the second half of the bottle into a goblet. "Just made myself a Mom drink."

"Listen: Shannon Chang is here—"

"Who?"

"*Shannon Chang*? Six-figure Shannon Chang, by far the hottest girl at work? Anyway, she's a girl and she agrees with me, that you should go to her."

"Even if I decided to, I don't have the money for a trip like that."

"I'll loan you the dough. Just pay me when you get back. Sell your John Singer Sargent when the price is right."

"I sort of wanted to be the only one in the family not to sell Grandma's paintings."

"Don't be so self-righteous. Look, I'll wire you ten K. Now go retrieve Paula."

Paula. On anyone else, the name would sound so short and common, thought Charlie, but on her it was an ode to soft vowels. *Paula.* He closed his eyes and felt the peach of her navel against his lips.

"What time do you think the travel agent works until?"

*

John called the family agent, made all of the arrangements, and told Charlie to consider it a twentieth and twenty-first birthday gift.

"Buy a new outfit," John had said. "White. White Levi's and a white shirt, make it a button-down shirt, and tuck it in. She'll know you mean business."

He asked Martine for a week off and told her why.

"Of course. Good luck, Charlie," she said, her Sioux cheekbones consulting with her tribe's ancient American gods for a positive outcome overseas.

He was to fly out of JFK, via the TWA terminal that was shaped like the massive wings of a soaring phoenix, invoking his parents' golden age of travel, the 1960s. He got to the airport hours early, nervous, wanting to cultivate a golden age of travel pre-flight buzz. He'd watched a couple say their goodbyes: the teary girl going Charlie's way, and her boyfriend also blubbering, repeatedly bringing a keepsake to his lips. The girl had been gifted flowers. *I hope they make it alive all the way to wherever she's going.* He'd sit next to the girl later at Flute's, the terminal's champagne bar, part of his mother's lore. Always two glasses at Flute's for good luck. The girl was on her second. She seemed so carefree, now. No more tears. No more flowers. He needed to know they weren't discarded. He needed to know that her tears were as real as her boyfriend's, that international airport terminal bars can't just go and turn heartsick blood into *bubbly*.

"I saw you earlier," said Charlie.

"Huh?"

"When you were saying goodbye."

"Goodbyes suck," she said. "Where are you flying to?"

"Paris. You?"

"Same!" Her second flute was half-full, but she ordered a third. "I'm not such a good flier. Need to be just a little tipsy. I'm Mallory, by the way."

"Charlie."

"Are you on the 8:55?"

"Yep." John had booked him in first class. The odds they'd be seatmates were minimal. Charlie intended to use the flight to practice a new religion—one of deep thoughts of Paula. The Boodo Khan was loaded, both sides of the tape, beginning to end, "Comfortably Numb." Mallory wore a hippie vest, lots of beads. She'd already moved her barstool closer to Charlie and had slid her Zippo and Marlboro Lights into his drinking territory.

"Listen," she said. "I know this sounds weird, but we have, like, another two hours before we board. Do you want to hang out together? I get really nervous before these long flights."

"What happened to those flowers?" asked Charlie.

"Huh?"

"The flowers your boyfriend gave you."

"Oh, those? I left them in the ladies' room. He means well, but it's my junior year abroad. I've been with him since, like, freshman year, and—I don't know, I just left them on the baby-changing table in the bathroom." She waved her hand at the nuisance of flowers and lit a cigarette. "So, what's going on with *you*?"

"Nothing much. Listen, I'm traveling first class, and think I might go to the TWA lounge, so—"

"Oh, I'm traveling first, too. My boyfriend saved up and surprised me. Let's finish these, then we can go to the lounge together."

Fuck.

"What's your seat number?" she asked.

"2G."

"Shit. I'm 7B. Maybe we can switch?"

The boyfriend would be mortified, thought Charlie. He probably worked all summer to afford that seat.

"I'm actually going to the souvenir shop for my French relatives," said Charlie. "So maybe I'll just meet you at the Constellation Club."

"Say what?"

"That's the name of the lounge."

"Oh, I could totally go shopping with you. It's a specialty of mine." She laughed heartily, turning Charlie's stomach.

"Souvenir shopping for my French relatives is sort of sacred to me," said Charlie. "So, I think I should do it alone."

"I totally get it. Well, I'll see you in the Star Club. Happy shopping!"

Charlie waited till she was out of sight, then raced to a dim Houlihan's, lit like a New York subway platform. The demonic fluorescence will forbid her, he thought. And he never saw Mallory again—not in the airport, not when boarding, and not on the flight. It was possible she slipped by, though Charlie liked to believe the boyfriend came for her, proposing marriage in the Constellation Club. Or maybe she was struck by a rogue wave of guilt about the flowers and altered her life course.

Worse: perhaps while waiting for Charlie at the Constellation Club she fell asleep. Poor Mallory in her beaded vest, loopy from champagne. *Ah, well*, he thought, donning his headphones on the plane, *I will not drink on this flight. Nope—nor will I eat, until that first a.m. croissant.*

"Could you please wake me for breakfast?" he asked the stewardess.

After two champagnes and seven Houlihan's double screwdrivers he was drunk. *Drunk* drunk. Paula used to say "You can get drunk, but never get *drunk* drunk, at least not in front of me. It scares me."

Charlie began his loop of "Comfortably Numb."

"Any dinner for you tonight?" asked the stewardess.

"No, thank you," he slurred.

"Let me know if you change your mind," said the stewardess.

"Numb," he mumbled. "No pain."

"I'm sorry, did you say you wanted champagne before takeoff?"

"Is there a girl in a beaded vest behind me, in the seventh row? 7B, I think?"

"7B's actually our only empty seat."

"Sure, I'll have some champagne. She would have wanted me to."

I shouldn't have left her alone.

"No one should be alone, right?" he asked the stewardess. "Not even me?"

He fell asleep before the champagne reached his seat. The stewardess wrapped him in a blanket, turned off his seat light, and buckled him in, making certain no one was watching as she dabbed away his still-streaming tears.

Chapter Thirty

JOHN HAD HAD THE good sense not to book Charlie at the George Cinq. Instead, he chose the four-star Sofitel, across from the Gare de Lyon train station, where Charlie would depart in two days' time for Aix-en-Provence. The 4:15 p.m. got in at 8:20. A car with tinted windows would be waiting to whisk Charlie to La Villa Gallici, where he would remain, exclusively, until the following predusk, when the same car would drop him at the base of the Chemin des Vignes and he'd walk the half-mile to the mailing address Paula had provided, in his white jeans and white button-down shirt, her letter in one hand, a flower in the other. Wine and the Boodo Khan would round out his satchel.

While in Paris, at the Sofitel, there was a safe distance between Charlie and that half-mile walk. Two nights. *Oh, the gorgeousness of time left*, he thought on his first night in Paris, watching a waiter carve a leg of lamb right in front of his nose at the Gare de Lyon's elegant Le Train Bleu. The rosemary was sourced right from Aix-en-Provence, the waiter had said, and rubbed the rosemary garnish into his palms and brought them to Charlie's face.

"The smell of Provence," said the waiter. "Beautiful countryside and beautiful people there."

Upon his third and final leg of lamb meal, forty-five minutes before he was to board his train, the smell of Provence was terrifying. He'd forecasted their reunion every day for close to two months. The silence. The embrace, the life-clinging embrace that would bruise their rib cages but seal their souls. The lovemaking. No words for days. Then, one morning, she'd smile.

"Hi," she'd say, and a ray of morning sunlight would activate her azure eyes.

Please come true, pleaded Charlie, while the waiter collected his dish of barely eaten lamb.

"Not to your liking?" asked the waiter.

"No, just—" He rubbed his stomach, and the waiter returned with a shot of alcohol so profusely aromatic it burned his nostrils.

"Voilà! Also, from Aix-en-Provence," said the waiter.

Orange peel, more rosemary, maybe lavender? What is this bitter place where I'm headed?

*

Charlie couldn't get to his hotel room fast enough. Stepping off the train, his feet sharing Provençal bedrock with Paula was just too much. He thanked God for the car's tinted windows and the sullen driver's wordless ride. He would need every hour of the next twenty-four to prepare for her. Practice the first *hello* over and over. Ask the hotel to clean and iron his colorless uniform. Try to sleep. Try not to drink until T minus one hour. Or T minus two hours. Haunt the hotel's lobby and bar but cover his face with the *Herald Tribune* just in case. John had said that Aix was a small city through which coursed an advanced gossip network. "Like all the capillaries in your body. So lay low until the witching hour, and don't take no for an answer. She'll probably say no at first, Shannon Chang said that's how it would all unfold. What a woman, right?"

"Uh, sure."

The sun didn't set in Aix-en-Provence until around eight, and Charlie needed the cover of dusk. He'd been disciplined all day.

12–1: Brisk walk around the hotel grounds.

1–2: Lunch. No wine nor garlic.

2–3: Shower prep and outfit prep in room.

3–3:30: Long shower, careful shave.

3:30–4: Wear outfit. Tuck in shirt.

4: To lobby bar. Drink wine slowly.

6: Back to room for physical inspection of self.

7–8: Back to lobby bar for courage. Vodka, soda, with excellent local olives.

8: To car.

The sunset was among the most beautiful Charlie had ever seen. The fading light didn't soften the world, but clarified it, and Charlie couldn't help but employ that mother of all French countryside triteness: "It's as if I'm in a painting."

But what a painting. The car was to wait for him indefinitely at the top of the Chemin des Vignes, a rural road. Sunflowers, vineyards, fairytale cows with soft brown circles on their hides. Charlie momentarily forgot why he was walking down this heavenly path. *Nope, my pilgrimage will not be upstaged by a grove of olive trees.* He steeled himself against the hypnotic skim-milk light and narrowed his eyes to focus only on the farm structures in the great distance. This must have been how World War II soldiers marched through rural Europe. Necessarily oblivious to the ancient countryside, or else they'd abandon the mission and disappear into a field of lavender. He'd passed several, but they were dull with October. He could make out the weathervane atop the main house. Her house. A silhouette of an iron rooster pointing to an opening. Another lavender field, but unlike the others, this one was vivid. Electric. *This is what she wrote of,* thought Charlie. *This is her field.*

I am trespassing. He began creeping, rather than marching. Progress was difficult, and he entertained becoming the AWOL soldier.

But each step closer was the bravest moment of his life. Jee-Jee had once dispensed some wisdom: that for some people, walking across a room and shaking someone's hand could be as brave as winning a Purple Heart.

*

When he saw her at the far end of the field, he stopped, dropped, and rolled, staining his white ensemble, crunching his ribs. He'd learned the maneuver during countless fire drills in middle school, but those were performed on cushy gymnastics mats. And while the purple field seemed so billowy, its ground was rock hard. Worse, the hard earth had broken the wine bottle. The Boodo Khan, saturated with Cote-du-Rhône, sounded one last time: "Comfortably Numb." Then it burped and died.

"*Bonjour*?" asked Paula. When no answer came, she shrugged and continued examining the field and the sky. Charlie had never seen her move so gingerly. An adagio. Ballet. And that smile. He'd also never seen her—never seen anyone—maintain a radiance for so long. John had said that when girls smile in nature, it's a hippie affectation, "A pot thing."

This was different, a communion between the blue light of heaven and the matching irises that Charlie had claimed as his own. *They're no longer mine*, he thought. *They've never belonged to me. They're hers, as is this reverie. God help whoever disturbs her.*

Sometimes she would move close enough so that he could see her leather sandals and painted toes, tangerine orange. A new color for her. How cheerful. And with that, he prayed for her happiness to continue unfettered, forever; vowed to remove himself from the field as soon as she was safely distant. She didn't need to be rescued or saved. How absurd. How arrogant. How selfish.

"Stay lavender," he whispered, then trembled. He was cold with her warmth, like his one experience handling dry ice: Jee-Jee's delivery of Maine lobsters, the one huge claw that had defied nature to break its band and yawn at death. Charlie had been burned by a smoking piece of lobster ice. Delightful. Awful. But he let it remain in his palm, smoking cold but also smoldering.

Paula's quintessence had found his body, and he had never been more in love with her. Walking back to the waiting car, he beamed as his ethereal wife had; the ether had found him, too.

"At last," said Charlie. "The *Dignidad*,"

*

He booked a flight home for the following evening, then had his pre-flight lunch at the hotel bar next to a man in a green suit, whose foppish handkerchief poured out of his lapel pocket like a bouquet of dying Provençal flowers. The man was having a working lunch, going through stacks of folders, each containing a photograph of younger people, Charlie's age. He wondered if they were lost or wanted. The man wore a badge on his belt. *Criminals*, thought Charlie, although of the photos he could see, they all seemed perfectly innocent.

"Are they in trouble?" asked Charlie.

Bothered by the interruption, the man whipped around and frowned at Charlie. He was handsome, like Errol Flynn, but an ornery Errol Flynn for sure. Jee-Jee harbored great disdain for French bureaucrats, calling them *amateurs d'échec*. Failure lovers.

"They might be in trouble," the man responded. "You Americans like—how do you say? Car wrecks, yes?" He snickered and continued working.

At least the asshole was drinking wine at a work lunch, and a bottle all his own, at that. At one point, frustrated, the man slapped down a folder, which opened to the picture page, and there she was, Paula Katherine Henderson Green, smiling right at Errol Flynn.

"Oh my God," said Charlie. "That's—I know her."

"Yes? Well, she is here working without the visa. Tsk, tsk, tsk."

"What does that mean?" asked Charlie.

"It *means*, she is taking a job away from the French, and will be sent home at once. *That* is what it *means*."

Jee-Jee had also said that the failure lovers were, to a man, utterly bribable; these inducements were the reason they chose the petit bourgeois career in the first place.

"Well," said Charlie, "I happen to know that the girl in your folder will be a credit to your motherland."

At this the man simply shook his head and brushed away the notion as if he were shooing a fly.

"Well," said Charlie, wishing he'd asked his father about how exactly to *do* bribes, "I could, *monsieur*, offer you a reward for being optimistic about my friend staying in the country."

Slowly the man closed Paula's folder, patted it gently.

"You do know that it is a serious crime, bribing an officer of the nation? You, Monsieur, could end up in some serious trouble. The jails in Aix?" He whistled. "However, much could be forgiven if you made a donation to, maybe, the local zoo?"

"The zoo?"

"Yes, it is a place I like to go on my day off. The animals are French animals. Brave and beautiful."

He's crazy. "What sort of donation?"

"Including les insects, there are six thousand creatures, ten franc for each would amount to sixty thousand francs."

Ten thousand US, thought Charlie. His savings from Martine's, and the leftover funds John had given him for the trip: "How do I know you will let her stay?"

"Feel this," said the man, showing Charlie a raised seal on the front of Paula's document. "Without this official stamp, I cannot act. Case closed, as you Americans like to say."

"I don't understand," said Charlie.

"I will give you the raised paper for safekeeping." He slapped his hands, *finished business.* "However, I will need your passport number, and it will be entered on a list of people who may not ever again visit France. She has no use for bribe makers, monsieur."

"I can never come here again?"

"Oui. I mean non."

"The love of my life. I may never see her again?"

What a sacrifice, the man thought. *He puts her heart before his. He must be part French.*

"If she remains here, I'm afraid not," said the man. "If it is of any consolation, I salute you. Might you be part French?"

"I am."

"Bien sûr. Of course."

Charlie had John call the front desk and arrange for the clearing of the funds while the man waited in the lobby, maniacally grinning at a Côte d'Azur vacation brochure. Within a half hour, the bills were counted out in front of Charlie. What crisp bills, the five-hundred-franc notes. The sound of French money: somewhere in between the sound of a whip and the sound of the wind. *No more France for me*, he thought. *American bills don't sound like anything at all.*

"Here's your envelope," said Charlie to the man.

"And here is your friend's paper. The zoo animals also salute you, monsieur."

"I guess this is the beginning of a beautiful friendship," said Charlie.

"The French do not care for the Casablanca movie, monsieur. *Très irréaliste*. Not realistic. Non."

Chapter Thirty-one

IT IS ONE HELL of a soup to die in a bubble bath. The body exacts final revenge on the now-neutered brain, purging it all, from the large intestine to the soul itself. Soup to nuts. It was Charlie who found his mother, aptly surrounded by bubbles and a bottle of her beloved 1976 Roederer Cristal Brut Millesime, which bobbed next to her, the livelier of the two. Charlie had returned home from France. Martine's had been closed due to a kitchen fire, although gossip had it that Martine was in some sort of trouble, something about a young girl. He took a moment alone with his mother, kneeling next to her, leaning in, hoping there were sparks left in the eyes that could capture one last look at her baby boy. Jee-Jee was in the kitchen, melting Brie, decanting the dinner bottle, selecting the CD, tweaking the lights—what joy it had given him, these last three decades, to be early-evening *rich* with his wife. And now as Charlie approached his father, so awkwardly, so carefully, Jee-Jee dropped the cheese knife. He saw and knew, touched Charlie's face before making his way upstairs.

*

"Jews are excellent at death," said John.

They were sitting shivah. Charlie, Jee-Jee, and Angelina, who had flown in with her ancient mother, who now wore her daughter's apron in the kitchen, plating sandwiches and making lemonade for a hundred. But there were no visitors; adult alcoholics exhaust their friends at a breakneck pace. There was one other guest, also in the kitchen, dutifully assisting Mama: Monica Miller. Somehow she had heard the news, maybe read the obituary, or just sniffed out the demise. *John was right. Jews are amazing at death.* Monica Miller knew just what to say. Just how to touch him. She was the one who ordered the food and who cleaned the tub.

"You know," said Monica Miller, offering her very few guests mini pastramis on rye, "we will all be with Rose in eternity soon enough, so it's probably in our best interests to make the most of our time here, before we are all reunited."

She wore a sleek pantsuit. Slimming and conservative. She looked great. A real twenty-year-old. Firm, and firmly in control.

"Thank you, Monica," said Jee-Jee. "Rose always liked you for our strange Charlie."

Charlie didn't mind the designation. He was floating. The death of a parent is a little forgiving that way, at least at first. You float, like in a Chagall painting, while staring at the Chagall painting that hung above the fireplace. Sometimes Monica Miller would put her hand on his head. Sometimes she would bring him a glass of water. Or put a blanket over his napping body. In just seven daylight hours, she had become the woman of the house.

*

"Come here, Charlie," said Angelina. She'd grown younger. More cosmopolitan. Chic, even, with a silk scarf tied around her neck, and the Jackie O sunglasses she'd inherited from Rose Green.

"I am proud of you," said Angelina. "You became a man so quickly, I can tell. We were worried if you would ever become a man, and now you have. Mother wrote me many times about you, and the girl you met. She was proud of you. But now you must do even more. This is *your* family now."

"John's taking care of all the will stuff."

"Your brother is sweet, but he is permanently a child. And children should not have children. He will never be a papa. *You.* You must give Mother a grandchild so that she can rest in heaven."

"Huh?"

"This *chica* Monica, she turned out nice."

With that, Angelina licked a finger and, for the very last time, rubbed a mustard smudge from Charlie's cheek.

So that's the plan, thought Charlie. A life with Monica Miller, who would give us a child, and the Green name will withstand the death of the matriarch. Got it. *Fuck*, he thought, feeling for his beeper.

"Are you happy?" he asked Angelina.

"Only sometimes," she said.

"I understand now," said Charlie.

*

It was Rose Green's wish to be cremated; her ashes poured off the back of a Bateaux Mouches tourist craft into the Seine. Jee-Jee called a friend at the French embassy, and it was confirmed: Errol Flynn had kept his promise. Charlie was on a list of American citizens forbidden to enter the motherland.

"I'll look after him," Monica Miller told Jee-Jee.

"Thank you," said Jee-Jee. "You know, Monica, I see Rose in you."

Mother comparisons? The kiss of death, thought Charlie. But he needed her now, so he clung to her, like he'd clung to Angelina as a child when she'd led the way in the Haunted Mansion, a walk-through attraction at the Jersey shore, his eyes closed, his fist full of his nanny's blouse, while college kids dressed as demons popped out at them.

"*Estupido* monsters. *Vamos*, Charlie."

A dead mother was the mother of all monsters, and she'd visited him the last several nights, in nightmares, wearing a dress train full of empty vodka bottles, like Jacob Marley and the clamor of his chains. Jews can suffer *A Christmas Carol*, too.

"Did your mom like Paula?" Monica Miller asked Charlie. They were in his bedroom while his family packed for the Concorde; Jee-Jee had even booked a seat just for his wife's ashes.

"Do you think the urn will wear a seatbelt?" Charlie asked.

"Maybe. Was she really pretty?"

"Who?"

"Um, Paula?"

He was lying in bed, Monica Miller behind him at his desk. The arrangement struck Charlie as psychiatric, a configuration he used to generate non sequiturs and avoid answering questions about Paula. He hadn't thought about how it would feel to return to New Hope. Paula might never return. Before, he'd held daily hope that the beeper would sound, but now it just felt impossible. Or perhaps the death of his mother cast a pall of impossibility over everything, except Monica Miller.

"Do you want me to make you a snack?" she asked. "Angelina gave me free rein over the kitchen. Can you believe it?"

Jee-Jee had asked Angelina and Mama to join them on the trip, and they'd agreed.

"I think Mama will like the Concorde," said Charlie. "Although I think Mama complains even more than Angelina. Angelina never got to meet Paula."

"You still love her, don't you?"

"I think I'd like another mini pastrami on rye."

*

"Give me a hug," said John.

Jee-Jee was loading luggage into a hired limousine, in which Angelina and Mama waited. Charlie could make out Mama's stoic profile through the tinted glass. The chiseled bones of *Dignidad*.

Mom would have liked the limo, he thought. It was so rectangular, so vitally 1978.

"A hug?" he asked John.

"Yeah, we should do that stuff more often. You've been through a fucking lot. Hey, you want anything from France? Sucks that you're blackballed, but trust me, girls will find that sexy. A whole country versus Charlie Green. Hot."

John left without giving Charlie the promised hug. Jee-Jee, an expert hugger, came through.

"We will be back in one week's time," he told Charlie. "Your Maman left you and your brother some things. Quite a lot of valuables, cash too, Charl, and we should discuss this when I get back. Will you be here, or in Pennsylvania?"

"I'm not sure." He watched Mama play with the automatic tinted window, opening and closing, opening and closing.

"Mama sort of looks like Sitting Bull," said Charlie.

"She is a good friend, your Monica."

"I think she's taking a shower." The thought excited him. A naked girl. But only for a moment, then back came death.

Jee-Jee kissed Charlie on his mop of wavy brown hair and got into the car, in the seat next to the driver. Jee-Jee always sat next to the limo driver. *He's humble*, Charlie thought. *He grew up poor, in a good way. A very good way. I hope I have some of that in me.* Then went back inside and shut the door. He'd never been alone, or at least without family or Angelina, in the five-story town house. He could hear Monica Miller in his shower. Without the noise of water, he'd hear the sound of death. A still tub holding a dead body. What did Hemingway write? "Death in the Afternoon"? *Shower longer, Monica Miller. Shower forever.* But soon enough the shower ended, and he fainted.

*

Charlie awoke in the arms of Monica Miller.

"How long was I out?" he asked.

"Just a few seconds."

"It felt like forever. My Mom's gone."

"Everything will be okay. I'm taking off from school so I can be with you."

"I don't think I can be in this house. It's awfully silent here."

"We can go wherever you want, even New Castle."

"It's New Hope."

*

New York City girls are so easily impressed, thought Charlie, watching Monica Miller shake her head in awe of the Delaware River. Then again, so had he been. He remembered that first time on the banks of the river with Paula, how the rural sun kissed the golden hair of her arms.

"God, I love little antique stores," said Monica Miller, whose arms were perfectly hairless, devoid of clues.

She'd bought an antique broom for twenty-five dollars. Wealthy New York City girls who never use a broom buy expensive brooms they will hang on a wall. *In a hundred years a Monica Miller will buy a Dustbuster for display.*

They'd been there a week, at Charlie's house; they'd slept in Charlie and Paula's bed. Charlie was sure to sleep on Paula's side, and they didn't have sex. Although he could tell she wanted to. He could tell she was wearing him down. In full girlfriend mode. Nurturing, sweet, available. She even slept in the nude, which struck Charlie as savage and impressive.

"You know," she'd said, "I have plenty of room in my apartment at NYU. I mean, it would be so easy for you to transfer. This New Hope is a little slice of heaven, but it feels like the type of place you leave on your way to New York or maybe Philly, you know?"

He saw New Hope through her eyes, her brown New York eyes, and tended to agree. With Martine's now closed indefinitely—Martine was being sued by the parents of a fifteen-year-old girl—and with the absence of Paula, New Hope felt unalive. A place without yellow cabs. A place without a central park. No pigeons. No Plaza Hotel. Bad pizza.

*

After it was decided that Charlie would move to New York, to Monica Miller's fifth-floor walk-up in Greenwich Village, they began making love, and she began making plans: the bar they lived above would serve them their famous cheese fondue; her best friend's boyfriend would become Charlie's best friend, and then they could order the fondue for four.

"We'll smoke cigarettes on the fire escape late into the night," she'd told him. "And listen to the sounds of the city that never sleeps, our city, where we were born. At the same hospital in the same year."

Charlie didn't mind her forecasts; it was all cozy enough. Even their perfunctory sex was comforting. The biblically scaled nights with Paula should be retired forever, he thought, like how great baseball players retire their number. Lou Gehrig's number 4. The luckiest man on the face of the earth, Gehrig had said, despite terminal illness.

"I'm the luckiest man on the face of the earth," Charlie had told Monica Miller. She knew nothing about baseball, so didn't get the reference. She didn't know that lucky Charlie needed to feel for his beeper when another girl exuded the scent of Paula's shampoo. *Not being with Paula is my Lou Gehrig's disease*, he'd think, then hug and kiss Monica Miller. It's just what people do. They make concessions. Small talk over fondue. Missionary style. The bass line from Snap's "I Got the Power" finding the open fire escape window while she smoked her postcoital Marlboro Light.

*

Martine opened the bar for Charlie's farewell party. He'd invited Francis and the Lacrosse Girl, leaving them a message on their answering machine that they didn't return.

They've moved on, he thought. *Good for them. No, great for them. We'll catch up in a future decade, a recessive decade when my hairline will have receded. Life prepares you for death, slowly but surely. It's the singular job of life: death. But Francis and the Lacrosse Girl will be immune to this fact. They will be happy. I will be balding.*

"Whatever happened to that girl?" *they'll ask.*

"What girl?" *I'll ask, Monica Miller tethered to my arm, our face-less children cowering behind our adult legs.*

Ah, well. Things got interesting for a little while there, back in 1987, 1988. Now it's time to settle in, get comfortable. A middle-aged paunch inside an argyle sweater. Let life work its deadly magic.

*

Miss Pettibone, Gary, and Monica Miller were the only attendees at Charlie's party. He'd also invited Mrs. Henderson, who would have attended, but she was already on her way to Italy on a Perillo Tour—thirty-five Mrs. Hendersons and the Tower of Pisa—which would con-clude with her visiting Paula around Thanksgiving. Mrs. Henderson didn't know the part Charlie had played in her daughter's open-ended expatriation. He didn't want Paula to know; if she thought she was taking a French girl's job away, she'd put an end to her lavender reverie and move to another country, a less safe one, like Tommy's Italy. She was safe amid flowers. She had earned her paradise.

"You want me to tell her anything, Charlie?" Mrs. Henderson had asked. "About your mom, or anything?"

"No, I'll write her a letter and explain things."

But he had no intention of telling her about his mother's death. *She'd pay me an unnecessary sympathy visit*, he thought, *and then go back to her color purple. A kiss on the cheek? Unbearable.*

"Well, I'll tell her you say hello," said Mrs. Henderson.

As far as Mrs. Henderson could tell, Monica Miller was just a family friend visiting New Hope during a tough time. "You Jewish people stick together, don't you, Charlie? I think it's real sweet. Plus, maybe this Monica likes you? You should ask her. I won't tell Paula. You deserve your happiness, we all do, but especially my Paula. Sorry, hon, but she comes first."

"I tend to agree with you, Mrs. Henderson."

Chapter Thirty-two

"To one of my favorite boys, in all the years," toasted Miss Pettibone. "It was only a few sessions, but you were so so . . . so special to me."

She was drunk. Charlie thought. Amateur drinkers talk too much; it's the pros who become deathly silent. God bless the toxicity monks in the bar's darkest corner, wondering at which drink it all went to hell.

"So pleased you will be matriculating to NYU next semester," said Miss Pettibone, slurring her words. To Charlie, it sounded like "you will be masturbating a Jew next semester." He looked over at his brunette girlfriend and her shiny brown hair. *There are worse fates, I suppose.*

"Watch, he'll forget all about the townies," said Gary.

Gary, shirtless, was also drunk. He was going to miss Charlie. "You made this little town a little more interesting, Charlie Green," he said.

Martine was upstairs, going through business documents.

"I'm going to check on Martine," said Charlie.

The Smiths bartender was playing "Is It Really So Strange." Gary hunched over his seventh beer, asking Miss Pettibone if she'd like to touch his recently acquired nipple ring. Martine had lit the fireplace, first of the season.

I'll miss this stuff, thought Charlie. I'll miss how brisk it gets by the river in October, how the town wears its seasons. The bounty of hearth smells, twelve months out of the year. Walking upstairs, he saw Miss Pettibone pull at Gary's nipple ring and giggle. *God, I love humans*, he thought, deciding he was not an actual human, just someone who loved them.

*

"I will really miss this place, Martine."

"And we will miss you, Charlie."

"Before I leave, do you need anything? Anything at all? My dad knows really good lawyers. I mean, I heard you got into some—"

"Just do me one favor," said Martine. She rose to hug him. "Make love your top priority, even if it kills you."

"I think it already has," said Charlie. Martine's Indian arms were so strong, he thought from inside the hug.

"No," she said. "There's more for you."

The hug lasted too long, and when it was over Charlie felt sluggish, infected by a soul too old for his body. Or maybe he'd donated whatever was left of his youth to the wise if heartbroken Martine. He hadn't had a real drink since his mother died, but now he needed a vodka.

Downstairs at the bar, Miss Pettibone and Gary were deep in conversation, while Monica Miller swayed to the Smiths, Rolling Rock in hand.

"Rodin saw gods in slabs of white marble," said Gary to Miss Pettibone.

"And I see gods everyplace that I shouldn't," said Miss Pettibone.

They're going to have sex tonight, thought Charlie. He poured himself a vodka, went over to Monica Miller, and moved with her.

"Is It Really So Strange," sang The Smiths.

No, he thought. Unfortunately, it's not anymore.

*

As the river receded into highway, Charlie felt canine, looking out the open window, trying to make sense of the whirring world. Monica Miller drove, and spoke about upgrading to a king-size futon; about how they should both be psych majors; about a girl in her year who had already gotten married.

"Not that there's any pressure," said Monica Miller, then squeezed his thigh. "I know a perfect place to hang that painting. Is it really worth two million bucks?"

It was, maybe more. And then there was the inheritance from his mother, a sum he didn't care to know. A coffin nail of a number which, once revealed, would surely erase her once and for all.

"Maybe I'll just give it all away," said Charlie. "Start from scratch."

"No, don't do that," said Monica Miller. "I mean, it's your money, of course. It's just that one day you might have a family, and you'll need it for things like college, and the house."

The house, he thought. *She means* our *house*.

The smell of another's house. The smell of another's life. Monica Miller's apartment. Something *chicken cutlet* in the kitchen. An insufficiently cleaned ashtray by the famous fire escape window. A scented candle in the bathroom. Apple Pie.

"Maybe we should buy a different candle," said Charlie. "One that smells like L'Oréal shampoo."

"You're so silly. Hey, let's hang up that painting."

*

There was something cozy about a tepid romance, thought Charlie. *A blanket of adequacy is draped over us.*

Their first few weeks together, Monica Miller attended NYU, and Charlie roamed neighborhoods. A strict rotation. Chinatown on Mondays. Little Italy on Tuesdays, where he'd had a brief affair with a cannoli maker's plump daughter. No guilt, none at all. She was older. Beautiful accent. And listened well to Charlie's stories about Paula.

Paris. *I've turned into my mother*, he thought, babbling about the old country and an old romance.

Those weekend nights, Monica Miller insisted on the neighborhood bar, the one with the fondue for four. The other couple included a guy named Reginald, who was older, already on Wall Street at John's firm.

"Your brother's a fucking legend," he'd said. "Took me for my first haircut with his special barber."

Haircut, thought Charlie.

"Charlie has a thing about haircuts," said Monica Miller. "But I do like your hair short, Reggie."

Apparently they'd dated at some point, and much to his own surprise, it threatened Charlie. While he wasn't in love, Monica Miller was his source of femininity, quite possibly his life's permanent placeholder for Paula; losing her would mean losing Paula again.

"But you like my hair messy, right, Monica?" asked Charlie. "Tousled."

It means messy, Haircut, he thought. *Human, fallible, real. I'm no Haircut. I have irrational hair.*

"Yes, I do, sweetie," said Monica Miller and grabbed a handful.

*

Her Perillo Tour had further hardened Mrs. Henderson about men; over a bottomless carafe of Pino Grigio at the Leaning Tower Trattoria, one in her group admitted to offing her philandering husband.

"He had a heart condition, Paula, so Mrs. Rosato put on a werewolf mask and popped out of the closet. The cheating asshole dropped dead."

Mrs. Henderson and Paula were having dinner at La Villa Gallici's bar, the only American bar in Aix-en-Provence.

Charlie would like it here, thought Paula.

"Not all men are evil, Mom," she said.

"Oh please, dear, of course they are. What the heck is salade niçoise?"

She'd arrived the night before in time for the family meal, chirping about Perillo Tours. Paula's French family were greatly amused by the loud, round American, who insisted on doing the dishes. Paula had missed her mother; she missed seeing someone she knew. There had been one night, after a literally sensational stroll in her beloved lavender field, that she was tempted to page Charlie's beeper, but what if he didn't call back? And what if that meant he'd found someone else? What if all men *were* evil?

Maybe Mom is right, she thought. *I'll just date myself forever.*

"Excuse me, monsieur?" said Mrs. Henderson to a man at the bar in a yellow suit, wearing an outrageously foppish handkerchief.

"Mom, don't."

"Oh, shush, Paula."

"Monsieur, what the heck is in a salade niçoise?"

He gritted his teeth. "Tuna, madame. And the oeuf, and the haricot vert, and of course the potato, and then—Audrey Hepburn. Look who it is!" he said, pointing at Paula.

"I'm not following you, monsieur," said Mrs. Henderson, herself annoyed after weeks of language barriers.

I don't look anything like her, thought Paula.

"Your daughter is Hepburn, and of course her boyfriend thinks he's Bogart, Madame," said the man. "Americans are good at pretend, oui?"

"I don't have a boyfriend," said Paula.

The man held up a finger, then rifled through a folder. "*Alors*, Mister Charles Green."

"What about him?" asked Mrs. Henderson.

"Let us not play games," said the man. "What is done is done."

"How do you know Charlie?" asked Paula. Now she stood, bothered by the man's coyness and the grandeur of his handkerchief.

"I met him here. Right over here," said the man. She did have a nice figure, he thought. For an American. "He made quite the sacrifice for you, just like his hero, Humphrey Bogart." He snorted out a laugh.

"What sacrifice?" asked Paula.

"Yeah, what sacrifice?" asked Mrs. Henderson.

"Let me put it in a way you will understand: Without his donation to, eh, le zoologique, you, mademoiselle, would have been sent home. You cannot work in France without the visa."

"Oh my God, he was here," said Paula, collapsing back into her bar seat. "I know the night. I know it. I sensed him. I even think I heard his stupid Walkman."

"What the hell's going on?" asked Mrs. Henderson.

Again, the man put a finger in the air, and again he rifled through his folder, and again he said, "*Alors*, Mister Charles Green."

"Charlie and Paula have called it quits, just so you know," said Mrs. Henderson. "He broke her heart, with this other girl. Typical."

Paula poured herself a glass of wine from the man's bottle.

Ordinarily, the man would have slapped a person—man or woman—for such brazen behavior, but he let it go. *This is a woman that men fight for*, he thought. *That they will die for. Très Français.*

"So, he did exactly what?" asked Paula.

"He was *très français*; loving you from, ah, how do you say . . . *distance sacrificielle.*"

"Excuse my French," said Mrs. Henderson, "but you can please speak a fucking language that I can understand?"

"*D'accord*," said the man. "But only for her ears." He whispered to Paula while Mrs. Henderson shook her big head and asked yet another customer about the meaning of salade niçoise.

"He did that for me?" asked Paula.

"*Pour toi.*"

"I felt him that night."

So rare to witness such passion, thought the man. This young couple could really be French.

"I felt his sweetness," said Paula. "His Charlie-ness."

"Oh, please," said Mrs. Henderson.

"No, she should obey these feelings," said the man. *I have no feelings*, he thought. *I did once as a child, but I am French, so they will not return until I am old and then they will kill me while another old man plays the accordion. D'accord? D'accord.*

Paula took the man's hands and kissed them, then rose to leave the bar. "I need to make a phone call."

"I'll order for you, hon," said Mrs. Henderson. "I'll order us that crazy-sounding salad. The kids these days," she said to the man, "they think they invented romance, but it was our generation, am I right, or what?"

"No, Madame. It is them."

Every generation thinks they invented sex, he thought.

*

Charlie and Monica Miller took Reginald to lunch at Adam's Rib. He'd recently been dumped by Monica Miller's best girlfriend and was apparently heartbroken—although, to Charlie, his heart seemed perfectly intact, as was the case with all Haircuts who couldn't handle the opportunity cost of true love.

"Let's go to the Carlyle Hotel next week for Thanksgiving," said Monica Miller. "The three of us. My parents are doing their soup kitchen thing."

"Maybe *we* should do the soup kitchen thing," said Charlie. Angelina would approve, he thought. She'd had to work every Thanksgiving of his young life.

"Maybe we could go to Puerto Rico, you know, just us, and surprise Angelina by cooking her Thanksgiving dinner," he said.

"I'd be down for some Thanksgiving," said Reginald. "I have much to be thankful for." He winked at Monica Miller.

Thanks for nothing, Reggie, thought Charlie.

"The Carlyle it is, Reggie," said Monica Miller. "Maybe before lunch, we could all go feed the homeless. Just, like, go around Washington Square Park and give them plates of food."

"I'd be down for that," said Reginald. "I want to be a better person."

Such bullshit.

"Really sorry about your horrible breakup," Charlie said to Reginald. Haircuts didn't get sarcasm. Literal bastards.

"Thanks, man. Your brother's been totally supportive at work. And you guys are the best. Love hurts, man."

Then why are you smiling?

Reginald had barely touched his Eve's cut of roast beef. There was an Adam's cut that came with a bone, but the Eve's cut was boneless and more petite. *Haircuts watch their figures,* thought Charlie. *I've gained twenty-three pounds of muscle since my first day of college; I could kick Reggie's ass.*

"Charlie and I are here for you, Reggie," said Monica Miller. "Let's get lemon meringue pie for dessert. It's Charlie's favorite."

"I once wrote an entire short story about the two constituent colors of that beautiful pie," said Charlie. "Canary Yellow. God's Beard White. To think there was a time I wanted to be a writer. Why not just observe the colors in silence? Impress your God with your restraint. You can ruin a perfectly good slice of pie by writing about it. I used to ruin everything."

The words that precede a life bookmark are tattooed on God's bicep. He must have a huge bicep. Something about stuffing. Something about vegetarian stuffing. Something about vegetarian stuffing with Italian sausage. Something about stuffing.

"For Thanksgiving," said Monica Miller. "The Carlyle Hotel makes an amazing vegetarian stuffing, but with all of this Italian sausage."

Then it's not really vegetarian.

"I'd be down for some complex stuffing," said Reginald.

For the rest of her days, Monica Miller would swear that for a brief moment, Charlie's brown eyes flashed the lightest teal. Then came the techno-jouncy jingle: "I'll Be Home for Christmas."

Monica Miller was horrified by Charlie's beet-red face, his hands so desperate to capture the beeper, and then his eyes: they must have become half his face reading the exotic numbers. How he jolted up from his seat.

"I'm sorry," said Charlie, backing away. "I need—I need—"

"What?" asked Monica Miller. "You need what?" But she knew. "Go," she said. "Call her."

"Yeah, man," said Reginald. "Take your time."

"Quiet," she told Reginald. "Just be quiet."

*

Before Charlie could even ask, the Adam's Rib bartender had produced the shiny black rotary house phone.

"But it's long distance," said Charlie.

"Not a problem," said the Adam's Rib bartender. "What's the number?"

"It says +33 4 42 23 29 23."

The Adam's Rib bartender took his own sweet time dialing all the numbers, finally holding the receiver above them both, so that Charlie could hear that queer French double beep.

"Here you go," said the Adam's Rib bartender.

What a shiny old phone, thought Charlie. I bet someone cleans and polishes it every night in the hopes that one day it might be used for the most important phone call of a man's life.

"Hello?" asked Paula.

"Hi," said Charlie.

"Hi," she said. "Hi."

And then, the Adam's Rib bartender? He vanished. Into thin air. But not before slipping a coaster beneath his customer's elbow; his customer who was on the horn to Europe, who was smiling, who didn't know where he was. That he was at a bar.